RAMPAGE!

An Aries Adventure

About The Author

Julia was born in Stafford, has lived in Australia, Stockport and Oxford and now lives in Warwickshire with her partner Jim and Bosworth the dog, who is half-cocker-spaniel, half-poodle (and all teddy bear). She has had lots of jobs, including keeping a photographic library of petrol stations for an oil company, deciding what colour packets sausages look best in and teaching history to eight-year-olds, which was when she and the children first discovered the Ancient Greeks, their fabulous monsters and the problem with wearing a chiton on a windy day.

Also available:

FLEECED!

RAMPAGE!

An Aries Adventure

JULIA WILLS

Piccadilly
PRESS

For my mother, Dorothy May Wills, cherished gold.

First published in Great Britain in 2015
by Piccadilly Press
Northburgh House, 10 Northburgh Street, London EC1V 0AT

A CIP catalogue record for this book is available from the British Library.

ISBN: 978-1-848-12477-6

1 3 5 7 9 10 8 6 4 2

Typeset in Adobe Caslon Pro by
Palimpsest Book Production Ltd, Falkirk, Stirlingshire
Printed and bound by Clays Ltd, St Ives Plc

www.piccadillypress.co.uk

Piccadilly Press is part of the Bonnier Publishing Group
www.bonnierpublishing.com

Prologue
The Wicked Witch of The Quest

SMASH!

The ancient amphora of red roses crashed against the wall, narrowly missing an oil painting of Lord Nelson at the Battle of Trafalgar, before exploding in a shower of shards, water and blooms that slithered to the floor.

WHAM!

A two-thousand-year-old Greek urn spun through the air, slammed into a watercolour of Queen Marie Antoinette's pinkly smiling face, and splintered the glass across her neck.

CRACK!

The heel of an airborne stiletto shoe (with the latest sapphire-blue sole) struck the sketch of King Harold, slap-bang in the eye, and sent the picture tinkling to the ground.

Pausing for breath, Medea the immortal Greek sorceress, surveyed the pictures of all the other famous people, now shattered and hanging wonkily on the walls of her secret room tucked deep beneath her London boutique. Beside each person's ruined portrait hung a framed sketch of the clothes they were wearing in the picture, showing the sorceress's designs for their outfits – ones that she had later hand-stitched for them.

The ones that they had died in.

She turned to the earliest portrait. A pretty Greek woman smiled back from beneath the broken glass, radiant in a headdress of cream roses, dressed in a snow-bright wedding **chiton**. Now little more than an image on crumbling parchment, it still gave Medea an icy thrill whenever she looked at it.

Princess Glauce.

Her first 'customer'.

Faintly soothed by the sweet memory of that success, Medea began walking along the row. Here was Julius Caesar, the Roman emperor, with a wreath of laurel leaves in his hair, draped in the handmade cloak of damson purple, on the day he was stabbed to death. Beside him, a papyrus sketch of Cleopatra clad in the cream linen kaftan she'd been wearing when the poisonous asp bit her. Several pictures along, Anne Boleyn, the English queen, stood quietly glamorous in a silvery-grey gown in front of the executioner's axe. A cheering General Custer in his buckskin jacket and a big hat with gold stars stitched on its band was next, leading his last charge, at the Battle of the Little Bighorn, and further along Captain Edward Smith beamed from beneath a gold-brocaded cap as he stood on the top deck of the RMS *Titanic*.

Medea smiled coldly as she strolled past the images of each of her celebrity clients.

Until her gaze fell upon the last 'picture' in her

collection, nothing more than an empty frame, hanging beside a sketch of a gorgeous pink gown. She glowered at the teasing blank glass and felt a snarl curl in her throat. It should have held a picture of Hazel Praline, the teenage pop sensation, all candyfloss-coloured cheeks and blonde ponytail. She flinched, hearing a thin echo of the girl's voice, twittering like a Texan sparrow on the stage at Leicester Square, at the premiere of her movie.

The last time she'd seen her.

The last time *anyone* was supposed to see her.

Three weeks ago.

Turning away, the sorceress caught her hand on a sprawling vine. Standing in its own gravel bed, it had been a luxury lolling spot for Hex, Medea's familiar,[1] a deadly black mamba snake, who'd loved snoozing in its crags, his coffin-shaped head gorgeously ominous. Actually, as far as the sorceress was concerned, lolling, snoozing and *looking* ominous were the only things Hex was ever any good at, since he'd preferred them to anything as messy as magic. Which was why she'd planned to dispose of him.

Horribly.

Except that he'd even managed to spoil that fun by deserting her first.

Three weeks ago.

Swiping the vine with the back of her hand, she sent

---

1 A familiar is a witch's pet, traditionally a black cat that stalks around looking spooky and catching rats for spells. However, they can be any type of animal and the best ones talk, make pots of tea and answer the phone too.

it clattering to the floor in a storm of snapped branches and scattered stones.

Now, those of you who weren't brave enough to read about Medea in my last book might be surprised at this sort of behaviour. After all, you probably expect an Ancient Greek sorceress to be a beautiful woman, trailing the skirts of her long green velvet dresses around a workshop tangled with ivy whilst she gazes dreamily at vials of indigo-coloured potions. Rather than, say, using her private art gallery as a firing range?

Well, reboot your brain.

Because whilst it's true that Medea was certainly beautiful, with wide silver eyes, a tip-tilted nose and long black hair, brightened by a single streak of violet, the only trailing she did was of bitter curses. Stroking was reserved for the snugly-wuggly fur on tarantulas' tummies and, as for dreamy, well, only about as dreamy as a lizard seconds before it flips out its carpet-roll tongue and snaps up fly-breakfast.

And I'm afraid it gets worse.

You see, for hundreds of years, Medea had been horribly busy, stitching the glittering curls from the Golden Fleece into her own range of handmade clothes created for the rich and famous, the special few whose pictures now hung on the walls around her. The Fleece, as you might already know, was a ram's coat made of dazzling gold ringlets and its rightful owner was Aries, who was indeed a ram, now a ghost ram, and a bald one at that.

Long ago, the Fleece had hung in a sacred grove in

Medea's homeland of Kolkis, or at least it had until Jason, a Greek prince, arrived with his fifty men, the Argonauts. (The full story is in the back of this book, because frankly I don't feel like talking about it now.) Falling deeply in love with him, the sorceress helped him steal the Fleece, and together they'd sailed off into the moonlight.

And lived unhappily ever after.

Because, you see, no sooner had the confetti been swept from the palace steps than Jason left Medea for another woman, Princess Glauce. Yes, that's right, the lady in the first portrait. However, in deserting Medea, Jason had unwittingly condemned his lovely new bride to the sorceress's Changing Room of Doom. Now mixing sorcery and stitchery for the first time, Medea used the Fleece to fashion the most magnificent wedding dress as a gift for Glauce. Beautiful and shimmering, it wreathed the young princess's body like mist and pooled in pearly ripples at her feet. But, as she cooed over her gorgeous reflection in the looking glass, the gown burst into flames and killed her.

And the rest, as they say, is history, because ever since that day the sorceress had snipped and stitched through the centuries, feverishly sewing twists of golden wool into the clothes of the richest, most powerful and glamorous people on Earth. Banned by the Greek gods from the Underworld[2] for her wickedness, she'd simply

---

2 This is the land of Ancient Greek ghosts, which sits plum in the centre of our Earth like the bubblegum ball in the middle of a gobstopper.

vanished for decades at a time, only to reappear years later, bright and talented, at the courts of new kings and queens and emperors, military leaders and film stars alike, creating their most glorious outfits, the ones that they died in.

Gasp!

Thud!

Aaaargh!

Thud!

Urgle!

Thud!

Like that.

But all things, even *bad* things, come to an end, and finally so did the Fleece.

Three weeks ago.

Oh, it had been with sadness that Medea had used its last curl in Hazel Praline's dress, but it had been with mind-numbing, blood-freezing, cat-squealing fury that her plans for creating a hundred more Golden Fleeces to power her evil magic had been foiled. By Aries, together with his best friend Alex, a ghost boy, who'd returned from the Greek Underworld to find the Fleece. Up in modern London, they'd met Rose, who, in case you're wondering, wasn't a ghost but an ordinary twelve-year-old schoolgirl, who helped them to defeat a sorceress. Which, when you think about it, makes her rather un-ordinary. A fact that, unfortunately, Medea had already noticed, so that even now after everything that had happened, remembering Rose's sweet face made the sorceress's heart flutter like a poisonous octopus in a warm tide. Which is thoroughly *bad* news, because believe me, being the object of a sorceress's soft spot is absolutely not what you want to be.

You'll see.

Medea slumped down on to the sofa and clenched her fists. Oh, how she ached to fling deadly curses at Aries and Alex, to squash them like June bugs. Just thinking of Aries with his mad rammy face squashed up against Rose's wild red ringlets as she hugged him, and that goody two-sandals, Alex, made the blood thunder in her ears. If she ever saw those two again, she'd turn them into toads and stamp on them and paint her bedroom walls with the goo and dye some fabric in what was left over to make a matching set of curtains and, well, you get the picture because, without their outrageous interference, not only would Hazel be nothing more than a downloadable tinkle of songs featuring the late tragic star but Medea would still have serious sorceress power of the cruellest, wickedest and most grimly gruesome kind.

Because, you see, without power – the particular sort of power that a Golden Fleece provides – sorcery is rather like trying to make a decent brew without a kettle. You end up with a cup of cold water, a sorry-looking teabag and nowhere to dunk your Custard Cream. Thanks to Alex and Aries, Medea had been reduced to the level of a common-or-garden witch, an elementary witchette with a few dribbly-magic tricks that even the most hopeless Brownie working for her first badge in Supernatural Wickedness could pull off.[3]

She scowled.

Was it any wonder that she'd lost it when the police flooded into the theatre that day and she'd punched those officers? It was their own fault for buzzing around her like houseflies and stopping her from getting her hands on the boy and the ram. Whilst those two had scuttled back to the Underworld, where she could never reach them, she'd been arrested, spent a night in a grubby cell on a bunk bed with a scratchy blanket and been sentenced by a judge who looked like a walrus with a beard to three weeks of community service.

She, Medea of Kolkis, forced to spend the last twenty-one days polishing policemen's boots, cleaning the toilets at the local library and washing up after banquets at the Mayor's offices! Giving herself a quick mental shake, she reminded herself that now was not the time to reminisce. There were far more important things to think about. Her Plan B, for finding a new source of magical power. Quickly stepping out of the scattered mess of vine on the floor, she swept her hair into an untidy bun and turned back to the group of portraits from the seventeenth century. A row of snooty

---

3 What do you mean, that's not the sort of thing they do? Don't be fooled by all that camping in the woods and helping old ladies over the road malarkey.

women with powdered white faces and tight red lips regarded her as she passed before stopping in front of a portrait of two men. A father and son, they smiled out kindly, sharing the same handsome, heart-shaped faces, shoulder-length dark hair, beard and neat moustache. Walter Raleigh, a nobleman at Queen Elizabeth I's Court, and his son, Wat, who'd explored the New World[4] together. Ever the seamstress, she paused for a moment, admiring her handiwork on their linen shirts and stiff lace ruffs, recalling how the Flanders lace had made her fingers sting. But it had been worth it. Her efforts always were. Chuckling, she recalled the news of their delightful deaths.

She quickly lifted the picture off the wall to reveal a small safe. A few taps and twists later, the door creaked open and she lifted out its contents: a tattered roll of parchment and a blue velvet bag. The parchment was mottled the colour of weak tea, and steeped in a pungent smoky smell that made her nose tingle. Unfurling it gently, she was delighted to see that the four-hundred-year-old writing and picture, scrawled in chocolate-brown ink, was still clear. Next, she snatched up the bag and glimpsed inside, catching a glint of engraved gold.

Clutching them both to her chest, the corners of the sorceress's mouth twitched upwards and her eyes grew

---

4 The New World is the name that was given to North and South America back in the sixteenth century when pioneers were exploring the continents. However, despite its name, it was just as scuffled and dusty as everywhere else.

dark, flat and dead as a shark's when it senses a vibration in the water and, with a flick of its tail, turns towards the splashing of swimmers by the shore.

I
Jungle Belles

Well, that's quite enough of that.

Medea is most definitely not my favourite person and, to be honest, I'd rather not talk about her any more, nor murder, man-eaters or mayhem for that matter. To be honest, there's far too much of that in the rest of this book and I've only just recovered from our last little excursion in the summer. But it hasn't escaped my hawk-like skills of observation that masses of mean words all start with the letter 'M'. Like murk and menace and mischief and malevolent. (And, *quelle surprise,* as they say in *la belle France*, the name of a certain personage.)

So, excuse me, but I'm going to leave the misfortunes[5] of that miserable[6] underground mooch-hole[7] to tell you about something a lot more exhilarating, which is what Rose was doing a couple of weeks later.

Rose was flying high above the Amazon rainforest,

---

5 *See, there's another.*

6 *And another.*

7 *What d'ya mean, 'mooch-hole' isn't a word? It is now.*

gazing out of the plane window, astonished at the vast sprawl of jungle beneath her. Down below the whirring propellers of the plane's pink-tipped wings, ancient teak trees, taller than tower blocks, thrust their branches into the sky. Neighbouring Brazil-nut trees snagged wisps of mist that floated about their crowns of frothy yellow flowers as, blinking, she tried to take in quite how enormously, overwhelmingly gigantic they were. Yet nothing her mother had told her – and what with her mother being an archaeologist who specialised in Amazonia, that had been *plenty* – had prepared her for the sheer spectacle of the rainforest. Pressing her face up against the sun-warmed glass of the window, she gazed further down their teetering trunks at the canopy, the swell of leaves and vines that lapped about them like an emerald ocean. As she peered, eager to glimpse a troupe of monkeys bouncing over the branches or a toucan circling in the warm air, her mother's voice floated back into her mind. Did she know that the Amazon was the biggest river on Earth? Or that its rainforest helped the Earth breathe? That quinine, the drug that cured malaria, grew in the bark of its trees? That mining, oil drilling and ranching ripped it to pieces every day, ruining great swathes of the forest that could never be replaced?

No, no, no and no.

Rose bit her lip, thinking guiltily back to those last awkward moments at the airport, wishing again that she'd been able to tell her mother the truth about this trip. But even though she'd always hated lying, despised it so much that it actually made her stomach hurt, she absolutely couldn't. What? Tell *her* mother that she'd been given the coordinates of Rose's missing father, by a magical All-Knowing Scroll? Confess that she intended to head deep into the eastern Brazilian rainforest to find him, even though search parties had given up six months ago, based on the help that a couple of Greek ghosts had given her? Her mother would have gone horribly pale, whipped Rose's suitcase back from the airport check-in desk and dragged her to some sort of specialist the same morning.

Rose sighed.

If only her mother was like other girls' mothers. The sort who believed what their daughters told them. And noticed them occasionally, instead of dragging them endlessly from one city to the next and one school to the next, whilst switching jobs from one famous museum to the next, elbow-deep in the relics of old Amazon tribes, trying to accept that they'd never see their husband again.

Rose shook her head. She knew she was being unfair. After all, her mother only did it to distract herself from her own grief.

Still, as she now reminded herself, trying to soothe her conscience, it was hardly her fault that she'd been forced, yes, that was it, *forced*, to pretend the trip was simply a thank-you from Hazel, for helping to save the pop star's life, in what the newspapers reported as 'a terrible theatre accident'. She bit a fingernail. That bit was nearly true, at least. The trip *was* a thank you, even if the accident at the theatre had been nothing to do with sloppy stage dressing and everything to do with the whim of a vicious bloodthirsty sorceress.

Rose shivered.

Despite the sunshine streaming in through the aircraft window, thinking of the sorceress made her skin prickle icily. She reached for the gold locket around her neck and rubbing its familiar oval smoothness, took a long, deep breath. A present from her parents for her eleventh birthday, it was now the most special thing she owned, because it had been only a few months later that her father had vanished on his expedition.

Twisting the locket between her fingers, she wondered for about the millionth time since the Scroll had given her its answer how her father would be when she found him. After all, the Scroll had told her that he was alive, hadn't it? So what had stopped him, or any of the others, from coming home? Or making contact? Her mind returned to the day the expedition left, hearing the men's shouted goodbyes as they boarded the plane at Heathrow, all khaki trousers and smiles, intent on finding the site of the village of some old Amazonian tribe, one whose legendary chieftain had dusted his skin with gold and danced in the moonlight, and pondered, yet again, what could possibly have gone wrong.

(Me, I'd already be thinking about those monstrous jungle spiders, big enough to throttle a finch, or merciless anacondas, ready to wrap round you like a taco and squeeze you till you're human guacamole.[8])

Sighing, she turned her attention to the stands of towering trees rocketing out of the endless canopy like flagpoles topping a ginormous circus tent. Pushing her forehead against the window, she stared at the swathe of leaves, knowing that he was down there somewhere, hidden far below, in the shadowy world beneath them. She would find him, she told herself, *she would*, and then they'd be a proper family again.

A sudden explosion of red, blue and gold from the treetops made her jump, as a flock of macaws burst screeching into the air.

'Did you see that?' gasped Rose, now bolt upright in her seat, blinking as the birds swirled and squawked in wide noisy circles.

She turned to Hazel, the only other passenger in the private cabin, who was seated across an expanse of pink carpet in a raspberry-coloured squishy chair. The young pop star was wearing pink cotton trousers and a pink T-shirt with a pink eye-mask snapped firmly over her eyes, her blonde ponytail swishing from side to side as she bobbed to the music playing through her earphones. And yes, they were pink, too.

---

8 Monstrous? Merciless? What did I tell you about those 'M' words?

'Haze?'

Rose watched as Hazel reached absently into the basket beside her seat for yet another bottle of French spring water (specially imported for the flight) and held it out like a microphone out in front of her, miming the words and blowing kisses to her fans. Punching one hand in the air, she kicked out a spangly pink sneaker. 'Got to see me, baby!' she trilled.

Rosc giggled, hardly able to believe that it was only a few weeks ago that she had met Hazel Praline – *the* Hazel Praline – and now they were actually friends. Sinking back into her seat, she was still faintly amazed that she, boring old Rose from Camden, was travelling with Hazel Praline in the megastar's private plane. Hazel Praline whose posters were tacked all over the wall of her bedroom, whose Saturday morning TV show, in which Hazel played a fearless horse rider rounding up cattle between bursting into song, Rose watched every weekend, whose concert she'd been so desperate to attend. And who now – even if it had felt like forever rather than a few weeks to Rose as she waited for Hazel to finish all her London interviews and film publicity and blah blah blah – had personally brought her out to the jungle.

But then, there had been so many unbelievable things this summer.

Like meeting Alex and Aries. At first she'd hardly even believed that they were ghosts. And small wonder since Ancient Greek ghosts, as some of you already know, look just as solid as you and me.[9] Now she felt her heart lurch, wishing they were with her and, stifling a snort of laughter, she imagined Aries uncomfortably buckled into one of the squishy seats, hooves in the air, complaining loudly, and Alex hopelessly trying to cheer him up. She'd never known anyone like them, so totally brave and funny and loyal. She wondered if they'd had the heroes' welcome they'd talked about when they returned to the Greek Underworld. It was funny really, she reflected, because before meeting them she'd only ever thought of Greek heroes as muscle-bound and brimming with confidence. Not a boy and a ram as bald as a pickled onion.

'My stomach!' squealed Hazel, jolting Rose from her thoughts as the plane dropped abruptly.

Snapping off her eye-mask, the young star blinked in the sunlight as the tannoy crackled into life and the pilot's voice crooned across the stylish deck.

'Good afternoon, ladies! In a few minutes we will be starting our descent into Barcelos Airport. Buckle up!'

'We finally there?' muttered Hazel, reaching for the giant sunhat on the seat beside her. 'I'm gonna fix us some watermelon coolers when we arrive!'

'Sounds good,' said Rose, clicking her seat belt together,

---

9 Unlike other ghosts, they don't waft, waver or go 'Whoo!' Nor do they haunt houses, lurk in wardrobes or loom menacingly. And they'd never be seen dead under a drooping sheet. In fact, they eat, drink, blow their noses and do all manner of boringly ordinary things just like us. Yes, including going to the toilet. Thank you for mentioning that.

freshly glad that Hazel was with her for company. She'd been such huge fun back in London.

Rose looked out, feeling her stomach loop the loop, as gaps opened up in the jungle through which the broad Rio Negro, its water black as liquorice, twisted and writhed. The town of Barcelos seemed little more than a cluster of whitewashed buildings nestled into a long curve of dark water and, closer now, catching her breath, she could make out houses with grey corrugated iron roofs, criss-crossed by narrow palm-lined roads. A blue bus rumbled sluggishly past a schoolyard filled with playing children.

'Here we go!' trilled Hazel, as the plane's tone changed, and it turned towards the runway. Catching sight of Rose's face, she smiled broadly. 'Won't be long now, Rose. We'll find him. You'll see!'

Rose stared down, watching as the plane flew over a row of grander waterfront buildings, dominated by a church, its big blue doors propped open at the top of a flight of steps that ran down to the river. Red fishing boats bobbed against the bank. A four-tiered river cruiser gleamed at the end of a whitewood jetty.

Now for those non-Brazilian geographers amongst you, Barcelos is a long way north-west of the coordinates the Scroll had given Rose, but Hazel had insisted they fly here, rather than Manaus which was closer, because Manaus was also the biggest, hippest, city in the jungle and bound to be *a-brimmin' with fans a-circling her like flies in the Texan heat*. Besides, she'd pointed out, after everything that'd happened to them in London, wouldn't Rose prefer a relaxing river cruise, too? Rose, as you might have imagined, wouldn't. She'd hated the thought of leaving her father a second longer in the jungle than she had to, but had bit back her impatience. After all, as she'd had to remind herself, it was completely amazing that Hazel was taking her at all.

As the plane lurched again, Rose spotted the runway, little more than a thin strip of tarmac, and a few seconds later the plane bounced down in a squeal of hot rubber tyres and rumbled to a stop.

'C'mon!' cried Hazel, dragging an overstuffed bag and three hatboxes behind her as the flight-attendant, a slim woman dressed in a neat pink uniform, opened the plane door.

For a moment, Rose stood in the doorway as Hazel clattered down the metal steps. Heat punched her in the chest, bringing with it the mingled smells of pineapple and sun-warmed bananas. Faint shrieks and howls rang out across the runway from the trees encircling the airport perimeter and, stepping out, Rose felt her stomach fill with butterflies. Then, quickly shaking her head, she hoisted her rucksack on to her back and scolded herself silently that whatever lay ahead it couldn't possibly be as daunting as squaring up to a sorceress and surviving her wrath.

She rolled her eyes.

What was she doing even thinking about Medea? After all, she was thousands of miles away, wasn't she?

On a different continent, scrubbing floors and buffing boots, doing her community service?

Which unfortunately brings me to yet another of those troublesome 'M' words.

Mistaken.

II
Chiselled Swizzle

At that moment, several miles below Rose's feet, down in the Greek Underworld, Aries, the ghost ram of the Golden Fleece, was snorting at his marble bottom. Now, since a marble bottom is likely to make anyone snort, I'd better explain that the bottom in question actually belonged to his statue. And statues, as we all know, are often made of marble, making a marble bottom perfectly fine and, indeed, much better than, say, having a bottom made of jelly. However, I don't know why you want to talk about jelly bottoms when I'm trying to tell you about his statue.

Ah, yes.

Truly splendid, the statue was a gift from Athena, the goddess of wisdom, who always rewarded Greeks returning from a quest with a prize. Gleaming creamy-white, it stood on a lawn in the Underworld Zoo, home to the ghosts of all the Greek monsters. The life-sized figure captured Aries perfectly, showing him in a furious battle charge. Its broad back reared upwards, its massive shoulders braced tightly, its front hooves hovered above the ground, as though he was poised to hurtle forwards.

Two glorious gold-dusted horns – horns that had taken the sculptor days of tippy-tapping until they curled precisely like Aries' own and were quite as twirly as Danish pastries – tilted forwards ready to butt anything, or anyone, out of his path.

Not that Aries was in the mood to admire any of that today.

No, because at that moment his attention was fixed on the crude wooden target that had mysteriously appeared on the statue's derriere and from which three arrows jutted.

'He's done it again!' he fumed, recognising Jason's latest attack.

The day before yesterday, he'd found his statue wearing a wide-brimmed straw hat. Last week, a black curly moustache had appeared painted beneath its magnificent muzzle. A moustache, Aries scowled, that had taken Hex, Medea's ex-familiar black mamba, two days of rubbing (and grumbling) to polish clean.

Now, staring at the offending arrows, he felt his brain start to simmer furiously.

Wasn't it enough that the leopard-skinned twerp had stolen the Fleece all those years ago? Leaving him, Aries the noble ram of legend, doomed to an eternity of bald ghosthood in the Underworld? Not to mention his being stupid enough to let Medea get her icy-white fingers on his golden coat for her cruel magic? Clearly not, because even now Jason insisted on treating Aries like some big, silly, walking joke. A joke that everyone else always found hugely amusing. Aries snorted furiously. If only they knew the truth about their so-called hero. What if, like him, the dancing girls had actually been in the forest that night and seen Jason's knees knocking whilst Medea sorted out all the scary bits? The dancers wouldn't be as pink and giggly then, he was sure. And would Athena still be simpering around him, cupping her face in wonder as she listened to his bragging? Hardly. His flanks began quivering with rage at the unfairness of it all, certain that things would be very different down here if they'd seen what had truly happened for themselves. And sighed. In the Underworld, people lapped up the story of a handsome hero over a bald ram every time.

He glared at the arrows and harrumphed bitterly. Just imagining Jason's ridiculous grin as he'd fired those despicable arrows sent a shudder down his spiralling horns, the sort of shudder that made them positively itch to butt the swaggering hero into the nearest pile of steaming **Minotaur** doo. For years Jason had picked on him, and it had become ten times worse since the ram had come back from London.

Rearing up, Aries threw his shoulders into the air and paddled his hooves over the grass, for a moment perfectly mimicking the statue in front of him.

Which was when he heard a familiar voice.

'Aries! You'll knock yourself out!' it yelled.

Sliding his treacly-brown eyes sideways, Aries saw Alex running towards him, tall and rangy, waving his arms wildly in the air, whilst Hex swayed up from the boy's shoulders in a silvery question mark. Then, undeterred, he hurled himself forward, galloping towards the statue in a blizzard of dust.

Veering sideways at the last second, Aries seized the edge of the target in his mouth, snapping its rope and with the flourish of an Olympic discus thrower entertaining a cheering crowd, tossed it into the air. Clopping after it, he speared it as it landed. Then, imagining it was Jason, he flung it down onto the ground and stamped on it, smashing the wood and splintering the thin arrow shafts – *crack, crack, crack* – before snatching up the wreckage in order to hurl it into the nearby lake.

Which was when he realised that Alex was now standing right beside him, with his arms folded, sighing loudly.

'Feel better now?' he said, picking up one of the broken arrow shafts and tapping its feathers against his palm.

'Much,' replied Aries primly, fixing Alex with a stubborn right-eyed stare.

This was because his left eye was now hidden behind a shard of the smashed target, which despite much flinging had remained stuck firmly on his horns and now veiled half of his face like a hat worn at a jaunty angle.

'You shouldn't let Jason get to you like this,' said Alex, stepping forward to pull the wood free.

Aries sighed, wearily disappointed to see that the boy was wearing his 'zoo-keeper's face' again. The same old look he always gave Aries when the ram talked about Jason. Or when he listened to the Minotaur moan about **Theseus** or the Chimera[10] chunter about Bellerophon.[11] That same old mixture of patience and frustration that showed that whilst Alex was truly sorry about what had happened to the monsters, he was truly tired, too, at hearing yet again how fabulous animals hated the Greeks who'd killed them or, in Aries' case, stolen the Fleece he'd loved most in the world.

'But don't you see?' said Aries, yanking his horn back as Alex pulled off the last shard of target. 'Jason couldn't attack it if it was where it should be. In the Heroes' Pavilion.' He scuffed a hoof through the dust. 'With all the others.'

'The others-s-s?' hissed Hex. 'I thought that'd be the las-s-st place you'd want it?'

The others, as some of you will recall, were the statues of Greece's most famous heroes. All displayed in the Pavilion, it was Jason and his fifty Argonauts that held pride of place, gracing its grand entrance hall. Standing high on their plinths, majestic and awe-inspiring, they gazed blindly at one another across an expanse of black marble floor, lofty beneath the circlets of laurels that

---

10 *A fire-breathing lion with a goat's head halfway down its back and a snake's head for a tail, this monster scared the living daylights out of the Greeks. Those lucky enough to survive its blasts and fangs were, however, furious to discover later that during the fight the goat had scoffed their washing off the line.*

11 *The Greek hero who, fed up with having no fresh laundry, killed the Chimera by thrusting a lump of lead on the end of his spear into its mouth, melting the metal in its furnace-like jaws and choking it.*

were placed on their heads each morning after their daily dusting. However, Athena had flatly refused to allow Aries' statue, celebrating the courage he'd shown back in the summer, to stand with them.

'You told me,' hissed the snake, slithering down from Alex's shoulder to bring his face close to Aries' left ear, 'that the Argonauts-s-s were jus-s-st a bunch of braggers-s-s, bullies-s-s and thieves-s-s. And that Jas-s-son des-s-served to be their captain becaus-s-s-e he was-s-s the bigges-s-st fraud of the lot!'

'He is!' snapped Aries. 'His statue should be crunched up into tiny pieces and used for the **Nemean Lion**'s litter tray! But the fact remains that the Pavilion is the place that people expect to see Greek heroes. Not stuck in the zoo, halfway between that lot –' he glanced over his shoulder at the lake – 'and that!' he finished, glaring ominously at a nearby villa-shaped building behind him.

Ah, yes.

Well, there was nothing wrong with the crystal waters of the lake. In fact, it housed the fabulous Pipers of **Poseidon** – one of the more glamorous attractions in the zoo, a band of blue-skinned mermen and women who played a splendid watery symphony on their conch shells every afternoon at three.

No.

The problem was the neighbouring small building. This was because it housed the – how can I put this nicely? – zoo lavatories.

That's right, public conveniences.

And Aries did have a point. After all, who expects to see statues of heroes within earshot of toilet noises? I mean, imagine if Lord Nelson wasn't up on his column but down in the square below with his naval nose pressed up against a block of Trafalgar Square loos.

It's hardly dignified, is it?

Sighing, Aries looked at the plinth of his statue, now scuffed with sandal marks, from where Jason had clambered up.

'I know it's hard,' said Alex, looking into Aries' eyes, 'but that's just the way things are down here. Goddesses will always prefer statues of hunky men to rams in their Pavilion because that's what heroes look like to them.' He shrugged, glancing over at the trunk of a nearby oak tree riddled with arrows, and rubbed Aries' head. 'And look! He only managed to hit the target three times.'

'Despite the s-s-size of it,' added Hex, snapping his tongue back quickly as Aries swung round and fixed him with a hot stare.

Quickly realising his mistake, Hex dropped onto the ground and zigzagged between the ram's hoofs. Then, snagging a dock leaf on his fang, he slithered up onto the statue's horns and hung down to busily rub Jason's sandal scuffs off the marble.

'The important thing to remember,' he hissed, glancing up between polishes, 'is-s-s that *we* know what we did. Unlike Jas-s-son, who you keeping ins-s-sis-s-s-ting didn't do what he's-s-s famous-s-s for, we really did s-s-save Ros-s-se and Hazel.'

Aries sank down onto his haunches and stuck out his bottom lip sulkily. It was different for Hex, he decided, his eyes following the snake's circling snout as he rubbed at the statue again, because escaping from Medea's clutches had been prize enough.

And Alex?

Of course Aries knew that the boy wouldn't give a mouldy fig for statues or fame. Or, he sighed, toadying poets who wrote epic poems about quests. Of course flouncy Jason and his wretched crew had a whole book devoted to how they'd snitched the Fleece. Written by **Apollonius** some years after the voyage, from the account given by Jason himself, since the ship's log had been unfortunately lost overboard on the trip, ***The Argonautica*** was on the scroll-shelf of every god and goddess, soldier, schoolchild and citizen in the Underworld. Oh yes, Aries groaned inwardly, down here they just couldn't get enough of his glittering story of bravery and glory.

And what, precisely, did he have?

A statue adorning the zoo toilets whose bottom was used for target practice.

Hooray!

Snuffling, Aries decided to settle down and feel properly sorry for himself.

He snatched a sunlit nettle and began chewing miserably, brooding on the fact that ever since he'd come down to the Underworld he'd been treated as nothing more than a four-legged laughing stock, as bald as a barrel. Even their London quest hadn't changed the way people looked at him. Now, lifting his muzzle, he turned to watch Alex, the boy's glossy black hair flopping over his face as he sliced up bread, setting it out on the long picnic table beside the lake, together with pots of salmon paste and a giant bowl of eel trifle ready for the mer-musicians' lunch. Aries loved the boy with all his heart, but that only made it even more frustrating that Alex didn't seem to understand how furious he felt. And, after everything they'd done up on Earth, could the boy really just go back to buttering bread for monsters? To cleaning flotsam from **Charybdis**'s pool? And soothing **Scylla**'s sulks? Aries rolled his eyes. Only yesterday, Alex had spent half the afternoon leaning over the sea-monster's tank, whispering close to the water to cheer her up. But then again, what could Aries expect when the boy had even used his prize from Athena to buy new things for the **Stymphalian Birds**' aviary? Not to mention installing them himself, struggling with the man-sized ladders and ships' bells, all the time flinching just far enough away from the tips of the birds' bronze beaks as they pecked impatiently from behind a makeshift net of iron. And for those of you not bold enough to read my last book, and who might be wondering why Alex should need to be so careful around the monster birds, what with his already being a ghost, let me give you one word: *extinguished*. This is what happens when a Greek ghost is killed a second time and is snuffed out to nothing with little more than a shocked gasp and a cry of, 'Oooo! What was th—?'

Of course, such good friends might have taken the latest outrage visited on Aries' statue properly if Aries hadn't been quite so grumpy or Alex quite so busy.

And certainly if a beetle-black chariot hadn't at that exact moment appeared, careering along the far side of the lake, thundering towards them, its driver wrestling the reins of two ebony horses.

Aries blinked, recognising the plumes of gold and purple in their brow bands, his heart tightening in alarm at the sight of the chariot belonging to Persephone, the Queen of the Underworld. Jumping to his hooves, he raced over to Alex, feeling his ears quiver as the driver blew three long shrills on a bugle.

'What's happening?' he cried, staring up into the boy's astonished face.

Alex shook his head as Hex threw himself off the statue and wrapped his long grey body around the boy's neck, closing his eyes tight shut as the ground began to tremble with the pounding of hoofs.

Seconds later, Aries' view of the sky vanished completely behind a wall of snorting black horses. Rearing up, they spattered Aries with frothy dribble, their hooves pummelling the air above his head before each clanged down onto the ground in a frenzy of whinnying.

The driver, a stocky man with a cloud of wild grey hair, wiped his brow with the back of his hand, straightened the bugle hanging across his bull-like chest and stared down at them.

'Alex Knossos?'

Alex nodded, pointing to Aries. 'And this is —'

'I know about the livestock,' grunted the driver. 'Queen wants to see you both. Castle **Hades**. Now.'

III
A Ram, A Ma'am, A Ding-Dong

Rams don't make good charioteers.

This is because they can only cling on by their mouths, leaving their hooves to clatter madly in all directions beneath them like bad flamenco dancers that no Spanish frock or fancy fan-flapping will improve. Now, as the chariot sped around yet another bend, Aries' belly lurched, dragging his copious rump sideways, to flatten Alex and the driver in a double-ram-whammy against the front of the vehicle, resulting in a cacophony of splutters (Alex) and extremely rude words (the driver). Meaning that everyone was very relieved when Castle Hades, crouching like a disgruntled crow amidst the Mountains of Despair, finally hove into view.

Built from marble as black as squid's ink, the royal residence comprised a cluster of buildings, flat-roofed and blank-walled, each built around a courtyard and graced by a first-storey colonnade. Once, the king had greeted the newly arrived ghosts from these lofty corridors, nodding as they wailed around the walkways, sobbing into their shrouds, trailing their grief like toilet paper stuck to the soles of their shoes. In those days, the palace had rumbled with the snoring of bats, which hung about the place like forgotten Christmas decorations, their fuzzy bodies glistening with damp from the fog of eternal doom that billowed endlessly around the Underworld.

But not any more.

'Are we there yet?' yowled Aries, out of the corner of his mouth.

'Nearly,' yelled Alex, noticing the festoons of pink and yellow flags, cheerful as Battenberg cake, flapping against the dark walls.

Because you see, when King Hades had kidnapped Persephone from Earth and made her his queen, she'd found herself the only living person in a drab, drippy Land of the Lost. All that snuffling, snivelling and gloom had quickly depressed her and she'd turned her mind to brightening things up, transforming the palace (and the Underworld with it) from grave to groovy.

Out went the mist and the soggy bats.

Out went the stench-swamps, where the speckled frogs of insult abused the newly dead between fruity burps.

Out went the petrified forests and fountains draped with stone skeletons.

And in came the fragrant rose gardens and trilling nightingales, the crystal-clear pools skirted by butterflies of joy, and orange trees scenting the air around fountains carved with bouncing bunny rabbits.

And bunting.

Lots and lots of bunting.

But Alex didn't have time to admire the décor. Quite

apart from being squashed, winded and bruised, he was overwhelmed with worry about why she should summon them there in the first place.

Worry, and something else.

Excitement.

That's right.

Because what Aries would've been astonished to learn was that far from being content to return to his zoo job, Alex had felt horribly restless ever since they'd left London. Lately, he'd felt only flashes of frustration when Scylla soared from her tank to spatter the crowds with a watery mash of mackerel, when it used to make him laugh. And his new feelings upset him. After all, working in the zoo had always been his dream job and he still loved caring for the monsters more than anything. But, even so, he couldn't escape the fact that finding slippers to fit the Minotaur's hooves or settling the **Centaurs**' squabbles was nothing like going on a quest, not nearly as thrilling as fighting an army of Medea's enchanted mannequins or lying strapped to a tomb and using his last scrap of imagination to stop Hex from killing him.

Not that we have time to talk about that now.

Not with the chariot flying in beneath the castle's iron gateway, a fretwork of black skulls now interlaced with pink ribbons and into the palace grounds. There was a furious squeal of wheels as the chariot screeched to a stop, followed by two matching yells of pain as Aries crashed into Alex and then the driver for the last time.

'Sorry about that,' muttered Aries.

Giving himself a brisk shake, he clopped down on to the stone-flagged courtyard and glanced longingly at the olive trees dotted around.

'East wing,' growled the driver, scowling at Aries. 'Follow the path. Queen's quarters, top of the steps.'

Aries glowered at the man as he limped away, muttering loudly about not being paid enough to transport overweight sheep.

'Well, what a delightful man,' said Aries. 'Topping off a charming day. First my statue's used for target practice, then I'm bundled on to a boneshaker by a man with the manners of a windy bull, before being deposited like a sack of last week's turnips to meet royalty. I've got hoof-rub. Bruised buttocks. And as for my voice —'

'Will you be losing it soon?' teased Alex and gave Aries' ear a reassuring rub before setting Hex down gently on the ground. 'Come on. Why don't we find out why we're here?'

Following the marble path, they soon reached a large black door set beneath a columned porch decorated with carved skeletons wearing pink ribbons. Alex rapped loudly with the brass-skull knocker and a few seconds later one of the queen's handmaidens peeped out. Willowy and prettily dressed in a green chiton, her smile vanished as she caught sight of Aries snorting impatiently, with Hex wrapped around his horns.

'We're here to see Her Majesty,' said Alex, noticing the pink carnations woven into the handmaiden's plait and musing briefly whether the staff always dressed as though they were attending a party.

Snatching a glance over his shoulder at the palace path behind them, the maid showed them into an airy entrance hall and through an archway into a long corridor. Lined by a row of columns on the left, it bordered a sunny courtyard. In the middle of its lawn Cerberus, Hades' three-headed hellhound, lolled like an overfilled suitcase, chewing a ball in one mouth, a bone in the second and panting with the third. All of which, thought Alex with relief, meant that he was too busy to notice, smell or, worse, chase the gigantic ram clopping past with a juicy side-order of snake garnishing his horns.

A sudden burst of giggles made Alex jump and, looking up, he noticed three more handmaidens scanning the horizon from the flat roof of the opposite building. Something special was certainly happening today.

But what?

Unfortunately, before he could ask the young woman leading the way, she stopped in front of a heavy door edged by two sword-shaped hinges and tapped twice.

'The throne room,' she said, pushing the door open to reveal a cavernous hall lit by flickering torches and dominated at the far end by two enormous stone thrones. Alex and Aries stepped inside, blinking in the sudden gloom after the sunshine of outside.

'About time too!' squealed Queen Persephone, who was perched precariously on top of a pile of cushions stuffed on one of the thrones. Slight, golden-skinned and freckle-faced, she was the same bubbly young woman the king had married all those years ago. She stuck out her small feet and admired her sparkling green flip-flops. (Yes, flip-flops. And we'll come to how she happened to be wearing those in a moment.)

Beside her, on the second throne, the goddess Athena was reading, her owl snoozing on her shoulder and her aegis,[12] spear and helmet tucked at her feet. Glancing up for a moment, her grey eyes met Alex's and he felt a spark of excitement behind his ribs. For Athena to be here, he knew that something very important must be happening. After all, even though Athena was Persephone's aunt, everyone in the Underworld knew that the goddess was far too serious and stuffy for her niece to invite her over for a girly chat.

'Ma'am,' said Alex, bowing to the queen before turning to Athena. 'Goddess.'

Beside him, Aries touched his muzzle to his kneecaps.

'Approach!' said the queen, flinging her long russet-coloured plait over her shoulder.

Alex and Aries walked across the huge room, the blue and gold mosaic of its floor twinkling beneath their feet and hoofs. On their left the king's tapestries hung, depicting blood-soaked battles and funeral processions.

---

12 Aegis is the fancy name for Athena's shield. Pronounced 'eee-jis', she carried this shield with her everywhere, to bed, to the agora, even to the bathroom. This was because she could never be sure where a new battle might spring up and the shield had always been her help in aegis past.

On the right hung Persephone's, pastel pink and blue and bursting with lovebirds.

'Not the ever-hungry ram!' shrilled a small frantic voice in a chaotic crumpling of paper. 'Quick! Roll me up, someone!'

There was a flash of cream vellum and, craning his neck, Alex caught a glimpse of the All-Knowing Scroll as it shot from its cushion, bounced off the floor and somersaulted like a maiden's baton in the **Panathenea** to land behind a nearby stack of travelling cases. A moment later, it peeped out from what appeared to Alex to be a soft toy lizard, button-eyed and made from shiny blue silk, curled around the biggest trunk.

Intrigued by the curious-looking creature, he turned back to the queen. 'Have you been to Earth again, ma'am?'

She nodded brightly. 'Ibiza!'

Which brings me back to those flip-flops.

You see, for the last three thousand years or so, Persephone had been popping up to Earth like a piece of Underworld toast. The only inhabitant of the Underworld ever allowed to return, her holidays had started soon after King Hades snatched her, when her mother, Demeter, goddess of the harvest, had stomped down to the Underworld and jabbed her new son-in-law over and over again with her pitchfork, until he let Persephone visit her back home for six months a year. Nowadays, even though Demeter, like all the other Ancient Greeks, resided in the Underworld too, her daughter refused to give up her holidays. (Not that you could blame her, what with King

Hades spending most of his time in the royal shed, polishing his collection of bashed ribs, hips and crumpled helmets, which he grandly called his Museum of Messy Deaths.)

She sighed wistfully. 'Oh, it was wonderful! Swimming by moonlight, sangria on the beach, dancing until —'

'Never mind all that,' snapped Athena. She slid off her throne and regarded Alex, Aries and Hex sternly. 'Look at this!'

She held out the magazine she'd been looking at to Alex. He felt his heart tighten, recognising it as one just like Rose had shown them – an Earth parchment full of pictures and stories about famous people.

'The queen brought it back from Earth. Page thirty-one!' barked the goddess.

'I didn't know what to do!' said Persephone, as Alex flicked quickly through the pages. She jumped off her chair and slip-slapped across the room to stand beneath the most recent portrait of King Hades waving his Sword of Calamity. 'Of course, there'd be no point talking to him!' She nodded up at the picture showing the king frowning over his enormous beard, crumpling his face into his best doomladen expression, which unfortunately only made him look like a bad-tempered sultana. 'He'd only tell me not to worry my little head. It was the same when I warned him about that little minx, **Helen of Troy**. I told him her flirting would start a fight! Do you know what he said?'

'No, ma'am,' said Alex hurrying past page twenty, page twenty-one . . .

'That the roses could do with a pruning!' exclaimed Persephone.

Page twenty-two . . .

'Three thousand Greeks about to be wiped out, and Hades is talking to me about gardening! That's why I had to call Aunt Athena.'

Page thirty-one.

Alex felt his jaw drop.

'What is it?' demanded Aries, batting down the edge of the magazine with his muzzle. '"Fashion designer turns over a tropical new leaf"?' he read. Yes, read, because Aries, like Alex, still owned the gift of tongues that Athena had bestowed upon them earlier in the summer, the ability to read, speak and understand any language on Earth, including the Spanish in the magazine that the queen had brought back.

'*Tropical* leaf?' He looked up at Alex. 'I thought the police in Britain were dealing with her.'

Which was charmingly optimistic, really.

Don't get me wrong, London's police force is famous the world over, but even the capital's finest is up against two major problems with Medea. One, she's a crafty lying sorceress. And two, well, like I said, she's a crafty lying sorceress.

Which Alex might have pointed out, had the photograph not frozen him speechless.

In it, Medea stood at the centre of a group of men and women with black hair, cut high over their brows, and golden-brown skin. Like everyone else, she was wearing a printed sarong and a necklace strung with yellow and blue feathers. Silvery-eyed, she smiled out from beneath a spectacular headdress of black feathers, each of their tips splashed with white whilst her face was painted with ochre-red stripes that ran in lines over her nose and cheeks, making her look like a cat. A scratchy, spiteful one.

Seeing the sorceress's icy face again, Alex felt his heart start to hammer and, taking a second look at the wide paddle-shaped leaves behind her, he was grimly certain that their feathery fronds and the fire-red flowers cupped in them were nothing like the spindly trees he remembered seeing on London's streets.

'She's in Brazil,' explained Persephone, pulling herself back up on to the throne. 'The Amazon rainforest.'

'The Amazon?' said Alex, exchanging a nervous look with Aries.

There was a nervous snap of fangs as Hex squirmed through Aries' horns and stretched up into the air and looped about Alex's shoulders, in order to look at the magazine.

'According to this,' said Alex, scanning past pictures of a waterfall and a tall mountain of rock, 'Medea's heading into the jungle to make jewellery with a tribe in the Amazon rainforest. 'In an exclusive interview with our magazine,' he read out loud, 'she told our reporter that she wants to make amends for what she calls her terrible behaviour towards the police at the Leicester Square Luxe theatre earlier in the summer. "I can't imagine what came over me," she said. "I'm so ashamed. Now I just want to put it all behind me by doing something good."'

'Something good?' Aries groaned in disbelief.

'The magazine says,' replied Athena, 'that the Amazon Indians share their traditional skills with her and are properly paid for their wares in return. They call it Fair Trade.'

'Ssscare trade, more like,' muttered Hex. 'There'sss no way ssshe'sss there out of the kindnessss of her heart. Ssshe does-s-sn't have one.'

Aries turned and clattered over the floor to the pile of packing cases by Persephone's throne and pressed his muzzle against the Scroll.

'Oy! Paper knickers! You're supposed to know everything. What's she really up to?'

'As a matter of fact,' replied the Scroll primly, 'the Underworld is too far from Earth for me to pick up on that particular vibration. However, the article tells us that she is staying a long way north-east in Kaxuyana territory at Tatu Village.'

'Meaning?' said Aries, impatiently jabbing the Scroll with his horn.

'Meaning,' replied the Scroll, twirling onto its end and telescoping out to a point to jab Aries back, 'that she is heading to exactly the same place as Rose!'

'What?' squealed Aries, clattering backwards, his tail spinning.

The Scroll sighed. 'I'm afraid that Tatu Village lies on the coordinates that I gave to Rose to find her father.'

'Noooo!' bellowed Aries, making the castle tapestries tremble on their poles. He thundered back to Alex and began clopping around him in circles.

'Do you think Medea's going to take her revenge on Rose for what we did in the summer? Maybe she's out to punish her?' He flung up his head in horror, his eyes wide with panic. 'Or worse? Alex, what are we going to do?'

Except that Alex wasn't listening.

This was because all he could hear was the roar of blood in his ears. Guilt, like a hot tide, surged through him, making his head ring and his heart drum wildly. He couldn't believe it. Whilst he'd been feeling a bit bored with zoo life, Rose had been travelling into danger; whilst he'd been consoling Aries about his statue, Medea was planning and scheming in the jungle. Now, standing in the twilit throne room, he shivered, imagining her, squat as a bulbous spider in the centre of a web, picking up quivers on silken threads, waiting as Rose approached.

'Alex?' Aries tattooed his hooves frantically.

Snapping back from his thoughts, Alex looked down at the ram.

'We don't know what Medea's up to,' he said. 'But whatever it is, Rose is in danger. We have to go back to Earth and find her. We have to protect her from the sorceress.'

'Nooooo!' Hex vanished down the back of Alex's chiton in a blur of silver.

'It's all right,' soothed Alex, remembering the promise

he'd made to the snake in London: that he'd never have to see the sorceress again. 'You couldn't come even if you wanted to,' he continued.

'No?' said Hex, sticking his shivering snout out of Alex's collar.

'Of course not,' replied Alex, eager to protect the snake's feelings. 'You're far too important to the Zoo. I'll need you here to make sure the monsters are properly looked after whilst I'm away.'

'Really?' said Hex, slithering back onto Alex's shoulders.

'Really,' agreed Alex in his most serious voice.

'To be honest,' snapped Athena, 'this matter is rather more important than deciding who'll make the Minotaur's bean stew. That's why I brought you here.'

Prickling with worry about Rose, Alex watched Athena sit down and lift her shield on to her lap. He willed her to hurry up and explain herself. 'You see,' she began, 'ever since you and Aries came back, I've been worried about Medea and the havoc she's wreaked on that lot up there.' She nodded quickly towards the ceiling.

'The *mortals*, goddess?' said Alex, puzzled.

Athena blushed. 'Yes, I know! It must sound completely ridiculous! Me? Pallas Athena? Daughter of Zeus? Fretting about those silly little Earth people.'

'Totally ungoddessy,' agreed Persephone, leaning on one oversized carved arm, her chin cupped in her hand.

'Rather below you,' sniffed the Scroll.

'But you see, I had no idea that she had the Golden Fleece.' Athena leaned forward on the throne, her face serious. 'Nor that she was using it for such dreadful things.'

'But it's all used up now,' said Aries. 'And we stopped her from making any more.'

'Yes,' said Athena. 'But do you honestly believe that someone as vicious as she's turned out to be is really going into the jungle to string beads on to a piece of wire? Or that it's just a coincidence that she happens to be precisely where your little friend is headed?' Athena stood up and took a deep breath. 'As goddess of wisdom, I can't allow her to do any more harm. It's time she was brought to justice.' Athena fixed Alex with a cool silvery stare. 'The way I see it, it's the gods' fault that she's still on Earth in the first place. I've been talking to my father, Zeus, and the other **Olympians** and we all agree that if we hadn't banned her from the Underworld . . .'

'Then she wouldn't be such a nightmare up there now,' finished Persephone.

'Quite,' said Athena.

'Are you saying —?' started Alex.

'She's committed terrible crimes for centuries now. Whichever way you look at it, she belongs in Tartarus,' said the goddess.

In the silence that followed, Alex found his mind spinning with the stories he'd heard about Tartarus. The Underworld prison was a dark and terrible place, echoing with the moans and yells of Ancient Greece's wickedest criminals being punished in horribly inventive ways. Like Tantalus, starving and mad with thirst, but forever condemned to stand in a pool of water that seeped away when he tried to scoop a handful to drink and a bower of grapes that sprang beyond his grasp whenever he reached up.

'Now I understand!' said Aries. Tossing his horns in the air, he strutted over to the portrait of King Hades and swung his derriere round. Then, framed by two floor-standing candlesticks, he regarded Athena and Persephone nobly. 'This is clearly why you summoned us here today,' he said. 'Because such a mission will take endurance, talent and daring. Obviously, Alex and I have just such a proven track record of unflinching courage.'

'Actually —' said Persephone.

Aries slammed down his hoof, silencing her with a clang. 'The task will take someone who doesn't run from a terrifying ordeal!'

'Yes!' said Athena.

'Who stands their ground no matter what?'

'Of course,' agreed Athena.

Beaming at Alex, Aries threw back his head. 'Which is —'

'Jason!' Athena clapped her hands in delight as the leader of the Argonauts swaggered into the room.

Alex stared as Jason approached the thrones, suddenly realising why the palace maids had been so jittery and prettily dressed. Gleaming in his battle armour, the leader of the Argonauts looked magnificent, his famous leopard-skin flung rakishly over one shoulder. Watching him, Alex became slowly aware that Aries was starting to make a very strange noise, rather like a hornet trapped in a jar, a high furious keening, and sliding his eyes sideways, Alex saw the ram's face, sucked-in and rumpled, his muzzle so tightly concertinaed beneath his eyes that it resembled a Spartan's shield after a Persian battle elephant had trampled it.

'Jason will quest through the Amazon to find Medea!' Athena announced proudly.

'Not with me he won't!' boomed Aries.

'Of course not,' said Athena. 'Not *with* you. You're simply going along with the hero of this quest to carry the equipment he'll need!'

'What?' squealed Aries, his eyes wide in furious disbelief.

Catching sight of the ram's face, lined with rage and hurt, Alex felt the injustice like a punch and hearing a snigger he looked up to see Jason rubbing a tiny smear from his breastplate and grinning coldly.

'Is there a problem, Baldy?' he teased.

Persephone kicked out her feet and giggled.

Alex wrapped a reassuring arm around Aries' hot neck, feeling the ram's pulse like a spring stream throbbing through the veins of his neck. He understood his anger and wounded pride, but when a moment later Aries' chest ballooned against his shoulder as the ram raised his head, his lip curled back with a blistering reply, Alex grabbed hold of Aries' muzzle and clamped it shut. There were more important things at stake.

'How mwh-mwh-mwh!' Aries twisted against the boy's grasp as Alex met Athena's gaze.

'And why am I here?' asked Alex.

'Because you're a bright boy,' said Athena. 'And I think that your recent knowledge of Earth might be of some small use in helping Jason find Medea.'

'And then what?' said Alex.

'Then,' Athena stood up, smiling proudly, 'he'll give Medea this.' She turned and rummaged in her bag to pull out a small statue. Carved from black marble, it was of a woman with a cold, cheerless face and wings arching high above her shoulders. In her left hand she clutched a set of scales; in her right, a sword.

'Nemesis?' said Alex.

Athena nodded. 'The goddess of retribution.'

Alex wondered at the point of delivering the figurine. He stared at its thin, judgemental mouth and beak of a nose, perfect for gleefully sticking in the air when someone got his or her just desserts. Then he noticed odd little flashes of red, orange and blue light, glinting beneath the statue's smooth veneer.

'Although,' continued Athena, stroking the statue's bony shoulders, 'this time, she's more of a Wooden Horse.[13] You see,' she continued, clearly warming to her own cleverness, 'I've filled this statue with the Erinyes.'

---

13 The Wooden Horse was a gigantic timber gee-gee, left by the Greeks outside Troy. Pretending defeat, the Greeks sailed away and the triumphant Trojans dragged the horse into their city as a trophy. However, unfortunately for them, it was actually filled with an elite team of Greek fighters who crept out at night and threw open the city gates to the returning army who then destroyed the city and won the war. (Soon to be a major movie: Troy Story.*)*

Alex felt his skin freeze. Beside him, Aries stopped struggling, his eyes wide with shock.

Which was hardly surprisingly.

The Erinyes, you see, were spirits of vengeance. Three bat-winged women with the heads of dogs and eyes that cried blood, they used whips of live scorpions to thrash the guilty, whispering endlessly in their ears and forcing the culprit to face justice.[14]

'As soon as Nemesis is placed in Medea's hand, the Erinyes will burst out and drag Medea straight to Tartarus.'

'Placed in her hand?' said Alex nervously.

Athena rolled her eyes. 'Well, there's no need to look like that about it. Obviously Jason will do the tricky stuff. He's the one with all the experience and daring. And besides, he knows Medea the best. That means it'll be easy for him to get close enough to hand her the statue.'

Alex's mind reeled. Expecting Jason to hand-deliver a statue to Medea was like asking Herakles to leap into the Nemean Lion's compound at the zoo and present the creature he'd strangled with a gift-wrapped bone. He opened his mouth to protest. Then he saw the sugary-sweet way Athena was gazing at Jason and closed it again. Clearly, having picked Jason to go as her champion, Athena wasn't about to be moved. He felt his chest

---

14 Personally, I'd already have apologised charmingly in sixteen different languages long before those stinging swishers appeared.

tighten. Even if Jason was the most celebrated hero in the Underworld, brave enough to lead and fight and triumph over all the obstacles in his path, the goddess had sorely underestimated Medea and he felt his heart thump, certain that the ice-blooded witch they'd defeated in the summer wouldn't be happy to see anyone from the Underworld bearing gifts and particularly not her handsome ex-husband.

Not that they had time to argue about that now because up on Earth, Rose was every minute journeying into danger. Behind him, Aries nudged his knees and, releasing his grip on the ram's muzzle, Alex looked into his face. Beyond the resentment clouding his eyes, and the way his fury made his flanks tremble, the ram's brow was furrowed with the same impatience that Alex felt knotted tight behind his ribs.

He turned back to Athena. 'When do we leave?'

IV
I Scry With My Little Eye . . .

Deep in the jungle, Medea was scrying.

That's *scrying*, not crying.

Crying is what you do after you've plunged head-first into a muddy puddle in your hockey lesson, come indoors to face fractions in maths and still have an essay on the life-cycle of a teabag to write for homework.

Scrying is what witches do when they want to find out precisely what somebody is up to. It's a bit like a spooky Facebook, but you don't need a computer, just a strong stomach because it always smells dreadful. To do it, the witch mixes up lots of gloopy liquids in a big pot and sets this over a fire. Then she stares into the swirling mix, watching it bubble and spit, peering through the roiling steam and thinking hard of the person she wants to snoop on (without breathing in too deeply) until at last the mixture burps, squelches and rolls completely flat. At this point, a picture appears, rising up from the blackness of the mixture like an old-fashioned television crackling into life to play a silent movie of the person of her choice.

Which in Medea's case was Rose, on whom she'd

been scrying ever since the girl left England. What a clever trick. Except that now, blinking through the stinky smoke that billowed out of the great brass bowl, Medea felt anything but clever.

Hot?

Yes, since despite being lightly dressed in a pair of khaki shorts, T-shirt and boots, the humid jungle air clung to her skin like a lovesick jellyfish.

And bothered?

Certainly.

But not clever.

Scrying, you see, made her feel like she was twelve years old again, a girl spending summers with her Aunt Circe on the island of Aeaea[15] watching the real witch do all the exciting stuff. It was just so *babyish* – a piffling, tiddly little spell that fell so far short of the truly ghastly magic that she yearned to do that it made her teeth ache. Scrunching up her face at the stench of bad dragon eggs and Spartan stinkhorn mushrooms, she flung some more tendrils from the feather she'd long ago plucked from Hera's, the queen of the gods', pet peacock into the mixture and reminded herself that but for Aries and Alex she wouldn't be reduced to such bog-standard magic, swathed in smoke and stuck in the middle of a jungle. She wrinkled her nose, disgusted as a droplet of sweat dribbled down it and splashed into the mixture. Oh, but for their

---

15 Tricky to say, Aeaea is pronounced 'I-er–I-er' as in the phrase 'I, er, I, er, wish the place was called something easy, like Corfu.'

interference she'd have had a hundred Golden Fleeces sparkling at her fingertips, giving her more glittering power than she'd ever known in all her long and vicious life. Of course, with *that* sort of witch-power she'd have been able to magic up an iceberg, right here in the middle of the rainforest, one that could drip, drip, drip freezing silvery-blue water into a bucket for her swollen feet. Or conjure a swimming pool rippling beneath a tent of cool, mosquito-proof silk. Or a fan the size of a windmill that would work without electricity. But then, she fumed, if those two dollops of taramasalata hadn't ruined her plans in the first place, she wouldn't need to, would she? Because she'd still be in London, giggling with the rich, famous and soon-to-be-dead instead of in the back of the back of beyond, sweating horribly and living on bananas.

Behind her, the wall was lined with shelves – crammed with spell books, vials of inky liquids, tubs of glistening green lizard scales, jars of herbs and switches of strange plants that continued to bloom in the relentless heat. Not that any of the villagers who stepped into her hut would have seen them, of course. Simple obscurity spells were still within Medea's limited power and this one had worked beautifully, hiding that wall from view, meaning that ordinary people would see only the hut's rugs, its tattered hammock, boxes marked with the 'Fair Trade' logo and Medea's battered steamer trunk, on which the ludicrous black-and-white headdress the reporters had insisted she wear for the magazine shoot continued to slump like a reproachful ostrich.

Suddenly a gust of indigo smoke whooshed up from the pot and the mixture began to settle. Medea stared down, narrowing her icy gaze as ripples shot across the liquid and bounced against the sides. Around her, the air thickened and crackled like the static of a thunderstorm. Now the mixture spluttered, spat and stilled. A fug of silver crept across its surface, then slowly, beneath its misty top, strands of brown and white began twisting into shapes as a picture gradually emerged.

A luxurious white river boat.

A river the colour of black tea.

Leaning closer, closer, Medea began to smile.

The image sharpened to reveal a girl dressed in a grey T-shirt and cargo shorts sitting all alone on the top tier of the boat. Feeling a cold spike of joy, she watched as Rose tilted her face to the sky, noticing how the girl's skin was much more tanned now than when they'd met in London and that the Amazon sun had drawn out her freckles so that they lay dark over her nose and cheeks. But that chaotic snaggle of rust-coloured ringlets was still the same. And, even better, those trusting chocolate-brown eyes . . .

Rose sank back into the squishy leather bench set into the deck, dazzled by the shrieks and hoots and shrills and whoops ringing out from the rainforest that lay far away on either side of the gigantic Rio Negro. Above her, a canopy of silk fluttered in the wind, as flawless and blue as the sky beyond it. She gazed across the vast stretch of dark water and the green wall of jungle beyond, finally understanding why her parents had been drawn to this remarkable place. A cluster of huts gleamed along the bank on the right. Each was built high on stilts and she remembered how her mother had told her that in the rainy season this river swelled and surged, rising up until the houses appeared to float on its surface, like water lilies. Now, in August, their stilts were exposed and sun-bleached, and a patch of sandy land ran down to the water's edge in front of them, where five boys were playing football. Seeing the boat, they stopped and stared back.

And no wonder.

Rose had never seen a boat as luxurious as this in her life either. The *Tucano* was three storeys of polished wooden decks, its cabins sumptuous with floor-to-ceiling blue-tinted glass, making it a gorgeous, floating hotel of air-conditioned rooms, enormous beds and five-star cooking. Usually it carried twenty passengers, but Hazel had chartered it for just the two of them together with a crew of sailors, cook, kitchen staff, stewards, laundry workers and cleaners, all under the command of Captain Eduardo da Silva. Rose liked him very much. A sturdy, cheerful man of sixty-three, with a laugh in his voice, he had spent his life in the Brazilian Navy. Now he spent his days taking glamorous boats through the Amazon rainforest for glamorous tourists. Although Rose was pretty sure he'd never had quite such a glamorous tourist as Hazel.

Rose stood up and waved at the children who giggled

and waved back. A tan dog splashed into the water and barked merrily.

A moment later, the boys turned back to their game.

Behind them, the jungle seemed to loom like a barricade and staring into the thick green light beneath the trees Rose felt a strange prickle of cold. Quickly rubbing her shoulders, she felt the knot of worry that had twisted in her stomach ever since they'd arrived tighten as she wondered again what had happened to her father to keep him here.

The sound of Hazel's cabin door crashing open made her jump.

'Look!' cried Hazel, quickly climbing up the steps on to the top deck.

'I know!' smiled Rose, spotting a flock of scarlet and turquoise parrots flapping over the water. 'This place is amazing, isn't it?'

'No,' replied Hazel.

Puzzled, Rose turned back to Hazel who was stomping towards her, hot and sour-faced, waving her right hand dismally in the air.

'My nail!' whined Hazel, sticking her finger out for Rose to examine. 'It's chipped!'

'Oh!' said Rose, trying to sound sympathetic as she spotted a tiny chink in the glossy pink nail.

'Can you believe, I damaged it swattin' an elephant-sized moth? Course, I'm all but out of "Blossom of Shanghai" polish and there's so totally nowhere around here to buy any more.'

'Eduardo says we're stopping at a market this afternoon. At Acajatuba. We need supplies. Maybe we could try there?'

'Me? In that jungle?' Hazel wrinkled her nose and glared at the riverbank. 'Besides, it's nail polish I need, Rose. Not a bag of coffee beans and a new parrot!'

Hazel slumped down beside her, smoothed her pink T-shirt and scowled at the heaps of fresh fruit, cereal, juice and plates of meat set out for breakfast on the crisp tablecloth.

'What's that?' she said eyeing up a brownish-pink fish lying on a blue plate.

'Piranha,' said Rose simply. 'Grilled and salted.'

Hazel curled her lip. 'You have to be kiddin' me.'

'It's an Amazon speciality,' said Rose, as Hazel began prodding at the gloomy-looking fish with a knife. 'The chef made it as a treat.'

'Treat?' Hazel picked up her plate and flipped the fish overboard. 'RIP!' she muttered and poured herself a large glass of mango juice.

Rose sighed and looked away, wishing yet again that Hazel might lighten up.

You see, almost as soon as they had arrived, things had started to annoy her and just how, as she'd lamented over and again, was she supposed to refresh herself when everything about the Amazon was so *dang* uncomfortable?

First it had been the sun – *sizzlin' like a Texan branding iron* – making it impossible for her to sit outside on deck and sip coconut coolers with Rose after ten in the morning. Then it had been the afternoon rains – *beatin' down like a crazy showerhead* – that kept her indoors until five because it ruined her hair. The bugs – *bigger 'n nickels* – had totally splatted her cabin window – *thank heav'n they couldn't fly through glass* – though they'd surely spoiled the view from her Jacuzzi, whilst that *infernal whooping of monkeys* had so jangled her nerves she couldn't enjoy playing deck games of quoits. And as for the as for the captain's nightly talks, well, maybe Rose did find it *fascin-atin'*, but as far as she was concerned when Eduardo shone his torch along the riverbank, pointing out the ruby red lights that glinted back from the caimans' eyes – creatures just as horrible and snappy as the alligators back home – all she could think about was her rifle.

Rose groaned inwardly as Hazel began picking at a bowl of dry cereal with her fingers. Being a kind and thoughtful girl, of course Rose wanted her new friend to enjoy the trip and she felt a sharp sting of guilt that Hazel was so ill at ease. After all, it was down to Rose that the young star was out here in the first place, which was why, over and over again, Rose had tried to suggest things that Hazel might like to see or do or taste or try or visit. They'd got on so brilliantly in England. But now, after five days of Hazel's moaning and griping, it was truly starting to wear her down. Being in the Amazon rainforest with someone, Rose decided, was very different from sharing a hot chocolate in a swanky hotel with them and now, as she gazed out over the water, she found herself wishing yet again that it was Alex and Aries on board with her.

If only!

Certain she'd never see them again, her heart sank. She missed them. And, knowing how the Amazon would have fascinated Alex made her feel even more downcast. Like her, he'd have loved the armadillos waddling down to the water for a drink and the pink dolphins, the *botos*, which followed the *Tucano* each day. The howlers would have totally amazed him too – the giant russet-haired monkeys, hooting and bellowing from the trees, as raucous as dinosaurs. To be honest, they'd scared her at first, right up until Eduardo told her that according to the *ribereños*, or river people, their deafening chorus should be cherished, because when they fell silent, it meant evil was present among the trees. She sighed. Alex would have yearned to spot a jaguar lolling in the treetops, just like she did. She swallowed a giggle, thinking of how Aries would be much more worried about the jaguar spotting him.

'Where exactl' are we?' said Hazel, breaking into her thoughts.

'About two days from the Wedding of the Waters.'

'Two days?' Hazel made it sound like a jail sentence. 'Weddin' of the what?'

'Waters,' said Rose. 'It's where the Rio Negro meets the Amazon,' said Rose, trying hard not to sound like her mother. 'According to Eduardo, the Negro is so full of dark silt that it doesn't mix with the Amazon when they meet. One's black, one's brown, they stay stripy for miles and miles.'

'Miles and miles?' sighed Hazel.

Rose felt her own spirits sinking at how the star she'd been so in awe of could be so, well, disappointing in real life. In London she'd seemed lonely and tired of all the jetsetting and glitz, the interviews, the fame. Now she clearly missed her starry life and all her adoring fans horribly. She watched as Hazel fixed a poisonous stare on a huge moth that was sunbathing on the table before scooching along her seat away from it, and sighed, remembering how on her weekly show, Hazel rode wild horses and ran with the rodeo men. But in reality, far from being what her mother on the show called 'a tough cookie', Rose was discovering that Hazel was far more like a Custard Cream gone soft.[16]

'It leads into the capital of Amazonia,' said Rose finally. 'Manaus.'

'Manaus?' Hazel brightened. 'Then why don't we take a couple of weeks there? I've heard it's like a cross between London and Las Vegas! We could take a girly break from all this jungle stuff. Enjoy us some serious pampering. What d'ya think?'

Rose bit her lip and looked down. Once it would have sounded so tempting. If only it had been just a holiday, of course she'd have loved to explore the city, shopping beneath its silver skyscrapers, swimming at its beaches and visiting the opera house that Eduardo had told her about, the one built by Victorians in the rubber boom, all pink walls and a spangling roof of gold, green

---

16 And believe me, there's nothing more disappointing.

and yellow, that shone like a fairy tale palace in the middle of the jungle.

But how could she waste two weeks in Manaus?

Or even two days?

Or two minutes?

When every second of it was more time that her father would be out there, somewhere, lost in the jungle.

Seeing Hazel's expectant face, Rose bit her lip. 'Maybe on the way back,' she said. 'Because we'll have to go north to reach Tatu Village and find my father, long before the Amazon reaches Manaus.'

And then, thought Rose, leave the *Tucano* to travel the rest of the way by canoe and foot. She pushed the thought away, knowing that now absolutely would not be the time to remind Hazel about that.

'I do understand,' said Hazel, leaning forward and cupping her face in her hands. 'And I can't wait for you two to be back together again either. So, why don't I hire us a man to go into the jungle instead? Y'know, a native tracker to find your daddy for us?'

Rose shook her head and turned back to look at the river. 'I can't wait around for someone else to do it,' she murmured. 'And I won't be parted from him for a second longer than I have to be. I'm going to find him myself.'

The pictures in the scrying bowl vanished in a twist of smoke.

But Medea had seen enough.

Because even without hearing their conversation it

was perfectly clear how badly things were going. Feeling a fizz of excitement, she clapped her hands together, delighted to see Rose, the same earnest, serious girl she remembered, and Hazel, who looked like she'd sucked a lemon.

'Oh my!' drawled Medea, mimicking Hazel perfectly. 'I just love a-travellin' an' seein' the world! All those amazin' new things to discover!' she laughed. *From a mightily safe distance, of course*, added her mind spitefully. The sort of mightily safe distance, say, that you found between the back seat of a limousine and the gritty street outside or from your hotel penthouse down to the city several floors below.

Or from a luxury riverboat just far enough away from that squirming, scurrying, slithering jungle across the water.

Suddenly knowing what to do, Medea turned away from the pot and all but skipped to her steamer trunk without even glancing out of the window to indulge her favourite view. One that I'm sorry to say wasn't the majesty and spectacle of the jungle. Not as breathtaking as a soaring kapok tree or as sizzling as a scarlet orchid. Not even so much as a bad-tempered macaw with droopy blue feathers on its bottom. And to be honest, I'm not even sure I should tell you about it, what with things about to become extremely horrible, you'll probably only run away.

What's that?

You won't?

OK.

But perhaps I'll better build up to it gently just in case . . .

Outside the window of Medea's hut was a beautiful *barrigona* tree, a palm with a swollen trunk, which was home to a whole family of cheeping blue budgerigars that hopped along its frondy branches every morning.

Tweety-tweet tweet!

How charming.

What d'you mean, 'Get on with it, grandma?'

All right then, but don't say I didn't warn you, because beneath that bounce of budgies was a European man. Haggard and wrinkled beyond his years, he sat hunched against the base of the tree, his bony knees, sun-blistered and poking through his ruined trousers, drawn up beneath his chin. Around him the bowls of armadillo stew and gourds filled with fruit juice that the villagers brought him lay forgotten as he stared into the brown water of the nearby creek.

But, like I said, Medea couldn't savour a single second of that today, nor even congratulate herself yet again on just how well she'd hidden him (using her obscurity spell) from that pesky magazine crew who'd badgered her for hours, because she was far too busy. And now, with her mind as fluttery as a cave full of bats, she dropped to her knees and threw back the trunk lid, plunging her hands down, down, through layers of jungle socks and cotton tops, mosquito nets and malaria pills, frantically scrabbling about the base until her fingers touched something smooth, hard and familiar. A moment later, she drew out an object wrapped in blue silk and hastily unwrapped it to reveal a solid gold wrist cuff. Egyptian, and over three thousand years old, it would have been the star exhibit in any museum in the world, but it was worth much, much more to Medea.

Now as you already know, without the Golden Fleece, Medea's magic was about as impressive as a light bulb in a power cut. However, she'd hardly be the most successful, wicked, grimly spectacular sorceress in the history of the entire world if she hadn't thought ahead and planned for just such a magical emergency, would she? Which made this ancient piece of gold jewellery the equivalent of her box of candles under the stairs. A special something saved for those crucial moments in a sorceress's life when her down-at-heel magic simply won't do.

Now, holding it up in the sunlight, she watched its buttery surface twinkle as sunlight glanced off its engraved falcon- and crocodile-headed gods. Sighing, she felt her mind drift back almost a hundred years to Cairo and the sand-blown Valley of the Kings to the excavation of the pharaoh's burial site led by Howard Carter and his friend, Lord Carnarvon. She closed her eyes, conjuring up Carnarvon in her mind, so dapper in the cream linen suit she'd made for him, nodding back to her as he'd stepped into the black mouth of Tutankhamun's tomb.[17]

---

17 Lord Carnarvon died soon after, when a shaving cut led to blood poisoning. This triggered talk of The Pharaoh's Curse – a death-spell said to strike down anybody who intruded into King Tutankhamun's tomb, and indeed, another eight people were to die in spooky ways soon after. However, the

But there was work to do. Giving herself a quick mental shake, she stood up and turned to the shelves, lifting down an ornate wicker box with a brass catch shaped like a dragon's face, its snout clasping a shining blue stone. Setting it down on the worktable, she heard a scuttling from inside and felt her fingers tingle with pure nastiness.

Because with just one blast of full-strength sorcery, courtesy of that gorgeous Egyptian bangle, that little Texan fly in the ointment would to be out of the way for good.

Leaving Rose utterly alone.

---

truth was that they'd all admired Lord Carnavon's tailoring and had asked for the name of his seamstress so that they could all become customers too.

V
Greeks Bearing Gifts

Meanwhile, down in the Underworld, Alex and Aries were ankle and hock-deep in the cold, salty water of the Cave of Acheron. Squinting in the grey light of the cavern, Alex was trying to make sense of the map he'd torn from Persephone's magazine whilst Aries was chewing on a clump of rather tasteless seaweed and considering whether the low tide would give him foot rot, which given the day he'd already had would just about put the tin lid on things.

The cave, in case you're wondering, is the place where the rocky barrier between the Underworld and the Earth is at its thinnest. Back in Ancient Greece, the place was a sort of drippy drop-in for heroes like **Odysseus**, who'd pop in for a chinwag with a clever ghost. Of course, in those days the River of Pain had gushed through it, a river well-named as far as Persephone was concerned, what with all those bad-tempered carp and snappy eels, so you won't be surprised to hear that she'd drained it (more or less) and fixed some cheery iron torches into its walls. More importantly, however, she'd used its closeness to Earth to install her own set of royal portals. Not for her the grubby old way back that Alex and Aries had used in the summer. What? Trudge through the Desert of Disappointment in her best holiday sandals? Cross the River Styx in a creaky boat filled with cave spiders? I think not.

Anyway, don't distract me. The thing is, for Greek portals to work they need to supernaturally connect with Ancient Greece's lost treasures, those old pots and columns and splinters of shield that were left back on Earth and transmit their energy back to the Underworld like satellites from space. Luckily for Persephone and her vacations, such treasures have long been scattered across the globe by armies and archaeologists, collectors and curators. And so, with the help of the ghost Greek engineers and a goodly dollop of godly magic, the queen now had her own network of shortcuts, quickly linking Hades' palace to cities on Earth as easily as a hotel lobby leads to its bedrooms.

The portals were arranged in five rows, carved high into the cave walls. Each row was reached by its own boardwalk, edged by a guardrail and festooned with stripy blue bunting, leading to a long flight of steps, damp and glistening, carved out of the rock.

On any other day Alex would have loved to explore what lay behind each portal door, shining beneath the exotic names painted above them, names like Marrakech, Paris, Tokyo and Rome. But this wasn't any other day and, already changed into the jeans and white T-shirt that Rose had found for him in the lost-property room of the British Museum back in the summer, he felt restless to leave.

Not that Jason was quite ready yet.

'Just look at them,' muttered Aries.

Quickly stuffing the map into his pocket, Alex glanced up to see the Argonaut, who was also dressed in jeans and a T-shirt (lovingly made by the palace seamstresses) framed by the arch of the cave's mouth. Leaping over a patch of damp sand, he twirled and jabbed a stick of driftwood in a mock swordfight with Persephone and the other goddesses. Even Hera, queen of the gods and the wife of Zeus himself (and who Alex thought must be at least three thousand years old and should've known better) stood tilting her face up to him, beaming.

'If we could make a start!' cried Athena, straining to be heard over the chorus of giggles as the Argonaut spun round and tapped each of the goddesses' noses in turn with the tip of the stick.

Aries snorted impatiently and Alex reached down to rub the ram's head. It felt hot with anger and Alex sighed, knowing how hard it would be for the ram to return to Earth with Jason in charge. Of course, Alex had no more time for Greek heroes than Aries did. He hated all that swagger and bluster too, and the way that everyone went weak at the knees for a flash of armour or an arm bulging with biceps. But since the summer and what had happened in London, he'd been surprised to find himself feeling a little bit different and, frankly, rather curious about how the famous quests had actually been done. And despite his best friend's frustration, he still couldn't quash his own growing excitement at returning to Earth. Of course he was fiercely determined to protect Rose from whatever Medea was planning, but he was quietly thrilled too, delighted to be on another adventure, and he thought that maybe this time, in going back to Earth with Jason, he'd have a chance to learn how the heroes always managed to win – a sort of boot camp to find out how they planned and thought, fought and stayed brave even when things were terrifying.

Not that he'd be mentioning that to Aries any time soon.

Obviously.

Alex watched the goddess of wisdom as she turned away from the little group, slipped off her sandals and scooped up her skirts, to walk into the cave. Her owl swooped in behind her, as bright as a snowball in the gloom, and nestled on her shoulder, twittering, as she waded towards them through the water. A flurry of maids splashed after her and quickly stacked an assortment of strange things on a nearby ledge, jutting out from the glistening wall. She waited for them to finish, curtsey and hurry away again, and then, stepping up on to a low flat-topped rock, she set the statue of Nemesis down on top of everything else.

'Jason!' she barked and slapped her shield with a resounding clang.

Glancing over, Jason flung down the driftwood and, offering an arm each to Euterpe, the muse of music, and Aphrodite, goddess of love, escorted them inside, stumbling and giggling, to look at the strange display.

Of course, it's traditional for Greek heroes to take a

magical gift or two on their quests – a pair of winged sandals perhaps, or a cape of invisibility – but usually they don't take quite so many. But then, you see, unlike Alex and Aries, who'd left the Underworld with only the All-Knowing Scroll and the gift of tongues,[18] it seemed that every other goddess wanted to give Jason something to help him on his special quest, too. And since we don't have time for a proper rummage now, let me quickly tell you that already heaped up were:

1) One of Zeus's lightning bolts.
   Made by Hephaestus, the blacksmith god, this zigzag of magical iron could be thrown like a javelin to conjure up an electrical storm.
2) Hestia's Tinder Box.
   A gift from the goddess of the hearth, this tinder could start a fire in the dankest, drippiest anywhere.
3) The Winged Cocktail Stirrer of Dionysus.
   A funny little silver contraption, shaped rather like a beetle. However, having never been invited to one of the God of Wine's snooty gods and heroes soirees, I have no idea what's so special about it.
4) Persephone's Purse of Infinite Wealth.
   This drawstring pouch tipped out coins in the

---

18 Which Athena had already bestowed on Jason, with an extra smattering of lurve words in all languages.

right currency for wherever the queen arrived on Earth.

5) Three pieces of fine embroidery sewn by **Penelope,** showing delightful scenes from old Greece to remind Jason of home.
6) A charming pocket-sized portrait of Zeus.
7) Three ornate fans made from **Pegasus**'s long white feathers for keeping cool.
8) Artemis's Arrows that Never Missed.
   Bundled into a leather quiver, these arrows from the goddess of hunting were trimmed with pink feathers, which I agree was a bit on the girly side. However, this wasn't the first thing you noticed when one whistled over your head and pinned your hat to the tree.

Staring at the odd assortment, Alex felt twitchier than ever, restless to leave. Time, you see, passes a lot more quickly up on Earth and he knew that whilst only a few hours had passed since he and Aries had left the zoo, above them days were flashing past, days where Rose was drawing closer and closer to Medea.

Meaning they should be going.

Right now.

Around him, the goddesses' giggles continued to echo around the rocky walls and he felt a spark of annoyance as he saw Euterpe stepping forward and realised they hadn't even finished yet.

'The Lyre of **Orpheus**,' said the muse of music,

pulling a small golden instrument from her satchel. She strummed its strings lightly, filling the cave with its thin bird-like notes. 'Made from magical adamantine, it will withstand the roughest voyage, soothe raging beasts and bring sweet harmony to any group.'

Sweet harmony, thought Alex. He glanced at Aries, who was glowering at Jason, who was scowling back, and felt his heart sink. Even for a godly gift, it was a big ask from a small harp.

'Me next!' squealed Aphrodite.

Sweeping all the other gifts out of the way, the goddess laid a roll of sapphire velvet on the rock.

'My *pot pourri* of love and desire,' she said, fluttering her eyelashes.

Aries groaned loudly as the goddess unfurled the bundle to reveal a cluster of delicate pink petals, each crystallized and twinkling with sugar.

'Passionflowers,' she explained, 'coated with my special love elixir. Slip one into Medea's food and she'll melt the moment she sees you. I mean, she will anyway, but . . . ' She paused, making a small *moue* with her rosebud mouth.

'But what?' prompted Jason in a gooey voice.

'Oh, Jason,' she sighed. 'You will come home quickly, won't you? I mean, you haven't forgotten it's my birthday at the end of the week?'

'How could I?' said Jason. He held a petal playfully to his lips and gazed into her eyes. 'Shall I test them?'

'No!' squeaked Aphrodite, plucking it from his fingers.

'Just one nibble and you'll be hopelessly in love with the very next person you see.'

'Impossible,' cooed Jason, 'when I'm forever in love with you.'

'You are?' said Aphrodite, delighted.

'Of course he's not!' barked Hera, barging forward and pitching Aphrodite sideways into the surf with a wallop of her hips. 'Never mind all that lovey-dovey stuff,' she went on, turning to the scabbard hanging from a belt on her dress and slowly drawing out a wide double-edged sword. 'This belonged to **Achilles**!'

'Achilles?' said Jason.

His eyes lit up as he took the leaf-shaped sword from her and expertly twisted it in the air, its blade glinting like a swarm of fireflies in the flickering torchlight. The goddesses stared adoringly. And even Alex, who was desperately willing them to hurry up and stop sighing like **harpies** with tail sag, felt a sharp twinge of admiration, imagining what it must be like to be that confident, that sure of yourself. More than that, his mind added, for everyone else to be so sure of you too.

'Ladies!' Jason smiled broadly and laid the sword down with the other gifts. 'You've all been so generous, but,' he turned down his lip in regret, 'much as I'd love to stay here with you, I think it's time we loaded up the beast of burden!'

'Beast of bur—!' spluttered Aries, whose voice was immediately lost under a ringing slap as Artemis walloped him on the rear.

Ignoring his furious cry, she dragged a tangle of ancient leather straps and buckles from her bag. 'I thought this might be useful,' she smiled, holding out the crackled old harness from her chariot of nightfall.

Back in old Greece it had been her evening duty to draw the moon over the sky in her chariot, pulled by two magnificent stags. Now, even from where he stood, Alex could see how grubby the harness was, stained with sweat and deer doo doo. But before even Aries could complain – which gives you some idea of just how fast she was – her hands had buckled the heavy bellyband under Aries' stomach, secured its back strap along his spine and tightened the breeching around his rear.

Aries grimaced, jutting out his lower jaw as the others hurried to tuck the gifts into the leather strapping on either side. Fingers fluttered all over him; cold metal and tickly feathers twitched his skin; giggles rang loudly in his head.

'I'll take that,' smiled Jason, plucking the purse of infinite wealth from the last saddlebag and tucking it into his back pocket. Grinning, he gazed round at the goddesses. 'After all, I'll need something to buy you all souvenirs of my trip!'

As the others laughed and clapped, Alex looked over the gifts and, feeling a fresh stab of worry, turned to Athena.

'We'll need something to protect us against the sorceress,' he said.

'Protect us?' laughed Jason. 'But that's my job!'

Feeling his face grow red with embarrassment, Alex looked back at the loaded harness. Perhaps lyres and thunderbolts, horse-feather fans and love potions had their uses on a quest (although being a thirteen-year-old boy he had seriously big doubts about the last one), but didn't the goddesses understand?

They were going back to Earth to face *Medea*.

'Alex does have a point,' said Athena finally.

Alex glanced up to see her smiling indulgently at Jason.

'After all, we don't know what she's up to in the jungle and we want you back safe with us.' Solemnly, she stepped forward and set her aegis down on the rock. 'That's why I've decided to lend you this.'

Everyone gasped. Eyes grew wide in the grey light. Even Alex felt his breath catch as he stepped forward for a closer look.

Athena's shield was *the* most revered object in the Underworld. Crafted from a wide circle of bronze and coated with silver, its face was dominated by the Gorgon Medusa's head. And I mean *the* Gorgon's head. You see, years ago, Athena's nephew Perseus had borrowed the shield to kill the snake-haired monster whose stare turned people to stone. Using the shiny inside of the shield like a mirror, he'd stalked Medusa through the cave-tunnels of her lair and, using her reflection to avoid her deadly gaze, had killed her. Triumphant, he'd brought back her severed head as a present for his aunt Athena, who'd magically fused it into the shield, seamlessly melding the monster's head beneath the metal, veiling Medusa's face in silver. The goddess never let anyone else carry it, never mind take it out of her sight.

Jason prodded the Gorgon's lumpy face rudely with his finger, making Alex flinch. You see, even though visitors to the Underworld Zoo still shivered fearfully from behind her ghost's stare-proof screens, Alex was truly fond of her. After all, it's hard to be terrified of someone once you know how they like their porridge in the morning, and now he found himself hoping that Hex would remember that Medusa liked hers steaming hot, with a squirt of grasshopper syrup.

'Observe!' smiled Athena and lifted her hands high into the air. 'I, Pallas Athena, command you to awaken and reveal!'

A sudden wind sprang up from the back of the cave and whistled around the shimmering walls, snapping at the curls of the goddesses' hair and making them squeal. Then, twisting back through the group, it rattled the shield furiously before sweeping out of the cave and gusting along the beach, leaving a trail of spinning sand dunes in its wake.

Alex stared. The surface of the shield was rippling, its lustrous coating running like liquid, shuddering over the Gorgon's features and dribbling over the etched scales of the snakes. Suddenly the Gorgon's eyes snapped open. Two orange topazes, glittering like fire, replaced the monster's deadly eyes and they sparkled furiously as five living snakes spiralled out around her head, like party poppers, from the squirming mass of asps below. With their tails held in the metal of the shield below, they rocked and hissed, slithering over one another, luxuriating in the cool air.

Aphrodite screamed and ran out of the cave whilst everyone else stepped backwards. Everyone else, that is, apart from Alex, who, recognising them from their ghost-twins at the zoo – the sandy-brown horned viper, an adder with a bumpy snout, a black-and-white striped krait, a rather elderly, copper-skinned cobra and a grass snake, no more than a whip of greenish grey[19] – wished he'd brought his jar of dried locusts with him.

The Gorgon slid her blazing eyes sideways to look at Athena. 'What do you want?'

'You've a mission,' said Athena.

'Miss-s-s-ion?' muttered Cobra, fluttering his collar sleepily.

'Is that it?' growled Medusa, screwing up her face. 'Wake me from the middle of a wonderful snooze for this, would you? I'd just dreamed that my cave was filled with a thousand statues of hunky men. Now it's blasts of wind under my chin, a deafening clang in my ear-holes and everybody up!'

'You'll be travelling with a hero,' said Jason smoothly.

---

19 Medusa had always been a fashionable lass and certainly not the sort of girl to let being turned into a monster with snakey hair cramp her style. Consequently she chose the most exotic serpents for hair extensions, weaving Egyptian cobras and Indian Kraits among the ordinary Greek wrigglers, to give herself the most cosmopolitan of hair-dos.

The Gorgon glanced in his direction. 'Oh, lucky me.'

Alex stifled a smile. After all, if it hadn't been for a *hero* like Perseus she'd still be wearing her head in its proper place: on her shoulders. He blushed as her blazing eyes caught sight of him and winked, knowing that her head was psychically linked with her ghost back in the zoo, and that she would realise that Alex was the one who cared for her.

Lifting the shield from the rock, Athena slid it on to her forearm and held it out in front of her as the snakes continued to writhe. 'These are the Serpents of Strife!'

'S-s-soldiersss in s-s-scalesss!' hissed Krait, swishing out so that his stripes flashed past like a zebra's tail. He quivered his pink tongue gleefully. 'We helped protect Medus-s-s-a for c-c-centuriesss! Picking up the s-s-scentsss of intrudersss —'

'Their vibrationsss,' continued Viper, ducking as Cobra began to wheel round happily.

'Their nas-s-sty s-s-swordsss and intentionsss,' muttered Adder, unfurling his brown, diamond-patterned body backwards as the old snake spun by.

'And made s-s-sure s-s-she didn't trip over all their los-s-st s-s-shields in the dark,' said the little green one.

Alex smiled. Grass Snake was the only non-venomous serpent in the gang and had always been more of a ringlet than a tress in Medusa's terrifying hair-do.

'S-s-so,' said Viper, narrowing his yellow eyes as the doddery cobra twirled past yet again. 'Where are we going?'

'The Amazon,' said Athena.

'A new battle!' hissed Krait and stretched bolt upright. Beneath him, the asps squirmed and rasped, twisting over each other in a tangle of knots. 'Attention! Let'sss make a s-s-start!'

'Cherry tart?' said Cobra, stopping abruptly to regard the other with dim, clouded eyes.

'No!' Viper prodded the old snake rudely with his snout.

'Besidesss,' explained Adder importantly, 'tart, cherry or otherwise-s-se, is a refres-s-shment enjoyed for lunch or s-s-supper. Were you to turn your aged s-s-snout towardsss the beach, you might s-s-scent how low the tide isss, clearly making it the middle of the afternoon.'

'Already?' said Alex, shocked. Snatching up the writhing shield, he looked at Persephone. 'We have to go. Which door is it?'

'This way,' she said.

Alex and Aries turned away from the syrupy chirrup of goodbyes for Jason, and followed the queen to the pooled blackness at the back of the caves. Stopping at the foot of the last stairway, she flicked her long plait back over her shoulder and reached for the hoop of keys hanging from her belt. For a moment she fumbled beneath the guttering torchlight until she found the right one and unclipped it from the others. It was a large iron key attached by a chain to what appeared to Alex to be a strange-looking wooden bird with blue feathers, but which we would have recognised as a parrot.

'This key opens the door to the Amazon,' she said,

looking earnestly into their faces as Jason caught up with them. 'From the Underworld to Earth and back home again from the rainforest. So, whatever you do, don't lose it!'

'We won't!' breezed Jason, plucking it from her fingers and leaping onto the staircase.

Flying up the steps, taking two at a time, he then sprinted over the walkway, pausing for a moment to stand beside the portal, hand on hip, waving the key over his head.

'See you all soon!' he announced to the cheering crowd. He glanced down at Alex. 'I'll lead the way! You, boy, bring the luggage!' Then turning, he vanished through the door behind him.

'Luggage?' snorted Aries. 'Boy? Did you hear him?'

'Come on,' urged Alex, looking into the ram's furious eyes. He unfastened the sword – the heaviest of the gifts – in the hope of reducing Aries' now dismally sagging back and, turning away from the goddesses, leaned closer to whisper in Aries' ear. 'Remember, this is all for Rose.'

Aries nodded and, clearly summoning up his last remaining scraps of dignity, turned away and thundered up the surf-slicked steps. Rams are amazing climbers, with tough hooves able to snag rocky cusps and soft pads as grippy as any climbing shoe, and I'm delighted to tell you that happily the craggy steps gave him no trouble at all. Soon at the top, he glanced back over his shoulder at Alex before turning and clattering along the boardwalk.

Relieved to finally be leaving, Alex followed him up the stairs, clutching the sword and shield tightly. How he wished that his parents could see him now. He smiled, remembering how proud they'd been that morning, their faces pink with delight, when he'd rushed back to tell them that he'd been chosen to travel with Jason – yes, mother, *the* Jason – and now, reaching the top of the steps, his whole body buzzed with the excitement of another quest, imagining Rose's delighted face when she saw them again, bursting out of the jungle to help her.

So, it was unfortunate that the old wood of the boardwalk chose that moment to start clacking rudely beneath Aries, thunking like a warped xylophone, whilst the lyre, bouncing in the narrow gap between the ram's bustling haunches and the wall, began to twang. Miserably. Far from being the sort of melody that would charm birds and soothe lions, it sounded to Alex more like something that would make the fire-breathing bulls hurl themselves on to the ground and fling their legs up in surrender. Awash with the dreary sound, Alex felt his burst of optimism fade away and with it the image of Rose's face as he realised the enormous danger of their mission. Because not only did they have to survive Earth, armed with a cocktail stirrer, a picture of Zeus and some rather attractive pieces of embroidery, *and* trek through a vast jungle filled with Hades-knew-what to face the wrath of a scheming sorceress at the end of it, but for them to have the teeniest chance of success, Aries and Jason would need to work together.

As if in reply, the lyre gave its longest mournful sigh yet and, feeling a cold shudder of worry, Alex hurried after Aries as the ram bustled noisily through the portal.

Gifts, thought Rose, who was at that moment stretching in her bed, blinking in the wash of morning light. Wasn't it totally amazing how they always managed to make people feel so much better?

Yawning, she murmured a whispered thank-you to the unknown but utterly determined fan who'd sent Hazel such a fabulous present the day before.

And changed the star's mood completely.

Rose sat up and leaned against her plump pillows, recalling how Hazel's face had glowed when the steward handed her a gift-wrapped box, giddily festooned with pink ribbons, at dinner the night before, explaining that it had arrived only a few minutes ago, by courier, out here in the middle of nowhere. *Dang*, how determined her true fans were, said Hazel, gasping that she simply couldn't believe it.

And neither could Rose – the change in Hazel's mood, that was, because for the first time since leaving Barcelos airport over a week ago, Rose had caught a glimpse of the fun girl she'd met in London. The one who'd reassured her so confidently that they would find her father together; that everything truly would be all right. Rose smiled, recalling the sparkle in Hazel's eyes as she'd ripped off the ribbons and flipped back the lid of the box to discover the most spectacular chocolate-coloured lily inside. Breathing in the scent of its cherry-red centre, Hazel had taken the box to her cabin bedroom and placed it proudly in the middle of her dressing table.

Rose hoped that the old, good-humoured Hazel would be back again today. She stood up and slipped on her trainers, pleased to discover that the tightness behind her ribs – born of the niggling worry that perhaps the star's world of pink planes and pink-faced fans really was too different from her own life of grey T-shirts and grey days spent in museums for them to be real friends – had finally disappeared.

And all thanks to a flower delivered in the weirdest little wicker box that had a brass catch shaped like a dragon's face, holding a dazzling blue stone in its mouth.

Hold on a minute . . .

Brass dragon?

Dazzling blue stone?

In. Its. Mouth?

Oh dear.

I don't like the sound of this, and I don't expect you do either. But, really, there's not point looking at me all worried, with your face scrunched up like a constipated squirrel.

I mean, what can I do?

VI
Snake Your Booty

At about the same time as Rose was brushing her teeth, Alex was grinding his in frustration. This was because ever since they'd stepped on to the plush red carpet of the portal corridor – only a few minutes before, though it felt much *much* longer – Aries had barely paused for breath.

Grumble . . .

Moan . . .

Snort . . .

Twang . . .

'Didn't I say that we couldn't trust him?' muttered Aries, shimmying his shoulders to make the harness more comfortable and sounding like a one-ram band.

'Only about a hundred times,' sighed Alex.

The Serpents of Strife hissed curiously from the shield, unfurling and twirling, tasting the air for scents.

Rude word . . .

Jingle-jangle . . .

BOOM!

Thunder rolled as Zeus's bolt thwacked the walls.

'Of all the low-down sneaky tricks!' said Aries. 'Can you believe he's left without us?'

'No, I can't!' replied Alex. 'Because he hasn't. He's simply gone on ahead to check things out!'

'Rather like the s-s-scoutsss who rode in **Alexander the Great**'sss cavalry,' said Adder loftily. 'A clas-s-sic tactic used by the bravessst of men to check out the lie of the land.'

'Who asked you?' grunted Aries.

'Well, really!' Adder curled himself into a sulky knot.

Having once belonged to the old mathematician **Pythagoras**, Adder[20] had long-considered himself the brainbox of the bunch and certainly wasn't used to such rammy rudeness.

'Stop it, Aries!' insisted Alex. 'We have to hurry up. We need to get to the Amazon. We don't have time to moan.'

Except that Aries always had time to moan.

And never more so than when he found himself on a long, gloomy corridor cut through black rock that twinkled in the firelight and that was distinctly Jason-free. Bustling his rear importantly, he looked up crossly at Alex.

'That's easy for you to say,' he muttered. 'You're not the one trussed up like a cheap sideshow at the **agora**, are you? All these ridiculous gewgaws!'

'Who you calling a gewgaw?' hissed Krait, sticking out his white chin indignantly.

'What'sss a gewgaw?' asked Grass Snake.

---

20 Well, what sort of snake would you expect a mathematician to have?

'A gewgaw,' sniffed Adder, from under his coils, 'isss s-s-something pointlesss and s-s-showy.'

'Like Jason,' finished Aries, giving the wall an extra hard wallop with the lightning bolt, making the corridor tremble with thunder.

Alex sighed.

If he'd had an **obol** for every time Aries had raged about Jason since they'd been down in the Underworld, he'd be sitting on a mountain of money taller than Mount **Olympus** by now. Down here, listening to Aries mutter and scorn (and twang and rumble and spark) he wished again that for the sake of their friendship he could join in and wholeheartedly side with his best friend.

Truly agree that Jason wasn't all he was cracked up to be.

Rail against the way he was still fêted as the golden boy of the Underworld.

Except he couldn't.

Not when he hardly knew him.

Back in old Greece, Jason had been captain of the *Argo* whilst Alex had been just a boy, up to his elbows in cold, wet clay, learning how to be a potter. To be honest, all Alex was absolutely certain of when it came to Jason was the memory of a dull ache between his shoulder blades, born of hefting trays of pots in and out of the kiln all day, and eyes that itched with tiredness from painting him on pot after pot after pot, late into the night: Jason guiding the *Argo* through the Clashing Rocks, Jason fearlessly yoking the fire-breathing bulls,

Jason climbing over the giant snake **Drako**'s back, high into the tree, to snatch down the Fleece. In his mind's eye, he could still see the rows of pots, gleaming black and orange on the shelves, ready for the townswomen who'd buy them the next morning, cooing over them like besotted pigeons, delighted to buy a crock showing the latest adventure that Jason had sent news of by messenger dove. Smiling, he remembered his grandfather closing the door after they'd gone and shaking his old, grey-haired head, muttering about what an extraordinary man Jason must be.

How could they all be wrong?

His family, the townsfolk, the gods, the goddesses, the poets? Everybody in the Underworld?

It was too ridiculous.

You see, to Alex, Aries' claims were rather like us having your best friend insist they've seen a flying saucer. You want to believe them, truly you do and you check the news, read the papers, search the net for a UFO sighting. But when there's nothing about it, when every other person you know rolls his or her eyes and insists your friend's addled, it makes it horribly tricky. In the end, it's only when you see something spinning with lights land in your back garden, watch it flip open a ramp for something green and slug-like to wibble out and poke you in the ear with its finger that you're likely to be convinced.

'I s-s-smell Earth!' squealed Viper.

Snapped from his thoughts, Alex narrowed his eyes

and squinted beyond Viper's wildly writhing body to make out the shape of a door, fuzzily gold in the distance. His chest tightened in a mixture of excitement and nerves.

'Where?' said Cobra, swaying up to face the wrong direction.

'It's that way,' whispered Alex, gently turning the snake's head.

He watched the old snake straighten like a spear. Back in his heyday, Cobra had slithered with the Athenian Army and been called the Purge of the Persians[21] for his extraordinary talent to scent the enemy from miles away. But now, rather long in the fang, Alex knew that his heyday, much like his razor-sharp sniffing, lay far behind him.

'According to Persephone,' said Alex, 'the last time she used this portal she stepped out into the middle of an orange grove. There was a garden party that day, with lots of people drinking and laughing around a fountain with one of our statues of Orpheus at its centre. That statue's the nearest portal to the Scroll's coordinates. Hopefully it's still standing in that orchard.'

Tightening his grip on the sword, Alex began walking more quickly now, curious about what Jason had actually found behind the door. And, he brightened, what sort of advice he might need from him to come up with a plan

---

21 Most famously, he'd once tripped King Xerxes himself down the palace stairs by stretching out like a skipping rope across the top step.

for their first move. A few moments later, they arrived at the door, which had been left slightly ajar for them. Pulling it open a fraction more, Alex frowned, puzzled to hear the faint strains of music. Hissing with curiosity, the snakes spiralled out and arranging their heads in a snaky totem pole at the gap and sniffed deeply.

'Dus-s-st!' confirmed Krait.

'Bees-s-s-wax-x-x!' added Viper.

'But no orangesss,' squeaked Grass Snake.

'Hmm,' Aries thrust his muzzle through the door and breathed in noisily. 'So, when exactly was the queen here?'

Alex bit his lip. 'About a hundred and fifty years ago.' Feeling his heart start to thump harder, he looked down at the others. 'Seems like things have changed. Remember, whatever is out there, we need to find Jason quietly. That means we mustn't do anything to draw attention to ourselves.'

Drawing back from the column of snakes, Viper narrowed his eyes. 'Defenc-c-c-e positionsss, ladsss!'

The snakes whipped back on to the shield and quickly froze in silver curls around the Gorgon's head.

Steeling himself, Alex pulled open the door.

❋ VII ❋
Flower Power

The scream tore the morning in two, shattering the chatter of the jungle and sending the Capuchin monkeys shrieking into the highest branches.

Electrified by fear, Rose sprinted on to the deck and turned towards Hazel's cabin as a second scream, even shriller than the first, exploded from it. Footfalls slammed over the wooden boards behind her. Snatches of panicked Portuguese burst out all over the boat.

Ahead of her, she glimpsed Eduardo, two stewards and the chef, still fumbling with the belt of his dressing gown, fly up the steps at the end of the deck. She raced after them and saw them hurl back the cabin door, and now, already halfway up the stars, she gasped, catching sight of Hazel, screeching puce-faced on the bed, pointing at something on the floor. Throwing herself up the last few steps, Rose skidded into through the open door and froze.

A big brown spider was standing in the centre of the floor. Easily the size of her hand, its legs were hunched and bony and, as she watched, it began to tap one front leg against the boards, almost as if it were amused.

I felt somethin', a-crawlin' on my arm,' sobbed Hazel, her voice hoarse from screaming. 'I sat up to check and, and —'

She burst into fresh tears.

Rose took a step towards her.

'No!' commanded Eduardo, his face slick with sweat, shining, as he scanned the room, searching for something to trap the spider with.

'It's a Brazilian Wandering Spider,' hissed one of the stewards, urging Rose to edge back against the wall. Rose noticed the panic in his eyes. 'It's one of the deadliest things in the Amazon.'

Turning back, Rose saw the creature lift its front four legs into the air and paddle them over its head, flashing its red fangs. She felt a sharp chill of unease. Something about the creature's appearance, those chocolate-brown legs, that patch of cherry-red, seemed uncomfortably familiar.

Now hardly daring to breathe, she watched as Eduardo, keeping his feet planted firmly on the floor, slowly extended his right arm and seized the wicker box sitting on the dressing table. Bouncing instantly back onto all eight legs, the spider raced headlong towards Hazel's bed, its feet tappity-scratching over the boards.

'Do somethin'!' cried Hazel, throwing her hands on her head and squeezing her eyes tight shut.

Deftly, with the grace of a dancer, Eduardo leaped forwards and threw down the wicker box, covering the spider completely. For a second the box lay still. Horribly still. Then it jerked into life and began juddering across the floor. Cursing under his breath, Eduardo pulled the sleeve of his jacket over his hand, dipped down and flipped the box over, scooping up the spider and shutting the lid in one fluid movement.

Rose edged back, her skin prickling with icy dread, as he walked past.

Suddenly Hazel began gabbling madly. She fell to her knees and began tearing the sheets off her bed, bunching them up and hurling them into a heap on the floor. Then she jumped down and began ripping out every drawer of her dressing table, throwing them on to the floor, spilling jeans and scarves and glittering pink tops.

'Check it!' she sobbed, kicking at the pile of clothes. 'Check it all!'

'Hazel! It's all right!' Rose reached out to hug Hazel, but the young star was hysterical.

Batting Rose away, she began emptying the wardrobe. Hangers skittered over the floor. Sandals flew through the air. Then, with one wide sweep, she sent her bottles and jars tumbling from the top of her dressing table, and threw herself, face-down, sobbing, on to the bed.

And even though Rose reasoned and soothed, promising her friend that the spider had gone, that it was a fluke, that it must have snuck in on the bananas the chef brought back from the market yesterday and they could check every single centimetre of the boat three times over, all she was truly sure of was the hot thumping of blood in her ears.

Not because of the spider, although that had been terrifying enough. But because, now, as she turned away from Hazel and watched the stewards clearing up the mess, the strange flower, delivered the night before, was nowhere to be seen.

VIII
It's Not Over Till The Fat Lady Screams

Ugh.

Well, that was all tremendously unpleasant, I must say. So let me calm my nerves with a sip of tea.

Ah, that's better.

Now, no doubt your teacher has banged on about how the Ancient Greeks gave us theatre, geometry, democracy, the Olympics and blah-de-blah-de-blah-de-zzzzzz.

Well, forget all that.

Because what the Ancient Greeks *really* gave us was lots of statues of men and women waving their bottoms in the air whilst frolicking with harps and flutes. And the thing about statues is that they're always moving about. Not by themselves, of course – that would be silly – but because of art collectors who over the centuries take a shine to them. Luckily for Persephone and her holidays, there's long been a particular sort of person who enjoys nothing more than snapping up Greek statues to decorate their lobbies, dining rooms or indeed orange groves, which meant that she often found herself in new and exciting spots for her holidays. Sometimes the flute-tootling **nymphs** and shepherds ended up gracing the swimming pools of Hollywood stars. Sometimes they topped the staircases of grand liners or adorned the foyers of swanky hotels. But occasionally they ended up on a pedestal, tucked in a curtain-draped alcove, in an elegant corridor that echoed with music.

Like this one.

Which was, as I'm sure you've noticed, most certainly not part of an orange grove. This was because this particular statue had been on the move again, having several years ago been donated to its latest plinth by a Lady Lavinia Snodgrass, the wealthy Victorian widow of a man who'd made his fortune from a certain fruit plantation high above the rainforest.

Harrumphing, Aries wedged his muzzle up against Orpheus's marble ankles. At least they were familiar, he thought, recalling the same puffy pair he'd seen dangling in the nymphs' pool two days ago in the zoo.

Unlike everything else.

Untangling his back hoof from the curtain, Aries bustled out into the twilit corridor and felt his hooves sink into the thick red carpet.

'I wonder where we are,' said Alex, as the portal door closed, its edges melting into the creamy alcove of marble.

Stepping out behind Aries, he cautiously scanned the luxurious corridor, glad to see that it appeared to be deserted. A row of doors, each topped by carved scrolls and festooned by curtains, stretched away along the right-hand wall. Lights shaped like falling showers of ice twinkled from the ceiling, casting a buttery glow on the gold frames of portraits clustered on the walls.

'And where Jason is,' muttered Aries, his ears now twirling round and round in time with the distant strains of music.

'I hope he's all right,' said Alex, scanning the pictures for any clues they might hold as to what this building was. In them, men with curled moustaches and women in dresses that billowed like ships' sails loomed, each one's mouth making a perfect 'O'.

Then, noticing that the door beyond them lay open, Alex edged his nose inside.

'It's a theatre!' he whispered, glancing back at Aries over his shoulder. 'Like the one Hazel sang in. Come on, we need to find Jason and tell him everything we know about them.'

Curious now, Aries craned his neck around the door-frame for a proper look. Seeing the small space, filled with gold chairs, and walled either side by panels of fancily twisted wood, he realised that this theatre was much snootier than the one Hazel had performed in. Rings of small enclosed spaces like the one he and Alex were standing in, that'd we'd recognize as theatre boxes, stretched around the circular wall, brimming with pink-faced men and ladies, staring over a lavish gold balcony into the crowded auditorium below.

Noticing a rather frosty old lady fanning herself in

the next box, he hunched down and began to creep, commando-style, along the carpet. Rams, as you might imagine, aren't made for stealth. It's just one of the reasons you never see them serving as soldiers in the British Army. Quite apart from the fact that they keep making horn holes in their berets, their derrières are easily spotted from miles around. But undeterred and determined not to draw attention to himself, he slumped down and stuck his muzzle through the balustrade.

At the front of the auditorium, musicians were playing. The men wore black coats with tails like swallows. The women were dressed in shimmering purple. Everyone plucked and strummed and blew, watching a scrawny man at the front whirl a small stick in the air. Aries swivelled his eyes, right and left, looking across row after row of heads and hats for a glimpse of Jason as slowly the sumptuous theatre curtain rose to reveal a man and a woman, singing, on what appeared to be a little humpbacked bridge.

Suddenly feeling an unceremonious poke on the flank, Aries twisted back to see Alex framed in the doorway, gesturing furiously for Aries to join him.

Huffing at the indignity, he quickly reversed out and followed the boy down the corridor.

'We have to keep out of sight!' scolded Alex, checking back over his shoulder.

Behind him, Aries was still busy pulling a face, when the boy stopped in front of a door marked 'No Entry to the Public' and quickly pushed it open to reveal a grimy stairwell. 'Come on! We should be able to keep out of sight this way.'

A minute later, they found themselves at the end of a long, well-lit corridor, lined with doors and hung with more pictures of singing people. Large wooden boxes were stacked against the walls. A mop leaned against a wall, stood in a red bucket.

'"Dressing room",' read Alex uncertainly, leading Aries past the first door. He walked on, reading out the signs on the other doors. '"Make-up", "Wardrobe", "Green room".' Then he stopped. 'This looks better,' he said, nodding towards its sign, which said 'Store room'.

Gently turning the handle, he opened the door a fraction to see a room jumbled with piled-up tables and chairs, more boxes and two rails of clothes carelessly jammed against the wall.

'Wait here,' he instructed, ushering Aries inside and glancing up and down the corridor. 'And do not step through this door. I'll find Jason and then we'll both come back for you. All right?

All right?

Hardly.

Ten minutes later, Aries lay gloomily on the floor, with Alex's instructions still echoing in his mind, thumping into each other like bad-tempered rabbits in a burrow. *'Don't move!' 'Remember what happened last time we stepped on to Earth?' 'We don't want to cause a scene again, do we?' 'Well, of course I have to look for him. He's leading the quest!' 'Don't pull that face!' 'Are you listening to me?'*

Sighing, he stretched out his back legs, accompanied by a small sour twang of the lyre. Less than half an hour into their new quest and golden boy had already abandoned them.

Not that Aries was surprised.

The only surprise was that Alex had immediately decided to shunt him in here. Greek heroes were never stuffed into cupboards, and yet here he was, bundled away like an unwanted stage prop whilst the boy searched the building to try and find Jason and remind him of what they were supposed to be doing in the first place.

A sudden snatch of conversation, out in the corridor, made Aries prick up his ears. The voices sounded horribly close. What if someone decided to come in? He hunched down – which, when you're the size of a chunky chest of drawers, doesn't make a lot of difference – and sank his head against his chest. What could he do? A cold fear now curdled his earlier frustration, knowing that if it were only the two of them, Alex would never have chosen to leave him on his own.

A few seconds later the voices faded away but, still feeling rattled, he turned his attention to a framed poster leaning against a nearby table. Gold letters at the top spelled out 'Manaus Opera House'.

Wondering what a Manaus was, Aries glanced at the picture below. In it a woman with a powdered-white face, a small red mouth and lots of black hair piled high on her head looked sadly at a branch of blossom. 'Madama Butterfly' announced the words at the bottom, which, as you might imagine, what with Aries being a ghost Greek ram, meant nothing to him.[22] However, that blossom, so succulent and juicy, was quite a different matter, and now, licking his lips, he realised that he was feeling rather peckish.

Of course, worry and frustration always makes rams horribly hungry, and now with his spirits drooping somewhere around his hocks, he swung his head back to re-examine the items hanging from the infernal contraption Artemis had strapped to him, just in case there was anything that might pass as a snack.

Like the roll of blue velvet hanging from his right shoulder, perhaps?

He'd been so furious back in the cave that he'd hardly listened to what each gift was, but the fabric certainly looked tasty. And, surely a little nibble couldn't hurt? Stretching his neck, he managed to clamp one corner with his mouth and, tugging it towards him, began to chew, surprised at how delicious it tasted. Not only was the fabric soft and yielding but it seemed to be flavoured by something sweet and flowery. Quickly beginning to feel brighter, he took a second bite, then another, ignoring the twinkling passionflower petal that spun away to the floor. Much calmer now, he settled down properly, bustled

---

22 *And in case they mean nothing to you too, let me explain that* Madama Butterfly *is an opera about a Japanese lady. However, despite its name, it doesn't have a single butterfly in it. This is because such creatures only have teensy-weensy voices that nobody can hear properly and, worse, they tend to flap out of the theatre in fright as soon as they spot the audience.*

his rear into a rail of sparkly jackets, aware of the sound of a woman singing. As her lucid notes floated into the room, he took another mouthful and found his mind drifting to the orange blossom and harbours and fine days of her song. Soon, his ears began spinning, scooping up the beautiful trilling like twin spoons in his favourite oatmeal. Not for one moment – as his heart soared, his hooves tingled and his nostrils flared – did he suspect that it was the work of the love mixture Aphrodite had given to Jason. All he knew was that her voice was the most perfect, the most exquisite thing he'd ever heard in his life, or death.

Who was she?

Where was she?

And, more importantly, how could he find her?

Suddenly propelled by an irresistible urge to discover the owner of such an intoxicating voice, he scrabbled up on to his feet and without a second's thought for Alex's stern warnings, butted open the door and hoofed out along the passageway in the direction of her voice. He paused, tilting his head, to listen. It was definitely coming from somewhere behind that pale green door up ahead. The one marked 'Stage'.

Rosita de Bonita, the world-famous opera star, was as curvy as a cello. Now, standing in front of a paper-walled house on stage, she cast a formidable figure as Madama Butterfly, bundled into her black-and-pink whorled kimono, her silk sleeves trailing to the floor as she flung out her arms, warbling at the top of her lungs, yearning for her love to return.

Aries gaped.

She was the single most beautiful woman he'd ever seen.

Oh, how his heart leaped as he gazed at her from the wings: her dark kohl-rimmed eyes, her luscious thick, black hair piled high into a bun on top of her head, decorated with a small bunch of cherries and combs dangling with strings of yellow beads, the way she raised her hands, like two chubby pink starfish reaching out into the crowd, calling for her lost love.

And here he was.

Positively bursting with affection, he could stand it no longer and he edged his head coquettishly around the curtain. 'Yoo-hoo!'

De Bonita's eyes shot sideways and grew larger. Now her perfect note began to slide upwards, rising unsteadily through one octave after another. As she hit a perfect top C, the audience burst into a flurry of applause and then stopped abruptly as her note carried on rising, rising, thinner and shriller, into an ear-detonating screech.

The violinists crossed their eyes. A wine glass on the second tier exploded and drenched three nuns below with vintage port. A cat on a nearby roof began to wail.

As de Bonita finally spluttered to a stop, Aries stomped out from the wings and clopped into full view of the audience. The orchestra slithered to a squealing halt. On stage, Suzuki, Madama Butterfly's trusted maid,[23] screamed and tried to run away. Instead, her legs tangling in her tight kimono, she flew over backwards, pulling a cardboard tree down on top of her.

Someone sniggered from the front row of the audience.

Sidling over, Aries leaned against de Bonita's hip, gazing lovingly into her shocked face, and puckered up expectantly. Horrified, she leaped backwards and, producing a paper fan from her belt, began thwacking Aries on the forehead in time with her croaked words.

'GET . . .'

Aries took another step forward, smiling widely as paper blossom rained down like a snowstorm.

'. . . OFF . . .'

Cherries ricocheted from Aries' muzzle.

'. . . ME!'

In reply, Aries gave de Bonita's ankle an amorous lick, sending her shrieking on to the humpback bridge as the funny little man from the musicians below scrambled up on to the stage and began jabbing Aries in the rump with his short stick.

'Call the police!' bawled de Bonita. 'A vet! A farmer!'

She spun away furiously. It was unfortunate that as she did so her Geisha wig, made for sitting prettily rather than running away from rams, flew off, whirled over the stage and landed on the head of a man in the front row. Now the audience erupted into gales of laughter, as an

---

23 No, not Madama's motorbike.

appalled de Bonita patted her head, horrified to discover her wrinkled stocking cap, skull-tight over her hair and leaving her looking like a bank-robbing walrus.

Which was when Aries noticed Alex race on to the stage.

'You didn't!' he cried, grabbing hold of the torn blue velvet roll around Aries' neck.

Aries looked up at him, bewildered.

'Get him out of here!' bellowed de Bonita, scooping up her fan and what was left of her dignity to race off stage.

Alex threw his arms defensively around Aries as a gang of burly stagehands dressed in black raced in from the sides of the stage. 'He doesn't mean any harm!'

Grabbing a ram, in case you haven't tried it, isn't easy at the best of times and particularly when they are as big as Aries. Now, trying to curtail a furious Aries, loaded up with a thunderbolt, lyre and a quiver of slapping arrows, it was like being sucked into a mad game of Buckaroo. In desperation, Alex grabbed hold of Aries' horns and forced him to look into his eyes.

'It's the love petals, Aries! That's all!'

Aries blinked. 'Love petals?'

At which Alex shot off the ground, dragged backwards by three pairs of hands. Suddenly, several more hands laced through the leather straps of the harness on Aries' back and began towing him behind Alex, off the stage and out into the corridor.

But on the up-side, at least they saw Jason.

He was happily strolling down the corridor in the opposite direction, whispering to a woman with curly brown hair tangling down her back.

'Jason!' yelled Alex. Aries heard the gladness in his voice, so relieved to have found him.

From the other end of the corridor the woman yelped and clamped a hand over her mouth as Jason glanced back and blanched.

'We're over here!' called Alex. Struggling against his captors, he looked down at Aries. 'Thank Zeus!' he gasped. 'He'll help us sort this mess out and we can be on our way to Rose again!'

Which was when Jason muttered something to the woman, wrapped his arm around her . . . and they vanished around the corner together.

'Jas—?' shouted Alex.

Aries snatched a last glance of the boy's face, crumpled in confusion as they were hauled away, their feet and hooves sliding over the tiles, yanked out of the corridor into a glittering foyer in the direction of a grand, gold-framed door.

A door through which five Brazilian policemen were now charging, brandishing handcuffs and ropes.

Which was just great.

IX
Look Who's Stalking

Things weren't going terribly well for Medea either.

Glowering at her spell book (flung face-down on the floor) and her chart of tropical moon phases (crumpled into a ball and stamped on), she clenched her fists, brooding yet again why ever since she'd woken up that morning thoughts of Jason had swarmed through her head like a plague of locusts, whirring and skittering and making it impossible to concentrate on anything else.

Her astral calculations were all wrong. Her mixture of lizard blood and scorpion sting had curdled miserably. Even the moments spent scrying on Hazel as she discovered that glorious spider crawling up her bedsheets had been ruined by her ex-husband poking his annoyingly handsome nose into her mind.

But why?

Frowning at the sudden chatter of budgies outside her window, she realised that she hadn't felt this sort of mental itchiness for centuries. Not since she'd been a fledgling witch had her natural ESP – Extra Sorceress Perception – been helpful to her by alerting her to things before they happened because since then she'd always had far more powerful magic at her fingertips to answer any questions she had.

Yet it was bamboozling her now.

Then a strange thought crossed her mind.

Surely Jason hadn't – *wouldn't* – come back to Earth? Jason? *Her* Jason? Leave the Underworld paradise he'd been partying in for years to do anything as dangerous as step back on to Earth? The thought was so absurd it made her laugh out loud.

Her mind spun her back to the palace she'd shared with him years ago on Iolkos. Bitterness flooded through her veins as she saw herself lying in her shuttered chambers, the Golden Fleece abandoned at her feet, jamming her fingers into her ears, trying to escape the sound of the city bells announcing Jason's engagement to Glauce. Of sobbing until her eyes burned and, in despair, throwing herself on to the scratchy curls of the Fleece, hating it, cursing it, blaming it for ruining her life, and in her furious misery pummelling it with her fists, tearing at its ringlets until her fingers bled.

When it had begun to glimmer with new life.

Back in the hut, she slowly turned her hands palm upwards.

The scars were still there.

Growling, she set her scrying bowl down with a violent clang, determined to find out why her ex-husband was stomping through her thoughts. Obviously, she scolded herself, muttering as she snatched up her potions and lit the flame, this would be a complete waste of time. There was no way he'd appear because there was no way he'd be back on Earth. (Scrying, you see, simply isn't powerful enough to see into the Underworld. Something to do with all those rocks and roots and buried dinosaur bones, not to mention a barrier of godly protection, overwhelmed such first-grade magic.)

Except that a few minutes later she found herself transfixed, watching the colours in the liquid spiral out to reveal a magnificent pink-walled building beneath a domed roof of green and gold mosaic, sparkling in the rain. Abruptly, the view zoomed dizzyingly down to the building's front doors as they slammed open.

And Jason strolled out.

He.

Was.

Back.

On.

Earth.

There was absolutely no doubt about it.

Feeling her breath snag in her chest, Medea leaned in closer, willing her brain to believe what her bewildered eyes were seeing: Jason, son of Aeson, hurrying down a flight of steps into an empty town square, his arm wrapped around the shoulder of a young, dark-haired woman.

That bit, at least, was easy to believe.

Stunned, she forced herself to calm down. Then, sensing her heartbeat dwindle to its usual crocodile slowness, she looked more carefully at the building behind them, at its domed roof twinkling like a giant mirrorball in the rain, and knew that she'd seen it before. From the plane – that was it! – on the day she'd flown into Brazil.

The Manaus Opera House.

Leaning closer, she watched Jason and the woman splash away through the puddles, feeling her curiosity prickle as he tapped the long and – now she came to consider it – curiously old-fashioned key sticking out of his back pocket.

She began pacing the hut, running her hand through the violet streak in her hair, thinking, thinking. Clearly the boy and the ram must have blabbed to the Underworld about her awesomely terrible magic and some bothersome do-gooder like Athena had decided to stick her snooty little nose in. Yet they'd known that without new fleeces she had no real power left. So why had Athena sent her shiny Jason back to Earth? To spy on her? To stop her from trying something else? Stop her, indeed! She sneered, imagining the goddess of war prancing around with her big silly shield. Soon, oh, so very soon, she'd wipe that smug little smile off her face for good. And how much more delicious would it be if she were to use Jason to do just that?

To and fro, fro and to, her jungle boots thudded on the mud floor as her thoughts grew colder and colder still, slowly crystallising into a new and delightfully poisonous plan. After all, wasn't it perfect that he should reappear precisely when she was on the cusp of seizing more magical power than she'd ever known in her long and malicious life? Because couldn't she, with a little careful planning, use him as her own finishing touch, like drizzled honey on her baklava of evil?

But, first things first.

Like the small matter of making sure he actually arrived to see her. After all, knowing him, he'd probably already be thinking of just how quickly he could get that impossibly handsome face of his back to his Underworld fans. She stood, framed by the hut window, her eyes dark as thunderclouds.

Which would have been one of those splendidly dramatic moments, had the scrying bowl not chosen that precise second to let out the most disgusting rumbling belch. The sort of belch a podgy hippo might produce, with a belly full of water, should it attempt a graceful riverbank roll, and, rudely snapped out of her reverie, Medea scuttled over to the bowl again.

'What the —?' she spluttered, gasping as she saw Alex and Aries, decorated like a peddler's mule, being dragged out of the building through the very same door that Jason had stepped out of only a few minutes ago. Except that the boy and the ram were leaving backwards, squealing, in a flurry of hands, feet and hooves, escorted by several gruff policemen.

Medea stared in astonishment.

Surely those turnips had learned their lesson the first time? So, why were they back again? To help Jason? *Aries? Help Jason?* The thought was absolutely ludicrous and yet there he was, as big and bald and mad-looking as ever, and, moreover, clearly loaded down with godly gifts for the quest, whilst the boy was struggling to hold on to Athena's enormous shield.

No, of course it wasn't for Jason, she chided herself. Rolling her eyes at her own silliness, she realised that plainly when the Underworld had discovered that she was in the Amazon – where their beloved Rose had been heading to find her father – they'd decided to come back and make sure their little pal was safe.

Well, how sickening.

But, perhaps, how perfect, too.

Because even though Alex might be as annoying as a mosquito, he was also smart and, coupled with the ram's blundering determination, that meant Jason would have the help he needed to actually be able to find her out here.

Just so long as he had a real reason to look.

She closed her eyes and found her mind returning again to that strange-looking key. Then, knowing exactly what to do, she raced across the hut, flung back the lid of her trunk and, slipping on the gold bangle, twirled around the room, congratulating herself on her own terrible cleverness.

Meanwhile, outside the window the little bunch of blue budgies continued to trill merrily, flapping their wings in the sun and tottering along the branch as though everything in the jungle was lovely.

Which, I'm afraid, is budgies all over for you.

X
Jailhouse Shock

Someone who most certainly wasn't trilling at that moment, or indeed bouncing along a branch for that matter, was Madam Rosita de Bonita.

Sopranos' voices, you see, are as delicate as porcelain and just as easily shattered by shock,[24] meaning that when Aries had turned Madam's aria into an *aaargh*-ia, he'd strained her voice horribly, warping her scales to wails, her trills to shrills and turning her Top-C turvy. Worse, with a leading lady moaning from her chaise longue with her singing voice sounding like a spaniel trying to yodel, the opera company had been forced to cancel its show.

And Alex and Aries had been arrested.

How unpleasant.

Now, unlike the city's opera house, which is as pink and giddy as a beautifully iced cake, the yard of the South Manaus Police Station is a miserable place. Open to the sky, it consists of a scrubby patch of ground bordered on three sides by the blank whitewashed walls of the police

---

24 Exactly the sort of shock suffered by turning round to discover a giant ram behind you puckering up for a big sloppy kiss. Just ask any shepherd.

station itself and on the fourth by a pair of tall gates, railed with iron struts and ending in sharp tips, that lead out on to the street and city beyond. Or at least they do when they're not chained and heavily padlocked, shut firm to imprison a boy and a giant ram. This is because cells, as you might have guessed, aren't built to accommodate oversized rams (or indeed ram-sized ones) and having seen the calming effect that Alex had on Aries, the police had decided to keep both of them outdoors.

'I suppose you're blaming me for all this,' sighed Aries, scuffling up a cloud of dust made silvery by the moonlight.

'No,' replied Alex patiently. 'I'm trying to get us out of here. Do stand still!'

Clambering up on to Aries' back, he steadied himself against the gates and stood up gingerly. Then, balancing like a stunt rider, he stretched up and closed his sweat-slicked fingers high around two bars of the gate.

And in case you're wondering, yes, one of their many gifts – say, the lightning bolt to zap the gates, or the cocktail stirrer to pick the padlock – might well have been useful at this point. Unfortunately, however, the Chief of Police, Inspector Gonzales – a rather gruff little man with a bristly moustache like a toilet brush – had seized everything and locked it safely away in his office.

'It's no good!' announced Aries. 'I can tell by the tone of your voice that you're cross with me.'

'Well,' admitted Alex, twitching his nose as a drop of sweat rolled down it, 'I suppose it might have helped if you'd ignored your stomach.' Lifting up his right foot, he braced it against the gate, took a deep breath and swung up his other leg. 'You know . . .' he grunted, grasping the bars more tightly, 'just . . . till . . . we left the . . . building.'

'I see,' muttered Aries. 'I notice you're not blaming Jason.' Aries stepped back to look up at him, frowning. 'Even though he's the one who made us creep around the opera house in the first place and didn't help us when the police arrived.'

Alex grimaced as the metal bit into his fingers. Steeling himself, he tried lifting one hand higher. But it was hopeless. The bars were sharp-edged and his hands were clammy, useless for holding on. Now, wholly losing his grip, his hands slid painfully down the bars.

'Aries!' he yelped, landing in a heap on the dusty ground. Frustrated, he kicked the gates hard, making the metal rattle wildly. 'Aren't things bad enough?'

'That's what I was just say—'

'No, you weren't!' snapped Alex, wiping his brow. It was hot and sticky, itchy with grit. 'And I don't want to hear it!'

'But if he'd owned up to knowing us —'

Alex threw his hands in the air.

'Then what? He'd be stuck in here too, wouldn't he? Locked up like us! We can't all make fools of ourselves, Aries, get caught and bundled into prison, you know. Some of us have to manage to stay out of trouble for five minutes to lead the quest.'

Aries' eyes widened in shock and Alex caught his breath, wishing that he could snatch the words straight back again. For a moment he simply stared at Aries, almost willing the ram to furiously stick out his lower lip and start the old argument they always had whenever they talked about Jason.

But he didn't.

Instead, Aries' face crumpled with hurt and he turned silently away, trudging over to the other side of the compound to slump down, his big bottom turned towards Alex.

Alex stood up and leaned against the gate, pushing his face against the warm bars. He glared at the narrow road beyond, littered with wooden trolleys piled with rotting fruit, and felt his heart grow heavier than Achilles's sword. In the distance he could hear the blare of the city – people laughing, music playing, the blast of horns from the sort of metal chariots they'd seen in London – and felt dismally glad that the other boys from the Underworld – the ones who hung round the zoo, teasing that he was more Ancient Geek than Ancient Greek for bothering with a load of smelly old monsters – couldn't see him now. Or his father, who'd doubtless still be bragging to the market traders in the agora about his clever, questing son who'd been chosen to help Jason. Biting his lip, he craned his neck, trying to see a little further down the street, wishing that Jason would hurry up and find them. Come back and show them how to escape. Show them how to stay calm when everything was going wrong.

Like now.

The thought sent fresh panic spiralling through his chest. They should be on their way to Rose by now. They should be heading into the jungle. If only they hadn't made such a spectacle of themselves in the opera house, Alex felt sure that they would have been.

'Alex?' Aries' voice was small now, little more than a whisper.

Turning, Alex looked over at the ram lying in a pool of moonlight and, seeing his sad, flattened ears, felt his heart tighten. He walked over and sat down beside him as Aries looked up, his muzzled scrunched up with worry.

'What is it?'

Aries paused for a moment. 'Supposing Jason doesn't come back?'

Alex laid his arm across Aries' neck. Usually a remark like that would annoy him but now he felt too exhausted to argue.

'Don't be silly,' he shrugged. 'He'll be here soon.'

Yet even so, as Aries slumped back down again, Alex found himself wishing that the ram hadn't chosen that particular moment, what with their being trapped in a strange, unfriendly place, hot, hungry and sickeningly worried about Rose, to suggest that they'd been abandoned too. Somewhere across town, a bell rang seven times and, feeling a sudden chill, Alex drew his knees tightly up beneath his chin.

Of course Jason would come back for them.

Alex just hoped he wouldn't take too long about it.

XI
Love and Roamin' Ants

Oh dear.

I'm not really sure how to start this next chapter, what with everything being so dreadful already. In fact, maybe it'd be better if you just put this book down and switched on the television instead.

What's that?

You still want to know?

All right, then. But don't say I didn't warn you and do try to remember that even though they killed the messengers in ancient times when they brought bad news, it is absolutely not the same for storytellers.

You see, as Alex and Aries huddled together, hot and miserable in the dust, Jason was relaxing on a bar stool.

That's right.

Relaxing.

Oh, he'd heard those seven bells ringing too, but now, taking another sip of his mango fruit cocktail, they'd only made him wonder why Estella, the beautiful woman he'd met in the opera house that afternoon, was a little late for their date. Around him, the bar began throbbing with hot samba music played by four men wearing shiny green blazers and big grins in the corner. Jason smiled broadly too, tapping his toe in time with the beat and toasting his reflection in the mirrored wall behind the bar, lined with shelves of bottles.

Manaus, he decided, was definitely his sort of city.

He chuckled, amused by the memory of what had been a freezing shock that morning when Athena had demanded he return to Earth to sort out Medea. That alone would have been enough to send anyone's spirits diving like a sea turtle sucked into the whirlpool of Charybdis's maw, long before the goddess had breezily added that he'd be travelling with Zoo Boy and Baldy.

Of course, that was the one drawback of being such a celebrated Greek hero: the fact that your reputation was only as good as your last quest. Like a shield, fame needed buffing to a fresh gleam whenever you were called upon to help, meaning that when the Goddess of Wisdom and War told you to do something, you did it. Whether or not you wanted to do what she'd asked. Which, frankly, he did not.

Which was why he was so delighted that now he wouldn't have to bother.

That's right.

You heard me.

Surprised?

Perhaps that's because like everybody in the Underworld (apart from Aries, of course) you thought that that he'd be bristling with impatience at the promise of a new quest? After the flamboyant way he'd bid the goddesses goodbye and raced on ahead, you thought he was desperate to swash and buckle through the jungle? Twitching to slap that statue of Nemesis into Medea's icy little hand and dispatch the sorceress straight to Tartarus?

Well, I'm afraid not. Because the last time he'd seen his ex-wife, she'd been glowering at him from behind the helm of a chariot drawn across the sky by snorting dragons. Looking down as she'd risen into the clouds, she'd flung furious curses at him for betraying her, screeching like a tormented seagull as their palace at Iolkos burned to the ground behind him. Which, however you look at it, is hardly your 'pop-round-and-see-me-next-time-you're-in-town' sort of toodle-pip, is it?

In fact, it was the fear of her scorching hatred that had persuaded Jason to take every single gift the goddesses had brought him that morning. Supernatural, bizarre or downright pointless, he'd been more than willing to accept every one of them and pile them on to Aries' back. He remembered the baffled look on Alex's face, clearly puzzled as to why they'd need to carry quite so much, and worried, no doubt, about overloading that ridiculous blimp of mutton. He smirked. Now he wouldn't need a single thing: no thunderbolt, no arrows, no singing lyre. Not since Estella had told him that the police would keep Aries and Alex locked up for days on end, leaving him plenty of time for some fun before returning to the Underworld.

(Without them.)

There, I've said it.

Please note that I did try to break it to you gently. I mean, don't you think putting it in brackets made it a little less shocking? You don't? Well, I'm sorry.

Unlike Jason, who wasn't remotely sorry about any of it. No, he was already planning the story he'd tell the Underworld and imagining the delighted look on Aphrodite's face when he stumbled, scratched and bruised, into her birthday party. With his clothes torn and his hair stylishly messy, he'd make a great entrance, breathlessly explaining to her and all of her guests how Alex and Aries had deserted him, running away at the last minute, leaving him to face the sorceress alone. The goddesses would gasp, find him a seat, a drink, a plate of peacock steak, a clump of grapes, as they listened in horror, pale-faced and tut-tutting, appalled at how their hero had been betrayed. Whilst he would simply shake his head in anguish, frustrated that he'd been unable to hand the statue of Nemesis to Medea, because those two had scarpered with it.

Now, chuckling quietly to himself, he tapped the key to the Underworld, tucked safely in his back pocket, and turned to watch the couples step out onto the dance floor. Shimmying and sashaying to the rising music, their laughter mingled with the frenzied trumpets as his mind continued to run on, delighted that he would finally be rid of Aries. Even though no one ever listened to the raging ruminant's version of events – thank the gods

– he'd still be glad to be rid of his endless bleating. Then, for a moment he thought about Alex. Perhaps it *was* a pity about him, though. Feeling a small twinge of remorse, he recalled the stories he'd heard about the boy. If they were true, then Alex did seem truly bold for his years, because even Jason had to admit that leading a flock of sheep across a strange city to defeat the sorceress was pretty impressive for a boy who usually spent his days wiping the snouts of drippy old monsters. Maybe there was even something quaintly daring about his search for some silly little Earth girl? He shrugged. Not that any of that mattered now. Besides, Jason reflected, wasn't it Alex's own fault that he'd never be going home again? After all, choosing Aries for a best friend hardly made him one of history's winners.

And anyway, he certainly wasn't about to spoil his evening worrying about those two. Not when he'd just spotted Estella stepping in though the door. He waved to her as she picked her way through the dancers to join him. She was dressed in a red top and white trousers, with a red flower tucked into her long dark hair, and he smiled, noticing that she was even prettier than he remembered.

Of course, what he should have noticed was the rather large ant that had just fallen from the hem of her trouser leg, turned and scuttled after her, weaving behind her red-sandaled foot as she strode across the flashing dance floor. Or the one that now plopped down behind it, or the next . . .

Three . . . four . . . five . . .

Eight . . . nine . . . ten . . .

Thirteen . . . fourteen . . . fifteen . . .

all snapping their huge chompers[25] in a funky ant-conga across the floor.

And in case you're thinking, don't be so silly, ants are far too diddly-widdly to notice, let me tell you that these were Amazon army ants. Unlike the tiddlers you see in the park, you know, ant-sized ants no bigger than ■, these were magnificent specimens, big enough to blot out whole words, like this ■■■■■. Such gi-ants were rarely seen anywhere but the rainforest floor and never ever in city bars unless, say, some sorceress had been using an old gold bangle recently.

But of course Jason didn't see them because he was far too busy beaming as Estella leaped up on to the bar stool beside him and planted a kiss on his cheek.

'You like to samba?' she chirruped.

Jason shrugged uncertainly.

'Come on!' She nodded towards the dance floor and pulled him to his feet. 'I teach you!'

Taking his right hand, she led him out between the swaying couples and wrapped her arms around his neck. Then, wiggling her hips, she began stepping forwards and backwards. Jason laughed, copying her steps. The

---

25 Or mandibles, being the fancy name ant-scientists use when studying them. You can easily spot ant-scientists – they're the ones in white coats and Wellington boots up to their armpits.

dance was fast and intricate. The trumpets jangled in his ears.

Which was when he felt something drop down the back of his neck.

He flinched and carried on dancing as a second tickle, this one beneath his right ear, began to annoy him. He batted it away quickly, feeling something stick to his fingers. Looking down, he was disgusted to see a gooey, leggy mess on his palm and wiped it quickly on his jeans before smiling brightly and taking Estella's hand. Spinning her under his raised arm, he hardly noticed the squirmy feel of her fingers at first.

At least not until the first needle-sharp jab of pain on his wrist.

And the next.

Glancing up at his hand, he felt his blood freeze in his veins. 'What on —?'

Ants.

Thousands of them.

Swarming through his fingers and tumbling in a treacly waterfall over his wrist. Whippy-legged as spiders, squirming from a ghastly brown mass that now seethed around Estella's hand, enveloping it like a living glove before storming up his bare arm towards his shoulder.

'Estella!' he shrieked, turning back to face her.

Except it wasn't her any more.

A human-shaped column of ants stood in her place. They scrambled in a mask over her forehead, tearing the red flower in her hair to shreds. They dripped from the tip of what had been her nose. Streaming over her neck and shoulders, they dribbled into thick swinging pendants of scuttling bodies that crumbled and dropped in clumps to explode and scatter around the heels of her shoes.

Jason felt a scream die in his throat as the phantom of roiling brown and black now gracefully lifted its other writhing arm and clamped it firmly on to his opposite shoulder. Immediately the ants moved as one, their wriggly platoons skittering up the twin bridges of her arms to pour over his body. Snapping and biting, they cascaded down his chest, his back and legs, enfolding him like a living mummy case, one lined with tiny fangs that sent bolts of pain searing across his skin.

Behind him, he was dimly aware of the band screeching to a stop as people fled past him, screaming and shouting, scattering tables and chairs in their wake as they swerved away from his flailing arms and the ants that rained down in a glistening shower on to the floor. Desperately scooping handfuls of insects from his face, Jason saw the swarm abruptly turn towards the door and charge towards it. A single glint flashed from the legion of their scrabbling bodies, the glimmer of the Underworld key as it was jostled along on their backs, the little parrot bouncing merrily, as they carried it like a trophy, out into the street.

'No!'

Roaring, he leaped blindly after them. But the ants were faster. Surging like a black tide, they turned sharply and poured down a storm drain. Taking the key with them.

For a split second Jason blinked after them, his body throbbing with bites, unable to believe what had happened. In agony, he lumbered towards the fountain and, heaving himself in, sank gratefully into its cool water. A few blissful moments later, he stood up again, dazed and dripping. Even in the moonlight the swellings were red and furious and, gingerly touching his face, he squealed, feeling his handsome features as crumpled as a fallen peach.

Dizzy with shock, he clambered out and stumbled away, swatting and scratching, still feeling as if a million tiny legs were scurrying over his skin. In fact, he was so distracted by the terrible sensation that he didn't even notice the red fire truck parked in front of Estella's apartment. Nor the clapping as the real Estella, the one who'd been trapped in the building's lift for the past three hours, stepped out of the doorway, flanked by a couple of firemen.

But he did hear a woman's eerily familiar laugh. High and chiming, it tinkled in amusement along the street behind him, echoing off the buildings as he limped away into the shadows.

XII
The Lone Star[26] Lone Star

Well, I don't know about you, but all those ghastly ants have made me want to throw myself into the nearest fountain too. Do you know, I've gone itchy all over? Prickly and tingly, the way you do when you watch one of those Sunday night documentaries about creepy-crawlies, only to find that you can't enjoy your cup of tea any more because of the sensation of something scooching up your leg.

Ugh!

Let me think of something nicer.

I know!

A kitten!

Not a real cuddly-wuddly one that meows and flops over so you can tickle its tummy – but one made from platinum, a pendant shaped like a kitten and the one that Hazel was admiring at that very moment, dangling

---

26 No, you're not seeing double. 'The Lone Star State' is the nickname for Texas. Every American state has its own moniker. Florida's called The Sunshine State; Georgia, The Peach State; and Kansas, The Sunflower State. However, since none is known as The Custard Cream State I shan't be emigrating any time soon.

in the window of the jewellery shop tucked inside Manaus's glamorous Hotel Esplendido. Curled into a ball, its nose and collar were set with pink diamonds, and now, lifting up her sunglasses for a better look, Hazel just knew that it would go fabulously with her strawberry-coloured suede jacket. And, what a snip at $5,000! Then her eyes slid sideways to the platinum poodle displayed on the necklace beside it, with a pink-diamond bow on one ear, and frowned because that was rather gorgeous too.

Kitten?

Poodle?

She frowned, strangely unable to make up her mind this morning. Heaven only knew she deserved a treat after that terrible ordeal on the boat and expensive, glittery things usually cheered her up. But not today. Frustrated, she turned away and walked across the marble-floored foyer to sink down into a green velvet sofa. Stretching back, she felt relieved that the shop didn't open for another twenty minutes, giving her plenty of time to think about it properly.

Above her, ceiling fans whirred and, listening to the tinkling piano being played in the lobby behind her, she glanced round at the women chatting over low tables set with silver tea pots and blue china; the old gentleman briskly turning the page of his ironed newspaper; businessmen in linen suits barking down mobile phones; and her own bodyguards, flown in last night, who stood blearily drinking coffee at the palm-fronded espresso bar.

She loved being here at the hotel. The way its floors didn't rock beneath her feet. The way she couldn't hear the endless slip-slap of water. The way the air smelled grubbily full of city and cars and not jungle. And most importantly, the way it wasn't squirm-full of hulking great spiders slinking up the duvet towards you. Of this she was absolutely certain, having insisted the bellboy[27] check her suite, demanding he look underneath all five beds, seven tables, thirty-three chairs, inside ten wardrobes, beneath the pool table and under the seats of all twelve toilets (twice). Now, leaning back against the marsh-mallow-soft velvet, this was, she decided, the only way to see the Amazon, although technically, of course, she couldn't actually see it at all from here. Only pictures of it, like the one of a golden jaguar stalking through the treetops on the wall beside her, which suited her fine.

So why then did she feel so twitchy?

She swallowed, uncomfortably thinking back to Rose's face the day before as the helicopter Hazel had chartered from Manaus slapped down its floats on the Rio Negro. Feeling a sharp jab of guilt, she remembered the disappointment etched into Rose's sunburned brow,

---

27 *A bellboy is a hotel porter employed to carry guests' luggage and attend to room service. It is not, as the name suggests, someone made of metal that ding-dongs each time they walk by. Such a person would cause havoc in a hotel by luring towel-draped guests from the shower into the corridor seeking imaginary ice-cream vans and play havoc with the manager's exotic fish, who'd doubtless suffer fin-flump from all the ting-a-linging vibrations in their water.*

her tight mouth, the sparkle gone from her eyes and felt her own heart tighten. But, she consoled herself, that ghastly spider on the boat really had been the absolute last straw. Her second near-death experience in as many months, it had been the giddy limit, the tin lid on the cattle shed and the sugar frosting on her Dallas doughnut – and much as she wanted to help Rose, she knew she had to leave the jungle. Recalling how Eduardo had told her that it was the most venomous spider on Earth, she shuddered. A deadly critter like that, ugly as a mud fence, climbing up *her* bed? The captain had been bewildered by how the, the *thing*, had managed to crawl on to the boat in the first place and, wringing his hands, he'd explained how his staff were always so careful, shaking out the bananas and coffee sacks and boxes of supplies they brought on board. Yet nothing he or Rose could say had made the slightest difference to her decision to leave, and so, utterly unravelled, Hazel had quite literally abandoned ship.

Glancing at her watch, she felt her heart thump. Rose and Eduardo would have left the *Tucano* by now, to canoe – *canoe!* – into the jungle. She imagined them paddling up some dark stretch of water, soupy with swimming snakes and tangled with vines. Just how could Rose entrust her safety to something so flimsy, so small, so *sinkable*, over that endless murky green water?

'You'll miss the anaconda nests lining the river,' Eduardo teased as he'd loaded Hazel's cases on to the helicopter.

She rolled her eyes and quickly shook the thought from her head. Nests, where she came from, were for little biddy chicks, not enormous great snakes that flung themselves round you, squeezing you tighter and tighter until they stopped your very lungs before unhinging their jaws, and . . . and . . .

Well, that was quite enough of thinking about that.

She twisted forwards on the sofa and tried to force her mind back on to the jewellery glittering behind glass a little distance away.

Except that her heart was no longer in it.

If only she'd been able to persuade Rose to let her hire some professional to track down Professor Pottersby-Weir, some capable sort with scorpion-proof shorts and a big grin, who'd machete his way through the greenery and come back, fly-bitten but triumphant. It wouldn't have mattered how much it cost, or what supplies or help he'd have needed. She was willing to pay for it all.

But Rose wouldn't hear of it. She was so impatient, so determined to do it for herself.

Now, sliding lower down the sofa, Hazel pulled her phone from the pocket of her pink jeans and flicked through her photos: her and Rose trying on matching sunglasses in London; her and Rose drinking lime coolers on the plane; her and Rose trying on huge floppy hats at Barcelos Airport. Flicking to the last picture, she felt a lump rise in her throat. In it, Rose stood alone on the deck of the *Tucano* waving as the helicopter turned away towards the city. Hazel tucked the phone away and glanced dismally at the jeweller's window, knowing that no diamond-studded cat or dog was going to change the way that that made her feel. Whichever way she looked at it, and however good her reasons were, she'd let her friend down. Even the GPS, the emergency flares and the army phone she'd had flown out to the boat as soon as she arrived in Manaus hardly soothed her conscience. Not when she could imagine Rose simply tucking them into her rucksack with a sad little shrug, puzzling at what half of them were for, and wishing that she had her friend beside her instead.

A sudden scrape of high heels over the floor startled her and she looked up to see a tall thin woman in a grey suit clattering over to the reception desk where a hotel employee was primping pots of thunder-orchids and ferns.

'It's completely unacceptable!' exclaimed the woman in grey, slamming down a crumpled poster of a Japanese lady and making the receptionist jump. 'My husband and I flew halfway round the world to see Rosita de Bonita perform!'

'Madam,' soothed the hotel receptionist. She raised her palms in the air apologetically. 'I am sorry for your dreadful disappointment. Obviously the opera house regrets —'

'Reee-grets?' shrilled the woman, stamping her foot on the marble floor.

Wincing, Hazel shrank down into the sofa and returned to her gloomy thoughts, consoling herself that at least Rose would be safe with Eduardo. Reliable as an old teddy bear, he knew how to survive the jungle.

Heav'n only knew he'd told them often enough about taking his granddaughters trekking through the rainforest to watch baby monkeys swing through the branches or spot owlets bustled like blobs of cotton wool in rotted tree trunks.

Meanwhile, over by the desk, the irate woman's voice was growing more furious and, glancing over, Hazel saw the receptionist take a big step backwards, nodding madly.

'Yes, madam. I agree,' she spluttered. 'It is appalling that they've had to cancel *Madama Butterfly* and close the opera house. But the management is offering full ticket refunds.'

'Reee-funds?' squealed the woman, her voice now wild as a toucan with its tail covered in termites. 'How can anyone possibly reee-fund the experience of hearing Rosita de Bonita as Butterfly on opening night?'

The tinkling piano stopped tinkling. The chatterers stopped chatting, the newspaper readers stopped reading, the sippers stopped sipping as everyone now turned to watch the woman's face grow as purple as the orchids topping the desk.

'But then,' the woman fumed, 'how can anyone be so careless as to allow a boy and a gigantic bald ram to ruin her performance in the first place?'

Hazel snapped off her sunglasses and threw them onto the sofa.

A boy and a gigantic bald ram? Goosebumps swept over her skin as though someone had thrown a bucket of iced water over her.

Alex and Aries?

Here?

In Manaus?

Was the heat frying her brain? How could it possibly be them? And yet, even though she knew she must be going wholly la-la, she found herself sprinting across the lobby – sending the jeweller, now busily unlocking his shop, careening headfirst into a large prickly palm – to skid to a stop in front of the desk. Because if it really were them, she reasoned breathlessly, there was only one reason that would bring them back: Medea.

Shunting the furious woman out of her way, she leaned over the counter until she was nose-to-nose with the bewildered receptionist.

'Tell me!' she demanded, as a pot of orchids smashed on to the floor. 'What happened to them?'

XIII
SURPRISE, SURPRISE!

Miles to the west, not to mention miles hotter, grubbier and wearier too, Rose stood waist-high in ferns, blinking the sweat out of her eyes, as Eduardo chopped through yet another thicket of bamboo.

For the past two days they'd been trekking through the jungle proper, hacking their way through the rain-forest understory, the tangled cage of tree trunks, ferns and palms, of prickly plants and pathless green that lay far below the canopy of leaves and criss-crossing lianas,[28] shut off from the sunshine above. Hot, thick and clammy, the air down here was murky, tinged with a mossy light, so soupy and green that it reminded Rose of the water in a forgotten fish tank. Worse, it stank of rotting leaves and fungus.

Snatching her breath in small gasps, she quickly

---

28 Lianas are vines that twine around tree trunks to reach the light above the canopy. Making woody tightropes high in the rainforest, they're used as sky-highways for tree-dwelling animals. Every day, they bustle with lizards, rats and monkeys, and ring with the swearing of sloths, who having chosen to snooze hanging upside-down from them, wake to find their tummies covered in paw-marks.

checked the bark of the closest tree before leaning her aching back against it, exhausted. She tilted her face up and watched two tiger-striped *Heliconia* butterflies flutter past the tip of her nose and spiral away like sparks, vanishing into the shadows between the trees. She felt swimmy-headed, dizzy from the sticky heat and the strain of hour upon hour spent picking their way over roots and toppled trees, of listening for falling fruit, of shrinking away from scorpions sunbathing on palm leaves, of splashing through small creeks and trudging through mud that sucked your feet down into it after the daily downpours. Then, wriggling her damp toes in her boots, raw and uncomfortable in their thick, bristly socks, she smiled so hard it made her cheeks hurt.

Because every aching, grubby, scary, exhilarating second of it had been worth it because they were almost there.

Tatu Village.

The thought sent a sudden swell of excitement surging through her body like an electric current jittering every exhausted cell, every nerve, every muscle back into life. Now, stretching up on to her tiptoes, she craned to see past Eduardo's bulky frame and caught her breath, snatching a glimpse of scrubby land beyond the broken fence of bamboo.

This was it!

Finally, the moment she'd been dreaming of, the moment that made lying to her mother all right, the moment that made the heat and the grittiness and the slamming rain and the discomfort and the fear bearable. Trembling with impatience, she felt a sudden stab of longing for Hazel because even though her head totally understood why Hazel had had to leave, her heart missed her horribly now. She bit her lip, tasting the tang of salt and wishing Hazel were beside her again – moaning, smeary-face and fizzing with bad-temper, of course – but actually *with* her now that she had finally, finally arrived at the outskirts of the village. Of course, Eduardo was kind and protective and strong and told her lots funny stories to keep her spirits up. But it just wasn't the same as having a friend by her side.

Her head was throbbing now, thumping with the crunch and splinter of bamboos beneath Eduardo's machete. Her heart thumped, pounding in time with the ceaseless trilling, screeching, shrieking, hoppity-clicking bang and rasp of the jungle around her. Of course, if she hadn't been quite so elated or quite so woozy with weariness, she might have noticed that the howler monkeys had abruptly stopped adding to the din about twenty minutes ago.

And it might have worried her.

But she didn't.

Because all she could think of was her father – only minutes away – running towards her – only minutes away – arms outstretched to scoop her up into a bear hug – only minutes away – speechless with astonishment to see his own daughter racing out of the trees to greet him.

'Rose!' Eduardo's voice rang back through the trees

in triumph, sending unseen parrots squealing into the air high above the roof of leaves. Pulling off his cap, he wiped his brow and stepped through the gap in the bamboo. He turned and looked back at her. 'Come and see!'

Euphoria exploded inside Rose like fireworks dazzling the night sky. Stumbling away from the tree, she forced her legs to run, even though they felt as though they'd turned to rubber, and stamped through the clumps of ferns to plunge through the bamboo after him, careless of the scratches on her face and arms.

In the distance, beyond the patch of cleared jungle, stood a wide circle of wooden huts. Rose swallowed hard, stifling the mad giggle that threatened to bubble up in her throat, and blinked. Thatched with palm leaves bleached by the sun, the huts stood like sentries around an enormous *molucca*,[29] the longhouse, outside which a family of armadillos were hoovering through the dirt like leathery vacuum cleaners. Suddenly, desperate to run the rest of the way, to search every centimetre of the place, she took a step forward and felt Eduardo's hand on her arm.

'Remember what we discussed.'

Rose nodded irritably and tried to tamp down her impatience by thinking back to the wide patches of

---

29 The molucca is the big hut in the middle of the village where the tribe meets to make important decisions. It's a bit like a town hall, only with monkeys instead of a fancy clock on the roof.

brown and treeless earth she'd seen from the plane window. Eduardo had explained why the villagers would be suspicious of them, of any strangers, and now, as they began walking towards the village, she reached for her locket, rubbing it nervously, hoping that an old man and a girl didn't look like the cattle ranchers and oil prospectors he'd told her about, the sort of people who'd tear the villagers' jungle down and turn it into a desert of dust, leaving them nowhere to live and hunt.

Closer now, Rose searched the village with her eyes, scanning every hut, every doorway, desperate for a glimpse of her father. Women dressed in red and green and gold sarongs stood peeling knobbly brown roots and throwing the creamy middles into a pot, others smashed them to a pulp with paddles. A few sat cross-legged on blankets, sifting through tubs of beads and threading them on to wires to make what looked like earrings. Around them, boys in football shirts chased one another around the huts, skittish as the dragonflies she'd seen flitting between the trees, whilst the girls helped their mothers and tufty-headed toddlers, some naked, some in red loincloths, giggled and crawled over blankets. A boy of about ten, wearing a halo of yellow parrot feathers, threw a stick for a thin, gangly dog.

By the time they reached the nearest hut in the ring, Rose could see that everyone's faces, even the babies', were painted with the same pattern of long red stripes, stretching from the tips of their noses and out across their cheeks, like whiskers.

Minus nought point eight three three. Minus fifty-seven point two.

Unbidden, the Scroll's voice drifted into her mind and now, despite her dry mouth and sweat-slicked hair, she saw herself back in London, surrounded by the icy white statues of the British Museum, hearing those numbers for the first time and turning to see Alex's and Aries' faces, bright with understanding, knowing just how much it meant to her.

If only they could have known she'd finally made it.

If only they were here with her.

If only!

Suddenly the boy with yellow parrot feathers noticed them, threw down the dog's stick and sprinted into the longhouse. Behind him, the women swept the toddlers into their arms and called to the other children, as five well-built men burst out of the building carrying bows and arrows. Their broad chests were hung with strings of something jagged and white that Rose thought might be jaguar teeth and now, tilting their chins up defiantly, the warriors stood absolutely still and stared at Rose and Eduardo.

For long moments it seemed like the trees were the only things moving, tipsy in the heat, and as the tribesmen continued to stare at them Rose felt another sting of impatience. She didn't have time for all this eyeballing, like the gunslingers in the corny old Westerns that she and her dad used to watch, and she was about to open her mouth and say something, although she wasn't quite sure what, when another man stepped out of the longhouse. He was tall and powerfully built and wearing a crown of yellow parrot feathers in his shoulder-length hair. Rose knew he must be the chief. He grunted something to the others and began striding across the dusty middle of the village, flanked by the tribesmen. The boy in yellow feathers caught up, his curious expression and pursed mouth a perfect miniature of the chief's face. Copying his father's walk, he regarded Rose suspiciously, whilst behind him, some of the smaller children, having broken free of their mothers' grasps, waddled like ducklings.

The chief stopped and stared at Rose. She held his gaze, feeling her cheeks grow hotter as he bent towards her, stretching out his hand, fascinated. Rose steeled herself as he took hold of a lock of her hair and teased a single curl between his fingers before looking back over his shoulder and barking something at the others. She glanced at Eduardo, feeling horribly confused, as the tribesmen began chattering excitedly.

'Fire hair,' translated Eduardo uncertainly.

Rose blinked up at him.

'He's saying —' Eduardo paused to listen to another burst of speech, 'he's saying that they've seen it before, Rose. On the pale man who sleeps beside the creek.'

A minute later, Rose sprinted away from the others in the direction the chief had pointed, diving between the huts and out towards the creek. Leaping the roots of a kapok tree that loomed like a giant elephant's foot blocking her way, she skidded to a stop beneath an arch of leafy ferns and gasped.

Slouched beneath a tree with a bulbous trunk was her father. She took in his hollowed face, his blistered skin, his beard, always so groomed and soft when he hugged her, now wiry and snagged with leaf litter. The sight of his knee, bony and bruised, sticking out of his ruined trousers made her heart hammer in her chest like a frantic woodpecker.

She began walking uncertainly towards him. 'Dad?'

Startled by her voice, a few blue budgerigars flapped out of the tree above him, tweeting furiously and flying away. But he didn't see them. Now, as an awful tightness clawed at her throat, Rose willed him to turn his head and look at her. Instead he simply continued to watch the brown water beyond, snaking away around a bend in the trees.

'Dad?'

She hunched down beside him and laid her hand on his thin shoulder, trying hard not to notice the jab of bones beneath her fingers nor the way his body stiffened at her touch. Biting her lip, she looked into his eyes, foggy and bloodshot, searching for a spark of recognition, a glimmer, a flicker in that blank emptiness. 'It's me, Rose. Your daughter?'

The words felt like stones in her mouth and as her father continued to stare through her, unseeing, she felt herself starting to tremble. She waited for a few seconds more, feeling a heaviness sucking at her bones and flooding her whole body with a dull aching coldness.

She hardly heard Eduardo's anxious voice – *'Aqua! Aqua!'* – as he ran, shouting, down the path towards them, but a few moments later he thrust a clay beaker into her hands. Mechanically, she brought it to her lips and then dropped it.

How could her father not know her? How could he look through her like a patch of air?

Hot tears prickled her eyes. She tried to blink them back, realising that even the terrible day when her mother had waited for her, tear-streaked behind the school fence, to tell her that the Royal Geographical Society had called off the search for him, she hadn't felt this desolate. This lost. Then, she'd blankly refused to believe that he was gone. Her head pounded and stifling a choking sob, she covered her face with her hands, shutting out the villagers, who now chattered like mynah birds around her.

Eduardo reached out and steadied her. 'There's a long way to go.'

A long way to go?

She shrank back, unable to reply.

Wasn't travelling halfway around the world a long way to go? And crying yourself to sleep for months on end? Lying to her mother? A long way to go?

Seeing the pain in her face, Eduardo took a step towards her father and laid his hands firmly on his shoulders.

'Your daughter, *señor*!' He spoke loud and slowly. 'She has come all this way for you. Is Rose? *Sí*?'

Her father stared back blankly at him. Frowning, Eduardo took a firmer grip and tried to pull her father away from the tree. '*Señor*, you should —'

'No!' Her father's yell roared in her ears.

Raw and primitive, it sounded like an animal in pain.

Scooting backwards in the dust, Rose shrieked, gaping as her father kicked out his legs out in panic, catching Eduardo's shins to send him sprawling backwards on to the ground. She stared, unable to believe what she'd seen, feeling a curdling mixture of horror and bewilderment flood through her as she scrambled uncertainly to her feet and swayed towards the other villagers who were trying to help Eduardo.

Which was when she noticed the woman watching her.

Rose stopped and tried to take in the pale, willowy figure standing a little distance away, dressed in a T-shirt and khaki shorts. She peered at the plait of black hair over the phantom's shoulder, the black hair streaked with violet, and growled under her breath, cursing her stupid brain. Clamping her eyes shut, she blamed the soul-splintering shock of finding her father so damaged and the throttling heat and the crushing exhaustion she felt for conjuring up such a terrible hallucination, counted to three and opened them again.

But the figure was still there.

Except it was closer now.

Rose blinked, furious at the way her devious mind had even painted a treacly look of concern on the imaginary sorceress's face, making her look like some lavender-scented aunt with a big bar of chocolate in her handbag. She almost laughed. As if Medea could ever be the sort of person to brush your shoulder with her hand and murmur a soothing, 'My poor Rose. I'm so sorry about your father.'

Making it all the more startling when she did.

Rose felt her touch like a sliver of ice dragged over her skin.

Sharp, cold and, worst of all, undeniably real.

She stared up into the sorceress's grey, glinting eyes, aware of the screeching jungle around her fading away as surely as if someone had turned down the volume on a giant radio. The world wobbled beneath her feet, jolting the trees and stopping the birds flying in mid-air. Lurching sideways, her gaze fell on a clump of scarlet fire-flowers, blooms that suddenly swelled into huge red trumpets and furiously rushed up to fill her vision.

Just before everything went completely black.

XIV
Holding Out For a Hero

'Is magnificent tea-tray! I think is silver!'

Chief Inspector Gonzales, head of South Manaus Police Station, pressed the phone hard to his chubby ear and admired the rather splendid silverware he'd confiscated from the boy and the ram the day before. Unlike the ugly little statue, lyre and other oddments he'd seized, which were clearly only cheap stage props that the odd pair had managed to thieve from the theatre, it looked valuable. Now, with his plump behind perched on his desk, he waited for his brother Leonardo, an antiques dealer in Belem, to tell him what he thought it might be worth. At the other end of the line, Leonardo huffed again.

'You say it has a lady's face on it?' he said.

Usually his dithering infuriated Gonzales, but not today, because today the Chief Inspector was far too busy totting up dollars in his mind, the dollars he was certain they'd make when Leonardo sold the tray to some well-heeled tourist. In fact, he was so busy counting that he didn't hear the low whisper of snakes behind him.

'*Si!*' barked the Chief Inspector. 'Though she looks like a cat's bottom.'

Nor the sharp intake of Medusa's breath, following by fits of hissing giggles.

'Bring it to the shop at the weekend, Gonzales.'

And he didn't even notice the flop of five bellies dropping one after another on to the stone floor behind him – *plop, plop, plop, plop, plip* – as four deadly serpents (and Grass Snake, who was doing his best) now slithered straight towards him. Sliding in SWAT[30] formation, their coffin-shaped snouts instantly homed in on the tang of his cheesy feet.

Of course, seeing them would have been the most dreadful surprise.

Maybe it's surprised you, too?

Which just goes to show what you know about shields belonging to Ancient Greek goddesses, because even fancy-pants ones like Athena's, that really do look rather like something a posh butler would serve afternoon tea from, will always revert to being a 'Where-do-you-think-you're-sticking-those-scones, Mister?' sort of deadly weapon on a quest. Making it extremely lucky that as the snakes began rising around the legs of Gonzales's desk there was a bright, 'Hot dang! Anybody home?' from the public office beyond, followed by a most impatient rapping on its glass screen, obliging Gonzales to waddle off, leaving the snakes snapping

---

30 Scaly Weapons Action Team

their needle-sharp fangs hungrily in the air behind him.

Luckily, world-famous pop stars, cute as cupcakes, can charm even the grumpiest of police inspectors into letting their prisoners go. Particularly when that inspector is left blushing like rhubarb from a 'You're so sweet!' kiss on his cheek, has been bamboozled by a handful of free VIP tickets for his daughter to 'Hazel Praline's Rio Rockfest', holds the full bail money in one hand and a thousand dollars for the ritzy antique tea tray (and all the other clutter the boy refused to leave without) in the other.

Meaning that half an hour later, Alex and Aries were up in the central living room of the penthouse suite of the Manaus Esplendido.[31] Huge and airy, with one wall lined by three big glass doors that opened on to balconies giving spectacular views over the city, it was sumptuously decorated. Chandeliers made of green and pink glass hung from the ceilings. The floor gleamed with honey-coloured marble. A grand piano stood in one corner. In the centre three leather sofas were arranged around a low wooden table, against which Alex had leaned the now silent and un-squirming shield.

Hazel was sitting on one of the sofas, fanning herself with a Pegasus feather fan despite the air-conditioned chilliness of the place, watching as Alex paced the

---

31 *What? You're surprised that Aries was up there? That the hotel entertained rams? Well, ever since the Esplendido had allowed a certain pop star's pet chimpanzee to stay, they'd become famous for accommodating pets of the rich and kooky.*

length of the living room. Up and down his sandals slapped against the marble as he fretfully snatched glimpses of the jungle lying distantly in the gaps between the skyscrapers that loomed about the hotel. Meanwhile, Aries soaked his aching hooves in a tub of 'Promise of India' bubble bath. Their sleepless night spent cross and worried, locked up in that unpleasant police compound, had left his four stomachs in a tight knot. Now, having recently been rudely bundled into Hazel's bodyguard-driven SUV, 'helped' on board by being prodded in places he didn't care to mention, he was feeling more miserable than ever and trying to cheer himself up.

And failing.

According to the blurb on the bottle, sinking into its frothy embrace was supposed to leave him ready to dance like a princess whilst smelling of Darjeeling roses.

But it wasn't working.

Of course, he thought gloomily, what he really needed was something that would foam up into a big figure of froth and jab a bubbly finger at Alex, forcing him to believe that what Aries said about Jason was true, something that would stop the boy wasting time waiting for the Argonaut to appear again so that they could leave Manaus right now and head into the jungle and find Rose. He could see how desperate the boy was to leave, how he couldn't eat, couldn't settle, couldn't even stop worrying long enough to sit down. All of which made him feel even more frustrated, and feeling like a four-hoofed Cassandra.[32]

In the hour or so since they'd arrived up here, there'd been hugs and thank-yous and cheese sandwiches and big glasses of iced chocolate-milk topped with cream that neither of them could face. Astonishingly, and I know you'll find this hard to believe, but even the olives glistening in their bowl had tasted like greasy pebbles to Aries today. True, his spirits had rallied briefly when Hazel had told them she'd never heard of Jason, and thought Argonauts were some sort of cookie, but they'd swiftly plummeted again when she'd told them how she'd left Rose on her own. Worse, at the mention of the sorceress, she'd promptly burst into tears, wailing about that *appallin' witchy-woman* and *heaven t'Betsy she'd a-never a-left Rose if she'd known*.

Which had thoroughly disappointed them both.

Aries looked up at her again, at her shiny blonde ponytail and her polished nails, pink as seashells, and realised that despite being so modern she was just like Alex's sisters, ready to scream and scamper into the villa at the first crash of thunder.

She wasn't a bit like Rose.

---

32 Cassandra was blessed with prophecy, the gift of being able to see into the future. Because of this, she tried to tell people that the Greeks would hide inside a wooden horse, sneak back into Troy and burn the city to the ground. Unfortunately she was also cursed so that no one would ever believe a word she said, and so no one did. Or at least not until their houses went up in smoke . . . WHOOSH . . . just like that.

'We should be in the jungle by now!' said Alex, glaring out of the window at the sweltering city.

'And we would be,' replied Aries, noticing how quickly the light was fading from the sky, draining it from blue to grey, 'if Jason were here.'

'I thought you said he was a hero, Alex?' said Hazel. 'Why isn't he leading you on the quest?'

'That's a very good question!' harrumphed Aries and stepped noisily out of the bubble bath, shaking each hoof in turn.

'Something must have happened to delay him,' said Alex.

'Then let's go on alone,' said Aries.

'Alone?' hissed Adder, suddenly lurching out of the shield and sloughing off its silvery veneer in an instant. 'That'sss not wis-s-se!'

Squealing, Hazel blanched and drew her feet up on to the sofa.

'It's all right,' Alex reassured her quickly as the other snakes began to stir and zigzag up. All apart from Cobra, who snoozed happily with his collar tucked over his snout.

The Gorgon flicked her golden eyes open. 'He's right,' she sighed, glancing coolly at Hazel's horrified face. 'Much though it pains me to say it, he's the only one who's likely to get close enough to Medea to give her the statue.'

'S-s-she wouldn't accept a pres-s-sent from either of you two,' said Viper. 'Even if you s-s-survived long enough to try.'

'Hero plusss gift equalsss victory,' said Adder, nodding sagely.

'Bes-s-sidesss,' hiccupped Grass Snake, boggle-eyed with alarm as the silver vanished and became green again. 'He'sss got the key home!'

'But we can't just stay here waiting,' protested Alex, thumping the back of the sofa. 'Rose is out there. And so is Medea!'

In the moment's silence that frosted through the room at the mention of the sorceress's name, Aries watched the boy's face, crumpled with a mixture of frustration and confusion.

He felt a tingling in his tail.

Was Alex finally beginning to wonder about Jason? About what exactly was taking him so long to find them? If indeed, he was even trying?

'Then let'sss s-s-start planning tacticsss!' hissed Krait, wrapping his coils excitedly around his head and rasping his scales. He peeked out of the tangle of loops. 'If we do have to go alone, we're going to need them.'

'Tactics?' said Alex.

'For the battle ahead, of cours-s-se!' cried Viper. 'Didn't your father teach you anything? The firs-s-st duty of a s-s-soldier isss to know the lie of the land.'

'Vantage pointsss to s-s-spy on the enemy,' said Adder. 'Ground cover, s-s-shelter and outcropsss for s-s-surpris-s-se attacksss!'

'And hiding placesss,' added Grass Snake, shivering on the Gorgon's brow.

Huge and round, Hazel's eyes slid warily from one writhing snake to the next as she nervously reached down into the big pink leather handbag at her feet and pulled something out. 'In that case, maybe this'll help?'

Everyone stared blankly (apart from Cobra, who was now muttering drowsily about grasshoppers).

'It's a book,' she explained, handing it to Alex. 'All about the Amazon. And there's a map tucked into the back.'

Alex read the title dismally. '*Glamazon Gals*?'

Aries shuffled over, and took a single olive from the tray Hazel had ordered from room service, before laying his head on Alex's shoulder as the boy began flicking through the pages. 'How to survive the rainforest and remain gorgeous', 'The five best heat-resistant lipsticks to wear in the jungle', 'Perfumes that do not attract bugs'.

'I'm not sure,' said Alex.

'Oh, I know,' said Hazel. 'Maybe it's not like, totally ideal for a boy and a ram, but it'll still tell you what you need to know. The bugs and gigantic spiders, what critter'll be tryin' to eat you in the trees, on the path, in the air, under the water —'

Aries felt his throat tighten around the olive, gulped it down loudly and looked at the book a second time.

There were pictures of a river so wide it made Aries think of the sea, and lots of strange-looking animals: a 'jaguar', all big and toothy, and rather like the Nemean Lion, except that it was still wearing its golden, black-dotted fur, instead of wobbling around, pink as a blancmange (thanks to Herakles); a craggy-dragon called a caiman; and pigeons, like the ones that were doubtless, at that very moment, decorating his statue with poo, but with dusky pink feathers, the colour of a sunset, not drab and grey. Glancing up at Alex, he saw the surprise on his face. Surprise, and something else: excitement.

Aries felt a spark of hope. Maybe, just maybe, if Alex read enough and thought enough, he'd feel confident enough for them to leave together? Couldn't he see, after everything that they'd done in London, that he was brave and smart enough to lead them through the jungle without the 'help' of old brawn-for-brains?

Alex took the map out of the back of the book, unfolded it and spread it out across the low table. Next, he pulled the crumpled page from Persephone's magazine from his pocket and carefully began comparing the two. Meanwhile, Aries pushed over a few more pages with his muzzle, eager to find out more. The back of the book was devoted to the rainforest's history: drawings of men cutting into rubber trees;[33] men mining for gold; men chopping down the jungle and driving cattle on to it; men wearing strange armour – 'conquistadors', the caption said – which was apparently Spanish for old soldiers. Aries snorted. Soldiers? They looked completely mad, dressed up in ballooning trousers and ridged metal hats that drooped with feathers.

---

33 Don't be fooled by the name. Rubber trees don't bend or wobble and when you accidentally run into them you still hurt your head.

A sudden knock at the door made them both jump and Hazel hurried across the ocean of marble to answer it.

'Miss Praline?' Aries watched as one of her bodyguards, a thickset man dressed in a black suit and sunglasses stepped into the room. 'I'm sorry to disturb you, but the receptionist just rang to tell me they've something of a fruit loop in reception. A young man, demanding to come up.'

Beside him, Alex turned and gave him an 'I told you so!' look, sending Aries' hopes diving, like a harpy spotting dinner at the bottom of a cliff, and taking his pipe dream of the two of them setting out as the A-Team[34] with it.

'A fan?' said Hazel curiously.

'No, miss.' The bodyguard glanced into the room. 'Actually, he's come from the police station where these two were held. It's Alex he wants to talk to.' The man hesitated, rubbing his chin thoughtfully before he went on. 'Insists he's a Greek prince.'

Jason hadn't felt less like a Greek prince in his entire life and ghosthood.

Having spent most of the night slinking through the shadows, he'd used every second since daybreak searching for Alex and Aries, dodging the strange chariots that hooted and smoked as he scurried through the city streets

34 The Alex-and-Aries Team.

to call at all the police stations, only to arrive at the right one an hour or so after they'd left with some singer, and he had been told to try at the Hotel Esplendido. Everywhere he went, faces froze, eyes gaped and children burst into squeals, horrified by the raging bites that had turned his golden skin fiery red and as bumpy as a monster's bottom.

Grunting, he glared at the two burly men now flanking him. Both were sturdy and thick with muscles, built like **Cyclopes** and with manners to match, and had bustled him into this infernal mirrored box with doors that slid magically shut and then shot upwards, leaving his stomach feeling as though it'd been left on the ground far below. He should have been back in the Underworld by now, he seethed, the guest of honour at Aphrodite's party. Instead he was raw, sore and absolutely furious that Medea had forced his hand like this, snatching the key and sending him skulking back to the quest he thought he'd so luckily managed to avoid. Worse, far from being worried that he'd been sent from the Underworld to find her, it seemed that she actually wanted to see him. Why else steal his key home?

Wanted to see him? The curious thought startled him and, feeling an odd little shiver down his spine, he found himself wondering whether she might actually still have feelings for him – the fluffy-wuffy lovebird sort, that is, rather than the scorch-your-pants-off dragon variety – because now that he considered it more calmly, he realised that she hadn't actually chosen to kill him, had she? She'd simply sent a special calling card that left him with an irresistible reason to come and see her. Was it possible she still loved him? She had done once. Deeply. And weren't her romantic gestures always a little, well, eccentric? After all, as he now reminded himself, this was the woman whose wedding gift to him had been to chop up his uncle and boil him in a giant pot because he refused to give Jason back the throne, which as presents went, certainly beat a fancy new pair of sandals hands-down.

Brightening, he lifted his chin and looked at his reflection, turning his head this way and that. With luck, the bites would fade in a few days, leaving him as handsome as the day he strode into her father's palace on Kolkis.

A moment later, the lift doors swished open and he looked out to see a short hallway lined with pale wooden doors in place of the grand lobby from where the two men had bustled him in. Stepping out behind them, he followed them to the double doors at the far end and stood impatiently, waiting as the shorter of the two stuck his head inside the room.

'Miss Praline?'

Shunting him out of the way, filled with fresh purpose, Jason strode into the room only to be instantly yanked back by four hot hands.

'It's al' right!' said a blonde girl dressed in pink jeans and T-shirt, clearly, Jason realised, the Hazel something-or-other the chubby police chief had been so excited about. The men released their grip and he nodded curtly at her, snatched up a jug of fruit juice and drained it noisily.

On the other side of the room, Alex was watching him, his face a mixture of relief and shock at his appearance. Unlike the ridiculous old windbag sheep, who looked as though he'd swallowed a cattle cake whole. Wiping his mouth with the back of his hand, Jason set down the jug and scanned the room, marvelling at its sheer size and comfort, at the trays heaped with food, the sofas and twinkling stars of lights, the huge windows.

'So this is where you've been relaxing, is it?'

Alex shook his head, unable to take his eyes off Jason's swollen face. 'What happened?'

'Medea happened,' said Jason.

He heard Hazel gasp behind him. 'She's in Manaus?'

Jason turned to her and shook his head, instantly regretting it, wincing at the flash of pain. 'No,' he replied, 'just the phantom-woman she sent to trick me last night, one conjured from ants.'

There was a sudden, wet squirming of asps around Medusa's face.

'Antsss?' muttered Cobra, rising up from the others and scenting the air.

'Yummy!' said Adder.

Behind him, Krait curled himself into coils and rolled his eyes from side to side. 'Did you bring any back?'

Feeling his bites itch at the cheek of such lowly creatures, Jason stomped across the room and booted the shield, sending it clattering – *clang* – *hiss* – *clonk* – wildly over the floor. Watching the snakes whirl dizzily around the Gorgon's puffed-up face made him feel a little better. At least until it crashed into the wall and Alex, ever the monster's nanny, rushed after it, carefully lifting it back on to its edge and checking the Gorgon and each of the serpents in turn, pausing to give Adder's nose a consoling rub.

'Will you put those Worms of Waffle down!' boomed Jason, throwing his arms in the air. 'Haven't we wasted enough time already?'

The boy stood up, blushing furiously.

'Wasted time!' snorted Aries, clopping in front of the boy and lifting his horns high in the air. 'That would be thanks to you and your running away!'

'Running away?' cried Jason. 'How dare you? But then, I'd hardly expect a farm animal like you to have the first idea about quests.' Jason walked up to him, and pushed his face close to the maddening animal's muzzle. 'You see, after you'd helpfully ruined our stealthy entrance by making sure that absolutely everybody in the building knew that we'd arrived, I was left to set about our mission alone. It was down to me to find out as much as I could about the place, talk to the locals, rack my brains about how we're actually going to find Medea.'[35] Jason glanced at Hazel as she hurried out of the room. 'Meaning that whilst you two were safely dozing at the police station —'

'We weren't dozing,' protested Alex.

---

35 Ooo! Liar, liar, pants on fire! And indeed, things would have been much clearer at that moment if Jason's underpants had started to smoke. But, unfortunately, they did not produce so much as a teensy flickerette.

Jason continued as if he hadn't spoken. 'I was actually in danger.' He paused, momentarily distracted as Hazel bustled past to set down a small case with a red cross on it on the table in front of him and watched as she clicked open its lid and pulled out a bottle of dark liquid, together with some tufts of spun cotton.

'This will help soothe the bites,' she said, upending some liquid onto a blob of cotton.

Sitting down, Jason winced as Hazel began dabbing at his arm. The liquid stung and it smelled revolting.

'Attacked by Medea's minion!' he growled. 'Left in agony! Blinded with pain! Then, forced to scour the streets for you without a single thought for my own welfare.'

'You're so brave!' Hazel gazed at him, pink-faced.

Aries groaned loudly.

'Thanks,' smiled Jason. 'Although it was tougher on the *Argo*.' He flicked a cool look at Alex and Aries. 'But now I'm back and ready to deal with Medea.'

Beyond them, he was glad to see that at least the godly gifts were still safe, piled high on a table by one of the windows. Perched on top, the statue of Nemesis gleamed back at him, its three flashes of light vivid as fireflies skittering inside the black marble.

Hazel nodded, following his gaze. 'You and your littl' ladies of justice?'

'That's right,' said Jason, turning back to the girl's brightly smiling face, certain that she wouldn't be nearly so cheery if she were to see those *littl' ladies* burst out, dog-headed, bat-winged and flinging their scorpion whips in the air. Mind you, he realised with a shudder, neither would he. Curbing a cold wave of panic, he reminded himself of the rosier thoughts he'd had back in the lift. If he were right, and the more he thought about it, the more certain he became, then dealing with Medea wouldn't be nearly as terrifying as he'd imagined. After all, if his ex-wife really was more swoony than loony, why couldn't he just flirt and flatter her into handing the key back to him, then hightail it home to the Underworld and leave the wretched statue, all wrapped in a big pink ribbon for her to find when he'd gone? The plan was brilliant. Cheered, he grabbed a handful of olives from the nearby tray and stuffed them into his mouth. Of course, he reflected, eating a few more, it wouldn't do for Alex and Aries to see quite how easy it was all going to be. But that was simple, too. He'd just insist on going it alone, privately schmooze her with his charm, and then tell them what a terrifying ordeal it had all been, before returning triumphant to the Underworld with an epic new tale to dazzle everyone.

Now, as Hazel packed away her medicine case, he noticed the crumpled map on the table and poked it with his foot. 'So, Alex,' he said, chewing noisily. 'You've had time to study that. What can you tell me?'

The boy beamed, clearly pleased to be asked, and sat down quickly beside him. Close up, Jason was surprised to see that Alex's hair was still matted with last night's dust and his sunburned shoulders were smeared with mud. Despite the luxury around him, Jason realised, the boy had clearly forgotten all about his own comfort since leaving the Underworld.

'This is the north-east Amazon rainforest,' said Alex.

Turning his attention to where Alex was pointing, Jason blinked, gulped and looked again. It was as if someone had simply painted the parchment green all over.

'And here,' continued Alex, actually sounding excited as he pointed at a black spot, which appeared to Jason to be about the size of a flea's baby and all but invisible in the expanse of jungle, 'is where Rose is headed. Tatu Village.'

'Tatu Village.' Jason nodded slowly. 'The same place as Medea. I see.'

'Tatu means armadillo,' said Alex.

'Which is what?' muttered Jason.

'A sort of animal,' said Hazel. 'We have heaps of 'em in Texas. Size a-hares but covered with bony plates like dinky suits a-armour. Rose said most likely the jungle round there'd be full of 'em and that's what gave the village its name.'

'Are they fierce?' said Aries, choosing that particular moment to thump his great big unwelcome snout over the back of Jason's seat and, worse, edge it within rammy-dribbling distance of his shoulder.

'Nah,' smiled Hazel, giving the ram's ear a tweak. 'Just fat and smelly.'

Jason glanced at Aries. 'So you'll get on fine,' he sniped.

He heard Aries open his mouth, clearly about to

retaliate with something extremely irritating, until Alex frowned at him, shaking his head.

'This is where we need to get to,' said Alex quickly, turning back to the map and tracing his finger along a thin line of blue south-west of the dot. 'There, where the Rio Negro turns north-east. See?' Jason nodded and waited for him to go on. 'Following its tributary, the Rio Trombetas, which according to Hazel is the same route that Rose was going to take by canoe to the village, we can trek through the jungle and arrive in a couple of days. More or less.'

'Hmm,' said Jason. 'I suppose that might work.'

Alex smiled up at him, like a sunflower turning to the sun, and reached into his jeans pocket to pull out the crumpled pages from the magazine Persephone had brought back. Tucking away the picture of Medea with the Amazon Indians, he smoothed out the photographs of the area around the village, pointing to them as he spoke to Jason. 'According to this, there's an enormous waterfall a few miles south of the village,' he tapped the page, 'and Pico da Nuno, moon mountain, lying to the west. It stands on its own. Luckily, it's got a really distinctive shape, dark and humped, so we should be able to spot it easily.'

Jason nodded, feeling slightly better. Maybe Athena did know what she was talking about in choosing Alex to come with him on this wretched mission. Because not only was Alex keen in the way that most boys of his age would be if they were lucky enough to be travelling on a quest with him, but he was smart too, already having mapped out a route through country of which he'd had absolutely no experience. 'And where are we now?'

'Here.' Alex pointed to a spot a long way west of Tatu. Stretching out his palm, he touched the turn in the Rio Negro with his little finger. 'Hazel said it normally takes about ten days by foot to get there.'

'Ten days?' groaned Jason.

Aphrodite's birthday party burst like a bubble in his mind.

'Normally, I said!' Hazel clapped her hands. 'Not this time, though, 'cause I'm going to hire y'all a plane. Fly you a lot closer to Tatu.'

Seeing Jason's puzzled face, Hazel threw her arms out straight on either side of her body and tilted to and fro.

'It's like a big metal bird that flies in the sky!' She frowned, dropping her arms to her sides. 'Course,' she sighed. 'I should-a flown Rose straight there too. But I was so dumb keen for us to have a vacation.'

Alex stood up and wrapped a comforting arm around her shoulder. 'It's probably just as well you didn't,' he said gently. 'Because you'd only have flown her faster into Medea's trap.'

The girl brightened. 'I can get y'all the stuff you'll need, too,' she said, turning back to Jason. 'Hammocks, nets against the bugs, things to make the water clean to drink, GPS to find your way.'

Rising to his feet, Jason looked out of the windows

at the grey sky faintly pocked with stars, feeling a lot more heartened. 'When will all that be ready?'

'Tomorrow,' said Hazel, pulling what appeared to be a wafer of metal from her pocket and starting to tap the front of it. 'First thing.' Turning away, she held the metal box to her ear and began talking into it.

Outside, the city lights glimmered, smudgy in the night rain. Jason watched Alex's reflection in the darkened window as he neatly folded up the map and tucked it in his bag, frowning at something the ram was whispering into his ear. He thought back to the Underworld and the chatter about Alex that he'd heard in the Heroes' Pavilion, on lazy afternoons spent drinking with Theseus and Herakles: of how the boy had talked Medea's deadly snake into helping Aries and him into escaping, how he'd whipped a flock of sheep into shape to defeat Medea's automatons, how he'd stormed a theatre and saved Hazel's life. Back then, he'd simply assumed that the stories were embroidered, made bigger and better and full of bragging, the way heroes' tales always were, but now, well, now he wasn't so sure. Because one thing was absolutely certain about what had happened back in the summer: Alex had survived his quest. Even with only that barmy ram's dubious help, the boy had returned in one piece from modern London. And Medea. Better still, Jason now realised that despite everything the ram must have filled Alex's head with about how he stole the Fleece, the boy was clearly still very much in awe of him.

Suddenly a fork of lightning flashed across the sky, silhouetting the jungle, which lay crouched and dark on the horizon, and, shivering, Jason turned back into the room. Flopping down on the nearest sofa, and ignoring the glowering stare from Aries, he listened as Alex talked to Hazel, making a list of the things they would need. He smiled, feeling himself relax.

Alex was going to be very useful indeed.

XV
Deal Or No Deal?

Rose stood on the riverbank, staring at the enormous Amazon water lilies, each the size of a child's paddling pool, bobbing up and down on the sluggish black water. Lush pink flowers bloomed in the middle of their pads, except for the one in the middle, on which her father sat hunched like a lily-hopper, staring blindly into the green-tinted air.

Cupping her hands to her lips, Rose shouted out to him, so hard she thought her lungs would burst.

Yet no sound came out of her mouth.

Instead she felt a violent tug at her feet and gasped to see the thick mud sucking away from her boots as a freak current twisted through the river. Suddenly yanked down, she was slammed backwards against the bank, only dimly aware of the wet snap of roots as each lily ripped free of its moorings to be whirled away like fairground waltzers, vanishing around the river bend and taking her father with them.

'Dad!'

Rose woke herself up with a start and blinked frantically in the dingy light. Around her, the world swayed and, looking down, she discovered that she was lying in a red-and-white-striped hammock, a hammock now swinging violently beneath her, its ropes creaking around two posts either end, stretching up into a palm-leaved roof above her. Slowly, as her eyes adjusted to the gloom, she made out other hammocks strung around her, hanging like striped chrysalises, and, peering harder, she could see the shapes of women and children, curled up tightly in them, sleeping soundly. Faintly comforted by their low snores and mutterings, she turned her head slowly, noticing the mosquito nets at the windows, fluttering like ghosts, the woven mats scattered over a mud floor, a rough wooden table dotted with flickering night-lights held in gourds.

'Hello, Rose.'

Rose jumped. Jerking her head round, she felt as if she'd been punched in the stomach. Medea was leaning against the far wall of the hut, her pale face dappled by the firelight of the lantern she carried. Rose pinched herself, certain that she must still be trapped in her horrible dream. Then, when that didn't make any difference, she jammed her eyes tight shut and opened them again. But, as she was rapidly discovering, not all nightmares end because you happen to wake up and however many times she blinked and looked again, the sorceress was still there, still watching her with those silvery-grey eyes all creepy with concern.

The sorceress walked across the hut to the table, poured something from a clay jug into a beaker and turned towards Rose. 'Thirsty?'

Shaking her head, Rose drew back against the scratchy fabric of her hammock, feeling fear coursing through her, searing her nerves like an electric shock and flipping her mind back to the last time she'd seen the sorceress. Now, as Medea picked her way deftly towards her, stepping lightly around the sleeping villagers, Rose remembered her turning circles between the red velvet seats at the Leicester Square theatre, drawing down her vicious magic, her face hollowed out like a crescent moon as Hazel screamed and screamed on the stage.

She bridled, edging away from her as the sorceress held out the beaker. The smell of pineapple juice made her stomach lurch and she bunched her hands into fists to stop them from shaking.

'Oh, Rose,' sighed Medea. 'That's not very friendly, is it? Don't you even want to know why I'm here?'

Rose stared up at her, trembling. 'Where's Eduardo?'

'He's gone back to the *Tucano*.'

'He's *what*?' Rose's head swam with panic.

'Such a sweet man,' sighed Medea, before taking a sip of the juice herself. 'He wanted my autograph for his granddaughters, you know? Said they'd read all about me and the jewellery I'm making out here, in some magazine or other. But you see, he's about to become a grandfather again, so obviously he wanted to go back home.' She examined her fingernails. 'Even so, you wouldn't believe how much convincing he took to leave you behind. But in the end, he had to accept that you weren't up to travelling back through the jungle right now. And so I told him I'd take extra-special care of you until you were strong enough to call him yourself. Look, you can see that your satellite phone's there by the side of your bed.'

Rose squeezed her eyes shut in absolute dismay, wishing with all her heart that Eduardo had waited a little longer so that she might have told him about Medea, about who she really was and all the terrible things she'd done. Even though she could already imagine the blank look on the old captain's face as soon as she said the S-word, she yearned to talk to him now.

'Now don't be like that, Rose,' said Medea.

Rose flicked open her eyes and watched Medea set down her beaker on the floor, lift a three-legged stool over to the hammock and sit on it. 'At least it gives you plenty of time to decide what to do.'

'About what?'

'Your father, of course,' said Medea simply. In the glimmering light the sorceress's face looked pallid and moon-like. 'And the offer I'd like to make you.'

Rose shook her head furiously. 'You must be joking!'

'I hardly think this is the time for jokes,' replied Medea stiffly. 'So hear me out, because either way, you'll still get to hate me. You can either hate me and watch your dad suffer, or hate me and cure him.' She leaned in closer until Rose could feel her breath against her skin. 'Choice is yours!'

'Cure him?' Rose whispered furiously, glancing quickly at the other sleepers. 'I'm not going to cure him. He's alive, that's all that matters. I'm going to take him back to London with me. Then he'll have doctors and hospitals and proper people to look after him and —'

'How?' interrupted the sorceress. The word hung between them, dead and heavy, like the clammy air in the hut. 'Hmm?' The sorceress leaned back and tapped her chin with a long white finger. 'How are you going to take him to London, Rose? Surely you haven't already forgotten how terrified he was when Eduardo only tried to get him to stand up and leave that tree? The way he squealed and fought like an animal to be left alone? Now, I'm no expert but I'd have to say I think it makes it rather unlikely you'd ever be able to entice him into a canoe, say, or a boat, or a plane. Especially,' she gave Rose a cold little smile, 'when he hasn't the faintest idea of who you are!'

Rose flinched. The sorceress's words struck her like spiteful little slaps. Feeling her eyes start to itch with tears, she blinked them back and took a deep breath. 'Then I'll get the doctors to come out to him,' she said.

'I see,' said Medea. 'And how long do you think they'd be prepared to stay out here in the jungle, standing around under that tree, before they started jabbing him with needles? Or restraining him? Tying him to a stretcher and bundling him out of the jungle, squirming and struggling? Is that *really* what you want? Your father taken against his will, back to England, to stare blindly through some rain-streaked window of a mental ward for years?'

'Of course not!' Rose hissed, annoyed at a tear that now ran hotly down her cheek. She pawed it away quickly so that Medea wouldn't see.

'Then listen to what I have to say! Your father is dreadfully unwell. Something must have happened to him and his team out here in the jungle.' Medea paused and raised an eyebrow archly. 'Because the others aren't here, are they?' she said simply. 'They're gone. And I think that whatever happened to them must have been so dreadful that it's shocked your father's mind into numbness, shutting it down like a locked room with the lights off.'

Rose stared at her, appalled, feeling her heart twist. She hadn't thought it was possible to feel any worse than she had that afternoon.

'I know what I'm talking about, Rose. In fact, I'm absolutely certain, because I've seen this before.'

'What are you talking about?'

The sorceress tossed back her head. 'A hundred years ago, I was seamstress to the most important officers in the First World War. Always in demand, I hand-stitched their dress uniforms for fancy dinners with the generals. But I saw things, Rose. Soldiers so badly damaged from being bombed in the trenches that they were left trembling wrecks, unable to eat or think properly, unable to recognise their own reflections in the mirror. In their minds they were still knee-deep in mud, their ears ringing with the blast of bombs raining down on them. They had that same glassy look in the eyes as your father, made the same gibbering noises. Most took years to recover.' She shrugged. 'Some never did.'

Rose stared at her, horror-stricken, feeling her breath leave her body as she recalled her father and his smiling team, all those months ago, waving as they boarded the plane in the sunshine. Now she saw them hollow-eyed, their clothes torn and filthy, stumbling blindly through the jungle thickets, and for the millionth time she wondered just what had happened to the expedition. She shivered as a feeling of sickness crawled up her throat.

'Why let your father suffer when between us we could make him well enough to leave for London next week?'

'Next week?' Rose gasped, shaking her head, bewildered. 'I don't believe you!'

'You don't?' Medea lowered her voice and shrugged lightly. 'Then let me prove it to you. Let's see! When you were six years old, your father bought you a spinning top, an old-fashioned one, didn't he? It had pictures of dogs on it, spaniels wearing red bows.'

A shiver raced up Rose's spine.

'But, dearie me,' continued Medea, 'that very same day you accidentally knocked it down the stairs. It was so dented, it wouldn't work any more, leaving you inconsolable and crying your little heart out. So the next day your father drove to almost every toy shop in London to find an identical one for you.'

'How could you possibly know that?' exclaimed Rose.

Ignoring her question, the sorceress went on, holding Rose's now furious and bewildered gaze. 'Your parents used to call you Rosebud when you were a toddler. In fact, there's an engraving of the same flower on the back of that locket you're wearing.'

Rose reached instinctively for the necklace. 'But —'

'That locket is made from a nugget of gold the Yanomani people gave to your mother on your parents' first trek into the rainforest, isn't it?'

'How? How could you know?'

'Because he told me, Rose.' The sorceress grinned triumphantly. 'He told me all of those things.'

Rose shook her head, blinking furiously. How could it be true? The man she'd seen under the tree couldn't even have told her his own name.

'Sweet Rose. Wouldn't he be pleased to know you're still brave as *The Wolf-Cub Who Waited In The Snow*? That *was* the name of the book he was reading to you, wasn't it, the week before he left to come out here?'

'Stop it!' Rose almost screamed.

Somewhere in the darkness a baby began to cry.

'I brought him back!' hissed Medea. Standing up, she ran a hand through the violet streak in her hair. 'For a short while he was the father you knew again. Then,' she snapped her fingers over her head, 'he was gone. Blown away again like a leaf on the wind. But the cure could be permanent if you help me.'

'Help you?' Rose sank back, appalled.

'Oh, Rose. You know you already have the talent to

be a fabulous sorceress. Why not use it to heal your father?'

'No!'

'Why ever not? Back in London, you couldn't wait to try out some magic. You were so keen to become my assistant and maybe learn a few tricks. But now, now you have a great big problem that desperately needs your skills and you're just going to give up!'

'It was different then,' protested Rose, feeling a flood of shame at the memory. 'I had no idea of how vicious you were then! What you were capable of!'

Medea leaned closer. Her breath was warm and smelled of honey.

'We're talking about *your* magic! Not mine. Magic that can bring your father back to you.' She paused, and breathed deeply. 'And all you need to do in return is be my partner for a few days.'

Rose reeled back, horrified at the suggestion. It was so astonishing, so ridiculous, so downright outrageous, it might actually have been funny if it hadn't been quite so repulsive. Help the woman who'd used the Fleece to try and kill Hazel? Who'd already murdered so many innocent people? Who'd tried to destroy Aries for a new coat of magical gold?

'Just a teensy bit of help, that's all,' said Medea. She held out her hand, her finger and thumb bracketing a tiny distance. 'Teensy weensy! You see, thanks to your meddling little friends, I no longer have any real power for my magic. No Fleece,' she shrugged, 'no magic. Which would have been a tragedy worthy of **Euripides** himself, except that there's something even more spectacular out here in the jungle.' Rose watched the sorceress's eyes gleam like cold stars in the twilight of the hut. 'Something wonderful that could totally transform my sorcery. But, you see, I can't seize it all by myself. I need the help of another sorceress.' She turned back to Rose, smiling thinly. 'And that's you.'

'Help you gain more power again?' Rose shook her head furiously, feeling her eyes well again with tears. 'Never!'

'Never?' The sorceress sprang to her feet. '"Never" belongs to that dream you cherish, you know the one, where you and your father walk down the aeroplane steps at Heathrow together. "Never" is leading him hand-in-hand as your mother runs towards him. "Never" is the chance of ever having him at home and being a family again! Unless you help me and change both your life and his.'

Tears now ran freely down Rose's face.

'This is your chance, Rose, if you're wise enough to take it,' said Medea. 'You've done so very much already, coming out here, finding him. That's amazing. Now you can make it all worthwhile.' She turned and walked across the hut, pausing to turn at the doorway. 'I'll leave you to think about it. After all, you've been through an awful lot. Today must have been heartbreaking for you.

So, give me your answer in the morning. I'll be right here waiting for you.'

Oh dear.

You're probably wondering just how bad a bad day can get?

Well, the glummest humdingers of doozy-days stretch right through the sunshine and way into the night, which was why several hours later, Rose was hunched at the hut table, in the light of the flickering gourd, with questions still bouncing around her head like lottery balls: how could she listen to Medea? What was the matter with her father? What if he really had forgotten her? How could she get him to the doctors he needed? What was the source of magic that Medea needed, out here in the jungle? Could she actually become Medea's partner?

Medea's partner?

Even the words went together like slugs and custard.

Worse, what, exactly, did the sorceress want in return? What *talents*, as Medea put it, could she – ordinary, boring old Rose from London – possibly have that would make her so perfect as a sorceress?

What's that?

You've been pondering that, too?

Well, maybe you do have a point as it's not the sort of job opportunity you normally see advertised in the newspaper, tucked between vacancies for dinner ladies and postmen, is it? But if it were, it'd probably read something like this:

<u>Vacancy: Trainee Sorceress</u>

Must be clever, trusting and loyal.

Able to learn quickly and believe in crazy things.

Good at keeping secrets.

Bravery essential.

Happy to deal with sudden lightning storms, ferocious monsters, cupboards of live spiders and frogs of every shade of green.

The ideal candidate will have previous experience of being a lonely child, preferably with horribly busy or missing parents, resulting in a fierce determination to sort things out for themselves.

Which made Rose an ideal choice.

Unfortunately.

Yet, out of all the questions jostling to be heard in her mind, there was only one that she absolutely had the answer to: who could she ask about this?

Answer: nobody.

Hazel, even if she were here, would already have fled squealing from the hut. Her mother would be far too busy telling her that sorceresses didn't exist in the first place to ever advise on dealing with the offers they made.

And her father?

If he was well, she realised, her heart lurching, then he'd insist that she leave right now and run as far away from Medea as she could, because she absolutely couldn't be trusted, no matter what she said or promised. Except that as Rose now realised, if *she* were the one sitting out there under the tree, he'd do anything to help her. It was so much easier being a parent, she decided. You could run into a burning house, dive into a stormy sea, clamber down a cliff face on a piece of fraying rope – in fact, do any mad thing to protect your child and people would still think it was totally normal.

It was different for kids.

In desperation, she rummaged through her rucksack, found a pad and pencil and, turning to a blank page, drew a line down the middle.

A few minutes later, she stared at what she had written:

Reasons to take Medea's offer:

Medea must have brought Dad back once

Medea is the most powerful person I have ever met

Medea is here

No one else is

Reasons not to take Medea's offer:

Leopards don't change their spots

What an odd little saying if ever there was one. I mean, really, what would they change them for? Tartan? Green stripes? A flouncy pink number with a matching net hat? But of course, as we all know, what Rose actually meant was that evil, real evil, never changes and it runs through the veins of murderous sorceresses like the Amazon pours out into the Atlantic Ocean. Meaning that whatever the sorceress wanted her help for, it wasn't going to be good.

She rubbed her eyes and glanced towards the window. Daylight was tingeing the air beneath the trees a thick, musty green. Sighing, Rose screwed up the paper and tossed it on to the floor, imagining how Aries, if he were here would stamp on it furiously and snort gigantic wet raspberries so deafeningly that parrots for miles around would spin beak-first from their branches to land in feathery heaps on the ground.

To even think, imagine, joke that she would help Medea, whatever the reason.

And Alex?

He'd pale with horror and tell her – no, he'd beg her – to realise that she absolutely, without a doubt, mustn't do anything, ever, ever, that Medea asked, no matter what wonderful thing she promised, because there would always be a terrible price to pay.

All of which made Rose glad for the first time since leaving London that they weren't with her.

Because they were absolutely right.

Agreeing to become Medea's partner was like diving into a swimming pool filled with sharks. It was ridiculously dangerous. Worse, it was stupid, irresponsible and vile. Why, if she sat here all week, she realised, she couldn't imagine anything more downright brainless to agree to.

But then, Alex and Aries weren't the ones whose father had vanished in the jungle months ago, a father who even though he was sitting beneath a tree a few metres away was still as lost as ever, a father who had no idea that his own child was so close.

She walked over to the window and looked through the mosquito net, standing for a moment to gaze at the sun rising beyond the far bank of trees. A couple of giggling children ran past her, through the doorway and out, eager to play in the morning cool. Turning, she followed them and strode out beyond the circle of huts towards the creek, aware that the morning chorus of whoops and shrills and shrieks was the only thing that still felt normal around her. A few minutes later, shielded by a screen of ferns, she watched her father mutter and rock beneath the tree, and felt her breath tight in her lungs as he drew strange patterns in the air with his hands, and understood that her choice was no choice at all.

XVI
The Sorceress's Apprentice

'Ooh, don't do it!'

'Come back here!'

'Right now, Mrs!'

How I wish I could have dragged a stepladder into Tatu Village that morning, and climbed up it next to Rose as she stood watching her father drowse beneath the tree and offer just such sagely words of wisdom. A bright 'Hellooo there!' through a handy megaphone, followed by a cheery 'Have you forgotten something? The fact that Medea's a low-down, lying, cheating, no-good, ice-blooded, vicious sorceress, for example?'

Not that it would have made a jot of difference, I'm afraid, because when your mind is beguiled by the promise of something you so desperately want, it's a lot easier to ignore all those troublesome little things like reality and consequences. And really, can you think of anything more beguiling to Rose than the promise of rescuing her father? Of bringing him home as the same cheerful man who'd left London all those many months ago? I can't. And certainly not me hanging off a ladder twittering into her ear-hole, that's for sure. Not now she'd steeled herself to agree to Medea's offer lock, stock and broomstick.

And yes, of course I'm shocked, too.

I mean, we all know that until today, *sensible* ran through Rose's nature like the letters down a stick of Blackpool rock, clear and unfailing, from the tips of her trainers to the neat black barrettes in her hair that stopped it flopping into her eyes when she was trying to think.

Now, turning away from her father, the *old* Rose, the Rose who'd walked into the village with Eduardo only the day before, would have been fascinated to see the line of tribesmen, their bodies striped with red plant dyes, stalking through the long grass towards the trees; or the chief's wife sitting cross-legged beneath the roof of the *molucca*, brushing a leopardskin pelt; or the sloth hanging upside-down from a nearby fig tree mumbling in his sleep.

But she didn't notice any of that.

Because all of her attention was focused on Medea, who was now leaning against the wall of the nearest hut, her arms folded against her chest, waiting to hear Rose's decision.

Feeling a cold drench of sweat, Rose began walking towards her.

And since I really don't think you need me to tell you how thrilled Medea was to hear the decision that Rose had unwillingly made, or the way that apprehension made Rose's words tumble out in little more than a jumbled whisper, I won't.

Thank you very much.

'Sorcery,' said Medea, leading Rose into her hut and closing the door firmly behind them, 'is all about changing life to suit you better. Like places!'

She snapped her fingers and broke the obscurity spell inside the hut. Instantly, plumes of silver stars exploded from the floor, rising like glittering fountains about Rose, as though from lines of invisible Roman-candle fireworks, spinning and twinkling through the warm air around them. Despite her fear, Rose stared in amazement as their sparkle faded to reveal that the wall beside her, the one that only seconds before had been hung with pans, now groaned with loaded shelves. Clay pots jostled against jars brimming with greenish scales and polished stones and bones and lumps of moss that almost looked as though they were breathing. A sheaf of russet feathers bristled beside a small bundle of creamy ones whose silky fronds curled over a box of splintered wood; glass domes enclosed prickly plants and lone branches that bloomed with black flowers. At the end of the middle shelf, an oversized iron key lay on top of a sloughed-off snakeskin and, spotting it, Rose frowned, surprised by its cheerful parrot charm that looked strangely out of place.

'And things,' added Medea, stooping down to playfully tickle the chin of a rather grumpy-looking stuffed toad, squatting at the end of the lowest shelf and dismally acting as a bookend to several ancient and battered books.

Rose gasped as its crackled grey skin began to glisten. Turning from grey to brownish-green, it flicked open mustard-coloured eyes and tilted its rocky head to regard the sorceress as she stroked its brow. Then it croaked once before hunching down and becoming lifeless again.

Peering at the dead creature, Rose blinked, hardly able to believe what she'd just seen. Then, reminding herself why she was here, she turned back to the sorceress and looked into her silvery-grey eyes.

'And people, too?'

Medea nodded.

Beyond her, Rose caught a glint of metal and noticed a deep, brass bowl that she was pretty certain hadn't been there either when she'd walked in. Balanced on a makeshift brick stand above a stack of glowing coals, it puffed up clouds of grubby grey smoke. Intrigued, Rose noticed its engravings of what appeared to be Ancient Greek soldiers and a tired-looking peacock feather drooping against the nearby wall.

'What's that?' said Rose.

Feeling slightly bolder, she began walking towards it. Whatever it was smelled dreadful, like bad eggs and cabbage mixed together, and it made her already nervous stomach roil sickly. She wondered just what the sorceress might be boiling up but before she could reach it Medea snapped her fingers again and the smoke vanished.

'Nothing to interest you,' she said.

Which was a great big porky, because if Rose had been quick enough to snatch a glimpse over the rim, she'd have been *extremely* interested to see Alex, Aries and a dazzlingly handsome – if horribly bitten – young man boarding a silver float-plane whilst Hazel, in big pink sunglasses, waved them off. Spotting them would also have made this book much shorter and jollier and by now we'd all be settling down to a splendid cup of tea and a Custard Cream. Except that unfortunately Rose didn't see or suspect a thing and, frankly, we're all still stuck in the middle of a horrible predicament.

Instead she was left to stare as the coals instantly darkened and turned cold and the smoke sucked back into the pot. Faintly frustrated, Rose turned back to inspect the shelves more closely. Every pot, jar and box was labelled with a scrap of parchment, written on in turquoise-blue ink, but the words themselves were little more than jumbles of capital letters, triangles and circles with lines through their middles. Rose guessed they must be in Ancient Greek and she was just about to turn around and ask Medea what they all meant when she felt the sorceress's cool hands on the top of her head.

'First things first!' said the sorceress briskly, sliding her hands down to cup Rose's ears for a few seconds before laying her hands over the girl's eyes. Rose heard her heart thumping in her ears as the sorceress began to chant.

*'**Hecate**! Mistress of the moon*
Hear your maid's appeal
Let secrets hidden in plain sight
To Rose, their truths reveal!'

Rose hardly dared breathe as Medea lifted her hands from her eyes and watched the sorceress begin to turn, her head thrown back, her arms stretched towards the roof, as she repeated the spell. Around them, the air seethed with low muttering, like the voices of mean-spirited people sharing a spiteful joke. Time seemed to teeter as the sorceress continued to spin, the whispers whirling about them both. Then, just as quickly, the murmuring vanished and the hut filled with the shriek and chatter of the jungle outside again. Medea stopped turning and, meeting Rose's eyes, nodded towards the shelves. Snatching her breath, Rose turned to look at them too.

And gaped.

Now the strange symbols on each label began swimming together, the circles and triangles darting in and out of one another, swift as blue fishes, changing into English letters and twisting into streams of words that Rose could read. The box of shattered wood was marked 'Wooden Horse of Troy – Use: Nasty Surprises'. The jar of green-tinged scales, 'Scylla Skin – Use: Sinking Ships'. The rust-coloured feathers were from Zeus' eagle, 'Use: Winning Battles', and the pearly ones were from Aphrodite's doves.

'Aphrodite,' murmured Rose, spotting the word

'romance' scrawled on the feathers' tag. 'Wasn't she the goddess of love?'

'Goddess of annoyance, more like,' muttered Medea sourly.

Rose glanced over her shoulder at the sorceress, who had walked over to the window and was studying a giant, blue-winged butterfly strutting over the sun-warmed sill. 'Flouncy little madam with a brain like a Jelly Tot, if you ask me,' she continued, leaning closer to the creature and reaching for the tall glass dome from the table behind her. 'Did a lot of damage with her romantic meddling! But then, goddesses are all the same, tripping around Olympus in their fancy sandals and cooing over the flying ponies daddy bought them. Far too important to talk to people like me and Aunt Circe.'

Rose winced, biting back a twinge of recognition at the sorceress's words. The way Medea talked about the Greek goddesses reminded her of some of the girls at her latest school, the ones with the most fashionable clothes, the glossiest hair, the trendiest boots, the ones who only ever glanced coolly in her direction but never actually spoke to her, boring old Rose from Camden with her too-curly hair and her too-flat shoes. She forced the thought away. After all, she absolutely didn't want to have anything in common with Medea or be like her. She just needed her help to cure her father.

She watched as Medea deftly brought the glass dome down around the butterfly and slid a wooden base beneath it. Sensing danger, the creature flapped up inside, beating its wings against the walls of its glass prison. 'Something small for your first spell,' said Medea lightly and set the bell jar down on the table. Rose swallowed, as the giant butterfly twisted and fluttered. The sight of it, fragile and panicked, so easily trapped by the sorceress, made her feel oddly uncomfortable and she turned away to see Medea wrestle down a big black book from the shelves. Mottled with age, its cover was decorated with a faded picture of a full moon over water, making it look like something out of a fairy tale, and Rose was surprised to feel excitement, as well as a cold rush of apprehension, as Medea laid it down on the table.

'We'll start with a basic reversal spell,' she said, lifting the book's creaking cover to turn its gold-edged pages.

'Reversal spell?' said Rose.

Medea looked up. 'It's quite a simple potion really, but that makes it ideal for a trainee witch. Besides, it's the sort of magic you'll eventually use on your father. Think of it as a magical reset button.'

Rose frowned. The only reset button she'd ever used was the one on the microwave, the one she used to change from defrosting her ready-meals to cooking them on the nights when her mum was late home from the museum.

Medea smoothed the yellowed page beneath her hand. 'Think about it, Rose. When your father left England there was nothing wrong with his mind, was there?'

Rose shook her head, thinking. 'So the Reversal Potion will turn him back to the way he was before he came out here?'

'Exactly,' said the sorceress, smiling. 'I knew you'd be a quick learner.' She ran her finger down the page, reading quickly. 'Now, according to this, we need twelve petals of Helios violets, plucked on the second day they opened, crushed with the sand from a stranger's footprint made under a new moon. Add half a goblet of Kolkis seawater taken at high tide on a New Year's Eve and heat with the tips of two phoenix feathers.'

'It sounds more like a recipe for cooking,' said Rose, thinking out loud.

Medea looked at her curiously. 'I suppose it does,' she shrugged. 'So, why don't you find the ingredients?'

Rose turned back to the shelves and noticed a tall jar on the middle shelf, brimming with long, scarlet feathers, their tips curly and soot-speckled. Quickly checking the jar's label ('Phoenix Feathers – Use: Fresh Starts')[36] she plucked out two and laid them on the table. The flagon of Kolkis Tidewater ('Use: Washing Away the Recent Past') stood on the lowest shelf, next to a pewter goblet, and beside it a tub filled with several scoops of beach and twinkling with pink seashells was labelled 'Trodden Sand – Use: Rewriting History'. She quickly set them all down on the table beside the feathers and, rising up on her tiptoes, spotted a small posy of violets, tied with string. These weren't labelled but, in case you're wondering, violets are famous for the way their heady scent vanishes one

36 Unsurprising since these fabled birds were famous for rising as new chicky-boos from the flames of the fire they'd flown into as scraggy old flappers.

minute only to return nose-zappingly stronger the next, which might, I suppose, make them ideal for reversal potions. Although obviously I am not a witchy-type person, so I could be completely wrong and it might simply be that they tint the potion a charming shade of purple.

Laying them beside the other ingredients, Rose looked up at Medea, who pushed the big, black book towards her.

'Read the spell,' she said.

Rose watched as the ancient text swirled into English before her eyes. Then, quickly following the first step of the spell's instructions, she peeled the papery violet petals apart and counted them one by one into a small bowl. Next she added the tidewater, sprinkled in the sand and began to grind them together with a stone pestle. Close by, the butterfly continued to thump against the glass, its wings a blur of blue inside of the jar. She glanced up at it and felt her heart tighten. She was going to use that in a spell – actually, she told herself importantly, going to *reverse* it.

The mixture darkened to a deep purple. It stained the sides of the pot as she stirred, and now, listening to the soft chink of her mixing, she felt the cold knot of fear in her stomach start to untangle, knowing that the concoction was the first step in bringing her father back to her.

Medea handed her a large pair of scissors and nodded at the feathers. Understanding, Rose snipped off the singed tendrils and stirred them into the mixture while Medea snapped a couple of twigs from a branch of grey wood, set them beneath a small tripod and flicked them with her fingers so that they started to smoulder.

Biting her lip, Rose set the pot on top of the flame.

'Now look at the incantation,' said Medea, nodding back at the book. 'You'll need to recite it turning widdershins.'

'*Widder*-what?' said Rose.

'Widdershins,' said Medea. 'It means anticlockwise. Magic, you see, needs movement.'

Magic needs movement.

The words echoed uncomfortably inside her mind and Rose swallowed hard, remembering how Hex had whispered the very same thing to her and Alex, back in the theatre, back when Medea was about to, to . . .

'Come along now, Rose,' said Medea, narrowing her eyes. 'Try the spell.'

'*Hecate! Mistress of the moon,*' began Rose, turning to the left. The words felt strange and dangerous in her mouth.

'*Spin back the hands of time,*' prompted Medea.

'*Spin back the hands of time,*' repeated Rose, now catching sight of a trail of blue smoke that was snaking out of the bowl and rising towards the roof.

> '*Reverse the damage of the days*
> *Restore! Reset! Refine!*'

There was a sudden bang like a gun being fired. Smoke funnelled up through the hole in the roof. The liquid spattered and boiled.

'Is it ready?' said Rose, startled by the long, orange flames licking around the bowl like tongues.

'The potion is,' said Medea, 'but that's only half of this spell.'

She turned and walked over to her steamer trunk, flicked a large feathered headdress off its lid and opened it up. 'To work, it needs the most important thing of all.'

'Something to power it?' said Rose, remembering what the sorceress had told her in the night.

She watched as Medea reached down into the layers of clothes to pull something out, something that glinted in the sunshine now streaming into the hut.

'Exactly!' said Medea, holding what Rose could now see was a wide golden cuff up to the light. 'Just like cooking needs an oven to bake cake mixture into a cake, potions need something to turn them into working spells.' Smiling, she walked back and handed it to Rose. 'Take a look at this.'

Rose turned the cuff over in her hand. Heavy and gleaming, its surface was engraved with pictures of people with the heads of crocodiles and falcons.

'It belonged to Tutankhamun,' said the sorceress, her eyes growing darker as she stared at it.

Rose felt her fingers tremble around the cuff. '*The* Tutankhamun?'

Medea nodded.

Rose brought it closer and, peering hard, made out a couple of spindly-legged birds, ibises who trailed a ribbon of hieroglyphics between them like a banner, and, blinking, she watched as the pictograms melted into words that she could read.

'To Osiris in the West,' she whispered.

Rose stared down at the glittering gold, her mind flitting back to the exhibition her parents had dragged her to, years ago, when the Museum of Cairo had allowed its treasures to go on display in London. Osiris was an Egyptian god – that was it – and an important one at that, although she couldn't remember what sort of god he was. She frowned, frustrated, fleetingly sensing a darker thought that fluttered through her memory and vanished as Medea spoke again.

'Remarkable, isn't it?' she said. 'It was taken from his tomb in the Valley of the Kings back in 1922,' said Medea.

Rose's mind returned to the exhibition. How she'd queued, seven years old, for hours with her parents in the rain. How she'd pleaded, sulky and wet, to go to the gift shop instead. Right up until she'd seen the pharaoh's dazzling death mask, twinkling in its bulletproof glass case, criss-crossed by red security lights and surrounded by dour-faced guards.

'It must be priceless,' breathed Rose.

'It certainly is,' said Medea lightly. 'It'd be worth millions of pounds to a collector or museum, but its value in money is nothing, Rose, nothing compared to what it can actually do for people like us.'

'People like *us*?' said Rose, uncomfortably.

'It's the power behind sorcery,' said Medea. 'The heat for the cake, Rose.'

'Gold?' Rose felt faintly disappointed.

'Not just any gold,' said Medea. 'It has to be truly remarkable.' The sorceress's eyes became glazed as she went on. 'Special and unique. Gold that has inspired men, captured men's imaginations. Gold that has changed the course of history.' The sorceress leaned over and stroked the edge of the gold as though it were the tiny hand of a newborn baby. 'How does it feel, Rose?'

Rose shrugged, confused by the question.

'Heavy?'

'What else?' Rose waited for a few moments before looking up at Medea.

'Warm?'

'That's right.' The sorceress's eyes grew darker. 'Like any metal, gold will draw the heat from your skin, but this gold, *our* gold, has drawn on something far more potent.' Medea plucked the cuff from Rose's palm and slipped it around her own wrist. 'Did you know,' said Medea, holding her arm out in front of her to admire the look of the cuff against her milky skin, 'that Tutankhamun was only ten years old when he took the throne of Egypt and yet his people revered him like a god?'

Rose watched as Medea turned her wrist as gracefully as a ballerina. 'According to the pictures inside the tomb, he wore so much gold that he shone like the sun and his people fell to their knees, dazzled. Can you imagine the wonder he inspired?'

For a moment Medea's face became quite still, transfixed by the sunlight dancing over the surface of the gold and Rose nodded, casting her mind back to the exhibition and a dimly lit side room, filled with old black-and-white photographs of Tutankhamun's tomb, hidden for three thousand years in a valley in the desert. She recalled her mother's face, pink with excitement, as she'd described the dead king's treasure room, shimmering like a gigantic jewellery box. Golden chariots and thrones, carved boxes and pots spilling over with crowns and coins, necklaces and bracelets, cuffs and golden ankhs; emeralds, sapphires, rubies, diamonds lay scattered underfoot; so much that crate after crate after crate had been needed to empty the treasure and wheel it away, month after month, over narrow, makeshift train-tracks to the Nile.

'All that power,' whispered Rose.

'All that love,' corrected Medea. 'Surrounding him as surely as the air he breathed, with gold like this right at its centre.'

'So, you're saying that the gold drew that sort of power into itself?'

'That's right,' nodded Medea. 'Feeding on it, drawing it deeper and deeper into itself until its very molecules were bursting with power.'

Feeding? Molecules bursting with power? Rose stared at the cuff, beginning to feel faintly silly. It was a funny way to talk about gold, she decided. After all, it was hardly alive, was it? Yet the way Medea had described it now made her think of a greedy aphid sucking the goodness from a flower stem.

'The Fleece was just the same,' continued Medea, her

voice becoming dreamy. 'Kings from all over the ancient world lusted after it, sending their bravest men to try and steal it.' Suddenly Medea's face stiffened. 'Even my own father became utterly besotted by it, standing in front of it, day after day, staring at it, adoring it.'

'And all that time —'

'Like the pharaoh's gold, it was gaining power,' finished Medea. 'Power that we can unleash. Watch!'

Taking a pair of tongs from the table, Medea lifted the bowl from the heat and dribbled a few drops of the potion onto the table, where it sizzled and pooled. Then she dipped the edge of the bangle into it and closed her eyes.

Her face became completely still, rigid with concentration, as a low moan filled the hut. Suddenly a flurry of white sparks exploded from the table and raced along its edge, trailing ribbons of blue and green smoke. There was a deafening crack and the edge of the table splintered outwards to reveal a gnarled tree branch in the gap. Rose stared, open-mouthed, as the branch grew before her eyes, feathering into smaller branches and twigs, each clustered with green leaves, unfurling like tiny fists as she watched.

'Back the way it was,' said Medea, her voice little more than a whisper.

Rose gaped. Even though she didn't understand all that stuff about gold molecules being infused with power, she couldn't deny what she saw in front of her. Or felt. Reaching out, she closed her hand around a cluster of new leaves, soft and real beneath her fingertips. She stared at the cuff and the fizz of purple bubbles dribbling over its edge, dumbfounded. Was that what made magic so special in the first place? The way you couldn't explain it away easily? The way you felt you were half-mad for even trying to bend your mind around it?

'Your turn now,' said Medea, setting the cuff down on the table between them.

Wordlessly, Rose quickly lifted one side of the bell jar up and drizzled the liquid on to the platform. The butterfly bashed against the top of the glass, as furiously as her mind, now bursting with questions. Maybe she just wasn't magical enough herself yet to understand? Maybe she was like those astonished Victorians huddled round-eyed around a glass bulb glowing with electricity, lighting up a darkened room?

'Concentrate,' said Medea gently. 'Now, as you use the bangle, force your mind onto an image of what you want the spell to do. You have to make the picture bright, like a photograph in your mind.'

Biting her lip, Rose picked up the bangle and quickly lifted the glass a second time, dipping it into the pool. A gasp of silver smoke spiralled into the air, sending the butterfly toppling down. It landed and teetered sideways, its legs sinking into the potion. Around it, the smoke thickened, rising like a miniature bank of fog.

'See what you want to happen in your mind!' commanded Medea.

Scrunching her eyes tight shut, Rose imagined the butterfly bringing its blue wings together over its back.

She saw their brown undersides fold gently down, as fragile as origami, as the butterfly sank on to its spindly legs, nestling its head as the potion seeped over it, enveloping it like a sheath. A sheath that became brown and translucent. Feeling her mind grow ever stiller, she watched it turn green. A moment later, she envisioned movement beneath its surface, a wiggling of tiny feet against its elastic sides. Finally, the sheath peeled away, and a fat brown caterpillar wobbled out.

Which was when Medea squealed with delight.

Her concentration shattered, Rose flung down the bangle and flicked open her eyes, astounded to see a caterpillar – a real, live, wriggling, wibbly-wobbly caterpillar – squirming around inside the base of the dome.

'I did it!' shouted Rose.

'What did I tell you!' exclaimed Medea, throwing her arms around Rose's shoulders. 'You're a natural!'

Rose felt like leaping for joy at Medea's praise. She felt like dancing around the hut. She'd done it, she'd actually, truly done it. Turned a living, breathing, flapping butterfly back into its caterpillar. She laughed out loud, unable to stop herself from imagining her father *reset* to the way he was back in London: big and broad and laughing, laughing, not lost, and the fogginess gone from his eyes, wrapping his arms about her in a bear hug. Laughing, she lifted the dome and scooped the caterpillar into her hands, feeling its furry body tumble around her palm. Then, she turned and hurried out through the door, setting it free on the dusty ground. A group of children ran over to see what it was and Rose laughed with them as they pointed and giggled.

Stepping back into the hut, she felt as though her heart would burst with impatience. In fact, she was already so busy imagining how her father's voice would sound the first time he said her name again that she didn't notice the squeals of the children outside as a swooping, white bird dived into their midst and snatched up the caterpillar. Nor did she see it flap past the window, the squirming creature trapped in its vicious sword-like beak, as it wheeled away into the trees. And even if she had, not being a bird-expert, she'd hardly have realised that it was a long-necked egret, rarely seen anywhere but on the river diving for fish and never, ever in the village.

But Medea certainly saw it.

And I'm afraid it gave her a nasty little thrill as she watched Rose sit back down at the table.

'So,' gasped Rose, 'how soon will I be able to cure my dad?' She picked up the bangle. 'Can't I just use this on the rest of the potion?'

Medea shook her head. 'I'm afraid there's not enough gold there to make the change permanent.'

'Not enough gold?' Rose shook her head, puzzled.

'Take a closer look at the bangle. See what happens when we use it.'

Rose brought the cuff closer, shocked to see that the engravings of the falcon- and crocodile-headed gods were blurrier against the sheen of the metal, the detail of their feathers and beaks and teeth rubbed out. Even the ibises, so stark and angular before, looked as soft as swans.

'You see, every time it powers magic,' explained Medea, plucking the cuff from Rose's fingers and drawing it to her chest, 'gold disappears. There isn't enough here to cure your father. And besides,' she added, tightening her grasp on it, 'it's the very last piece of gold I have. We'll need it in order to find more.'

'More special gold?' said Rose. 'Is that what you're looking for out here in the jungle?'

Medea nodded. 'Gold that will produce enough magic to heal your father completely,' she replied. 'The gold of El Dorado.'

'El Dorado?' Rose turned the exotic-sounding words over in her mind, thinking. 'I've heard that name before.'

She recalled her father in the days before he'd left with the expedition. El Dorado? Wasn't that the name of the chieftain he'd been talking about, the one who was supposed to have bathed himself in gold dust? No doubt he'd probably tried to tell her all about him, except that she hadn't wanted to hear it then and so she hadn't listened. El Dorado had been simply one more boring old archaeological someone or other, dull and dusty and dead, who'd take her father away from home again.

Now he was the person whose gold could bring her father back.

El Dorado . . .

Her mind ran on, the understanding spell turning

the Spanish words into English. 'The Golden One,' she said out loud.

'That's right,' smiled Medea. 'El Dorado was the name given to each new chieftain of a long-lost tribe that lived somewhere around here. In the months leading up to each new crowning, the tribe's people spent all their time working the gold they'd sifted from the Amazon, making chains and medallions, crowns, torques and statues of caimans, anteaters, capybara, monkeys, ready for the ceremony. When the time came, the gold was piled on to a raft and the chosen chief, his skin bright with oil and gold dust, would sit amongst it, to be rowed out at midnight, over the dark water, by his priests. Then, as the tribesmen played shell-horns and drums from the shore, El Dorado would throw the gold into the water to ensure the happiness of the tribe.'

'And that gold is still there?' said Rose, imagining the statues of animals shining like a golden zoo beneath the water.

'Yes,' said Medea.

'So where is it, this lagoon?'

Medea shrugged. 'I have no idea,' she sighed. 'So, it's lucky that I know how to find the man who does.'

She walked back to her steamer trunk and stooped to pull out the map she'd brought with her from her safe in the room beneath her London boutique. Rose watched, waiting as the sorceress gingerly unfurled the old paper, smoothing out its dusty surface and weighing down each corner with the pots and jars Rose had used in the spell.

'He's here,' said Medea, pointing to a clearing on the far left of the map.

Rose studied the area for signs of a village, a mine or a loggers' camp, anywhere that the man might be living or working. Instead, there was nothing but a patch of cleared jungle marked by a row of crosses. Puzzled, she read the words scribbled in brown ink beneath the biggest one.

'Wat Raleigh.'

The name meant nothing to her and she looked at the words written beneath it for a clue. '*Requiescat in pace*?'

She waited for the Latin to swirl into English. 'Rest in peace?' She turned to the sorceress, feeling her skin prickle. 'Isn't that what they usually write on graves?'

'That's right,' smiled Medea.

XVII
Is This The Way to Armadillo?

Is this the way to Armadillo?
All my fears are starting to billow
She's scheming schemes in Armadillo
Where Medea waits with glee!

Sha la la la la la la laa! Dark spells!
Sha la la la la la la laa! Bad smells!
Sha la la la la la laa!
Where Medea waits with glee!

What's that?

We don't have time for a song? Oh, really? Only I thought my re-working of a classic might cheer things up a bit, what with everything being so worrying at the moment. But if you're going to be like that about it, I shall stop.

See.

To be honest, Aries didn't feel much like singing either. The clammy heat of the jungle pressed against his brow, his back and clutched at his swinging belly like invisible and, frankly, very unwelcome fingers. Sweat ran off him like sheep dip, dribbling down his skin and over his knees, whilst prickly ferns attacked his hocks and sent showers of green beetles the size of Brussels sprouts cascading over his hoofs. Not only that, but a rather persistent pink butterfly that had flapped around his horns for several minutes had now chosen to settle near the tip of his tail, making him look rather like a hot, bald Eeyore, only much gloomier.

It was now over four hours since the funny little flying machine had set them down on the site of an abandoned gold mine – little more than a wasteland of cleared trees and dust – and buzzed off into the blue with a last twinkle of its wings. Of course, as he repeatedly tried to remind himself, glimpsing the sluggish Rio Trombetas twisting its way through the fern-swathed slopes, it was marvellous that flying here had shortened their trek by several days and brought them so much closer to Rose. And it had certainly been a relief to find that the plane-thing was a much cleverer invention than those waxy, feathery contraptions **Daedalus** hired out at his Underworld School of Flying[37] even if the flight had left his derrière so bruised that it now resembled a map of Greece and all her islands.

---

37 *Daedalus's flying machines comprised pairs of giant wings, made of wax and feathers, which you strapped to your arms while you ran round flapping in an effort to take off. Going too near the sun and having the wax melt was rarely a problem. Looking like an oversized turkey with windy indigestion was.*

But that still didn't stop his mind from fizzing with suspicion as he pondered what exactly could have triggered the sudden change in Jason. Despite the Argonaut's bluster back in the Underworld, Aries was sure that Jason would have been anything but keen to track down Medea. After all, he snorted, just look at the number of wretched gifts he'd insisted on bringing with them. Questions tumbled in his head. Why had he taken so long to find them? What had suddenly made him so keen to return to the quest when he arrived at the hotel? And just why was he being so nice to Alex, who Aries knew he'd seen as only a boy, a humble potter, a zoo-hand?

Up ahead, Jason was chopping down yet another thicket of prickle ferns with a bold flourish of Achilles's sword. Aries frowned, barely recognising the let-someone-else-do-it, is-it-over-yet? knee-knocking fraud that he'd come to know and loathe over the centuries. Because ever since Jason had stepped, green-faced, from the plane, he'd thrashed through thickets like a formidable, one-man mashing machine, swishing and bragging in equal measure.

Clearly he was Up To Something. But what? And worse, thought Aries, swallowing hard, what sort of danger did that mean for him and Alex?

Aries paused, lifting up each front hoof in turn for a scatter of scorpions to scuttle over the newly hacked path, and stared as Jason ripped more broken branches out of his way.

'I feel like **Sisyphus**,' he announced. 'Each time I cut

down one swathe, there's another, twice as tough behind it. Of course, he was an old man. Luckily, I'm young and fit and strong.'

'And modest,' muttered Aries, clomping on again hotly.

In front of him, Alex followed Jason, holding the GPS in one hand, the shield in the other. And in case you're wondering, unlike everyone else, who was either swishing (Jason), map reading (Alex), scowling (Aries) or crumpling up her nose and moaning about the mouldering smell of the place (the Gorgon), the snakes were in their element. Clearly thrilled by what appeared to them to be an Eat-As-Much-As-You-Can-Serpent-Canteen, they lolled out blissfully, snapping up moths and fire ants, commenting like chefs judging a cookery contest.

Aries sighed.

Either side of them, trunks of tall trees festooned with lianas rose in dizzying green walls, their branches closing over their heads like a roof, as tall and shadowy as being inside the old Parthenon.

Except a lot smellier, greener and hotter.

Oh, and livelier, of course.

Having stayed up most of the night to read Hazel's book from cover to cover, Alex was rapidly becoming something of an expert about the rainforest. He'd already pointed out a bird-eating tarantula crawling up a tree like a furry glove towards a small red finch, and a rotted tree-hollow filled with velvety fruit bats. Five minutes ago, he'd been raving about a hulking great snake, wallowing in a slick of muddy water, that looked just like Drako's grand-nephew but that Alex said was actually an anaconda, capable of dislocating its jaw and eating Aries whole, making the ram certain that this Amazon place was even worse than the stinky old forest back at Kolkis where his Fleece had hung in the Sacred Oak. Sure, it had been a miserable, squelching smog-bog, but at least nothing there was likely to sting, bite or wrestle you to death for looking at it the wrong way. Better still, he'd only had to endure Jason's company for one, albeit dreadful, night there. Not like now. He grunted, feeling his heart sink faster than one of the coconuts that every so often plunged from the trees into the river below as Jason began yet another recollection.

'Reminds me of the time I fought the bone men!' he declared.

SWOOSH!

'Aiming for the knees, the neck, the ribs!'

SWISH!

'Alex!' yelled Aries, certain that a large and rather rubbery millipede had just landed on his forehead. 'Something's got me!' He jerked his horns backwards to fling it off.

Turning back, Alex waded back through the hip-high undergrowth to take a look. 'I can't see anything,' he said gently. 'Perhaps you shouldn't have eaten the hat I made you.'

SLICE!

'Clatter, clatter! Exploding bones!' cried Jason.

'Will you make me another?' asked Aries, glancing

at Jason swiping down another thicket of green. 'With ear plugs?'

'Oh, Aries,' said Alex, rubbing the ram's head. He reached out and broke off a nearby palm leaf and began twisting it deftly. 'I thought you'd be pleased! Look at him – he's really into his stride now! We could never have made this sort of progress without him, could we?'

Aries shrugged glumly as Alex dropped the cone-shaped hat between his horns and set it straight. Jason was certainly strong, he couldn't argue with that. After all, he was made of muscles, wasn't he? They ran down his arms, his legs, between his ears . . .

Alex looked Aries in the eyes.

'I know it's hard for you but we have to think of ourselves as a team now.'

'A team?' spluttered Aries. He shook his head furiously. 'Alex, Jason doesn't do teams!'

'Aries!' sighed Alex.

'I mean it,' said Aries, peering along the path to where the Argonaut had stopped chopping and was looking back at him. 'I know you don't believe anything I say about him, but he doesn't! He only does looking after Jason.'

'Is there a problem?' called Jason.

Giving Aries one last exasperated look, Alex stood up, shook his head and ran back to the Argonaut. Aries watched him, feeling his spirits sink even lower as Jason slapped the boy cheerfully on the back and looked at the map with him. The sight of the boy's dark head leaning close to the Argonaut's blond one as they nodded together, discussing the route, felt like a jag of glass in his side.

'Hurry up, Aries!' shouted Alex, disappearing behind Jason through the latest hole in the undergrowth.

Aries thumped on, unhappiness weighing him down even more than the ridiculous lyre and the thunderbolt as Jason started gabbling about yet another episode from his past.

'"Ooh, **Atalanta**!"' Jason's voice floated back to him, about as welcome as a bott fly. '"Don't be worrying yourself with the Stymphalian Birds," I told her. "Let me have the arrows!" P-tow! Kerchow! Should have seen me . . . !'

'Ooh, Atalanta!' mimicked Aries, trying to cheer himself up by swinging his bottom and fluttering his eyelashes and ears for good measure. 'You'd better fire the arrows! You know my aim is rubbish. Last time I tried, Herakles was hopping around holding his backside for a week!'

Which is when he realised that Jason had stopped and was now glaring back at him, framed by a hole in a screen of prickle figs. Sweat slicked his long hair against his neck and glistened over his face.

'What's that, Aries?' He walked towards him holding out the sword teasingly. 'Did I hear you say you wanted to take over? Only you seem a bit ragged to me. And I'm not sure that hat is doing anything for you. Perhaps you're finding a real quest harder than that little stroll you took round Britannia back in the summer?'

'Why?' replied Aries, stomping up the path towards

him and feeling anger curdle in every one of his four stomachs. 'Are you finding it harder than that pleasure cruise you took on the *Argo*?'

'Aries!' hissed Alex, shaking his head angrily.

The Argonaut stuck his hands on his hips. 'That was an epic voyage!'

'Really?' said Aries. 'Let's see . . . An enchanted vessel made of magical wood and rowed by a crew of fifty strong Greeks. Sounds pretty cushy to me.'

'Not now!' growled Alex, walking back towards Aries.

Except that Aries wasn't to be stopped. 'Not to mention the protection of several goddesses,' continued Aries, booting a rather large scorpion off the path. 'Athena and Hera clucking round Olympus like a pair of mother hens. Even Aphrodite telling her little boy **Eros** to fire a love arrow into Medea's heart so that she'd do everything for you, all topped off with big wet witchy kisses! And wasn't she useful, eh? Stealing into the glade and—'

'And what?' interrupted Jason quickly. His ant-bitten face flared. 'Your trouble is that you're jealous. Rams don't get to be heroes in Greece, do they? They don't get the help of the gods, or the fame and the glory and, let me see, the statues. You know, there's a reason for that. It's because they're stupid farm animals!'

'Stop it!' shouted Alex, wincing at the Argonaut's florid face as Aries drew himself up to his full height, tilting his horns defiantly in the air.

Jason ignored him. 'Just smelly old windbags that get sacrificed to celebrate the real heroes' victories!'

'How dare you!' spat Aries, ready to charge as a sudden chord of music rippled through the trees and he felt a shiver chill his skin.

'Or wh—?'

Jason stopped abruptly and listened. Around them, the forest seemed to shimmer. Now, as the music floated into the trees, the monkeys high above ceased their chattering, and the frogs' incessant hoots, whoops and burps melted into a trembling harmony. Scarlet birds swooped from their airy reaches into the unfamiliar gloom of the forest floor, to settle on spindly branches and tilt their heads, curious at the strange and wonderful sound. For a moment, even Aries felt as though he'd been magicked to a sunny Greek meadow dotted with trees bowed down by luscious ripe olives.

'We're in this together!' said Alex, immediately whisking Aries' imagined countryside and, worst of all, olives away. He thumped past him and buckled the lyre back on to the harness. 'And we have to start acting like one. We need to forget our differences and start to trust one another. Don't we, Aries?'

Aries curled his lip, choosing to fix his attention on a rather dizzy-looking snake lolling from a nearby branch, its tongue dangling, clearly mesmerized by the memory of the sound. Despite being yet another creature that could probably kill him six different ways before breakfast, it still made him feel less uneasy than the prospect of ever relying on Jason.

'Jason?' said Alex.

The Argonaut shrugged lightly. 'First rule of being on a quest,' he said. 'Stick together.' He turned back and began to hack away at the next thicket.

'I know it's hard, Aries,' whispered Alex, as the sound of toppling bamboo filled the understory. 'But you have to try.' Lifting the harness briefly from the ram's back, he wiped the sweat away with one of Penelope's embroideries and glanced through the trail of broken plants at Jason, whose sword was a silvery blur, arcing against the green. Alex's face glowed with admiration. 'Just think, the rate Jason's going we should be there by this time tomorrow. Then we can get Rose to safety, help Jason deliver the statue to Medea and —' Suddenly, he gasped and his eyes widened in alarm. 'Jason! No!'

Alex's yell exploded the jungle around them as he turned and raced down the hacked path. Parrots screeched from the treetops, monkeys clattered away through the branches.

Aries blinked. Ahead of them, Jason was swinging the sword towards something white and oval, tucked out of his sight behind a bower of red flowers. The ram gaped as the boy threw himself forwards and grabbed Jason's arm, tackling him to the ground, sending them both sprawling sideways into a bank of ferns.

'What the —?' demanded Jason furiously.

'That!' said Alex, pointing above them.

In the eerie silence that now enveloped the jungle, Aries clopped through the undergrowth to join them. For a moment all three of them regarded what appeared to be a gigantic paper lantern hanging overhead. It reminded Aries of the ones the ancient Athenians used to carry through the city streets to celebrate Athena's birthday, only bigger. Its walls gleamed in the fading light, but unlike the goddess's lamps it pulsed with dark shapes squirming inside. Now, in the stillness, Aries' ears twitched anxiously, hearing a low angry buzzing from inside.

'Killer wasps,' said Alex, his voice thin with shock as he sat up and brushed the leaf litter off his shoulders. 'I saw pictures of them in Hazel's book.'

Aries felt a shiver of fear, watching as a single copper-coloured wasp, as long as a finger, landed on the skin of the nest and skittered around the rim.

'They can sting a man to death in seconds,' said Alex, reaching up to lace his hand around Aries' neck. 'Or a ram.'

Jason wiped his brow, visibly shaken.

'That's why we can't keep arguing,' said Alex, clambering back to his feet. 'We have to start looking out for each other. Right?'

Behind him, Jason scowled, irritably shaking the leaf litter from his hair. At least until Alex turned round to face him, whereupon he switched on his dazzling smile and nodded in agreement.

'Like a team,' he said, playfully punching Alex on the shoulder.

XVIII
Magic Moments

Magic is much more exciting than sewing a superhero outfit for your dog, juggling eggs or making a pet dragon out of a toilet roll. And it's way more thrilling than stringing one clay bead after another onto a piece of wire. Which Rose might have told you, if she hadn't been, well, so busy stringing one clay bead after another onto a piece of wire.

A couple of hours after her lesson with Medea, she was sitting cross-legged, hot and horribly frustrated, surrounded by the other women from the village, in the *molucca*, trying to make Fair Trade necklaces. Snatching a glance out through the doorway, where she'd chosen to sit so that she could still see her father slumped beneath the tree, she blew her sticky fringe off her forehead and tried again to jab at the tiny red ball, only for it to slip through her fingers and shoot on to the floor to lie dismally with all the others. Next to her, a young woman in a printed shift dress looked up and smiled sympathetically, the sun glowing against her coffee-coloured skin as she handed the bead back again.

Rose forced a smile.

It was all very well, she grumbled inwardly, squinting at the minute hole in the bead, for Medea and Eduardo to agree with the chief that she'd help make Fair Trade earrings in return for staying in the village until she was stronger, but how on earth was she supposed to concentrate on something so dull and annoying after what she'd achieved that morning? Dazzled by her own magic, every bone in her body had ached to practise more, to use the remaining potion to try and turn Medea's stuffed toad into one that would hop around the hut, or zap an iguana back into an egg. All of which made it feel like a punch in the stomach when the sorceress had then flatly refused to let Rose try anything else, because she said she had things of her own to do. Worse, she'd then promptly marched Rose over to the *molucca*, sorted a bowl of fish stew for her breakfast, sat her down with the other women in the jewellery workshop and then, half an hour later, stomped out of her hut, pink-faced, into the jungle.

Leaving Rose fretful and impatient, her mind crammed with squirming caterpillars and blue butterflies, with Egyptian bangles and tales of ancient Amazon chiefs dusted in gold and flipping over and again back to her last glimpse of the Reversal Potion, abandoned and glowing darkly in its clay bowl at the end of the bench, twinkling like an oasis in the desert.

Lifting her head, she sighed, watching her father trace patterns in the dust with his finger.

Then she focused her attention on the sorceress's empty hut.

'Rose Pottersby-Weir!' She could almost hear her mother's disgusted voice scolding her for even thinking of sneaking into someone else's house when they were out.

She turned back to the beads, feeling more annoyed than ever, certain that trainee sorceresses didn't follow the same rules as everyone else. For a moment, she wondered what Medea would have been like at her age. She couldn't imagine her stringing necklaces patiently if her Aunt Circe had just shown her how to turn sailors into pigs. Sorceresses, she was sure, were never held back by nice manners and doing as they were told.[38] Not when they were able to do far more spectacular things. Like sneaking in and using the leftover potion on their fathers.

Rose felt a jolt of pure excitement at the idea. Dare she? Actually creep into the deserted hut and steal it, together with the bangle, and go down to the creek? A sharp thrill of fear swept through her, jangling her nerves, and yet the idea remained, fizzing like a sparkler in her mind. Wasn't it worth any risk to see her father's smile, even if only for a few moments? Exhilarated and shocked, she could hardly believe that she was even thinking of such an awesome thing to do. But she still found herself flinging the beads into the pot and standing up anyway. Then, rubbing her hands, damp with nervous sweat, on her shorts, she picked her way through the other women,

---

38 They don't tidy their bedrooms, smile for the camera or clean out their hamster cages either.

stepped out of the hut and walked quickly over the dusty plaza towards Medea's hut.

Thanks to the understanding spell, Medea's obscurity charm, routinely flicked back on like a house alarm when she'd left the hut that morning, no longer worked on Rose. Now, stepping through the door, the pot was the first thing she saw, standing exactly where they'd left it earlier that day.

Me, I'd have noticed the scrunching noise, crumpling and crushing, like someone screwing up a big sheet of brown paper. Which is what Rose heard next, and discovered that it was coming from the branch, newly sprung from the table that morning, or, more accurately, the termites that now engulfed it. For a moment, she felt her stomach lurch at the sight of the squirming insects, thick as treacle, pouring over the fresh wood, the leaves and the glistening sap. Then she recalled Eduardo telling her that termites were kings of the rainforest, feasting daily on the leaf litter and wood, and felt her shock melt away, realising that it was hardly surprising that they'd been drawn indoors by a delicacy as rare as English oak.

Even so, she snatched up the remaining Reversal Potion as quickly as she could and carefully poured it into one of Medea's flasks. Then, stoppering it tightly, she stepped back from the writhing edge of the table to scan the hut for the bangle.

The place looked just the same as when she'd walked out of it. The spell book lay open at the same page, surrounded by a few spilled grains of sand and the crumpled phoenix feathers. The map had been rolled up neatly and left on top of the steamer trunk. Over in the corner, the brass pot gleamed in the sunlight, although Rose noticed that the peacock feather, which had earlier leaned against the wall, was now laid across its rim and there was a faint crackling sound from the coals beneath it, as if they'd been doused recently.

For the next few minutes, Rose searched the hut from top to bottom, rummaging through the sorceress's trunk, checking each tangle of clothes in case the bangle lay hidden inside, smoothed out the folds of her hammock and peeped under the pillow at the top.

Nothing.

She dragged a stool out from under the table, gingerly brushed off a few termites and, setting it down under the shelves, quickly climbed up. Then she scoured each shelf in turn, inspecting pots and jars, squinting beneath the lids of clay jars and flipping open carved boxes. She found jags of old hoplite spears and obols with pictures of owls, dried black plants, beetle wings, three desiccated bats and a swatch of glittering twig that reminded her of Christmas decorations.

But no bangle.

Finally she snatched up the stuffed toad to check underneath it, fleetingly glad that it felt cool and dead, and sent the sloping row of books it'd been wedging on the shelf clattering to the floor.

Still nothing.

Shaking her head in dismay, Rose realised that the sorceress must have taken the bangle with her. Frustration welled up in her like steam in a geyser as she stepped down from the stool and stared at the mess of books. She reached for her locket and dragged it to and fro along its chain, thinking hard. What good was the potion without the bangle she needed to make it work? It was stupid, as useless and raw as cake mixture when you wanted a slice of Victoria sponge. She bit her lip, feeling the heat of her anger rising inside her. After all this effort, screwing up her courage to do something so daring and un-Rose-like as steal into someone's house, she couldn't believe she'd ended up with a big fat nothing. She slid the locket again, listening to it ratchet over the chain, and glared down at the books, doubtless filled with even more spells to answer any heart's desire, unless it was for the gold that would make any of them work.

The thought was almost funny, except that she absolutely did not feel like laughing. Which was when she looked down her nose at the locket twinkling between her fingers. It was gold, wasn't it? Hardly on a par with Medea's bangle, of course, it certainly wasn't Ancient Egyptian and Rose was pretty certain it hadn't inspired anything so grand as a nation. But it had been special to the chief who'd given it to Rose's mother, hadn't it? Not made for a king like El Dorado, perhaps, but passed down as a lucky talisman through the tribe for generations. Didn't that count for something? Make it a teensy bit beloved? More importantly, mightn't it have just a gasp of power to use on the potion? Rose had absolutely no idea, but then, she had no other gold either.

Galvanised, she dropped to her knees and quickly scooped up the books, grunting as she hefted them back on to the shelf. Quickly jamming the stuffed toad against them, she was about to leave when she noticed a small, rolled-up scroll lying beneath the table. Intrigued, she snatched it up and unwound it a little way, expecting to see more spells and diagrams. Instead, she was surprised to see a sketch of a Greek ship and columns of writing crammed across the pages. Water stains blurred some of the words and the parchment felt almost crusty, but now as she watched, underlined words melted into English: 'Wednesday', 'Thursday'. Her curiosity prickled.

Clearly it must be somebody's diary, she decided.

But whose?

The writing was haphazard and squashed in tightly winding lines, as though written quickly and in secret. Halfway down the third column, the word 'Jason' swirled into English, making the hairs on the back of her neck tingle. She watched, mesmerized, as more English words bobbed out of the tangle of Greek – 'love', 'handsome', 'besotted' – as inviting as shimmering flies on a fishing line, drawing her in despite her anxiety to leave the hut. Could it be Medea's diary? Of course, the old Rose, the one who'd stepped into the jungle a few days before, would already have put the scroll back on the shelf, red-faced for even sneaking a peek. But then, that Rose wouldn't have crept into someone's empty house in the first place.

Now, as she watched, more words twisted into English, teasing her: *'to lovingly protect him with sorcery'* . . . Rose's eyes widened, and she positively itched to read on. Except that, obviously, as she scolded herself, she absolutely shouldn't. It was, as her mother might have told her, out of the question.

But her mother wasn't there.

And besides, the scroll was sucking her in like quicksand.

Suddenly somewhere nearby a parrot shrieked madly, making Rose jump, and snapped from her indecision, she flipped up the scroll and stuffed it into her shorts pocket. Then, telling her flabbergasted conscience that of course she could return it without reading it properly, she snatched up the Reversal Potion and ran out of the hut.

In the middle of the Amazon day, everything feels hot and sleepy and now even the frenetic buzz of insects skittering over the river sounded little more than a murmur in Rose's ears. Stepping into the dappled green light beneath her father's tree, she briefly laid her hand on his shoulder, steeling herself as he flinched beneath her touch.

'It'll be all right, Dad,' she whispered, curbing the unwelcome sensation that she was talking to herself.

Quickly checking that she couldn't be seen by the women chatting under the shade of the mango trees on the far side of the village, she dipped her locket into the potion and shivered as a lick of blue smoke, spangled with tiny grey stars, twisted from the neck of the flask. Spurred on, she drizzled a few drops of the liquid on to his head and jammed her eyes closed, forcing her mind away from the suffocating heat and the trickle of sweat running down her neck, willing herself to imagine what she wanted the spell to achieve. She cast her mind back, picturing him when he was well, the way he'd looked that day in April when he walked away from her and her mother towards the plane, turning back, waving, calling their names one last time. She scrunched her eyes tighter and tighter, conjuring up his face, hearing his laugh echo back as he boarded the plane with the others, and felt her whole body tremble as she compelled the magic to turn him back into the man he'd been before. Love curdled by desperation coursed through her, making her feel light-headed, almost as though she were floating, and when she heard his voice, for a moment she felt sure she was still creating it in her mind.

'Rose?'

She flicked open her eyes, and started, astonished to see her father looking up at her. Bright and curious, he pawed at the liquid that now dribbled down his face.

'Are you all right?' He glanced at his purple-stained hands and grinned up at her, bemused. 'What on Earth are you doing out here? Where's your sunhat?'

'Oh, Dad!' Rose threw her arms around him and buried her face against his bony chest, hugging him so tightly that she could barely breathe. Tears of delight coursed down her cheeks, soaking his filthy shirt until finally, reluctantly, she pulled back from him to look into his puzzled face.

'What's the matter, Rosy?' he muttered, his eyes clouded with confusion. 'How did you get here? Is your mother with you? James and the others will be so pleased to see you both. Do you know, we were only talking the other night at camp about the farewell meal we had at our house just before we flew out. That rubbery goose your mother cooked. Do you remember?'

Rose stifled a giggle, wiping her eyes.

'It was as tough as a football.'

He smiled broadly, and chuckled.

'Jeff said that we should have packed the peas for blow-gun pellets!' He paused and held out his arm in front of his face, frowning at his tattered shirtsleeve, the bony hand sticking out of the filthy cuff for the first time. He looked back at Rose in dismay. 'What's happened to me? I don't understand.'

'You will, Dad. Soon, I promise. When we leave for London.'

'London? But we're not finished here yet. There's so much more to do. We've only mapped a tenth of this region and we've already found traces of black soil, potshards, tools made from animal bones, Rose! You know what that means?'

'Evidence of that old tribe, Dad?'

He nodded, his face animated and filled with enthusiasm, the way it always was when he talked about archaeology. And for once, Rose was delighted to hear it too. In fact, she'd never been so happy to hear about a bunch of old bones and bashed-up crockery in all her life.

She smiled, urging him to go on.

'James thinks that the Royal Geographical Society will want us to come out here a second time.' He smiled, looking around at the river, and quickly squinted back over his shoulder towards the village. His face grew serious.

'What is it?' said Rose.

'The others?' said her father. Paler now, he turned back to her, his skin glimmering beneath a shimmer of sweat. 'Have you seen them?'

Rose felt her heart skip a beat. She shook her head.

'They were out on the water,' he muttered. He frowned and rubbed his temples with his fingers. 'That water was so dark, Rose, as black as oil. They went out to take readings and I stayed on the shore, collecting soil samples on the bank . . . and —'

'Dad?'

Noticing that his hands were trembling, Rose leaned over and took hold of one as he hunched lower, almost cowering. When he looked up at her again, his eyes were wild and shining with a sudden fear. 'Teeth . . .'

'Dad?' Rose stared, bewildered. 'What are you talking about?'

He drew his hand away, and together with the other, ran both through his hair, staring hard into the dust. 'Like shards of rock,' he said slowly. 'James and the others, they were in the dinghy, that's right, they were in the dinghy and, and . . .' His face crumpled with horror. Lurching towards her, he seized hold of her shoulders in alarm. 'I tried to warn them, but . . . '

'But what?' urged Rose. 'Dad?'

His brow lowered, as he searched for the rest of the memory. He looked up at her, panic-stricken.

'They're all . . . gone.'

Rose felt a ripple of horror flash over her skin. 'What are you talking about? What happened to them?'

But it was too late.

She watched helplessly as his face returned to its calm, blank mask. Then, sagging back against the tree trunk, he pursed his lips and stared into the flowing water once more, as if she hadn't spoken. Worse, as if she wasn't even there.

'Dad?'

But there was no response.

Hearing her own breath, short and stabbing, rasping in her throat, she wondered what on earth could have induced such terror. Teeth like shards of rock? It hardly made any sense. A cold prickling crept up her spine. Just what *had* happened to those men out on the water? *What* water? She shuddered, knowing that she must accidentally have stumbled on the memory of whatever terrible event had left him in such a wretched state in the first place, the dreadful thing that had shut down his mind, as Medea put it.

Shivering, she snatched the flask out of the dust and

buttoned it back into her cargo shorts. For a few long moments she sat back, listening to the chatter and shrills of the jungle, letting it calm her with its familiar, hypnotic lull.

'It's going to be all right,' she whispered, as much to herself as her father.

And slowly, slowly, despite the sick feeling squirming in the pit of her stomach at seeing his terror, she knew in her heart that it would be. Obviously, she reasoned, her rookie potion hadn't been strong enough to last more than a few minutes. But it had worked, hadn't it?

And, with the right gold, Medea's special gold from the lagoon, she would be able to make it permanent. The thought filled her mind, as big and bold and brash as an advert slapped up on a billboard, and she felt her earlier fear slipping away.

Things *would* be all right.

In fact, her mind now ran on, they were going to be very much more than simply all right. With Medea's help, they were going to be dizzyingly, life-changingly, unbelievably marvellous.

Above her, the afternoon rainstorm began pattering against the canopy of waxy leaves and she leaned back beside her father, listening to his breathing. She lifted her face to the sky and felt the cool water run over her sun-burnished skin.

She could do it.

She could actually be a sorceress.

As the rain soaked through her thin clothes and

plastered her hair to her head, she began to feel giddily happier than she had since leaving England and, leaning over, she kissed her father's filthy cheek.

Medea was right: magic really did change everything.

And, with the sorceress's help, just what couldn't she do?

Well, unfortunately, one of the things that she couldn't do was see what Medea was up to at that precise moment.

A few miles south of the village, the sorceress was turning rapid circles in front of a waterfall. The same waterfall, in fact, that had appeared in Persephone's magazine, and in case you're wondering, it was much more spectacular in real life, what with all those thousands of gallons of water gushing over its rim of grey rock and plummeting in a deafening whoosh into the eddies below. Yes, ringed with rainbows in the late-afternoon sunshine and twinkling with kingfishers' wings, it'd certainly be a much pleasanter thing for me to write about and maybe even draw a picture to go with it, instead of telling you about madam, who'd now stopped twirling round and was busily rummaging through the sack of old jaguar bones she'd brought with her. Trophies from the big cats the tribesmen had killed, these bones had adorned the wall of the chief's hut, and had been childishly easy to steal earlier that day with all the men out in the jungle, hunting. And now, picking out a long yellowed thighbone, she reflected that much as she hated being stuck out here in the festering jungle, the place did have its advantages.

Rather like a Do-It-Yourself store for sorceresses low on power, the place was full of its own sort of labour-saving devices. Not power drills, electric saws and paint guns or anything like that, but brimful of animals, plants and insects that were already so supercharged with the desire to bite, sting, throttle, squeeze and savage anything in their path to a mush of tapioca that it only took a small blast of magic from her to turn them into the most ghastly of weapons. Which was just as well, she reflected sourly, as she could hardly ask for Rose's help with what she intended to do now.

Sinking to her hands and knees, she began piecing together a skeleton in the dust: a cage of ribs, a column of vertebrae, a curve of tail, leg bones, toe bones, a butterfly of shoulder blades and lots and lots of teeth. Setting down each piece as carefully as a museum curator preparing a display for a glass case, she laid out the shape of a big cat in front of her.

Except that this one had three skulls at the top of its spine.

Yes, I know.

Things are not looking good.

This is because they aren't.

Next, she took the bangle from her pocket, aware of its coarser surface since the girl had used it in her magic that morning and, muttering dark curses, began dragging it down the ribcage and spine, the chinky-chink of dry bones easing her sour mood.

You see, since Rose's lesson that morning, the

sorceress's day had gone rapidly downhill. Having packed the girl off to make earrings, Medea had settled to her daily scry only to be rocked back on her jungle boots when she discovered how close Alex, Aries and Jason were getting to the village. She could hardly believe her eyes when the scrying waters had cleared to reveal Alex guiding Aries over the slick, flat stones crossing the Trombetas rapids, a few miles to the west. Soundlessly shouting instructions over the raging water, he'd kept the ram safe – wet, miserable and scowling after Jason who leaped the stones as gracefully as a gazelle – but safe. And, keen though she was to see each one of them for her own exquisitely poisonous reasons, it wouldn't do to have them clomp-hoofing in unannounced and totally ruining her plans with Rose. To be honest, the speed at which they'd coursed through the jungle thanks to that whingeing, wet sock Hazel made her want to spit lizards.[39] But, tempting though a vile sulk would be, she knew that a piece of unspeakably dreadful magic would do a lot more good.

Or rather, bad.

It had taken her hours of sweat and blisters to walk here, but now, as the earth beneath the bones began to judder, jiggling the bones where they lay, she felt her spirits lift a little. A whisper of low voices twisted around her as the bones began sliding jerkily together, as though yanked by invisible threads. The spine stacked like

---

39 A rather unpleasant habit that she hadn't indulged in since the age of ten.

building bricks, the rib cage closed like a bony hand and the skulls rumbled like grisly bowling balls to line up along the creature's neck.

Clunk,

clunk,

clunk.

And if you're squeamish, I'd suggest closing your eyes and running your finger halfway down the next page before you open them again, because this next bit is positively stomach-churning.

The rest of you, who're a little bit tougher, brace yourselves.

Pink flesh now knitted itself rapidly on to the bones. A heart bloomed like a red orchid behind the creature's ribs and began to throb; a stomach bulged and gurgled, two lungs puffed up like bellows. All over the creature's body veins spun out like cables, battening down the slabs of growing rubbery yellow muscle that stretched over the creature's broad shoulders, plaited over its back and pelvis, unfurling down its legs and wrapping about its toes. Teeth slotted into the hollows of jawbones and twinkled as the creature lay thickening and rounding, as wobbly as a jaguar-shaped jelly, and about as unappetizingly pink.[40] Its tail twitched. Muscles jumped and rippled along its back, fired by nerves, making its hips and shoulders jiggle, its legs shiver into life. Finally a tide of gold fur, dotted with black, surged up from the

---

40 No pudding for me, thanks.

tip of its tail over its body and heads, making Medea squeal with glee.

Instantly, six ears twitched at the sound. Six ruby-red eyes slid round to regard the sorceress. Medea chuckled and held out her hand as the creature stretched up on to its paws, arched its back and padded over to her. For a moment she ran her milky-white fingers lovingly through its fur, rubbing each of its ears in turn as it nuzzled its heads against her. Then, taking it gently by the scruff of the neck, she led it into the jungle, knelt down beside it and, leaning her forehead against the creature's middle head, began chanting her dark charms and imagining its claws tearing through Aries' flesh. In her mind's eye she saw the ram's horns vanishing one last time beneath a fury of pounding paws and felt a cold swell of delight as beside her the giant cat purred with understanding.

Finally drawing back, she tilted its middle head up and kissed its nose. 'Go hunt.'

A moment later, the monstrous cat sloped away into the darkening jungle, its heads keenly sniffing the air around it.

XIX

Things That go Bump! Hiss! Raar! Tippity-Tap! 'Eek! What Was That?' in The Night

Night falls quickly in the jungle, stuffing every nook and cranny with a thick, velvety blackness. Tree trunks veiled in darkness start to slither and squeak, hissing and rasping with secret visitors. Invisible ferns rustle with the snuffling of unseen rats. And scuttly-wuttly things with far too many legs plop on your mosquito screen like trapeze artists tumbling into safety nets.

Plunge!

Whee!

Splat!

Or at least they do until the bigger things slink down from the branches and gobble them up.

Which hardly made Alex feel any better.

Despite the sheer exhaustion that made his body seem heavier than a Spartan's shield, since falling into his hammock a few hours ago he'd lain awake, prickling at every screech and squeal and sudden snap of a twig underfoot. Not to mention the eerie three-voiced roar that repeatedly splintered the night, sounding louder and closer each time it keened, like a pack of wolves in the wilderness.

Actually, let's not mention that.

Shuddering, he stared up at the impenetrable gloom overhead, thinking of how the rainforest at night reminded him of the Underworld Zoo, in those hours after the visitors had gone home, when the most ferocious monsters stirred into life. Creatures like Hydra, the huge, many-headed lizard. Easily the sleepiest exhibit in the daytime, frustrating the crowds by lying like a grey hillock, snoozing at the bottom of her tank, things were very different in the dark. And, much as Alex loved her, whenever he caught sight of her greasy scales, big as dinner plates, pulsing against the glass wall of her pool as she dragged herself up into the moonlight, he was always hugely glad that she was enclosed behind monster-proof mesh.

Unlike the predators here.

Not that the eeriness of the jungle was the only thing keeping him awake, I'm afraid. No, his unease had started much earlier, soon after bundling Aries into his hammock[41] when he'd returned to chat with Jason over the campfire. Emboldened from having saved the Argonaut from the

---

41 Such beds, even ones bought by world-famous pop stars, are not designed for rams. This is because when the hammock is high enough off the ground to be useful, the ram can't clamber into it, but when it's low enough to step into, the ram is left standing up with his belly gift-wrapped. How delightful.

wasps' nest earlier in the day and feeling as though the three of them (and the Gorgon and snakes) were at last on the quest together, he'd shared his own ideas with Jason on how they could defeat Medea. The one where Alex would strum the lyre to momentarily distract her whilst Jason slipped the statue into her hand. The one where they could sneakily follow her out into the jungle, zap her with a lightning storm from Zeus's thunderbolt to freeze her long enough to tuck it beneath her arm. The one where Aries could butt her into the river and, when she stretched out for help, stick Nemesis neatly in her grasping fingers.

Sighing, he felt his face grow warm again, blushing with that same mixture of embarrassment and anger that he'd felt when Jason had simply smiled indulgently at him, as if Alex were just a child. 'That needn't concern you or Aries,' he'd said, flinging the rest of the fish bones from his supper into the fire, and watching the flames sputter with blue light. 'I'll handle it myself.'

Handle it himself?

Medea?

So much for working together, piped up a sour little voice in his mind, or for learning any hero tricks. Alex bristled, thinking back to the Caves of Acheron, of watching Jason sword-fight using the stick of driftwood, and wondering if he'd teach him to fight as gracefully too, and felt freshly foolish.

Yesterday, when Jason had punched him on the shoulder as playfully as a big brother, he'd really thought they were a team. But now he was beginning to realise that while Jason relied on him to read the map, catch the fish for dinner using Artemis's arrows, build the fire and cook, he clearly didn't think he was good enough to help with the important things.

Suddenly the triple yowl echoed through the jungle again, closer than ever, and, thoroughly rattled, Alex slid out of his hammock. Even if Jason thought he was only about as much use as a chocolate sandal, he consoled himself that he could at least protect the camp by stoking up the fire to ward off any circling carnivores. Beside him, Grass Snake shivered off the shield and began passing him twigs and kindling in his mouth to help. Back in old Greece, he'd been one of hundreds of non-venomous snakes who slithered around the floors of **Hippocrates**'s healing sanctuary on Kos where he'd loved nothing better than building lots of lovely sparkly fires for purifying water. (To be honest, it'd been much more fun than all the hissing and wriggling he'd had to do in the long, boring ceremonies dedicated to Asclepius, the god of medicine, where the priests would fling him round their heads until he felt almost as sick as the patients.) Now, watching the blaze and knowing it would scare off even the most determined prowlers, they both felt calmer.

On the other side of the clearing, Aries grumbled in his sleep, muttering uneasily, tangled in his mosquito nets. Yet Jason slept on soundly, the sword of Achilles laid alongside him in the hammock. Alex watched the splashes of firelight playing over his dirt-smeared features, lending him nobility even out here.

Trust them, he thought, to be stuck with someone who wanted it to go it alone, determined to be the hero and scoop up all the glory right to the end. Except that, now, the more he thought about it, the odder it seemed. After all, on the quest for the Fleece, Jason had had no fewer than fifty helpers, Argonauts who'd fought beside him, battled the harpies and boxed with a king who wouldn't let the *Argo* pass until someone stepped into the ring with him. And even though Alex knew that Jason had done all the dangerous bits by himself, he'd still taken a little of Medea's help, wearing her magical salve to protect him against the fire-breathing bulls and waiting until she'd enchanted Drako before he clambered up the deadly serpent's coils. So why wouldn't he even listen to anybody now? Was it really because it came from a boy and a ram? Even allowing for Jason's huge pride and achievements, they were still up against a vicious sorceress, and it hardly made sense to ignore every one of Alex's suggestions.

Jabbing the fire with a branch of mahogany wood, Alex felt a sour twinge of unease wrap itself around his heart, enfolding it like an anaconda. And, as he thought about how the other Greek heroes had achieved their missions, he felt it start to squeeze: Theseus had gladly taken Ariadne's ball of wool, spooling it behind him so that he could find his way back out of the Minotaur's maze; Herakles had asked his nephew to sear the stumps of Hydra's necks with a flaming torch after he lopped off each head, to stop more from sprouting. Alex glanced curiously at the shield and the snakes and Gorgon sleeping beneath its silvered veneer. Even Perseus had needed to ask for directions to find Medusa from the **Grey Sisters**. So why, if men like that could rely on princesses, boys and a group of hags with only one eye between them, would Jason flatly refuse their help? It didn't make sense. Unless, he thought, there *was* something Jason wasn't telling them about what he planned to do.

He looked over at Aries, still snuffling in his hammock and knew that the ram would have lots of suspicions and doubtless each would be more dreadful and unbelievable than the last. But even so, by the time the tree frogs began their morning burp-chorus high above him, Alex still hadn't come up with a reasonable explanation for why Jason was being quite so secretive and, slinging Artemis's bows and arrows over his shoulder, he headed down to the river, feeling more unsettled than ever.

XX
Great Puffballs of Fire!

Rose wasn't having the greatest of mornings either.

Squinting through the same early grey gloom as Alex, some ten miles west of her, she slipped and slithered over squelches of rotting leaves, catching a glimpse of Medea as she vanished behind the next twist of trees up ahead. Deft as a tarantula, the sorceress scuttled on, picking her way over tree roots, the rolled-up map tucked beneath her arm, whilst Rose gasped, losing her footing, her mind tumbling with the strange new words that she'd just been rehearsing.

Linque tenebras!

Leave the shadows!

Mihi accede, umbra!

Come to me, ghost.

They squirmed and spun in her head, dark and unknowable, writhing about each other like the tentacles of a bloated jellyfish. Medea had insisted they use Latin because Wat had been a learned man and it would draw him more easily. Shuddering, she stumbled into an acacia tree, seething with ants, and yelped. Latin, English, Greek? What did it matter? She still found herself wishing wholeheartedly that she'd been left in her hammock fast asleep. Rather than having been rudely roused by the sorceress's nerve-freezing whisper telling her that dawn was the best time for raising a ghost. Which, as alarm calls go, certainly beats a jangling clock on the nightstand.

The idea had horrified her and it still did. Things like turning a butterfly into a caterpillar, even fleetingly bringing her father back to talk with her, suddenly seemed like child's play compared to this fully fledged sorcery. But then, it wasn't as if she'd had much choice, because as Medea had calmly pointed out, the summoning spell was a truly difficult one, and if she had to do it all by herself, then she'd end up using so much of the bangle's remaining power that there simply wouldn't be enough of it left to retrieve the gold from the lagoon anyway. Meaning that if Rose were truly serious about bringing her father back, she'd have to steel herself to do it.

Rose turned and ran on again, feeling her breath snag in her lungs. A moment later, still trembling with nerves, she dipped her head beneath a low-hanging branch and found herself in a small clearing. On the opposite side, Medea stood poised, framed by the sprawling exposed roots of a huge mahogany tree. Between them, a few low stones jutted tipsily from the ground, standing in a line ending in a taller, more elaborately carved one.

Looking down at them, Rose felt a jolt. Obviously she hadn't imagined that a makeshift graveyard in the middle of the jungle would be like the cemeteries in

London – all tended lawns, primped yew trees and scrubbed stones set with urns of chrysanthemums – but even so, she felt saddened by the clutch of headstones, rain-eroded and forgotten, cloaked in moss. She walked along the row, pausing to read the single names carved into each one: Carlos, Matias, Enrique, Fernando. The names sounded Spanish and it struck her as odd – after all, Wat was an English name – and she might have asked the sorceress to whom they belonged, except that Medea was waiting for her with a face as tight as a limpet. Standing beside the grandest stone at the end, the sorceress held out her arms like half a bridge, clasping the bangle between her fingers.

Quickening her pace, and careful not to step on any of the graves, Rose hurried to stand opposite her and glanced down.

Wat Raleigh
Killed in battle
3rd January in the year of our Lord 1618.

The name, Wat Raleigh, seemed almost familiar, like someone famous enough that she might have learned about them at school, but history wasn't Rose's favourite lesson and she'd probably only have been doodling in her jotter when the teacher talked about the yawny old Tudors and Stuarts.

Stretching out her arms, she tried to slow her breathing to calm the thrum of blood drumming in her ears and took hold of the other side of the bangle, fleetingly surprised at how much thinner and rougher it felt than the day before. She waited, the pose reminding her of the turns they had to do in country dancing.

'Start walking anti-clockwise,' said Medea. 'And don't stop until I tell you.'

Rose closed her eyes and began to move, shivering as the sorceress started the spell.

'*Mihi accede, Wat Raleigh!*'

The words sounded weirder than ever, out here in the jungle dawn. Stumbling over the uneven ground, Rose took a deep breath and repeated her own part of the chant through dry lips: '*Linque tenebras*! *Mihi accede, umbra!*'

Over and over, their incantations wove together, twining up through the trees, sounding strange against the chorus of frogs now in full song above them. Rose tried to close off the jungle around her, concentrating hard to remember her own set of words and to curb the rising dizziness she felt as they revolved together over the soil. Each half of the spell was made to dance around the other to make the whole thing work, rather like the parts of those rounds songs you sing at school, 'London's Burning' or 'Frère Jacques', except that no matter how well you sing those, they'll never summon a spook.[42]

Suddenly the bangle jumped beneath their fingers. Startled, Rose's mind went blank for a second, but hearing the sorceress still muttering, her voice tinged with excite-

---

42 Not even if you ask the recorder group to join in.

ment, Rose screwed her eyes tighter shut, kept her feet moving and forced her mind back on to her words.

A breeze began blowing through the glade. It lifted the hair at the nape of her neck, cooling her. Around her, the air seemed to fizz and crackle, the way it did before a thunderstorm, and she felt her senses prickling, primed and ready for something to happen. Even so, she still jumped as a deafening swoosh of cold air slammed between her and the sorceress, freezing her face as surely as if she'd walked into an air-conditioned room.

Of course, had Rose had her eyes open she would have seen the ice-white bolt of lightning that had shot down from the canopy, blasting through the bangle like a ray of sunlight focused through a magnifying glass. She'd have seen it slam into the soil, zapping a nearby Bird-of-Paradise plant with so much frazzling power that its beak-like flowers were now clucking like a tree full of macaws, before toppling over, singed, on to the ground. And she might even have noticed how the fizzing energy trickled outwards, spilling on to the other four graves in flashes of light.

But she didn't.

To be fair, I suppose that the sound of one grave being drenched by magic – a sort of *whoosh-splut-zzzng* – is much the same as the *whoosh-splut-zzzng* that the other graves standing in the row behind it make when they're being doused, too. And besides, her attention was now wholly focused on the fact that the sorceress had stopped moving and chanting. Opening her eyes, she looked across at Medea, noticing her fair skin was tinged pink with effort.

'It's done,' she said, glancing down at the grave.

Rose followed her gaze and blinked to see a flurry of silver stars hovering over the soil.

Then she looked back into the sorceress's eyes.

Medea smiled darkly. 'Now we wait.'

Well, that's enough of all that.

I don't know about you, but all that grubbing about in the dark, worrying about ferocious great animals with more teeth than a shop full of piranhas only to break for a ghastly beckoning of ghosts has left me quite wibbly.

So, I'm off somewhere more genteel, where the manners are as polished as croquet balls.

Dorset.

Nestled on England's south coast, this county is home to craggy cliffs, harbours with little bobby boats and fields of pink-nosed cows that twirl their tails and make cream for scones. And the ghost of Wat Raleigh, of course, who at that moment was carrying his croquet mallet across the East Lawn of Sherborne House and chatting to his parents, Sir Walter and Lady Bess. Unlike ghosts from the Greek Underworld, who are as solid as you or me, English ghosts (and particularly those belonging to the aristocracy) are a far more traditional lot in their appearance and are quite invisible to ordinary people. True, they might occasionally allow themselves to be glimpsed along a galleried corridor or hover unnervingly around the chandeliers of a great hall, but for the most part they're as see-through as bubbles and almost as floaty.

Centuries ago, Wat and his father – as you may recall from the portrait hanging in Medea's private gallery – had been flamboyant explorers inspired by stories of the New World. But you wouldn't think so to look at Wat now. He hardly appeared to be the daring young man who'd been felled by a Spanish musket-ball in the middle of the Amazon rainforest, cut down in his prime, which, I'm afraid, is what four hundred years of playing croquet with your mum and dad will do for you. Instead, stooped over his mallet to take his next shot with his short cloak tucked back over his shoulders like wings, he looked more like a disgruntled crane,[43] an illusion compounded by the flamboyant puffball trousers he wore, from which thin, white-stockinged legs emerged and ended in over-the-knee boots.

He clacked the ball through the last hoop.

'Bravo!' said Walter, slapping his left hand against his thigh, a rather unpleasant sound and nothing like applause, but which had remained the old man's only option since his execution had obliged him to use his right hand for carrying his head centuries ago.

Dropping an elaborate bow, Wat was mid finger-flourish when he noticed the topiary[44] squirrels fronting

---

43 The water bird, not the one you find on building sites.

44 Topiary is the name for cutting hedges into amusing shapes such as giant

The Orangery beginning to twitch. He straightened up abruptly, feeling his eyes widen in alarm as the twiggy creatures then raised the nut-shaped clumps of privet clasped in their paws to their mouths.

'Zooks!' he gasped, as behind him the lake exploded with the trumpeting of hundreds of ducks lifting off the water.

But before he could twist round to take a proper look, something blazingly bright slammed into his stomach like an invisible cannon ball and flipped him off his feet to hoik him up, up and further up into the air. Flapping his arms uselessly, he stared down, horrified as the castle shrank beneath him, framed by his splendid purple shoes. Far below, his mother toppled backwards in a flurry of squeals and petticoats, whilst beside her Walter bellowed, holding his head high over his stumpy neck for a better view.

Sucked up into a tunnel of lightning, Wat spun through the air for several minutes, toppling cape over puffballs, to finally land with a dismal squelch. Dazed and blinking through a last drift of stars, he noticed his mud-soaked hose[45] and instinctively dabbed them with his silk handkerchief. Then he heard the chirruping cicadas whose tune had replaced the familiar chatter of sparrows. A lyrebird trilled high above him. As the last wisp of smoke vanished around him, he spied the buttress

---

rabbits, vampire bats and typewriters.

45 *For those non-historians among you, this is the correct term for the stockings seventeenth-century men wore. I'm just pointing this out in case you thought he'd brought something to water the jungle with.*

roots of a mahogany tree a few metres away, standing like polished walls around the base of the enormous trunk. Half-remembering it, he felt his bones chill beneath his phantom skin and, tilting his head back, he followed its column up with his eyes, knowing he would see a cloud of leaves halfway up, ringed by blood-red flowers. They were still there.

Just like on the day of his funeral.

'Welcome back,' said a woman's voice.

Jerking his head round, he saw Medea standing over him and felt his ghost heart begin to thump.

'Seamstress?' he gasped, fingering the soot-edged hole in his jerkin and rising to his feet. 'Witch maiden! Vile conjurer of curses! Architect of mine own death!'

Ah, yes . . .

'Minx of the stitching needle! Dreaded embroiderer of the Fleece . . .'

. . . Whilst he's going on, I'd better explain.

You see, ghosts have lots of spare time and they tend to get rather bored. Even floating around the ceilings of Buckingham Palace and sneaking in free to the movies becomes rather dull after the first hundred years. So, to jolly things up a bit, they like to throw parties. Of course, meeting all those new guests with a 'Hello and how did you die?' it wasn't long before Wat and his father discovered that lots of other spooks, despite living centuries apart from them, were all dressed in clothes fashioned by one and the same person: Medea. Strange enough in itself that a Roman emperor should find himself kitted out by the same woman who'd sewn an astronaut's socks, but odder still when they all discovered the cusps of golden wool sewn into the linings of their last-gasp clobber and found out what they meant.

'Jinxer with the Fleece! Dire mistress of evil! Demon-dabbler of decoration!' spluttered Wat.

'And it's lovely to see you again too,' said Medea, holding up her hands to stop him. 'But really, we don't have time for all this flattery.'

Flicking his eyes sideways, he spluttered to see a red-haired girl step out from behind the sorceress. Odder still, she seemed to be peering back at him, as though she could actually see him. Snatching up the head of his mallet, he jabbed its handle towards her, prodding the air around her, as though at an unwelcome mouse in the castle larder. She flinched. And so did he. Clearly, he realised, the Greek witch had granted the girl some sort of magical clear-sightedness to see things hidden from ordinary mortals.

'What vile trickery be this?'

'No trickery,' shrugged Medea. 'Her name's Rose and she's my apprentice.'

'Apprentice?'

Wat inspected the girl more closely. With her wide brown eyes and startled expression, she looked far too kindly to be tangled up with the sorceress. Worse, she appeared to be little more than a child, and now, despite his own shock, he felt thoroughly dismayed that she should be out here in the middle of the jungle in the company of such a dreadful woman.

Around him the cicadas began to roar in his ears and somewhere near by a woodpecker drilled into a tree, seeming to rattle his very bones. He hated this place and, feeling slightly dizzy with the heat, loosened his ruff with his finger. Sticky with heat, it prickled like a sleeping hedgehog against his neck.

'Why hast thou summoned me to this abominable spot?'

'Because we need your help.'

'Me?' spluttered Wat. 'Help the foul witch of Kolkis?' He felt a bitter laugh rise up his throat. 'Assist a lizard of deception, a rat in the barrel of —'

'Oh, don't start all that again,' snapped Medea. 'We don't have the time.'

'Then play me not as a ninny, madam!' cried Watt. 'Return me henceforth to mine estate!'

'No,' said Medea.

'No?' A tingle of icy shock rippled from his toes to his brow. 'Prithee?'

'Not until you take us to the lagoon of El Dorado.'

Wat's mind reeled. For nearly four hundred years he'd forced the memory of the place from his mind. Now, he felt himself whirled back, his head filling with images of dark water, ringed by caimans with snouts like tooth-filled mantraps. Trying to control his rising alarm, he lifted his chin defiantly. 'For what purpose, madam? Pray, what can such a vile place mean to you?'

'That's none of your business,' said Medea.

'Then,' said Wat, more boldly than he felt, 'perhaps I shall choose not to assist.'

'And perhaps,' returned Medea, 'I shall choose not to return you home.' She narrowed her eyes. 'Ever.'

Wat heard Rose snatch her breath and knew that he had been right, that the fledgling witch's heart was not yet as stone-hard as her mistress's. He turned back to Medea.

'Thou wouldst tether me to this place, madam? Forever prey to the frenzied rattle of wasp? The velvet taps of a spider's midnight rambling? An eternity beset by a veritable armada of ants? Thou surely wouldst not!'

Medea raised her eyebrows and crossed her arms firmly over her chest, in a gesture that said she most surely wouldst.

Swallowing hard, Wat heard the parrots in the tree-tops above burst into a riot of shrieks and trills as though mocking the dishonour of helping such a woman. Yet if he refused, he'd be condemned to this everlasting prison of green, wishing every moment to see his parents, the castle, even the lemon-faced gift-shop assistant whom he loved to annoy by hiding the pencil-sharpeners shaped like cannons.

Finally, and with what he hoped was a defiant flick of his cloak, he turned back to Medea.

'If I must,' he muttered. Then hoisting his mallet high in the air, he stepped towards the trees, aware of his fine purple-shoed foot slithering into the mud. 'This way, madams.'

XXI
Greeced Lightning

Alex's feet were even wetter.

So was his hair, his face, his clothes, his arms and his legs. This was because for the last half an hour, whilst Jason had marched on ahead, Alex had been leading Aries down the craggy staircase of rock that edged the waterfall south of Tatu and he was now drenched in the pounding spray exploding up from the furious cascade. His hands ached from holding Aries' horns and his ears were ringing from a torrent of the rudest rammy words you've ever heard, or rather you won't as I certainly shan't be repeating them here.

Rams, you see, are much better at climbing up things than picking their way down them. Worse still, once a ram starts sliding down a slope, it's anyone's guess where he will stop[46] and rocky ridges bordering waterfalls,

---

46 *This is why rams don't take skiing holidays. Quite apart from the fact they look ridiculous in bobble hats, they're extremely likely to rocket down the slopes and make ram-shaped holes in the wall of the chalet below. And believe me, nothing spoils your après-ski mug of hot chocolate more than a ram crashing through the living room, wearing one of the windows.*

splashed in water and steeped in moss, are the most treacherous descent of all for rams.

Of course, the waterfall was a much more dramatic affair than the little spurts of water that dribbled down hillsides in the Underworld, and despite the nerve-racking, slip-sliding, fly-shocking, tail-whipping trip down, Alex had been awed by the torrents of water thundering into the river below. But now at the bottom and gasping for breath, he was even more delighted to be leaving the fuming eddies behind.

Ahead of them the ground slowly levelled out. And, even better, the slippery rocks gave way to a spit of sandy land that ran along the river like a wide ribbon of beach.

For most of the day, the jungle had been slowly shrinking away from the river. Gingerly picking their way down, Alex had noticed that the bigger trees were thinning out, drawing the sweltering canopy away with them, and leaving clumps of bamboo and twisted shrubs in its wake. Now, down here on the lowland, the scene had changed again. Glossy ferns shimmered close to the river, hanging with clusters of dark purple fruit. Beyond them, a scrubland of hip-high grass, yellow and dotted with prickle thorns, opened up. Green mountains, wreathed in cloud, stretched away in the distance.

As Aries bustled down to the river's edge, muttering something about washing the tropical hoof-mange off his feet, Alex tilted his face upwards. Above them, the sky was a perfect, dazzling blue. Bright green parrots soared against it, stretching their wings wide, gliding on the warm updrafts of air, and for a few blissful moments Alex felt the sun pouring down on to him and let his aching limbs relax. Distracted from the need to talk to Jason again about having a proper plan and the worry that had gnawed at him all morning, he sank into a mixture of exhaustion and excitement, knowing that this feeling was what had been missing from his life back at the zoo. Or at least he did until the Grass Snake, who'd been sunning himself on the front of the shield, which was now hanging over Alex's left shoulder, unfurled himself and jabbed him impatiently in the ear.

'Are we there yet?' he demanded, stretching out to stare up from the tip of Alex's nose, his little black eyes twinkling enquiringly.

'Soon,' said Alex.

'What?' murmured Cobra, slithering up to drape himself over Alex's other shoulder. 'Back in Old Greec-c-ce?'

'Of coursssе not!' snapped Viper, whipping up beside him. 'Doesss thisss look like Athensss to you?'

Cobra narrowed his eyes and jabbed his snout at the horizon behind them. 'Well, is-s-sn't that the Acropolisss?'

Rolling his eyes indulgently, Alex turned round to look.

And blinked.

A few hundred metres away, Pico da Nuno lay basking in the sunshine. Feeling his heart punch behind his ribs, he pulled the magazine page out of his pocket, and, smoothing it flat, saw the perfect match of the mountain with its picture: the rock, piebald with moss, the sprigs of thin, pale saplings at its summit, the shape of its soft hump soaring from the scruffy vegetation about it like Scylla's back curving out of the water as she dived into her tank. He read the familiar caption beneath it, even though he already knew what it said:

'Pico da Nuno lies four miles west of Tatu Village.'

He turned to Aries, or rather the ram's rump, now waggling high above the water's edge and slapped it.

'Aries!'

Flinging up his head in alarm, Aries hoofed backwards and swung his head round.

'Look!' cried Alex. 'We're nearly there!'

Beaming, Aries stamped the sand with his hoofs. Yet, as well as the look of sheer triumph on the ram's face, Alex now saw something else: how absolutely exhausted Aries looked. His brow was scorched with sunburn, his face covered in scratches. Long stripes of pink chafed his shoulders beneath the harness and his skin was covered in mud and sweat. And, feeling a sudden flood of affection for his best friend, knowing just how much it had taken for him to come this far – the jungle heat, Jason, the insects, Jason, the discomfort, Jason – he threw his arms around the ram's neck and hugged him. His cheek against the ram's gritty skin, Alex let his mind run on, imagining how it would feel for the two of them to charge into the village and see the appalled look on Medea's face as the dog-headed women exploded from the Nemesis statue and dragged her down to Tartarus. Picturing Rose, ecstatic that the sorceress was finally banished from Earth, he felt a jolt of excitement shoot down from his head to his toes and, pulling away from Aries, he looked further down the river to see Jason cooling down with a swim, crossing the water with long easy strokes.

He would talk to him right now.

This quest wasn't about him and his glory. It was about dealing with Medea properly. And it was about protecting Rose. After all, she was their friend, he reflected. Not Jason's. They hadn't come back to Earth to be manhandled, locked up and trek through the sweltering jungle just to tremble like sparrows outside the village whilst he swaggered in and dealt with things himself. Not when they were the ones who could back him up and make sure that his plan worked so that the quest was a success. After all, that was the only thing that truly mattered.

He set the shield down beneath the shade of a nearby palm and rubbed Aries' ear.

'Wait here.'

It was a long walk and by the time he reached him Jason had stepped out of the river and was smoothing the water from his hair with his hands.

Summoning up his courage, Alex glanced back at Aries.

And froze.

Something was moving through the expanse of high grass towards Aries, carving a path through the burnished yellow stalks towards him.

'Jason,' he hissed, unable to drag his eyes from the movement.

Hearing Jason gasp behind him, Alex held his breath, watching as the disturbance reached the edge of the grass cover and three black noses edged out, noses that sloped up into three big, angular heads, each as hefty as Hephaestus's anvil, but covered in gold, black-spotted fur.

Panic exploded inside him as he took in the broad snouts, the white chins, the drooling mouths, fleetingly recalling the pictures of jaguars he'd seen in Hazel's book.

'Aries!' he yelled, 'Run!'

Startled by the boy's shout, Aries clopped back from the water's edge and looked towards him. Then, catching a flash of amber movement, he spun round and snorted in alarm as the jaguar glided out, its three heads sprouting from the same massive pair of shoulders.

Alex flinched in disbelief. The creature was weird and unnatural, clumsy as Cerberus, the guard dog of hell, and far more like a Greek monster than anything he'd seen in Hazel's book. Now, feeling a cold wash of dread, he knew instantly whose handiwork lay behind it.

'We have to help him!' said Alex, his voice tight with fear, watching as Aries brayed wildly, stepping back towards the water as the terrible creature slunk towards him. From beneath the tree he saw five dark wiggles drop down from the shield in alarm. 'Come on!' demanded Alex, reaching for an arrow from the quiver on his shoulder. 'Let's go!'

But glancing back at Jason, he felt his breath stop in his throat.

The Argonaut was standing rigid with fright. Terror glittered in his wide, appalled eyes.

'Jason?' urged Alex, feeling shock slam into him like a punch. 'Come on!'

Slowly shaking his head, and without taking his eyes away from the monster-cat circling Aries in the distance, Jason took a big step backwards. Then another. And another.

'We have to help him!' insisted Alex.

Behind him, Aries' war-bellow ripped through the hot air.

His mind reeling, Alex pointed down at the Argonaut's sword, willing him to step forward, to pick it up, to do *something*. But instead Jason made a small grunting noise and, looking at him one last time, his face a mask of horror, spun around and ran, as fast and as hard as he could, away from Alex in the opposite direction along the river bank.

Alex's stomach lurched. For a second he stared incredulous at the sand flying up at the Argonaut's heels, as the terrible reality slammed into his brain.

Jason was running away.

Jason was saving himself.

Winded, Alex felt a maddening rush of hot tears flood his eyes.

Jason was leaving them to be extinguished.

The thought sent a freezing bolt of determination through him. Adrenaline surged through his veins, energizing his muscles, and, spinning round, he saw Aries thundering towards the big cat, horns down. As the ram slammed into the creature's broad chest, sending it toppling over backwards, Alex began to sprint hard over the ground towards them. Furiously blinking away his blurred vision, he reached back for an arrow, skidded to a halt and fired. The arrow whistled through the warm air, arced down and struck the jaguar's shoulder as it twisted back up on to its paws.

'Yay, Artemis!' cried Alex.

Raising a fist, Alex thanked the goddess for her gift and reaching back for more arrows, sprinted along the sandy spit towards Aries. The big cat roared furiously, momentarily hurling its bouquet of heads round to glare back at Alex before turning back to Aries, who was already braced and quivering, head down, ready for him.

As the cat slunk towards him, Viper and Adder spiralled up from the grass, and flung themselves around its back legs, coiling over the bristling fur, hissing and jabbing their fangs into its thick skin. Krait rocketed out and latched on to its soft belly, biting hard. Yet it stalked on, as untroubled as if the snakes were no more than bothersome midges.

Snorting, Aries lowered his head and charged. Instantly, the cat reared up on to its back feet and narrowly avoided Aries' strike. Twisting round, it swiped at Aries' horns, slamming the left one with terrible force and shearing off a curl of gleaming gold to send it spinning into a clump of ferns.

Then, thumping down on to its haunches, it readied itself to pounce.

But Aries was faster.

Swinging his hindquarters round, he lifted his back hooves off the ground and caught the side of one of the jaguar's heads, knocking it into its neighbour, rattling them like coconuts on a shy. Stunned, the big cat staggered sideways, dizzy-eyed, and, seizing his chance, Aries swung back to face it and butted its flanks – once – twice – three times – knocking it, winded, into a tangle of prickle thorns.

The creature gasped, wrestling with the snaggling branches to squirm free. Then, lifting its heads, it squealed like a choir of demons, arched its back and sprang.

'Oh no you don't!' yelled Alex.

He fired more arrows, one after the other – *THUNK! THUNK! THUNK!* – each finding their target, piercing the animal's neck, its flanks, its legs. Bristling with arrows now, the creature shrieked and landed heavily, hunching lower and lower as the last of the arrows struck its chest. Stumbling, its legs collapsed beneath it and it gave one last blood-curdling roar and crashed down onto the ground.

'Aries!' yelled Alex, racing towards him again.

The ram was breathing hard, shuddering, staring at the cat lying on the ground. Viper, Adder and Krait slithered off its body and whirled around it in frenzy; Cobra and Grass Snake huddled behind the shield. For a moment Alex regarded the creature's beautiful coat, its long sinuous limbs, its grotesque cluster of heads, all peppered with arrows. He felt a stab of pity, knowing that but for Medea's wickedness it might have been an animal he'd have cared for at the zoo. Now slowing to a walk, he noticed the sweet thick smell of decay hanging about its body, like a hallmark of her poisonous magic, and hated her again for stitching such viciousness out of the creatures that lived here. Feeling the fear finally seep out of him, he turned to Aries and smiled, awash with relief that the ram was safe.

Which is when a sudden flash of movement caught his eye.

Jerking his head round, Alex saw the cat spring up and in one terrifying liquid move launch itself into the air towards Aries. Its claws glinted like daggers in the sunshine and for one gruesomely long moment it seemed to Alex to hang painted on the shimmering air before landing with a sickening whump on the ram's back. Aries' scream tore into the air. He bucked and spun. He threw his head backwards to try and gore the creature with his horns. He leaped and kicked out his back hoofs, twisting and throwing his body from side to side.

But it was no good.

Alex yelled in horror as Aries vanished beneath a flurry of pounding fur. Bringing down its terrible paw, the cat sliced through the harness, sending the godly gifts flying in all directions, before continuing to drag it all the way down Aries' flank. Five brilliant stripes of red sprang up as blood poured down Aries' leg and splashed on to the sand below. Bleating desperately, he lumbered backwards, his face twisted in agony.

The jaguar hung on, bouncing and tossed, riding like

some demented jockey. Drool whipped from its mouths, as it looked teasingly one last time at Alex, before bringing its three heads down on to Aries' back to sink its death bites into the ram's spine.

'No!' screamed Alex.

Gagging from the now overpowering stench of rot, Alex lunged forwards, seized the tip of the spilled thunderbolt and dragged it across the ground. Sparks burst into the air and scorched his fingertips as, with his shoulders burning from effort, he hoisted the dazzling zigzag of silver into the air and, spinning round like a shot putter, slammed it hard into the jaguar's side.

WHAM!

The animal squealed, jerking upright as power surged from the thunderbolt and engulfed its body. Darts of burning energy crisscrossed its tawny fur, singeing and hissing, tangling its flailing limbs in a net spun from lightning. Alex leaped back as sparks exploded around the howling creature as, paddling the air, it toppled sideways on to the sand. For a split second the jaguar lifted its heads towards him, its eyes dimmed with pain and confusion, before a deafening clap of thunder rent the air and the creature exploded in a cascade of black stars and yellowed bones that bounced down over the sand and splashed into the river.

Alex gaped, breathless, hardly able to believe that the creature was actually gone.

As the snakes coiled around his feet, he looked out into the river, staring as the last cage of rib-bones sank beneath the water and felt a ridiculous tickle of laughter rise in his throat.

Then he turned to Aries.

The ram lay on the sand, his chest barely moving.

'Aries?' whispered Alex.

Feeling a fresh flash of panic, he stared at the wide gashes in the ram's side, ragged-edged and livid. His broken horn glinted in the sunshine, the light twinkling on the gold dust peppering the twist of bone. A cloud of stained sand fanned out beneath his back and rump.

'Aries?' whispered Alex more urgently.

But there was still no response. Stumbling the last few steps, Alex dropped down beside him.

'We've done it!' he insisted desperately.

Leaning back, he shook Aries' shoulders, horribly aware of how leaden the ram's body felt beneath his fingers.

He stared, willing him to move.

A flicker of life trembled over Aries' eyelids.

Then there was nothing.

XXII
Glum And Glummer

A few hours later, Alex was certain that he'd never felt worse in his life (or death). Even being strapped to the plinth in Medea's crypt back in London, with a deadly snake on his chest, hadn't made him feel half as helpless as he did now, hunched over Aries' limp body, stroking the ram's brow.

In the time since he'd destroyed the jaguar, he'd kept everyone busy and particularly himself, in that rather desperate way that people do when things have gone so badly wrong that they can't even begin to think about them properly and choose to do something practical instead.

First he'd built a makeshift shelter around Aries to protect him from the sun. Slung together from straggles of bamboo, tied with hammock ropes and covered with palm leaves, it stood in an upside-down V-shape over them both. But now that they were finally inside it, he realised it was lop-sided and a bit wobbly. Worse, he'd missed a bit in the corner and, staring at the sunlight shining through, he felt a stark hollowness in his chest, knowing that if Aries were well, he'd be prodding Alex with his horns and pointing out that the sun was burning his hock, and how, precisely, was he supposed to make himself comfortable when his ankle was scorching? Except that, of course, Aries said nothing at all, and the only thing Alex heard was the dull thump of blood in his ears.

A lump rose in his throat and he tried to concentrate on inspecting the patchwork of grubby dressings he'd put on Aries' wounds. For these he'd used Jason's hammock – tearing it up furiously – before slathering each strip of calico with a paste of crushed Amazon buttercups. This was because Grass Snake had insisted that the yellow flowers growing along the riverbank reminded him of the pain-killing blooms Hippocrates had used to dress the injuries of Greek soldiers. Of course, no one could be sure if he was right or not, but they had nothing else to try and besides, all that wriggling along the water's edge, stuffing as many of the plants as they could find into their mouths before scooting back to spit them out into Alex's lap, ready to mash up, had given them something else to do.

Then whilst Gorgon had bossed Viper into collecting the spilled godly gifts and sent Adder slithering off to retrieve the sword of Achilles, Alex had searched the ferns to find the missing twist of Aries' horn and tucked it safely in his pocket.

Lastly, he'd built a fire to keep predators away.

But now that there was nothing else he could think of to do to help Aries, he laid his hand on the ram's quivering neck and gave in to the tidal wave of misery he'd felt in his heart ever since he'd killed the jaguar. Hunching his knees up below his chin, he sank his face down and cried. Hot, furious tears ran down his face, soaking into his filthy jeans as he wished with every cell in his body that he'd listened to his best friend when he'd insisted that Jason was a fraud. Sobbing, he realised just how frustrated and hurt Aries must have felt every time Alex refused to believe him. He felt his heart tighten with longing, desperate to tell him that yes, he believed him now, that he was right, that Jason was nothing but a cheat, a fraud and an absolute coward. And what was more, if they ever made it home again, he'd tell everyone in the Underworld too. He'd shout about their 'wonderful' hero from the roof of the Tropical House of the Zoo until he was too hoarse to yell any more. The thought stemmed his tears for a moment, at least until a darker thought overtook it: that Aries might not ever wake up again for him to tell him anything.

At that moment, the call of a solitary night bird echoed through the darkness, trilling the same four notes, over and over again. It sounded sad and bewildered, and, listening to it, Alex felt as though it was mourning his own miserable state.

If only he'd listened.

If only he'd believed Aries when he tried to tell him that Jason would always let them down, that he didn't do teams.

Moaning under his breath, he remembered how he couldn't, no, he *wouldn't* see it, because he'd been so keen to learn how to be a real hero. But he saw it now, clearly, and the realisation made him feel utterly stupid. Duped, and trusting as a puppy, he'd chased after Jason, desperate to learn, like some ridiculous mini-Argonaut.

They should have been walking into the village by now. They should have been on the cusp of completing their quest. Instead, Aries was badly hurt and they were abandoned in the jungle. Jason had fled and taken the key to the Underworld with him. Rose was still in danger and there was nothing Alex could do about it because he absolutely couldn't leave Aries' side. And, any time now, Medea would probably try something else.

Again, the bird's call echoed through the night, but this time, as he listened to its pained cry, Alex began to feel his remorse crystallising into something else.

Anger.

This was all Jason's fault.

He punched the sand and, startled, the snakes peered into the mouth of the shelter, their faces – hooded, horned, mottled, stripy and green – all wearing the same expression of worry, staring at him like a **Greek chorus** about to break into a miserable lament, and he knew that they wanted him to say something encouraging.

Like what?

Unbidden now, a memory returned to him of his grandfather's long-gone pottery studio in old Athens. He saw the rows of orange and black painted pots, drying in the sunshine, depicting all the marvellous things that Jason had done, and knew with cold certainty that the man he'd seen today couldn't possible have done any of them. Imagining knowing the truth about Jason all those years ago, his fingers twitched as he pictured himself pitching those shelves on to the floor, smashing the pots and stamping on the fragments until every line, every blush of paint, every trace of every last stupid, lying portrait of the *great* hero was no more than scattered rubble ready to dump in the rubbish pits of Attica.

Heroes didn't run away.

Not proper ones, as Rose would have said. They stood and they fought and they saw it through no matter how hopeless things seemed. They stuck together and they risked themselves for each other, because where was the glory in succeeding, of winning any prize at all, no matter how glittering, if you left your friends to die?

Now looking down at Aries in the fading light, he recalled him, hot and miserable, persevering through the jungle, enduring Jason's endless bragging. He saw him manhandled from the opera house and squashed into the little flying machine. He remembered his face, twisted in terror and absolute determination as he tried to throw the monstrous jaguar off his back and realised something else about proper heroes.

They didn't give up.

Oh, blimey.

Everything is going a bit pear-shaped, isn't it? And talking of pear-shaped, have you ever seen a picture of a Common Potoo bird? He's the night warbler that was trilling his little heart out so sadly in the last scene. Personally, as a pick-me-up at this most gloomiest of moments, I'd suggest cranking up the computer and checking him out on the net. Go on. Have a look! I guarantee he'll make you smile. He's like a flying feather duster with mad googly-eyes.

And indeed, how he might have cheered Rose up that night by zooming over her hammock. Except that, obviously, he didn't, meaning that Rose lay exactly as she had done for the past couple of hours, hot and horribly irritable. Tonight the snores around her seemed as loud as jets and her bed felt stitched from wire as she twisted over again, considering that ever since she'd left it that morning the day had grown steadily worse. Which, when you've already raised a ghost before most people sit down for breakfast, is saying something.

For starters, the lagoon had been nothing like the magical place she'd imagined from the way Medea had described it the day before. An eerily silent spot, secluded by jungle, it had been a wide stretch of night-dark water, and as soon as Rose had seen it, her father's frightened words flashed back into her mind, loud and clear: *Water so dark, Rose, water as black as oil . . .* Shivering, she'd stared across its glassy surface, trying to tell herself not to be so silly, because there must be lots of lakes, equally drear and desolate, dotted throughout the rainforest. Except that despite trying hard to rally her common sense, her skin still prickled icily under the heat of the sun, and her stomach raged with furious butterflies and she couldn't help but wonder if any of those other pools of black water gave off quite such a dreadful sense of menace.

Trying to calm herself, she'd studied the high bluff of rock that loomed at the northern edge of the lagoon, tracing its cracked face with her eyes. Ridged with terraces and crags, and dotted with outcrops scattered with stones, it looked ancient, majestic even. Yet all she'd been truly aware of was the way it cast its cold shadow over the caimans dozing in the treacly water below.

Whilst she and Wat had uneasily hung back, watching an anaconda, as thick as a car tyre, swim over the water's surface, Medea had skipped down to the shoreline. Delighted, she'd clapped her hands as gaily as if she'd happened on the most perfect of boating lakes, the sort that has painted rowboats, islands all clucky with ducks and a charming ice-cream café to boot.[47]

Right before she'd turned round, smiled icily and refused to return Wat to England again.

That's right.

Even though he'd kept his end of the bargain like a gentleman, she had simply shaken her head and walked away up the slope towards the jungle, explaining that really, she didn't have enough magic to waste on silly little spells like that.

Now bristling against her hammock, Rose remembered

---

47 So, let that be a lesson to you. Never go on a mystery trip with a sorceress, even if she promises to buy you a ninety-nine with two chocolate flakes.

how Wat had vanished into the jungle in a flurry of silk and lace, brandishing his mallet overhead, whilst she'd watched, her stomach churning like a mad concrete mixer filled with shock and dismay. All the way back to the village, Rose had been too furious to speak a single word to Medea and, despite the delicious smell of stew and freshly baked manioc bread wafting from the *molucca* as they'd arrived in the village, had found her appetite had completely deserted her too.

Throwing off the light blanket, she curled up into a ball, disgusted at herself for even feeling surprised at the sorceress's behaviour. After all, what was breaking your word to a ghost compared to the awful things that Medea had done in her lifetime? A big fat nothing, thought Rose. Apart from the fact that Medea couldn't have abandoned Wat here at all, if Rose hadn't helped her with the summoning spell. Making it just as much her fault as Medea's that Wat was stranded thousands of miles from home, from his family and from everything he loved and understood.

Just like her father.

Her face burned with the shame of it. And now, just to top off her wretched mood, some ridiculous bird had started crooning gloomily on the tree outside.[48]

Trying to soothe her conscience, she reminded herself that bringing Wat back had been an essential step in retrieving the El Dorado gold that would cure her father.

---

48 Yes, it's him again!

Yet at what cost?

She felt her heart sinking, imagining him out there, stumbling through the jungle in the dark. How could it *ever* be right to trade one person's happiness for another's? To break promises as carelessly as Medea? She sat up in the hammock, frowning indignantly. Surely she didn't have to let it happen, did she? Couldn't she use her own stash of Reversal Potion to send him home again? After all, it had worked on her father, maybe only for a short time, but mightn't it be powerful enough to put this injustice right? For a moment she settled back, feeling a cool calmness wash through her. Until, like a pebble tossed into a pond, a darker thought rippled through her mind: what if she was fooling herself? What if learning sorcery was bound to turn you into a bad person anyway, however hard you tried? What if its power warped you from the person you wanted to be and made you just as mean as Medea?

Freshly miserable, she found her mind returning to the scroll-journal that she'd picked up the day before and the phrase that had so surprised her: *'To lovingly protect him with sorcery'*.

Lovingly protect?

That hardly sounded like the Medea she knew. She scowled as the notion jumped about in her mind like an irritable flea until, certain that sleep was impossible, she slid out of the hammock and walked over to the window. Then, taking the scroll-journal from the pocket of her shorts, she unfurled it, letting the moonlight splash on to its pale vellum.

But only a few sentences into the first column, she felt her heart sink, realising that this wasn't Medea's teenage diary at all, or a diary belonging to any other young woman for that matter. Bridling her frustration, she looked at a detailed sketch of a ship drawn in the top left-hand corner, and waited as the Greek letters written beneath its bowsprit melted into the vessel's English name: *Argo*.

Rose's eyes widened in astonishment.

The parchment suddenly felt dusty beneath her fingers, musty and frail with age, and she scanned the first column of writing. It comprised a list of men's names written against the jobs that they must have done aboard ship:

Jason – captain
Tiphys – helmsman
Lynceus – lookout
Herakles – chief oarsman.

But there were stranger jobs too:

Orpheus – musician
Mopsus – talker to birds[49]
Atalanta – archer.

---

49 *Mopsus was able to predict the future by chatting to birds. Having tried this myself, I am delighted to tell you that next week's winning lottery numbers will be: 'Tweety-tweet, cuckoo, chook-a-chook and cock-a-doodle doo'.*

Rose gulped, understanding that what she actually held in her hands must be an account of the *Argo's* voyage. Of course, her mother would have fainted clean away by now, she realised, flopped out on the floor, the toes of her sensible shoes turned to the ceiling, flummoxed at discovering such a prize for archaeology. But Rose, more curious than ever to find out about Medea when she was younger, read on.

Skimming past maps of islands and a drawing of a harpy like the one she'd fought back at the British Museum, she noticed that someone, probably the journal-keeper, had scrawled his name at the bottom of the parchment. It was blurry with water stains, but she could just about make it out: Echion. Whoever he was.

She unfurled the scroll a little more and spotting the phrase that had snagged in her memory, began to read:

Wednesday
Our captain has insisted that the witch make him double quantities of the salve to protect him from the blaze of the fire-breathing bulls. She agreed, and took several hours to find enough herbs and strange plants on the island. She worked long into the night to lovingly protect him with sorcery and will do anything to keep him safe.

Feeling a tingle of hope, Rose carried on reading, trying to imagine a different Medea, one who'd actually used her power for good.

Thursday

Jason yoked the fire-breathing bulls and sowed the field with dragons' teeth. Yet minutes later, skeleton men sprang from the soil, wielding swords and shields. In the midst of the bone army Jason's eyes grew wide as discuses and he looked set to sprint from the field in terror. Truly, I feared we would return with neither captain nor Fleece had the sorceress not hurled a rock into the midst of the skeletons, sparking a fight amongst them, leaving Jason untouched in a storm of falling bones.

Rose frowned. In this version Jason hardly sounded like the rufty-tufty Greek hero she'd read about in stories and, for a moment, it struck her as strange. But then, as she reminded herself now, Medea was hardly turning out to be the way she'd imagined either.

Friday

Having refused to poison the terrible serpent who guards the Fleece, claiming it to be something of a childhood pet, Medea sang softly to it, dabbing its deadly snout with her mixture and stroking its head till it fell into a deep slumber.

Rose sat back and tried to picture the sorceress, cupping the monster's head, lulling its fearsome snout until its eyelids drooped closed, to protect it against the Argonauts. All right, it was a bit on the gruesome side, what with her pet being a massive man-eating serpent rather than, say, your average hamster or fluffy kitten with a tinkling bell on its collar, but she'd still shown it true kindness.

Despite this, Jason refused to set foot on its snoring coils and so Medea clambered up into the tree herself, to bring down the Fleece to him.

Quickly uncurling the rest of the parchment, Rose felt a small jab of disappointment to discover that it was completely blank. Water stains and patches of crusted salt mottled its vellum in place of any more words and for a moment she wondered if the scroll had fallen into the sea. That would certainly explain the crumpling and the lack of any more entries. Yet, if that was so, then someone, someone with more power than most must have summoned it back from the waves again and kept it safe. Which would explain why she'd found it amongst Medea's things. Rose gently rolled the scroll back up, imagining the sorceress, different back then, lovestruck and sentimental, retrieving it from the sea to keep as a memento of meeting her husband.

The fact that it stopped short of a full account hardly mattered. Not now that she had her answer. Medea had definitely been different back then. Kind and brave, she'd protected Jason from the bulls and saved his life from the bone men. She'd even collected the Fleece for him.

All of which meant that yes, you could be a sorceress

and still have a heart. Rose felt her mood lighten, reminding herself that all the bad things Medea had done had happened much later. Maybe the way Jason treated the sorceress had twisted her out of shape? Maybe it took centuries of using magic to make someone wicked? Or maybe there was something else, something darker still, which had changed the way Medea's magic worked?

But whatever it was, Rose knew that she absolutely wouldn't let it happen to her and, tucking the scroll-journal safely back into her shorts pocket, she promised herself that she would never *ever* let her magic hurt anyone.

Starting with Wat.

Her fingers brushed against the flask of her Reversal Potion and, buttoning her pocket, she looked out into the dark thickening of trees.

She just had to find him first.

XXIII
The Rammie Dodger

Extinguished, thought Aries gloomily.

Was there a sadder, more dreadful word in the whole of the Greek language? He fluttered his eyelids open to a foggy blur of green, certain that he was fading from the world. Damp crept up one of his hocks and, waggling it, he sighed, knowing that the suck of eternal nothingness had already begun wrapping itself about it like a wet sock.

He watched woozily as something glided past. Or was it someone? He couldn't be sure because his vision was as fuzzy as staring through a pair of Vaseline-smeared spectacles, and he peered harder. Yes, it was definitely some*one*, a rather short someone, wearing what appeared to be a bonnet of yellow flowers. Which struck him as odd. After all, extinguishing was meant to be about vanishing without trace. There wasn't supposed to be anyone else around, and certainly nobody in a mad-looking hat.

His nostrils twitched, then flared and, gradually aware of a delicious smell, they began flapping like frilly sea slugs in a spring tide. Was someone chopping up fresh figs? That absolutely couldn't be right either. His mouth watering, he took another tantalising sniff and wondered if the old Greek thinkers had got it all wrong after all. Perhaps extinguishing wasn't the way they had imagined, and you weren't snuffed out like a candle, but instead remained in some limbo-land, with scrummy snacks and dressing-up competitions?

For a moment it didn't seem quite so bad.

Until he remembered that there would be no Alex.

The thought hit him like a mallet and was so bleak, so stark and so appallingly dreadful that his appetite vanished in an instant (yes, it was *that* bad) and he thumped his head down in despair.

'Come then, cold doom,' he muttered bitterly. 'Sound the final trumpets!'

'Crumpetsss?' muttered a familiar voice. 'Yesss, pleas-s-se!'

Aries gasped as a tawny scaled face loomed above him.

'Can I have mos-s-squito jam on mine?'

'Cobra?' Aries gingerly lifted his head as the snake's face came into focus.

What was he doing here? And why was rain bouncing off his hood? And, now that he thought of it, why wasn't it bouncing off his own?

Quickly glancing over his shoulder, he realised it was because he was under a leafy shelter. Moreover, it was responsible for the murky green light, not the emerald fug of extinguishing at all. Although whoever had constructed it hadn't made a very good job of it, and a great gaping hole was letting in the water and soaking his foot. But before he could ask any himself any more muddling questions there was a deafening yell.

'Aries!'

Delighted by the voice, he jerked his head up, overjoyed to see Alex flinging down a handful of figs and scrambling towards him in the sleeting rain.

'You're awake!' exclaimed Alex, throwing his arms around the ram's neck. 'How do you feel?' he went on, now hugging Aries so tightly that he couldn't muster a reply. 'Only I was so worried. I thought, I thought . . .' He drew back as his voice grew wobbly and looked into Aries' face. 'Well, I'm just so glad you're all right!'

Aries beamed back. He'd never been so glad to see Alex in his entire death. Rubbing his muzzle against the boy's shoulder he felt a mixture of delight and relief swirl through his muddled mind, making his aching limbs twitch, eager to clamber up and get on with the quest. He wasn't extinguished. He wasn't lost. Sure, he had a terrible headache, there was something wonky about his left horn and his side hurt every time he breathed or moved or even thought about breathing or moving, but he was still here!

And so was Alex!

When they finally drew apart, Aries saw that the other Serpents of Wisdom had gathered around. Grass Snake bobbed from side to side at the end of the scaly line-up, his little face lost in the bunch of yellow flowers he clasped in his mouth. The hatted-figure in the mist, realised Aries, smiling at his own silliness, fleetingly wondering why Jason wasn't there too.

Now, jerkily, snatches of a darker memory drifted into his mind. Each like a patch of picture from a scattered jigsaw puzzle – a flash of amber fur, six blazing red eyes, a paw like a razor-edged punch bag – made his heart beat harder against his ribs. He looked up into Alex's concerned face, feeling a trickle of cold fear dribble into his stomachs as he began to remember what had happened to him. Suddenly the memories clicked together as one and he jumped, gasping as the terrifying three-headed cat pounced back into his mind so vividly that he could almost smell its terrible stench again.

He snorted in alarm, shuddering. Instantly Alex laid a hand on his flank.

'It's over now,' he soothed, meeting Aries' fearful stare.

Viper stuck his head up over Alex's shoulder. 'Becaus-s-s-e Alex killed him!' he announced proudly.

Aries turned to look at the boy properly. 'Killed him?' he said, filled with awe.

'I used the thunderbolt,' shrugged Alex. 'And Artemis's arrows.' He paused and pushed his heel into the wet sand, making a shallow trench. 'I'm only sorry I didn't put him down sooner. Before he could hurt you so badly.'

'Rubbis-s-sh!' insisted Viper. 'You were fabulousss!'

'Like Achillesss!' said Adder. 'You s-s-should be proud of yours-s-self!'

But, thought Aries, Alex didn't look fabulous or proud. Instead, he looked exhausted. His muddy face was lined with tear marks, palely scored down his cheeks, and he looked worried. Now, despite the boy's embarrassed grin as the snakes continued to compliment him, Aries could tell that there was something badly wrong, something that was upsetting Alex just as much as what had happened to him.

'What is it?' he said.

Alex turned to him, his eyes clouded.

'Aries, I'm sorry,' he said, running his hand through his hair.

Aries continued to stare, waiting for him to go on.

'I was so wrong about Jason. I should have listened to you.'

'Jason?' Aries glanced around again, looking for the Argonaut.

'He'sss gone!' exclaimed Adder, his large eyes glittering in outraged dismay. 'He ran away and left usss!'

Aries suddenly felt woozy in a way that had nothing to do with his earlier concussion. Jason had finally shown everyone who he truly was? Meaning he'd never have to protest or argue with Alex about him ever again? He paused, waiting for the surge of triumph, the victory flutter in his stomachs, the marching band of 'I told you so!' tramping through his mind, setting off firecrackers of glee the way he'd always imagined it, every time he'd let himself hope for this moment.

Except that he wasn't feeling any of it.

No surge. No flutter. No marching band. No glee.

Instead all he could think about was how defeated and miserable Alex looked. Listening as the boy went on – '*all those times you told me . . . I should have believed you . . . I was so stupid*' – and despite knowing that he would never again have to protest until his hooves ached that Jason was a big, cowardly, steaming fraud, his mind turned to how Alex must have felt when Jason fled, how his world must have tilted and all his certainties slid. Yet Alex had summoned up every scrap of courage he had, to run headlong into the fight against that terrible creature to save him, despite the odds. He thought of the worry he must have felt tending Aries' wounds, nursing him, sitting up with him through the long dark hours, uncertain that he would even recover, and understood one surprising thing: that sometimes being proved right wasn't much fun at all.

'Can you forgive me?' said Alex finally.

Aries rolled on to his stomach and stretched out his front legs like a bald and rather wobbly **Sphinx**, the Greek monster with the body of a lion and a woman's head. A right old know-all, each morning she fixed him with her indigo eyes when he took in her breakfast at the Zoo, challenging him to a new riddle. Not that he ever had a clue about the answers and nowadays had simply taken to answering 'haddock' to every question. But he dearly wished he had her cleverness now because then he'd know exactly what to say to make everything right. He sighed. Love for the boy, hatred for Jason, a sense of losing the frustration that had dragged about him all of these years tumbled in his mind. But you see, rams aren't known for their big words and flowery phrases and so all of those thoughts and feelings stayed tied up in a great muddled knot in his brain, and instead he just looked at Alex and nudged him with his horns. And you know, sometimes that can be every bit as profound as a poem or a speech, particularly when it's between best friends, and seeing Alex's brown eyes brighten, Aries knew that the boy understood.

'Well then,' said Gorgon, yawning loudly. 'I'm hungry.' She looked from Aries to Alex, her eyes twinkling a mischievous rusty-gold. 'Maybe now that you two have quite finished with your love-in, we could have some breakfast and get going?'

XXIV
Rose-Tinted Magic

At around the time that Aries was complaining about the fig seeds stuck in his teeth, Rose was sitting in the sorceress's hut admiring the six glittering vials of Levitation Potion[50] she'd made that morning. Since dawn she'd been busy, grinding ash that had spiralled up from the fire-ruined city of Troy, with the down of high-flying geese that had circled the peak of Mount Olympus. To this she'd added slivers of volcanic rock – jumping when they'd suddenly morphed from grey clumps of stone into popping red lava, rising in the bowl – and doused the entire mixture with melted ice that had floated on top of the pond of **Boreas,** the god of winter's snow garden.

Whirling, she'd recited the words from the ancient black book as she mixed the strange ingredients together, until finally Medea had produced the gold bangle, or what remained of it, snapped it in two and handed half

---

50 Levitation means making things rise or float up, rather like the parlour-trick of old Victorian magicians, who'd make tables, chairs and ladies in long frocks sail towards the ceiling stiff as a board, in front of them. And yes, I know it's a funny way to spend your time, but television hadn't been invented back then.

to Rose to supercharge the potion. Rose had been aghast at quite how thin and fragile the cuff had become since summoning Wat the day before. Of course, she'd have been even more shocked if she'd known the real reason – that most of the gold had actually been lost in Medea's jaguar-conjuring spell later that afternoon – but she didn't, and so she'd simply dipped it into the simmering brew. Slim as a chicken's anklebone, the gold had dissolved in a flurry of froth.

Meaning that now, finally, the Levitation Potion was ready.

Twitchy with excitement, Rose stared along the line of vials standing in an old-fashioned test-tube rack on the table, each glowing the dusky pink of a summer sunset and fizzing with glints of green light. Tonight, you see, they were going to raise the gold of El Dorado.

Actually, I think that particular announcement needs a little fanfare.

One moment, please:

TADAAA!

That's better.

And with a little more gusto, if you will:

TONIGHT
THEY WERE GOING
TO RAISE THE GOLD OF EL DORADO!

Feeling rather impressed with herself, Rose sat back and took a long, deep breath.

And immediately wished she hadn't.

As her mouth and nose filled with the revolting stench of what smelled like old socks and last week's sprouts, she coughed furiously and glared at the simmering brass pot in the corner. She'd been astonished when, arriving a few hours ago, Medea hadn't immediately snapped her fingers to extinguish the flame beneath it, and had instead let it burp and sputter and fill the hut with its stinky, grey smoke. Stranger still, the sorceress had been drawn to it over and again, lured every few minutes, as though tugged on an invisible string, to stand and stare, tearing tendrils from a saggy peacock feather to fling into the mix. All of which had made Rose positively itch with curiosity. What on earth was so special about a smelly pot and a feather? Not that there was any point in asking, of course, because despite being Medea's partner, she was hardly an equal one, was she? To be honest, working with the sorceress left Rose feeling like a little crocodile bird, one of those African plovers that perch on the heads of Nile crocodiles and peck the decaying food trapped in the reptiles' teeth. And crocodile birds don't ask too many questions either. Not if they want to stay *outside* the crocodile, that is, and especially when the crocodile was in such a snappy mood as Medea.[51]

Eyes watering, Rose looked up at the sorceress, who

---

51 Of course, some people might point out that crocodiles are always snappy.

was pouting at her reflection in the mirror for what felt like the ninety-third time that morning, and watched her apply yet another coat of red lipstick. Next she fussed with her hair, today styled in an elaborate up-do, with ringlets framing her face in a way that reminded Rose of the women on Greek urns. She frowned. She'd never seen Medea so fretful about her appearance – not even back at Hazel's concert in London, when the newspaper photographers had been flashing their cameras in a sea of white lights – and it struck her as strange. Perhaps, she reasoned, the sudden glamour was some sort of sorceress-chic, a glitzing up for your most important feats of magic, but it still felt faintly disappointing, when there were far more important things to be thinking about.

'Finished?' said Medea, noticing Rose watching her in the mirror.

Rose nodded and the sorceress turned, walked towards the table and plucked a vial from the stand. She held it to the window, letting the sunlight stream through it, and peered closer, like a scientist studying the results of an experiment, her eyes following the glittering green flecks as they trailed steadily upwards.

'Excellent,' she murmured.

Rose felt another flutter of pride, thrilled at how far she'd come in learning to be a sorceress. She stared at the mixture she'd made, knowing that it would bring them the gold they needed to cure her father, and smiled, the thought dazzling like a big shiny diamond in her mind. Everything was going to work out perfectly.

Just as long as she helped Wat first, she reminded herself.

'We need to talk,' said Medea, drawing a stool up to the table and sitting down opposite Rose. Her face was cool and serious. 'Tonight you're going to see some frightening things. But whatever happens, you absolutely must hold your nerve. OK? Because I can't do this spell on my own, Rose. Do you understand? It needs both of us.'

Rose nodded, feeling a shiver of unease prickling the nape of her neck.

'Good,' said Medea, reaching into her pocket and pulling out a black drawstring pouch. She opened it and began sliding the vials inside. 'You're a brave girl and I've always known you were capable of the strongest magic.'

Rose watched her, the jungle noise outside seeming to fade. In the fuggy stillness of the hut, the soft chink of glass grew louder as Medea slipped the last of the vials into the pouch, drew the strings tight and set it down by Rose.

'Don't you need any?' said Rose.

Medea shook her head. 'No. You'll take all of them when you go out over the water.'

Rose stared. '*Over* the water?'

'Yes,' said Medea. She stood up, smoothed her shorts and walked back to the pot. 'You'll have to be above the gold when you tip the Levitation Potion in.'

Rose felt a wave of fear ripple down her back. The lagoon had been scary enough when she'd simply been gazing at it from the shore in the sunlight, long before Medea mentioned taking a moonlit paddle over it.

Medea tutted. 'Well, there's no need to look like that about it,' she muttered. 'If it makes you feel any better, whilst you're pouring the elixir into the lagoon, I shall be dealing with far more unpleasant things on the shore.'

Unsurprisingly, this didn't make Rose feel any better. Not even a teensy bit. For a moment she stared at the sorceress, wondering what could possibly be *far more unpleasant* than taking a trip over what was frankly a gigantic bowl of oil-black anaconda and caiman *gazpacho*.[52]

But Medea was already staring back into the pot.

The conversation was clearly over.

Around her, the smoke had changed colour, billowing in indigo curls, and as Rose watched, the sorceress's face softened, the line of her mouth momentarily turning into a fond smile, before returning to its icy mask. When she looked up again, her eyes were as hard and grey as pebbles. Impatiently sweeping the room with a glance, she smoothed down her clothes and, primping her hair one last time, walked briskly to the door and glanced back over her shoulder.

'Be sure you're waiting here for me at six o'clock sharp.'

Rose opened her mouth to reply as the door slammed shut. For a few seconds she sat, bemused by the sorceress's sudden exit, and, staring uneasily at the pouch of Levitation

---

52 Cold soup to you.

Potion on the table, felt the memory of that dark water seeping back into her mind.

But, as she quickly scolded herself, this was what it had all been about and if she truly wanted her father back, then she'd have to get on with it, wouldn't she? Do whatever she had to, however scary it seemed. Besides, why was she sitting here, wasting time and thinking about herself, when she still had Wat to find and use the Reversal Potion, tucked in her pocket, on him? Giving herself a brisk mental shake, she stood up, ready to leave.

Which was when the pot rumbled again.

Rose turned, realising that in her rush Medea had forgotten to snuff out the flames. She stood, braced for the door to fly back open, waiting for her to thump back in and put out the fire. And, when nothing happened, she walked over to the window, just in time to catch a glimpse of the sorceress striding out between the huts towards the jungle.

Eager to sneak a peek before she left, Rose hurried over and peered into the pot. Inside, a thick lumpy sludge muttered like prehistoric swamp and, curious, Rose plucked up the peacock plume and tore off some tendrils, throwing them into the goo, the way Medea had.

Nothing changed.

Frustrated, she waited a few seconds more and then, thoroughly dismayed, tossed the feather back down on the floor. She didn't have time for this. Not when she needed to find Wat. Thinking of the enormousness of the task ahead made her heart feel heavier than lead. Where was he? Still at the lagoon? Keeping a lonely vigil at his grave? Or somewhere in between, lost and bewildered, in some patch of jungle that resembled every other patch of jungle around it? For a long moment she stood, recreating the horrified look on his face in her mind, seeing him again that last time, as he turned and stomped off into the trees in a flurry of lace and satin. Frowning, she imagined how unhappy and alone he must be and, curbing a fresh stab of guilt, turned to leave. Just as the pot let out an almighty belch.

Flinching from a flying gobbet, Rose peeped back in and was startled to see the mixture roll flat and lie completely still. Holding her breath, she stared as the surface began to sparkle with brilliant crystal colours, yellow and green and blue. Curls of purple smoke twisted from the surface as its colours merged and whirled, bouncing against the sides of the pot, before tumbling into patterns, shapes and finally a picture. Rose rubbed her eyes, at first wondering if she was imagining the familiar headstones, wonky and green with moss, basking beneath a perfect sky. But when she spied the croquet mallet, leaning against the buttress root at the edge of the clearing, she suddenly understood what the pot was for and that, somehow, thinking hard about Wat must have conjured this picture. Astonished, she stared down, knowing why the sorceress had been so obsessed by the smoking mixture. The brew must work like some sort of magical surveillance camera, she reasoned, enabling Medea to spy on whomever she wanted, and now, feeling slightly sick, Rose forced herself to concentrate harder. She stared at the mallet again, certain that it meant Wat was somewhere close to the graveyard, and squinted about the scene for a shimmer of satin between the trees. When something golden caught her eye, twinkling at the edge of the picture, she felt her heart lift, sure that it must be a button or strip of brocade.

Except that it was bigger than either. Hard and rippled, it curled round and round like a winkle shell.

Twirling.

Glittering.

Ridged with ripples.

Feeling a strange lurch in her chest, she dragged her hair off her face and leaned closer for a better look.

'Aries?' she whispered, feeling utterly ridiculous.

How could he possibly be up on Earth? Here in the Amazon rainforest? And so close to Tatu? Confusion fogged her brain, muddying her mind, yet her eyes insisted that it was unmistakably and absolutely one of his horns.

A moment later, he stepped properly into view and she burst into laughter, thrilled to see the familiar curve of his jaw, his flaring black nostrils, his muzzle crumpled up in puzzlement as he stared at something on the ground.

'Aries!' she yelled, punching the air in delight.

Blinking, she wondered at the lop-sided harness, tied crudely around Aries' girth. A lyre dangled over his rump. An ugly-looking statue poked out of a saddlebag. Then Alex stepped into the picture too, and Rose squealed again.

Leaning closer, she was amazed to see that he was

carrying what appeared to be a shield of living snakes. Most people, of course, would have felt alarmed at this. But not Rose, who giggled as the funny little green one dropped from the metal disc and squiggled over the earth. At least until a sudden flash of panic crossed her mind: was this what Medea had seen? The reason she'd been obsessed by the pot all morning and had left in such a hurry? Dread bristled in her chest, so hard and spiky that for a few seconds she could barely breathe, before a surge of logic lit up her brain, pointing out that the sorceress had actually headed into the jungle in the opposite direction from the graveyard.

Relieved, Rose grinned as Aries jabbed his hoof at something lying on the ground and swung his head up to talk to Alex. As they stared down, she peered closer too and felt her smile vanish. A heap of disturbed soil lay at their feet, and sliding her eyes sideways she saw that each of the Spaniards' graves was ringed with silver stars, just like Wat's had been when she and Medea had summoned him back[53].

Something strange had happened to them.

And, feeling a sudden fear for Wat and her friends replace her elation, she backed away from the pot, turned and raced out of the hut.

---

53 Remember that dazzling bolt of magic that spilled on to the other graves? Thought you might.

XXV
A Fright in Shining Armour

Alex gazed along the row of twinkling graves, feeling a prickle of sweat across his brow that had nothing to do with the humidity of the jungle.

'I don't like this,' he said.

Beside him, Aries drew a front hoof through the nearest spangling halo. Instantly the stars spun out, fizzing with tiny bolts of lightning, and then streamed up around his hock. Intrigued, Grass Snake stuck his snout closer for a better look, tilting his head one way, then the other, mesmerized by the lights.

'I think it'sss pretty,' he sighed, his eyes rolling round and round.

A clatter of branches echoed above them and, glancing up, Alex saw flashes of russet fur as an eerily silent troupe of howler monkeys swung away through the branches. Even the animals didn't seem to like it here and, sensing the hairs on the back of his neck stand up, he felt certain that there was something terribly wrong with this place.

'Let's go,' he said.

Suddenly the clearing exploded in a frenzy of yells and whoops. A high, thin laugh screeched through the trees.

'Lads!' commanded the Gorgon.

Instantly Viper whipped hold of Grass Snake and jerked him, befuddled, back on to the shield, where they instantly froze into defence mode with the others beneath the veneer of silver.

Alex gasped as a thickset man lurched out from behind the huge tree trunk at the far edge of the clearing and charged towards them. Dressed in a metal helmet, breastplate, striped knee-length pants and boots, he bellowed furiously, unsheathing a whip-thin sword, and Alex barely had time to lift the shield in front of Aries and himself before the man skidded to a stop, twirled his weapon above his head and brought it down with a whistling shrill until its tip quivered three millimetres from the end of Alex's nose.

Shuddering, Alex felt himself go cross-eyed as he stared up the shining blade to the snorting man at the other end.

'Who are you?' demanded the man in armour, glaring red-faced from beneath the rim of his gleaming helmet.

'Alex Knossos,' spluttered Alex, instantly understanding the question though not, of course, realising that it was actually asked in Spanish.

Alex held the man's gaze, his heart hammering hard, and slowly, slowly, inched his hand down towards Achilles's sword. Staring back at the man's neat black moustache and triangle of a beard, he wrapped his fingers around its hilt as three more men burst out of the stand of trees and stomped over the ferny ground towards them.

'Intruders, Carlos?' asked the tallest amongst them.

Thin and bird-like, he stopped and leaned forward to gaze down his pointed nose at Aries. Blond hair stuck out like straw from beneath his helmet.

'Thieves, Enrique,' muttered the first man, sheathing his sword again.

Alex shook his head, astonished at the suggestion. Thieves? What could they possibly steal in the jungle? Horrified, he slid his eyes sideways to look at the others: an old man with a grubby grey beard who stared back at him with rheumy, suspicious eyes and a small, weasely man with the leering smile of a gargoyle. He felt his stomach lurch as he realised that they were all dressed in exactly the same way, precisely like the picture of the old soldiers in Hazel's book. He searched his memory quickly for the caption beneath the picture.

Conquistadors.

But that was too ridiculous. Those men had ridden through the jungle over five hundred years ago. Yet here they were, dressed in the same uniform, even down to their helmets, ridged like walnut shells over the crowns of their heads. Feeling the blood drain from his face, he felt the unmistakable spider's touch of Medea's meddling once again.

The oldest one, the grandfather of the group, stepped forward. A rotted red and yellow sash hung over his breastplate. A tatter of red feathers drooped from his helmet.

Beside him, the wiry soldier grinned through yellowed teeth. Now Alex noticed that as well as his sword, he was carrying another, odd-looking weapon. Made from a long pole of wood, it made him think of spears, except that it had no pointed tip, only a hole drilled down its middle and a curled metal catch halfway down its length.[54] Alex held his breath as the man stopped and lurched forwards until he was nose-to-nose with him. 'Gold rats!' he hissed, his breath rank with the smell of onions and brandy.

Twisting away, he stretched out his arm, drawn by the sheen of one of Pegasus's fans tucked into Aries' harness.

'Pretty,' he muttered, stroking it with a filthy finger, before poking the bundles of embroidery and twanging the harp loudly. Then, spotting the Nemesis statue, his beady eyes lit up. 'Matias like this,' he grinned, starting to unbuckle it from the harness.

Snorting, Aries stamped backwards, taking the statue out of his reach.

Alex looked back at the other men. 'We're looking for Tatu Village,' he said as evenly as he could.

'Tatu Village?' said Enrique, in a high whine. 'Carlos? Do you hear that?'

Carlos stroked his beard and scowled nastily. 'There is no village in this hell of green!' he replied.

(Which, as far as Carlos and the others were concerned, was true. After all, when you've spent the

---

54 Actually a harquebus, or shotgun, not that Alex knew that, which was probably just as well, what with the way things were going.

last five hundred years or so haunting the taverns of Seville, before being accidentally summoned back to the jungle, you're hardly likely to know what's been happening in the Amazon, are you?)

'Is a dirty lie!' cried Matias.

He pulled a dented flask from his pocket, uncorked it and took a swig. Then, wiping his mouth with the back of his hand, he belched loudly as if to agree with himself.

'Charming,' muttered Aries.

The men froze.

Several seconds later an eyebrow lifted, a mouth snapped shut and a look of astonishment bounced between their grubby faces.

'What crazy sheep-animal is this?' demanded Enrique. 'What trickery?'

'Devil's work!' announced Matias and jabbed Aries in the belly with the harquebus, so that its butt left smoky-circle marks on Aries' skin. 'I don't think we like you.'

Aries flared his nostrils in disdain. 'I'm not much bowled over by you, either,' he grunted.

Matias reached for his sword.

'Everybody!' said Alex quickly, lifting his hands in surrender. 'This is all a silly misunderstanding. We didn't mean to intrude on you, er, gentlemen.' Hearing Aries snort derisively at the last word, Alex continued quickly. 'So we'll just leave you to it and carry on.'

'Leave you to it and carry on?' said Enrique. Looking round at the others, he held a finger to his cheek and looked up playfully as if to consider the remark. Then he looked straight back at Alex and leaned forward until they were nose-to-nose. 'No!'

'Kill the boy,' said *Señor* Granddad. 'Eat the sheep!'

Upon which four metallic hisses rang through the clearing as the men unsheathed their razor-sharp blades in unison. Four swords of Toledo steel glittered in the sunlight, forming a claw over Alex's head.

Aries reared up, clanking his horns against the blades.

'Get him out of the way!' demanded Carlos, as Aries paddled his hooves high in the air towards him.

Immediately Matias and *Señor* Granddad slid their swords back into their scabbards and leaped forward to gruffly seize hold of Aries' horns. Then, cursing wildly, they hauled him roughly out of the way. Aries struggled and snorted, dragging his hooves in the earth to try and stop them, but the ground was slippery beneath his feet and now, gasping at a bolt of pain in his wounds, he was unable to summon up his usual ferocious strength. Finally, jerking his head left and right, he tried to jab them with his horns.

'Oh no you don't!' squealed *Señor* Granddad, snapping off his rotted sash and quickly tying it across Aries' eyes as a blindfold.

'Let him go!' demanded Alex.

He stepped towards Aries, only to be abruptly stopped by the stinging tip of Carlos's sword against his chest. Alex looked back at the man, who smiled icily and with a deft flick of his wrist sliced open the fabric of Alex's T-shirt.

'Fight!' he demanded.

Aries snorted furiously. Blinded and disoriented, he

drummed his hooves against the ground and out of the corner of his eye Alex saw a flash of metal in the gloom as *Señor* Granddad slid a dagger from his boot.

'Quiet, stupid animal!' he hissed, holding the cold blade against the ram's throat.

'Do as he says!' shouted Alex desperately.

Sensing danger, Aries spun his ears round to find Alex's voice and immediately stopped struggling.

'Stay still,' added Alex, trying to sound calmer than he felt. Then, swallowing hard, he turned back to his opponents.

'*En garde!*'[55] announced Carlos.

Feeling dread, Alex pulled the heavy sword of Achilles from his belt with his right hand, trying to control the trembling in his arm, and, hearing a low hiss from inside the shield, lifted it high against his shoulder.

His heart hammered against his ribs as he looked at the men's faces, their smiles as cold and sharp as their swords. His own sword suddenly felt massive and unwieldy, horribly clumsy in his hand. Being Ancient Greek, it was cast from iron and, looking out from behind its broad leaf-shaped blade, he saw a look of amusement pass between the soldiers' faces. He swallowed hard, his mind racing. Before this quest he'd never even held a sword in his hands, never mind tried to fight with one.

---

55 Swordsmen, including Spanish ones, use fancy French lingo when they're sparring. This particular term means, 'Get ready, matey! I'm about to prong you!'

Suddenly Carlos and Enrique lunged forward, their front legs bent, their arms holding out their swords gracefully.

'Ready?' sniggered Enrique.

'Ready,' whispered Alex.

There was a metallic whoosh from the front of the shield.

'Ready!' agreed Gorgon, her voice low and menacing.

'Willing!' hissed Viper, unfurling to lurch out at the men.

'And able!' spat Adder.

Alex felt his heart soar as the snakes fanned out, hissing furiously, baring their fangs. He took a step forward.

Now the men's confident smiles were all gone and, stepping backwards, their eyes glittered, round with fear.

'More devilry,' hissed Carlos.

'Then it's lucky our blades are so sharp,' sneered Enrique.

Exchanging a dark look with Carlos, he sprang forward, the whistle of his sword sending a muddle of macaws flapping into the treetops. Beside him, Carlos matched his move, lunging forward, bringing his sword down like a guillotine.

The snakes spun backwards, away from the swish of silver, as Alex leaped at the men, reflexively swinging the sword left and right in front of him. The snakes ducked and curled, criss-crossing in front of the men, confusing them as Alex sprang to the side and slammed his sword against Carlos's blade.

The men pounded forward. Alex leaped back as the slices and jabs rained down like hail. Fleetingly, his mind flashed back to how flamboyantly Jason had wielded the weapon and saw clearly how easy that was when you happened to be six-feet tall with muscles like an ox and the only thing you chose to spar with were jungle thickets. Rather than, say, a gang of fight-hungry ghost soldiers who were completely bananas.

Freshly incensed at the unfairness of it all, Alex ran at the men, holding the shield high and throwing his full weight behind the sword, swinging it like a scythe. Alarmed, they scuttled away, momentarily framing Alex like a pair of brackets. Yet a split second later they were behind him, stabbing and lunging. Furious now, Alex spun back. Left, right, he swung the sword, deflecting the frenzy of blows, looking for a chance to charge at their undefended chests before all his strength was gone.

Never had he seen combat like this. In all the army tales his father had told him, the enemy had never danced about like crickets. Like the men's strange weapons, their fighting was light and fast too, all flair and flounce, with enough fancy footwork thrown in to rival an Athenian temple dancer. Full of parrying, *voltes*[56] and glides. Greek battles were all about brute strength, about cutting and

---

56 No, no idea either. And despite sounding like cakes, little ones, iced pink and sprinkled with hundreds and thousands, I couldn't see those being much use in a fight.

stabbing and rushing towards your enemy as one. They were about fighting as a unit.

Making it lucky then that Alex and the snakes were one.

Now, as Carlos and Enrique lunged, close enough for Alex to feel their breath on his face, he heard the Gorgon's voice.

'Attack!' she roared, her voice raw with fury.

In a single flash of movement, like nothing the Spaniards would have read about in any of their lofty books about sword fighting, all five serpents catapulted from the front of the shield and sped through the air like rubbery spears, sending Carlos and Enrique stumbling backwards in horror. Krait flung himself around Carlos's neck, hissing viciously. Viper and Adder each flew around one of his wrists and, quickly looping together, tightened into a pair of scaly handcuffs. Grass Snake lassoed his ankles, sending him tripping backwards over his own headstone to crash into a thicket of prickly figs.

And Cobra? Remembering his youthful military days, he curled into a tight ball and cannoned into Enrique's stomach, toppling him on to the ground in a fury of splutters. Then, as the man tried to stand up again, he slithered on to his chest and wrapped himself tighter and tighter.

Infuriated, Matias let go of Aries' horn and unsheathed his sword to leap at Alex.

Behind him, *Señor* Granddad leered and drew the knife to one side of Aries' throat, ready to kill him. Alex felt a sickening swell of terror. Aries snorted, aware of the danger beyond the blindfold. Ducking as Matias's blade now swished passed him a hair's-breadth from his neck, Alex thought furiously, swinging his sword in the air to deflect another furious lunge.

Then he had it.

'Aries!' he yelled, summoning up every ounce of strength to shout over the clatter of steel against iron. 'Remember to shut in the fire-breathing bulls!'

Aries whinnied in confusion. Then, suddenly understanding, he hurled his head up roughly, away from the knife, and rose on to his back legs. Spinning round, he dropped down, bringing his rump round, and gave an almighty kick with his back hoofs.

'What the?' spluttered the old man as Aries twisted up and away from his grasp.

The gate back at the Zoo had always stuck horribly, you see, jamming into the dried earth before it could close the creatures in safely and it had always been one of Aries' special jobs to shut it with a ferocious back kick, slamming it into the catch. Now, instead of an iron gate, his powerful hooves caught *Señor* Granddad squarely in the back and sent him sprawling forwards.

His cries chimed with the chorus of wails and moans from Carlos and Enrique. Which would have been a truly triumphant moment, except that Matias was back.

Red-faced and furious, he bounced towards Alex over the ground as if it were a springboard. Up, down, left, right, he danced, his sword tracing gleaming curves in the air as Alex held up his sword like a lance. The Spaniard's blade chinked and jangled against the iron, angry as a hornet. Then, dipping down, he clipped Alex's face. Alex felt the trickle of blood, hot over his cheek, and saw the conquistador's face, smiling as he sensed triumph, and stepped closer, sweeping his sword up from below. Galvanised by shock and fury, Alex brought his sword down, letting it fall under its own thundering weight, and caught the silver sword close to its hilt. The conquistador yelped, feeling the blow jar his hand as a sudden snapping noise, like ice cracking on a frozen pond, rang through the clearing and the blade, sheared clean from its handle, toppled into the dirt.

Yay!

Alex!

And *touché*, as they say in snooty sword-fighting circles.

'Villain!' roared Matias, just as Grass Snake slithered down into his boot.

Whoo-hoo!

Grass Snake!

Scaly star!

No longer the most timid of the snakes but the only one brave enough to share air with a five-hundred-year-old soldier's sock. Two seconds after the tip of his tail vanished, Matias's eyes grew wild and, shrieking, he hopped into the trees, waving his hands wildly over his head.

'What a team!' cheered Alex, running over and snatching the blindfold from Aries' eyes.

Rearing up lopsidedly to spare his injuries, Aries paddled the air with his front hooves and landed with a soft whump. Alex threw his arms around the ram's neck as Matias's shouts rang from the trees, squealing at the squirming around his toes. Groaning and mumbling, the other soldiers lay dazed, barely stirring as the jungle slowly returned to its jangle of shrieks and chatters.

'Victory!' trilled the Gorgon, rolling her amber eyes as Krait and Viper zigzagged back into place.

Which was when Rose's voice rang out behind them.

'I command you spirits! Be at peace!'

Astonished, Alex and Aries spun round to see her striding across the clearing towards them.

'Rose!' they cried together in delight.

Throwing down the sword, Alex ran towards her. Aries whinnied and galloped behind him, snorting in delight. She was safe! She was all right! They'd made it to her in time after all!

Except that she didn't reply or smile. Instead, with her face a mask of fierce concentration, she uncorked a small flask and began dribbling purple liquid on to the first grave in the row.

Alex and Aries exchanged confused glances, hearing her murmuring, her voice low and stern.

'Return to your rest!'

Instantly, a loud sucking noise echoed around the clearing and, behind him, Alex realised that *Señor* Granddad was struggling to his feet. Turning, he gaped as the old man's face lost its ruddiness and faded away to white. The colours drained from his striped pants. His helmet dimmed to grey, its feathers paled from red to misty pink. There was a shudder of movement at the old man's feet and Alex glanced down to see a silvered stream of air wrapping about the conquistador's disappearing boots. Slowly, like a cyclone in slow motion, the twisting air enveloped the soldier, higher and higher, rising like a magically spinning cocoon until he was wholly engulfed. Next, it lifted clear of the ground and began moving, floating over the earth and pausing above what Alex assumed must be the man's grave. Then, like a wisp of smoke, it was gone.

'Rose? What are you doing?' cried Alex, feeling bewildered and frightened as Rose turned to dribble liquid on the two neighbouring graves.

With a whistle, a second spiral of sparkling air swirled out of the trees, spitting out Grass Snake with a bump, before hovering over the next grave and disappearing. A third, smelling of onions, twisted furiously, sped past and vanished.

About to walk to the last Spanish grave, Rose smiled up at Alex, but her expression instantly flipped to one of horror.

'Behind you!' she shrieked.

Alex whirled round.

Matias filled his view, lurching towards him out of the bushes, bringing the strange wooden weapon up to his shoulder in one fluid move. Catching the tang of something acrid and bitter wafting from its tip, Alex stepped reflexively backwards, feeling shock course through his veins, shock that stretched everything into a terrible slow motion so that he could see the gleam in Matias's bloodshot eyes, the dirty brown stains on his teeth and hear the icy-cold click of something metallic halfway down the weapon's length. The small black hole at the end of the weapon jutted towards his nose as he heard Rose's feet pound past, sprinting headlong towards the man's grave. But she was too far away to use whatever was in the flask; she'd never make it in time. Beside him, Aries snorted in horror. Just as what appeared to be a large wooden hammer swung into view above Matias's head and struck him neatly on the head. There was a dull clonk as Matias's legs crumpled beneath him and the weapon tumbled from his grasp. Breathless with relief, Alex looked up to see a neatly bearded man standing where Matias had been. Wearing a ruffled lace collar, not to mention the maddest ballooning trousers he'd ever seen, the man beamed, twirling the mallet as he fell into a flamboyant bow.

'I see a kindred soldier also ill-met by Spaniards,' he said, his eyebrows shooting into his hair as the shield snakes stretched out for a better look. 'Wat Raleigh. At your service!'

XXVI
ALL THAT GLISTENS

Well, hooray for croquet!

And for trick shots like the one Wat had just performed, taught to him by the long-dead Duchess of Formby,[57] which had proved as useful on conquistadors' heads as it had been to thwack balls lying far from the next hoop and half-hidden under his mother's rhododendrons.

And hooray for Rose, too! For sending the conquistadors back to where they came from with an equally splendid flourish.

Oh, hang on a minute.

I appear to be the only one cheering . . .

Not that Rose had noticed because she was far too busy stuffing the cork back into the flask to stopper up the remaining potion – oh, and ducking the swirl of ghostly grey, the last spectral sparkle of Matias, whipping over her head to vanish into the soil of his grave – to notice the singular lack of applause. Exhilarated by her success, she beamed at Wat, now certain that she could

---

57 *A regular visitor to Sherborne, who was known to shamelessly flaunt her ankles every time she used the stunt.*

help him too, and, turning, flung her arms around Alex. Tears of happiness welled up in her eyes as she hugged him tightly and, reaching down to rub Aries' head, she could hardly believe that not only were her truest friends back up on Earth and right beside her in the jungle, but she'd actually been able to protect them with her magic.

Her *own* magic!

Which was when she noticed that Alex wasn't hugging her back. And, that Aries was edging away behind him, his eyes clouded and nervous, fixed on the flask in her hand. Even the snakes were coiled, quiet as worm casts on a beach, silently framing the Gorgon's face that now regarded her suspiciously through slits of glittering amber.

Stepping out of her embrace, Alex looked at her as coolly as though she were a stranger. Confused, she watched as he slowly lifted his hand to reach into her hair, fumbling with the tangled ringlets to draw out a lone spiral. Seeing his face crumple, she slid her eyes quickly sideways and gasped, astounded to see a streak of pure silver nestling amongst her curls as vivid and stark as the violet stripe in Medea's hair. She gaped, dumbfounded, and, seeing the revulsion on Alex's face, felt her triumph crash-land in the dust.

'Forsooth, boy,' muttered Wat, dusting his gravestone with his handkerchief before leaning against it. 'Art thou surprised? She's the witch's helper.'

'The witch's helper?' repeated Alex flatly.

Behind him, Aries whined in confusion and Rose caught her breath at the miserable sound. She wanted to step forward, to rub his head, to stop the terrible sound of his distress and, looking from him to Alex, at their matching expressions of confusion and horror, she felt her heartbeat start to gallop.

'I can explain everything,' she said. 'You see, I've found my father!'

A smile fluttered over Alex's lips and vanished. 'That's wonderful,' he said thinly. 'Really,' he added, running his hand through his hair. 'I'm glad for you.'

'But he's ill,' continued Rose. 'Really sick in his mind. Medea said he stumbled into the village a few months ago, but since then he just sits under a tree, staring into space, day after day. He has no idea who I am.' She heard her voice trembling as she thought back to his hollowed-out face. 'He doesn't even know who *he* is.' Rose took a deep breath and carried on. 'Medea told me that something truly dreadful must have happened to the expedition in the jungle, something that made his mind shut down because it's too awful to remember it. She said I'd never get him out of the village without her help.'

'And you believed her?' asked Alex, wide-eyed.

'Yes.' Rose stared back at him. 'You should see him, Alex! He totally freaks if you even try to move him. And she proved to me how easily her magic could bring him back. Like that!' she snapped her fingers in the air. 'She told me things he'd shared with her, things from before he went away. Things that she couldn't possibly have known any other way.'

Alex looked away and Rose felt a sour nervousness

curdle in her stomach. 'Medea promised that she'd show me how to cure my father if I helped her.'

'Oh, Rose!' groaned Alex. He looked up at her, his eyes bright with alarm. 'Please tell me you haven't helped her.'

'You don't understand,' said Rose defiantly.

'Understand?' Alex spluttered. 'Of course I don't understand! Rose, when we heard that Medea was heading to the same coordinates as the Scroll gave you, we thought you were in danger! We came back to protect you from her.' His expression grew cold. 'Or at least the Rose we thought we knew!'

'But I am still the same Rose!'

'Do you think so?' Alex shook his head. 'Only the Rose we knew wouldn't have listened to a word Medea said. She'd never have helped her. She'd never have used filthy sorcery on ghosts!'

Rose gasped. 'What was I supposed to do? Those soldiers were trying to hurt you!' Anger seared through her, scorching her face, making her head pound. 'And besides,' she added, 'I only sent them back to where they belong. I was putting things right again!'

Alex stared at her in disbelief. 'With sorcery, Rose? Think! When have you truly seen her magic do anything good?'

Rose tightened her grip on the flask. Staring into Alex's anguished face, she felt all her earlier doubts starting to trickle through the solid wall of reasons to help Medea that she'd built in her mind.

'Look, I know how it sounds, Alex. Really, I do. And it totally wasn't an easy decision for me to make. But you have to understand that this is my father we're talking about.'

'*And* Medea,' said Alex. 'After everything we went through in the summer, Rose, how could you be so blind? So selfish?'

'I'm not blind or selfish!' Rose felt her throat tighten with anger. 'I just want my father back! And helping Medea is my only chance to do that. She proved to me that it works. She said, she said —'

Rose scrunched up her face, searching for the right words. But all the right words had suddenly vanished under the rising swell of doubt that Alex had released. She tried to stem its flow, telling herself that if she stopped helping the sorceress now, then everything would be hopeless, certain of how the story would end for her father.

Shaking her head, she stepped backwards, wishing that she could simply jam her fingers in her ears and make him stop.

She didn't want to hear what he was going to say next.

She didn't want to hear any of it.

'Rose,' he said, reaching out to touch her shoulder. 'Nothing in the world, nothing at all, is worth helping Medea.'

Unstoppably, the truth of what he was saying now surged through her mind in a freezing torrent, sweeping away all her earlier certainties. She gasped, appalled as every reason she'd soothed her conscience with now bobbed, splintered and broken, in the deluge. She pressed her fists to her eyes, trying to stem the big, hot tears welling there, as an image of the London theatre returned to her. Seeing Alex beside her, huddled with Hazel on the stage with the pop star's screams dying away in her ears, she remembered the sheer relief of knowing that they had stopped the sorceress's cruelty.

'I've been so stupid,' she gasped.

She felt her chest tighten with panic and shame and remorse, knowing that every moment of learning from Medea, every yearning step on the way to helping her father, despite her best intentions, had been utterly and totally wrong. Deep inside she'd always known it – of course she had, she was sensible, kind Rose – but she'd been so desperate, so headstrong, so determined to make things right that she'd joined forces with Medea as cheerfully as boarding a roller coaster. Strapping herself in and setting her hands on the bar as the ride had started moving, she'd let it crank up the rails, taking her higher and higher with it whilst she'd made herself ignore the bumps and creaks of her own conscience, stuffing every clanking fear about what she was doing into a dark corner of her mind, simply so that she could get what she wanted.

Worse, she'd actually enjoyed it.

Now, as the tears began streaming down her face, she thought about the magic she'd performed over the last few days and felt the dizzying certainty that somehow curing her father made everything else all right vanish away to nothing, leaving her feeling absolutely disgusted with herself.

Gently, Alex put his arm around her shoulder and, feeling horribly unworthy of his friendship, she cried harder still. Minutes later, she finally looked up and wiped her face roughly with the back of her hand.

She'd never felt more wretched in her life.

For a long moment, no one said anything.

At least until Aries gave Rose a big, rough, rammy lick on the shoulder.

'We all fool ourselves sometimes,' he said, ignoring the shocked gasp from Wat.[58]

Flicking a knowing look at Alex, Aries settled his muzzle on her shoulder and continued.

'Even if we know deep down that something is wrong, we can still let ourselves be taken in by other people, by how they appear and what we think they offer us.'

'Fie!' said Wat. 'Thou art indeed a strange creature, but you speak the truth. We can all be made clowns. Like Lady Francesca of Windermere and me. She was so charming, I didn't know my beard from my elbow.'

'And,' said Adder, jabbing Alex rudely on the knee, 'jus-s-st like you and Jas-s-son.'

Alex glared at him and Adder instantly coiled back on to the shield.

'Jason?' said Rose, her surprise for a moment dousing her misery. 'Is he here too?'

---

58 Talking rams were not common at the Court of King James I.

'He was,' muttered Alex.

So that was why Medea had been so jumpy all morning, she thought. *Jason?* The man who'd betrayed her so brutally was back on Earth? *He* was the reason the sorceress appeared to have swapped her brain for a bath sponge?

Rose looked at Alex, willing him to go on.

'Athena insisted he lead us in the quest back to Earth,' he explained. 'She decided it was time that Medea paid for all the crimes she's committed over the centuries.' He walked over to Aries, unbuckled a saddlebag and lifted out the statuette she'd glimpsed in the scry bowl. 'That's why she wanted Jason to hand her this.'

Rose raised her eyebrows at Alex. 'A statue?'

'Not any old statue,' replied Alex. He turned it over gently in his hands.

Sunlight glinted from its sharp, spiky wings and unforgiving face. Now, looking more closely, Rose noticed flashes of red, orange and blue light skittering about inside it.

'It's filled with the Greek spirits of vengeance,' said Alex.

'Three goddesses,' continued Aries, under his breath, 'who'll drag Medea, kicking and screaming, down to the Underworld prison.'

Rose shuddered and looked around the clearing.

'So, where is he then?'

'Gone,' said Alex coldly. 'Ran away.'

Rose's mind flipped back to the journal she'd read the night before, and the way Jason had freaked out amongst the bone men and had flatly refused to climb the serpent's coils.

Grass Snake loomed up in front of her. 'Firs-s-st he refus-s-sed to help Alex when Ariesss wasss attacked by a terrible three-headed jaguar.'

'See,' said Aries, turning his left side to her to show her the tattered dressings beneath the harness before tilting his head down and rolling his eyes towards his broken horn. Feeling her heart clench at the sheared-off twist, Rose leaned over and kissed his head.

'And now he'sss run off and left usss behind altogether,' added Grass Snake, looking up at her with furious ball bearings of eyes. 'With the key!'

'What key?' said Rose.

'The key to the Underworld, of cours-s-se,' shrilled Grass Snake, flopping back on to the shield. 'I don't know how we'll ever get home again!'

As Grass Snake continued to wail, Rose recalled the enormous key on Medea's shelf and how puzzled she'd been to see it in a village without a single lock.

'Was it long and black?' she said. 'Attached to a little carved parrot on a chain?'

'Yes,' said Alex, exchanging surprised looks with Aries and the snakes. 'But how could you know that?'

'Because it's been hanging in the sorceress's hut for days.'

'Days?' said Alex.

Aries stamped his hoof in the mud. 'Then Jason must have lost it when were locked up!'

'Which is why he was so keen to get on with the quest when he came back to the hotel,' said Alex sourly.

'And,' sighed Aries, 'it explains why he came back to find us at all.'

'More lies,' muttered Alex. He shrugged sadly at Rose. 'I was so convinced I knew what he was like. Just like a stubborn goat.'

'More like a goat with a bucket on his head,' said Aries. 'Like this.' He started walking backwards, swinging his head left and right, warming to his theme, the harness jangling as he flung his enormous behind from side to side, and despite her dismay Rose had to stifle a small giggle. '"Oh, no Aries,"' he said, waggling the fans hanging from the back of the tackle. '"You are completely mistaken about him! Please don't say such rude things about Jason-Sparkly-Sandals."'

'Do you mind?' grumbled Alex, but Rose was relieved to see that he was smiling for the first time since they'd met again.

'Aries is right,' he said. 'I suppose we can all be taken in by what we want to believe. And I meant what I said about your dad. I'm glad you've found him. Truly.'

Rose blinked back a fresh threat of tears.

'Child,' said Wat. He laid a gentle hand on her shoulder. 'Perhaps you should tell us what the witch asked you to do.'

Taking a deep breath, Rose looked up at Wat.

'She needs me to help her raise the gold from the

lagoon you led us to. She said that it was special, special enough to make her magic work.'

Aries groaned.

Glancing uneasily at him, Rose went on.

'Because it has an amazing history.'

Whereupon Wat groaned, too.

Feeling a tingle of dread, Rose looked at each of their faces in turn, at their matching expressions of dismay.

'What is it?' she said. 'Medea said the gold in the lake would help me cure my father because it was just as cherished as the Fleece.'

'Oh, Rose,' sighed Alex, shaking his head slowly. 'She was lying. The Fleece wasn't cherished. Every strand, every single curl of it was cursed.'

'Cursed?' Rose heard her voice trail away to nothing.

'By Medea,' said Alex. 'The Fleece ruined her life from the start. From the moment her father hung it in the forest at Kolkis, things started to go badly wrong for her because he became so dazzled by it that he simply forgot all about his little girl.'

'And then,' said Aries, 'when Jason arrived she thought she'd finally be happy. She was so sure he loved her –' Aries sighed. 'As far as she was concerned, my Fleece ruined her life and so, in return, she poured her bitterness into it. Then, when it was brimful of her hatred, she used it in her magic. Every time she stitched its curls into her special clothes, the Fleece released her misery. That's what brought about the deaths of the people wearing them. I know it's true, because she told me herself, back in London, down in that terrible cellar, when she tried to extinguish me.'

Rose stared at him. '*Misery* was the real secret of its power?'

'That's right,' said Aries, looking at her with his treacly eyes dimmed by sadness. 'My beautiful gold coat used for something so terrible. Her misery poisoned the gold in the Fleece. And poisoned gold can only ever do poisonous magic.'

'But what can be so bad about the gold in the lake?' said Rose.

Wat turned away and looked into the trees.

'After what you've just told me,' he said grimly, 'I think I can guess.'

The others waited for him to go on.

'El Dorado,' sighed Wat, turning back. 'In my time, people believed it was the name of a city built from shimmering gold, hidden deep in the heart of the jungle. Even my own father, in his boyhood, would race down to Plymouth harbour each morning, eager to hear the returning sailors' stories of their quest to find it. Truly intoxicated, he yearned to discover it and years later his tales dazzled me too.'

'So, Medea *was* telling the truth,' said Rose. 'The gold did inspire men?'

'Inspire, child?' Wat shrugged. 'Perhaps some might call it that. Men were certainly provoked into trekking deep into the jungle to find it.' He looked around the clearing at the graves. 'Thousands of men, men such as these conquistadors, men who never returned.'

'Thousands?' Rose flinched. 'What happened to them?'

'Some drowned in the Amazon, some were attacked by deadly snakes, crawling pests or mauled by big cats. Some were sent mad by the strange berries and mushrooms they ate in their desperation and turned on each other like wolves. Yet more were bitten by the fever flies.'

Alex looked up at Wat.

'But if so many people were looking so hard for the place, then why could no one ever find it?'

'Because it never existed,' said Wat simply. 'There *was* no city of gold. Yet, in their greed, the Europeans tortured tribe upon tribe of native Indians to death, demanding that they tell them where this marvellous city was to be found.'

Dizzy with horror, Rose pictured the soldiers storming into a village like Tatu and rounding up the villagers, snatching the giggling women, the children playing happily on rugs, demanding answers that nobody could ever give, and felt her anguish turning into anger.

'During our months in the jungle,' Wat continued, 'we heard strange rumours. That El Dorado was not a city but the leader of a fantastically wealthy tribe – the Muisca, whose gold was so plentiful they even fashioned pans and cups from it. Gladdened, we made haste further north than anyone had searched before, towards the great lagoon by which they lived. Fain,' Wat laughed coldly, 'in happening on this true El Dorado, I wished verily to be dressed for my triumph.' He pulled back his doublet to show a ragged black-edged hole in the linen, and Rose caught a glimmer of gold thread. 'Some triumph,' he muttered. 'Thanks to the sorceress's needlework, I stumbled blindly into an ambush and was felled by a Spaniard's gun. Worse,' said Wat, almost whispering, 'when my heart-broken father returned to England with tidings of my death, the King was so furious that I'd fought with the Spanish that he marched my father to the Tower of London and beheaded him.'

Rose groaned, utterly sickened at just how many terrible deaths stained the El Dorado gold, and felt freshly foolish in her own misguided willingness to help Medea reach it. She saw how easily Medea had twisted the truth around her little finger, and Rose with it, duping her from the start.

Poisoned gold can only do poisonous magic.

Like a spiteful chant, a cold little voice piped up in her mind, mocking her, taunting her with the phrase. Her skin prickled. The gold in the lake was so saturated in misery and suffering that it could never, ever have helped her father. It could only make him even worse. Imagining it, glinting beneath the dark water, she realised something else and felt a judder of shock: that whilst the gold of Aries' fleece had only been powered by the unhappiness of a single woman, the gold of El Dorado buzzed with the misery of thousands. Meaning that if Medea succeeded in getting her hands on it, she'd be absolutely unstoppable.

Rose turned to Alex, a blistering fury scorching away the last of her earlier, drizzling despair.

'Show me that statue again,' she said.

XXVII
Love Isn't in The Air

There have been many passionate moments in the Greek myths: Paris whisking Helen away to Troy, Ariadne unravelling her knitting to give Theseus the wool to lead him from the Minotaur's maze, and Narcissus going all googly gaga over his handsome reflection in a woodland pool. However, thought Jason, now practising a seductive raised eyebrow at a rather elderly yellow-footed tortoise he'd found waddling in the long grass, his meeting Medea again wasn't likely to be remembered as one of them.

'Sweet rose of Kolkis,' he said, practising his newest chat-up line and offering the ancient reptile his best smile. 'How I've longed to see you.'

The creature regarded him blankly with big, black eyes and continued to gum at a clump of grass, churning it round and round in her lipless mouth.

'My dear and long-lost love,' Jason continued, as the creature lurched away towards the undergrowth, 'your smile is like the sun rising over the sea. It makes the water sparkle and the seagulls swoop, it, it —'

He paused, sniffed and, noticing a rather sour smell

wafting up from the ground, glanced down at the rear end of the tortoise, dismayed to spot a trickle of yellow liquid, seeping into the soil behind her crinkly back feet. Clearly he was losing his debonair touch. And small wonder. He'd been so stressed about meeting his ex-wife again that he'd given himself a crick in his neck from rehearsing his best hair flick, whilst his voice, usually low and syrupy, sounded as squealing and high-pitched as a piglet at teatime.

He'd have to do better than this if he wanted to smooch Medea into handing the key to the Underworld back to him. After all, as he reminded himself now, he really didn't need to be so worried.

You see, ever since he'd stopped running away from that ghastly big cat the day before and recovered from the raging stitch that running for nearly an hour will bring on, he'd started thinking. And, it hadn't been long before he'd realised something rather important: that just as the swarm of army ants hadn't killed him, the weird three-headed cat hadn't even seemed interested in him. After all, he must surely have passed the creature only moments before it attacked Aries and yet it hadn't so much as batted one of its six eyelids in his direction. Instead, it had been utterly single-minded, launching itself at Aries like a bleat-seeking missile. All of which had confirmed his earlier suspicion: that Medea clearly still reckoned he was the best thing since stuffed olives.

The thought brought a welcome surge of his old confidence and, setting his hand on his hip, he tilted his head boyishly and turned on his full-beam smile, staring at the tortoise's receding bottom.

'Light of the Greek isles,' he cooed, his voice low and smoochy again. 'How I've dreamed of this moment.'

'Why thank you, darling,' replied a woman's voice behind him.

Jason froze, open-mouthed.

For a second his blood seemed to drop in temperature until it clinked through his veins like an ice-slushy. The voice was instantly familiar, and even though he hadn't heard it – save in nightmares – since he'd been in the Underworld, he felt the hairs on the back of his neck prickle.

Forcing his mouth into an unwilling smile, he turned round.

'Medea!' he gushed.

The sorceress looked radiant, her hair gleaming in ringlets, her face tinged pink from walking, as pretty as a Venus flytrap in the sunshine. In fact, considering his own stained and torn T-shirt and jeans and the way he smelled like a Spartan's sandal after a hundred-mile march, she looked amazing. Rather, he thought, now complimenting himself on his own hunky charms, as if she'd been powdering and primping all morning especially for him.

'I've been expecting you,' she said.

She smiled, drawing red lips back over shiny white teeth and held out her hand. Taking it firmly, he curbed a small, telltale shiver as she laced her fingers through his, reminding himself that at this rate he'd soon have the Underworld key back in his pocket.

'Walk with me,' she sighed, looking up at him under her sooty lashes. 'It's a lovely afternoon and we have so much to talk about.'

Jason followed as she led him off the path that led into the village, and turned towards the jungle instead. Now, stepping in her footsteps, Jason recalled the way she'd guided him through the Kolkis forest on the night they'd stolen the Fleece. She'd glanced back over her shoulder and beamed at him, just the way she did now, and he felt himself start to properly relax, wondering why he'd been so worried about coming back to Earth at all. Women always forgave him. And who could blame them? He was irresistible.

Squeezing his hand, she picked her way under a low-hanging bough, thick with blood-red blooms. He squeezed back, knowing that if he played his cards right, she'd probably magic him back to Manaus, to the opera house, for good measure. Meaning that he'd be back in the Underworld for Aphrodite's party. And once he'd told them his story – his pained regret that Aries had run away with the statue, but what could you expect from a clonking great farm animal? And the sadness he felt for Alex, just a boy unready for a real quest (after all, the goddesses loved a troubled hero) – he'd be posing in his battle armour and leopard-skin for a new range of pots and urns in his honour. Better still, he'd have that old sop Apollonius fawning round him, ready to take down everything he told him again.

But, he reminded himself, first things first.

'I've missed you,' said Jason softly. Which was sort of true since he had missed her, even if it was rather in the way that people miss a terrible headache, say, or a giant spider lurking in the bath.

'And I've missed you, too,' replied Medea.

'My princess,' sighed Jason.

'My hero,' cooed Medea.

My foot.

To be honest, as Medea led him further and further into the jungle, their conversation became far too gushy, mushy and slushy for me to waste time and good ink on. So I shan't. Only to say that Jason was so busy flirting, flaunting and flattering that he was quite flummoxed when they suddenly stepped out of the jungle's thick shadows to see a wide, dark lagoon.

Yes, you know the one.

'Isn't it beautiful?' said Medea, gazing up at the craggy bluff of rock at the far side of the water. 'We used to take walks like this on Iolkos, when we were first married, do you remember?'

Jason did. As his eyes swept over the dark water, he found himself recalling the swamp of singing stink-toads that she'd loved to visit and realised that her taste in 'beauty spots' hadn't changed much.

Shuddering, he turned his face up to the sky and watched the wisps of white trail over the blue.

'Do you remember how we'd watch the clouds,' he said, 'seeing pictures in them? I'd always see stags and warships.'

'And nymphs,' muttered Medea quietly.

'Whilst you saw scorpions and dragons,' said Jason

'Sweetheart,' said Medea, tilting her face up to his and laying her hands on his shoulders. 'I'm so glad you came back.'

'So am I,' said Jason, shrinking beneath her embrace. 'But how could I not? As soon as I heard what Athena was planning, I volunteered myself for the quest. I knew that I had to protect you.'

'Protect me?' said Medea, wide-eyed.

Turning, she led him to a low tumble of rocks, close to the shore, sat down and patted the warm stone beside her.

'Yes,' said Jason, sitting down next to her, warming to his tale. 'Of course Athena took a lot of persuading. I think she was suspicious of why I was so desperate to return to Earth. Deep down, I'm sure she knows that my heart still belongs to you, my sweet.'

'My darling,' sighed Medea.

'But, I was determined. I demanded she let me return to find you.'

'Oh, captain of my heart!' sighed Medea.

'Of course it was a nightmare when she saddled me with Alex and Aries.'

'But they're gone now, aren't they? Tell me,' she said, bristling with curiosity. 'Was there a lot of blood?'

'Barrels of it!' said Jason, surprised to see the glitter of genuine interest in her eyes. After all, she must surely know that her magic would have dispatched them horribly? Or perhaps she simply couldn't resist hearing about the details first-hand from him? Between you and me, Jason might have been surprised to know that she wasn't actually sure of any such thing, since she'd been so busy preparing for meeting him. And not only in the lipstick and hairbrush department, I'm afraid. But, we'll come to that later.

'It was hideous!' Jason went on. 'Truly, I've never seen a monster more terrifying. The power of him, Medea, the span of those feet and claws. The ram didn't stand a chance.'

Medea clapped her hands together. 'And Alex?'

Jason shook his head, pushing the uncomfortable thought of the boy racing hopelessly back with those flimsy little arrows out of his mind.

'You really excelled yourself there.'

'So,' said Medea, resting her head on Jason's shoulder. 'Tell me about Athena's plan.'

'She means to send you to Tartarus.'

Medea regarded him evenly. 'How?'

'Using a statue,' said Jason. 'Filled with the Erinyes. Can you imagine, she actually wanted me to hand it to you?'

Medea waited for him to go on.

'As if I ever could!' he added, wishing that he had it in his hand now, wrapped in a big soppy ribbon.

'And you came back to sabotage her plan?'

'It's been my only thought!'

Medea looked up at him, saucer-eyed. 'My honey-baklava!'

'My rose-lipped princess!'

'My sweet prince of Iolkos!'

'My cherry-lipped queen!'[59]

Medea laughed girlishly and stood up, clapping her hands together.

'And now you're back with me!'

'But only for a little while,' said Jason, rather too quickly. 'I mean, it's awful, I know, but I'll have to return soon. We don't want Athena sending anyone else up here, do we?'

Medea shook her head sadly.

'That's why I think that you and I need a plan.'

'We do?'

Jason nodded, and took the sorceress's hand in his.

'I think I should go back and tell her that we've talked as ex-husband and wife —' said Jason

'As lovebirds,' interrupted Medea.

'As lovebirds, yes,' said Jason. 'And that you've told me how terribly sorry you are about the past and that you've turned over a new leaf.'

'Except that I won't.'

'Well, I know that,' said Jason. 'But she doesn't need to, does she? And, if you were a little less, well, flamboyant about things in the future, then she'd never find out.'

---

59 My! Pass me the sick bucket. Let's not start all this again.

'And it would be our little secret,' cooed Medea. 'A love secret?'

'That's right,' said Jason. Sitting back on the rock, he allowed himself a moment to imagine the word 'DIPLOMAT' being chiselled next to 'HERO' in the plinth of his pavilion statue.

'Sealed with a kiss?' added Medea.

'Maybe later,' said Jason, leaping to his feet.

For a split second, Medea's mouth drew tight before she gave him a wide, generous smile.

'And you'd really do this, just for me?'

'Of course,' said Jason, tossing back his head. 'We were so close once.'

Medea sighed happily and glanced towards the bluff of rock edging the far side of the water.

'But before you go, there's something I'd really like to show you.'

Masking his impatience, Jason put on his considering face and looked up at the sky to where a cloud, unpleasantly shaped like a spider, was chasing after a fluff of white that looked rather like a fly.

'Well . . .' he stretched the word out as he thought.

'Then I'll magic you straight back to Manaus, to speed you on your way?'

'All right, then,' said Jason, crumpling his brow into an earnest frown. 'You know how much I'd love to spend more time with you, but for your sake, I have to leave soon.'

'I know,' said Medea, a faint sliver of ice in her voice. 'But don't worry, darling. You'll be gone soon.'

II VIII
By a Creepy Lagoon

A few hours later, the lagoon lay like a slab of black marble in the moonlight.

Overhead, a straggle of ragged clouds swept across the sky and a few vultures hunched in the scatter of trees around the shore, their silvery plumage ghostly in the gloom. Rose trembled with nerves. Her fingers twitched. Clenching her fists impatiently, she told herself to get a grip.

But it wasn't easy.

As you know, this place had freaked her out right from the start, and now, steeped in darkness, it felt a million times worse. Menace seemed to ooze from its water and stalk the bluff behind her, and she shivered to see the small canoe, bobbing at the water's edge, moored to a low tumble of rocks. She rubbed her shoulders, hardly able to believe how excited she'd been only a few hours before, racing to find Alex and Aries, so giddy with her own powers and certain that sorcery held the key to her father's happiness.

But now everything had changed.

Now she knew how foolish she'd been to even think

of helping Medea. And on top of that, discovering the true history of the lagoon gold, so horrible it made her skin creep, she was absolutely determined to stop Medea's plans.

A few metres away, the sorceress stood half-stooped on the shoreline, her arms outstretched, whispering over the water. Her voice drifted back to Rose through the sultry air, eerie against the lisping cicadas, and although she spoke too quietly for Rose to make out the individual words, her tone was unmistakable. Playful and inviting, as though she were coaxing a cat into a warm house for the night, which, given the ghastly surroundings and complete lack of cuddly kitties or bowls of creamy milk, was all highly unsettling and so I'm not going to linger on it.

Thank you very much.

As Medea raised her hands to the moon, Rose caught a flash of what remained of the pharaoh's bangle twinkling in her fingers and felt a deep stab of revulsion. You see, after everything the others had told her, she'd started to wonder about the bangle's true nature, absolutely certain that whatever power it contained, it certainly wasn't distilled from the love of the Egyptian people.

Batting creepers and vines out of her way as she'd stumped back to the village, she'd recalled the sorceress's bright, lying face when she'd talked about the cuff and racked her brain over its weird inscription to Osiris. For several minutes the name had pinballed around her mind, bouncing off her recollections of the Tutankhamun exhibition, the glittering death mask, the glass cases of jewels and amulets and huge golden boxes. But it hadn't been until she reached the outskirts of the village and seen the tribe gathered together, singing in the firelight, that she'd remembered the painting.

Dominating one whole wall of the dimly lit side room at the exhibition, it had shown women dressed in the white of mourning standing beside red-robed priests huddled in the burial chamber, whilst behind them the slaves bricked up the doorway. From *inside* the tomb. Sealing themselves in to die. Because, as she finally recalled her mother telling her younger, sobbing self, dead pharaohs liked to have company in the afterlife.

Only then had she remembered that Osiris was the Egyptian god of the dead. And with a sickening certainty, she'd understood that Tutankhamun would only have worn the bangle *after* he died, clamped around his mummified wrist like a golden ticket into the Egyptian Underworld. Appalled, she'd pictured it nestled inside the dark sarcophagus, its gold feeding on the muted wails of the people dying around him, gorging itself on their misery.

Poisonous gold can only do poisonous magic.

Of course, Rose hadn't seen the grisly fate of the big, blue butterfly she'd turned back to a caterpillar, but she remembered the tree branch that had sprung from Medea's work table, and how, only half an hour later, she'd discovered it swarming with termites, their sharp little mouths ripping the new wood to shreds, and shivered.

Medea's magic was rotten to the core.

Meaning that when the sorceress had used the bangle to work her spell on her father to uncover those memories of Rose's childhood, there couldn't have been any healing. Instead, she must have damaged him more. After all, Rose thought, despite whatever had happened to the expedition, he'd still managed to reach the village, hadn't he? Yet, thanks to Medea's toxic magic, now he couldn't even leave his sheltering tree.

She glared at the sorceress, feeling hot fury stinging her cheeks, coupled with a sudden, biting impatience to be out on the wretched water so that Alex and the others could finally end Medea's reign of misery. And since by now you're probably wondering quite what Rose was doing there, all on her own, I suppose I'd better tell you about the plan that she and the others had come up with at the graveyard.

Having listened to everything Rose had told them, they'd quickly decided that it would be far too risky to try to overpower the sorceress at the village since the Kaxuyana people of Tatu would surely rush to defend their lovely Fair Trade lady. Instead, they agreed to sneak down here and wait for their chance to ambush her at the lagoon. And so, whilst Rose had returned to Tatu to accompany Medea here, Wat (who'd flatly refused Rose's offer to magic him back to England, verily insisting on doing his part to defeat the cruel minx of Kolkis, the jinx of the jungle, the vile vixen of — well, you get the picture) would lead the others through the jungle to the western side of the water.

Then, as soon as Rose was out on the canoe, and more importantly a safe distance from the sorceress's wrath when she discovered the girl's betrayal, they'd stop the spell and slam the statue into Medea's hand.

Simple.

And then Rose heard the first snap from the water.

Sharp as a guillotine, it sliced through the muttering jungle behind her and jerked her from her thoughts. She paused, stretched up on her toes, seeking out the water beyond the sorceress, but it lay darkly still and secretive. Silently scolding herself for being so jumpy, particularly when Alex had said it was important that she didn't do anything to arouse suspicion, she began walking towards the canoe, setting her face into a look of cool determination. It didn't help, of course, that she'd never been much good at acting, but she consoled herself that she wouldn't need to pretend for much longer because, if everything went according to plan, like Alex had described it, then they'd be able to strike soon, and long before she had to release a single drop of Medea's hateful potion into the water.

Which was when she heard a second snap.

And another.

And another.

Squinting, Rose made out a row of soft, triangular shapes break the dark surface of the water. For a long moment, the pale and fleshy throats of ten, twenty – maybe more – caimans loomed from the centre of the lagoon, glimmering like gravestones before they sank back down.

Rose made out the gleam of eyes at the bridge of each snout, as the reptiles knifed through the water towards her and Medea. Without warning, Rose's legs turned to rubber as she realised whom the sorceress had been calling.

'Come along, Rose!' Medea's voice was light and fluty, sugary as a hostess inviting someone to sit down at the table. 'Time to make a start!'

Rose stepped into the canoe, just as something big and broad thumped against its side. Suddenly unbalanced, she toppled backwards, landing clumsily. She spun round, horrified, as a huge caiman stumped past her, up on to the mud, only centimetres from her fingers. Swinging its massive tail, it slapped the canoe a second time, sending it skittering sideways out across the water, and Rose grabbed the sides, gasping as more and more caimans slunk out of the lagoon and surged up the shore towards the sorceress. The night throbbed with their grunts and snorts as they surrounded her like toddlers nuzzling a beloved nursery teacher.

A sudden cramping sickness clawed at Rose's stomach. There was no way the others could attack Medea if she was flanked by such a legion of toothy guards. Panic tightened her throat and she gaped, wordless, as the biggest caiman, a crack-scaled bruiser with a scar down its tail, rolled on to its back to have its belly tickled, drooling whilst the others jostled round, jaws snapping in glee, clambering to get closer.

'Oh, don't look so worried!' cried the sorceress, glancing up and seeing Rose's stricken face. 'It's all right!

They're with us. I'm enchanting them to collect the gold when you've raised it to the surface.'

Rose swallowed hard, her eyes widening as Medea began walking towards her, with the caimans like a dark, scaly stain around her feet. Still cooing at the swell of reptiles, Medea crouched beside the canoe.

'Right out to the middle, Rose!' she whispered. She pulled the pouch of Levitation Potion from her pocket and set it on the floor of the canoe before reaching over a couple of squirming caimans to toss the mooring rope into the boat. 'And wait for my instruction to start pouring.'

Start pouring?

Rose gulped.

The plan was meant to have worked long before that.

Panic fluttering behind her ribs, she leaned forward, took hold of the paddles and edged them over the sides of the canoe. The wood felt slick against her palms, wet with sweat, and she had to tighten her grip until her knuckles grew white. From the shore, an audience of caimans watched her, their teeth shining in wonky, stupefied grins as, steeling herself against the prickling fear now sweeping up her legs and back, she dipped the oars into the water and began to row.

'C'mon!' growled Alex under his breath, willing the caimans to move away from Medea as she walked back towards the rocky bluff. Like an assassin waiting for a clear shot, he could feel every muscle and nerve twitching, itching with impatience to strike.

Beside him, Aries snorted hotly behind the screen of yellow monkey-blossom as Medea paused at the base of the rocks and, tilting back her head, scanned its cracks and fissures, smiling.

'Fie!' hissed Wat, puzzled. 'What foul deed would she fain make now?'

'Foul deed?' quavered Grass Snake, slithering through the branches for a better look.

Alex drew him gently back and settled him among the others on the front of the shield, who were coiled in tight battle-springs, ready for action, and snatched a glance across the water at Rose. She looked so small and vulnerable, dwarfed by the long stretch of blackness, and, hardly daring to breathe, he turned back again, tightening his hand around the Nemesis statue.

Suddenly a low, guttural moan erupted from the rocky cliff face bordering the lagoon. The snakes bristled and Gorgon gasped as around them the jungle chirruping stopped instantly. An armadillo, which had been busily snuffling at the water's edge, jerked back its head with a squeak and waddled rapidly back into the undergrowth.

'What's happening?' demanded Aries, feeling his hooves beginning to judder beneath him.

Over by the sorceress, the caimans began edging away from the foot of the bluff as now the high-pitched whine rang out again. Eerie as a lone wolf's cry, it echoed through the strange stillness that hung over the water, making the hairs on the back of Alex's neck stand up.

'I don't like thisss,' whispered Grass Snake.

But Alex's attention was glued to the sorceress as she briskly fluttered her fingers at the caimans, like a teacher dismissing a class. Immediately, the creatures at the edge of the group peeled away. The others rapidly followed, slithering into the water behind them, to swim like a scaly flotilla towards Rose's canoe, meaning that finally, finally the sorceress was alone.

'This is our chance!' hissed Alex, above the rising grumbling of rock. 'We go now. Ready?'

Glancing down, he saw the fierce resolution kindling in Aries' eyes.

'Ready with ramming speed!' he replied.

Beside him, Wat nodded once and tightened his grip on his croquet mallet.

'On three,' said Alex. 'One, two —'

Except that nobody heard three.

This was on account of the ear-splitting roar that ripped out of the rock face and ricocheted like a thunder-clap around the lagoon. Half-emerged from the thicket, Alex and the others stared in disbelief as the rock splintered into a tracery of cracks, jagged as a lightning strike. Crags of stone snapped off ledges and tumbled down, splashing into the water as the rock groaned and wailed.

'What in Hades!' gasped Aries, as another whip-like crackle rent the air and a new darker fissure, thicker than the others, sped along the face of the rock, fizzing like a trail of lit gunpowder. On and on it bore, drilling through the stone in a riot of dust, outlining the shape of something big, something gnarled, something with a broad trunk-like body, a flat triangular head and a thickly tapering tail.

Wat stepped backwards, clutching his beard in horror as ripple after ripple swept over the surface of the centuries-old stone.

'I don't believe it,' he hissed.

Sandstone chattered and chipped, reduced to a jigsaw of shivering shards around the outline of a gigantic caiman, much, *much* bigger than the ones paddling across the lagoon below.

'Believe what?' said Aries, unable to drag his eyes away from the cracks that now spliced the rock to reveal four stubby legs, each topped by a clawed foot.

'The Lake Guardian,' said Wat.

The shape began to tremble.

No, it began to *breathe*.

Alex stared, awed, as the weird creature wrenched itself proud of the rock and stretched as though waking from a comfortable sleep. There was a scrunching sound, like a boat being dragged up a pebbled beach, and Alex realised that the creature's skin wasn't leathery like the other caimans. Instead, it was made of greasy-looking shards of rock that overlapped its head, back and legs, fitting it like a stony suit of armour. A line of jade bristled along its spine and twinkled greenly in the moonlight as it swung its head from side to side. Catching sight of Rose on the water below, it bellowed furiously.

'According to the old legend,' gasped Wat, wiping

his brow with his cuff, 'El Dorado threw gold into the water to appease the demon of the lake.'

'Demon?' said Alex, feeling his stomach turn over.

'Otherwise it would wreak misery on his people, stealing into the village at night and devouring them as they slept. Alack, I never believed in such a beast, what with it being some made-up creature from a flight-brained myth.'

'Made-up creature from a flight-brained myth?' muttered Aries.

'Fain, I meant no insult, ram!' soothed Wat, raising his upturned palms. 'That was before our paths crossed.'

Alex lurched backwards, looking across the water at Rose, white-faced, in the canoe. 'And if it thinks someone is taking its gold away – '

'He'll attack them,' said Wat.

'Then what are we waiting for!' cried Aries as the Guardian spun its head round and began to stalk down the rock towards the lagoon. 'We have to get Rose off the water.'

'Wait!' said Alex, suddenly noticing what the sorceress was doing.

Breathlessly, the others spun round and stared.

Medea was turning circles at the foot of the cliff, twisting her hands out in front of her. Abruptly she threw her arms over her head, releasing streamers of light.

Distracted, the Guardian dipped its head low and watched the dancing beams, fascinated, tilting its snout this way, then that, as she tossed the gleaming plumes higher into the air. Wreathed in dancing black stars, they crackled and spat with energy. Entranced, the Guardian took a lumbering step down the rock in her direction.

'She's drawing it away from the maid,' said Wat, his voice little more than a whisper.

And he was right.

All thoughts of Rose clearly forgotten, the Guardian's eyes flashed like lighthouse flares as it stalked along the top of the cliff, following Medea and her trailing ribbons of light far below. Alex stared, certain that luring the Guardian away before the gold was raised must be the 'much more unpleasant things' the sorceress had told Rose about. Relieved, he realised that as long as it was following Medea, Rose was safe.

Yet how could she keep it distracted for long enough?

As if in answer, the sorceress drew the light back towards her and kneaded it between her hands. Then, throwing it like a basketball towards a hoop, she hurled the glittering globe high up the cliff to spotlight a craggy outcrop just below the summit.

The Guardian turned its massive head, its neck crunching as Alex felt his jaw drop in horror.

Tied spread-eagled across a boulder, high on a rocky ledge above Medea, and struggling hopelessly against the ropes of creepers that bound his wrists and ankles, was Jason.

XXIX
Gang Ram Style

Flung back against the floor of the boat, Rose clung tightly to the canoe sides as it tipped and yawed, giddy as a see-saw on the boiling water of the lagoon. Clumps of rock smashed down either side of her, sending water slapping into the boat as she struggled to pull herself up. Her ears rang with the last of the thunderous rumbles and now she could hear someone screaming, shrill and terrified. Pawing her wet hair from her eyes, she saw the brightly lit outcrop of rock and the man tied to the boulder on it, his hair a flash of yellow against the grey stone. Despite her own terror, she knew that it had to be Jason and fleetingly imagined how clever Medea must have felt in giving the man who'd caused her so much heartache the best seat in the house for tonight's performance.

Suddenly her eye was drawn to a scuttling in the shadows above him, and horrified, she saw something enormous and lizard-like skittering down across the face of the cliff. Her stomach roiled as a gigantic rock-clad caiman edged into the pool of light and threw open its glittering mouth. Unable to drag her eyes away, she pulled herself upright and, pitched and bounced on the water, she stared upwards, utterly frozen with sudden knowledge.

Teeth like shards of rock.

As a wave of terror shuddered through her, she knew that this creature, this monster, this vile, vicious horror, was what her father must have seen when the men finally reached the lagoon. Her heart boomed in her head as the scene flashed in front of her. Daylight. Her father taking geological readings on the shore. The others in their dinghy, sinking their underwater cameras in the murk, and her father glancing up, to see that, that *thing* clambering down from the rock towards them, to stop them from what? Taking its gold? Certain of how the others had perished in the creature's terrible jaws, she scrunched her eyes shut and hunched low in the canoe.

'Rose!' The sorceress's voice splintered her thoughts. High and hectoring, it rang out over the lagoon. 'Start pouring!'

Rose looked across to Medea standing on the shore. She was holding her arms outstretched far beneath the monster, like a weird puppeteer, tweaking its movements on invisible strings, controlling it, enticing it towards Jason.

'Now!' she yelled.

Rose stared at the bag on the floor. What should she do? Biting her lip, she glanced up, desperately scouring the shore for a glimpse of Alex, Aries and Wat, knowing that they could never have imagined Jason turning up like this either. Plucking the first vial out with trembling fingers, she stared at the hateful green lights twinkling inside. She couldn't, she shouldn't, no, she *wouldn't* pour it into the lake. It had never been part of the plan she'd made with the others. She simply had to pretend, that was all. Pretend to be raising the filthy gold. Woo the sorceress into a false sense of security and then destroy her.

Yet, even as she thought it, she knew that it was thoroughly stupid. It was far too late for deception now. If she failed to pour the potion into the lake, Medea would know, she'd know and then they would all be in terrible danger. Her hand was forced. The others would need more time. She clasped the vial tightly in her left hand. For a moment it felt like a hand grenade and the cork its pin, and it was with every cell in her body willing her to stop that Rose yanked it out and tipped the potion into the water.

There was a hissing sound and a whoosh of silvery smoke, as the spangles of green melted together and rippled away like a shimmering electric eel into the depths.

For a moment nothing happened and Rose found herself hoping madly that she might have misread the spell, have added too much Trojan ash or not enough bubbling lava so that the whole charm would fail. As the seconds stretched on, her hope grew and she tried to empty her mind, refusing to picture the gold rising, trying to sabotage the spell.

But, suddenly, like a whale blowing spray, a plume

of lagoon water shot high in the air. Glistening in the moonlight, it churned and frothed, a pillar of water, rocketing out of the lake. Something glinted at the top, like an exhibit on a pedestal, bouncing in the foam. Then, slowly, the pillar of water shrank down and, blinking, Rose saw a narrow gold figurine jostled on its watery top. Closer now, she could see that it was a crudely wrought eagle, its hammered wings tucked tightly behind it. The pillar dropped down again and again, so that it was only a metre, then half a metre above the top of the lagoon, shrinking away to leave the gold nested in a ring of froth on the surface. A second later, a caiman's head bobbed up, then five or six more. There was a fierce wrestling thrash of scales and snouts as the caimans fought to snatch the prize, until one emerged victorious, carrying the eagle in its maw. Turning gracefully in the water, it began paddling towards Medea on the shore.

'The gold's coming up!' gasped Alex.

Aries stared, horrified.

Behind him, Wat gaped like a goldfish, mesmerized by finally seeing the treasure that had lured so many to their deaths. From beneath the bluff, the sorceress's laugh echoed back to them, sharp as shattering glass.

'I can make the distance in twenty strides,' hissed Aries, feeling his hocks trembling as Jason's terrified screams twisted through the air, 'before she gets her hands on it.'

'No,' said Alex.

'But it's the perfect moment,' persisted Aries. 'Look how distracted she is. We could —'

'No!'

Aries looked up into Alex's frowning face, knowing what he was going to say.

'You have to save Jason.'

Aries brain erupted with fury. Wasn't this whole sorry mess Jason's fault in the first place? He was a liar, a coward and a cheat. Twice he'd abandoned them to save himself. And now his sneakiness had finally caught up with him. He snorted hotly and threw back his head. They should just finish the quest, deliver the Nemesis statue and take Rose back to her father.

Except that however much his brain told him it would serve Jason right to perish up there, it didn't change the freezing frost around his heart at the thought of actually leaving Jason to his terrible fate.

'Aries?' Alex crouched down beside him. 'I hate him too, for fooling me, for making me doubt you. Mostly I hate him for the way he left you to be extinguished. But —'

'I know,' snorted Aries.

'Besides,' Alex smiled sadly, glancing up at the rock face, 'you're the only one who can make the climb in time.'

For what felt like a long moment, Aries looked into Alex's anguished face and bit back his anger that of all people it should be Jason who ruined their simple plan to overthrow Medea.

Then he glanced over the boy's shoulder. Over on the shoreline, the sorceress was stooped, calling out to a solitary caiman swimming back to her, with something chunky and gold clamped in its maw.

'You have to get her right now,' Aries said.

Turning, Alex pulled the shield up on to his chest and rubbed Aries' head one last time.

'And soon as we're done,' he promised, 'we'll come up and help you.'

Nodding, Aries stomped backwards out of the bush, wrenching himself free of the branches that snagged his harness. Determined now, he glanced back at Alex, confident that the boy could, no, *would* defeat Medea, and galloped towards the cliff.

The climb to the top was much steeper than it looked, but even with his injuries Aries made light work of it, deftly placing his hooves into every small indentation and sidestepping the clusters of loose shale that had shaken free when the Lake Guardian wrenched himself out of the ridge. Hocks stiffened, he quickly scrabbled up the narrow ledges and, wedging his front hooves into a couple of perfectly sized nooks, peered over the top of the bluff.

Jason was tethered a on a wide plateau a few metres below to his left, squealing and thrashing against the creeper ropes as the monster caiman circled him, its granite tail *chink-chink-chinking* over the rocks.

Instantly sensing the ram's presence, the huge creature paused mid-step and, in stomach-twisting slow motion, tilted its enormous V-shaped head round to regard Aries. Filmy eyelids flicked back over its eyes to reveal twin chunks of gleaming obsidian, twinkling like black glass. And, clearly amused to see Aries, it drew back its lips in a mockery of a smile, its jaws glittering with shards of quartz.

Aries held his breath as the Guardian lurched towards him. Just as suddenly, a flash of blinding white light exploded from the shore below. For a moment the monster froze, a black hump against the dazzling brilliance. A high-pitched yell rang up from the shore and Aries felt his heart soar, knowing that Alex had delivered the statue.

He'd done it.

He'd done it!

Medea was defeated.

Startled, the Lake Guardian now slammed down its foot and shot up the shallow slope, speedy as a sun-warmed lizard, towards Aries. But emboldened by Alex's success, the ram skittered down the slope to meet it, horns first, and, twisting his head at the last moment, caught the Guardian under its jaw with a resounding crunch. Of course, on a normal caiman the throat would have been a fleshy weak spot and might have sent the creature winded, squealing away. But there was nothing fleshy or weak about the Lake Guardian and as Aries stumbled onto the plateau in a clatter of hoofs, his head felt as though he'd slammed it against a brick wall.

Roaring in fury, the Guardian stumbled back into

the pool of light and launched itself a second time at Aries. But Aries reared up out of its way, paddling his front hooves in the air, yelping as the rock-caiman's snout glanced his belly, scraping it like the edge of a barnacled boat. As the Guardian twisted round, Aries brought his hooves furiously down and hammered them over the creature's back, before pounding its terrible muzzle. He lifted his head into the night and snorted in delight. Grunting, the Guardian drew back, pawing at its injured nose and dizzily shaking its head.

Seizing his chance, Aries leaped over its sweeping tail and skidded to a stop beside Jason.

The Argonaut twisted his head to face him, wide-eyed. 'I thought you were —'

'No thanks to you,' snapped Aries, positioning himself behind Jason's head, so that he could see the monster flailing a few metres away as he frantically began chewing at the first creeper.

Luckily, rams' teeth are great at grinding grass, and even though the creeper was tough as ship's rope, in only a few seconds Aries had snapped the first one in two. Then, hearing the crunch of approaching footsteps, he clopped round to Jason's other side, chewing and staring as the Guardian stalked back over the rock towards them.

'Athena preserve us!' cried Jason, reaching across to Aries' harness with his one free hand. He blindly groped for something from its buckles, and flung the first thing he found – the portrait of Zeus – at the Guardian.

Unfortunately, charming pictures of Greek gods are not known for their ability to stop furious monsters in their tracks and this one was no exception. Bouncing off the Guardian's head, a giddily grinning Zeus vanished in a blur of parchment and silver. Fans made from Pegasus's feathers aren't of much use either and despite Jason's furious lobbing, they still twirled into the night, as dangerous as a chicken aerobatics team. Now, finally snapping the last strand of creeper around Jason's second hand, Aries rolled his eyes to see Dionysus's flying cocktail stirrer whizz past his horns.

He snorted, wondering at the Argonaut's desperation.

Until he heard a low, curious grunt.

Twisting his head back, Aries was startled to see the stirrer flip out what appeared to be two metal wings and flap over the rock, looping and diving, stitching the night with a fizzle of orange. It dipped and twirled, fluttering in circles and spiralling down and around the Guardian's head. Fascinated, the giant caiman forgot all about Aries and Jason and began chasing it, lurching up and snapping at it, like the world's ugliest kitten chasing a dazzling dragonfly.

Paddle,

Whir,

Snap!

Paddle,

Whir,

Snap!

Aries lifted his head up from the creeper. 'About my

statue at the zoo,' he said, one eye on the Guardian as it flapped a webbed-foot after the stirrer.

'What about it?' demanded Jason, tearing uselessly at the creeper around his other foot.

Paddle,

Whir,

Snap!

'I want you to stop drawing moustaches on it and hanging targets from its rump.'

'All right,' gasped Jason. 'Just hurry up.'

'And no more funny hats?'

'No more,' said Jason.

Aries chewed again.

Paddle,

Whir,

Snap!

Paddle,

Whir,

Snap!

'And,' said Aries, spitting out the greenery, 'you promise to tell the truth about what happened on this quest?'

For a moment Jason hesitated and Aries took a step backwards.

'Yes,' spluttered Jason, hopelessly yanking at the creeper on his foot. 'Anything!'

Aries chewed again.

They were nearly there.

In just a few short seconds they'd be able to get

down from this terrible place, before the Guardian noticed.

Paddle,

Whir,

Snap!

Paddle,

Whir,

CRUNCH

Tinkle tinkle . . .

Duh?

Aries' ears shot up.

Beside him, Jason straightened up, hopping unsteadily, still tied by one ankle to the boulder.

Together, they stared down the slope.

The stirrer lay in a mangled heap on the rock. Its wings were buckled, its emerald glass shattered. The Guardian snuffled dismally at it, prodding it with its snout, trying to make it fly again. Then, dejected, it swiped the scatter of green glass with its foot and looked up sulkily at Aries and Jason. A flash of moonlight twinkled in the depths of its glassy, disappointed eyes. Just before it shot up on to its legs and thundered up the slope towards them.

Oh dear.

I suppose you've arrived down here on the lagoon shore hoping for some cheers and celebration about Alex having dispatched Medea to the Underworld.

So, this is going to be a shock.

But you see, that huge flash of light wasn't the Erinyes blasting out of the statue at all.

And the high-pitched yell wasn't even remotely triumphant.

In fact, well, perhaps it's best if you simply read on.

Surprise, they say, is the best form of attack. And so it was a great pity that as far as surprise went, Alex's and Wat's attack didn't have enough to cover a gnat's ankles. As soon as Aries had turned towards the bluff, they'd sprinted heads-down across the shore towards the sorceress, aiming to topple her like a poisonous skittle. But as they were closing in on her, just as they were in tantalising statue-slamming distance, she'd spotted Aries clattering up the rock face and, immediately realising that she was under attack, she'd spun round. In her hand she held what looked like a golden eagle, the first piece of El Dorado gold that the lead caiman had brought her. And as Alex and Wat ran towards her, she glimpsed the Nemesis statue, eyes narrowing as if understanding the danger (which, thanks to Jason, she did). Raising the eagle high over her head, she'd unleashed its terrifying power.

A brilliant flash of bone-grey light shot through the air, sending Alex stumbling backwards. He yelled – yes, I'm afraid *that* was the high-pitched cry Aries had heard – and dived out of the way as what seemed to be an octopus of streaming light loomed up in front of them, crackling and spitting, wreathing its ghostly legs out into the darkness around them. Its tendrils unfurled to curl around his neck, chest and arms. They coiled around Wat's mallet-wielding arm. Growing longer, they tangled about their ankles and, with a ferocious yank, sent them both spluttering to the ground. Alex crash-landed, sending the Nemesis statue flying out of his grasp and slap into the mud. Throwing out his arm, he brushed the tip of its base with his fingertips as the quavering light changed around him, thickening into what appeared to be a gelatinous wall. A split second later, it slid backwards, scooping him up like a snowplough. His fingers dragged through the mud as he was slammed back against Wat, and the quivering wall engulfed them, sealing them together into a giant rubbery bubble, which lifted into the air to float a couple of metres above the ground.

Alex punched, he kicked, he jabbed, he tore. Wat pounded the walls with the mallet handle, desperately trying to tear a hole, but each time he struck the sides, they stretched out like bubblegum. Hissing wildly, the snakes tried to pierce it with their fangs.

But it was hopeless.

The walls were unbreakable.

Beneath them, Medea watched, spider-eyed and triumphant, being careful to step quickly away from the Nemesis statute, lying upended in the mud.

Alex stared at it through the bubble. He could still see its base sticking out of the mud and his head hammered with frustration that it was so, so close and yet absolutely unreachable. Doubling over, snatching his breath, he pushed his face up against the clammy wall and watched the glints of red, orange and blue, bright beneath its mud-spattered veneer. For a few seconds more they twisted and bounced, and then, as if knowing what had happened to the Nemesis statue, they faded away to nothing.

Out on the water, Rose was far too horrified to scream.

Dimly aware of the Guardian playfully snapping at something on the rock high above, she gaped at Alex's and Wat's terrified faces as they pummelled from the inside of the trap, feeling sick in the pit of her stomach.

'That's better,' cried Medea, dusting off her hands. She looked across the lagoon at Rose, shaking her head in disappointment. 'C'mon, we have work to finish!'

'You must be joking!' shouted Rose. 'I'll never do another thing you ask. And I know about the gold, Medea. It's not cherished. It's disgusting and poisoned and can never ever help my father!'

'Oh my,' sighed the sorceress. 'I wonder who's been filling your head with such rubbish? As if I didn't know!'

She jabbed the golden eagle into the bubble and it instantly started to shrink.

'Still,' she added, stifling a giggle as the snakes stabbed at the approaching walls with their snouts, 'it'll be the last time they ever interfere. In a few minutes that bubble will be so small, so airless . . . well, you can imagine.'

'Let them go!' shouted Rose, scooping up the vials from the bottom of the canoe. 'Otherwise I'll throw these over the side and you'll never get the rest of the gold!'

Medea sighed. 'Oh, Rose. Why spoil things now when you've been such a marvellous partner?' She smiled spitefully. 'You do realise that I could never have got this far without you? I couldn't have raised Wat and I'd never have found the lagoon. I certainly couldn't have distracted the Lake Guardian and fetched the gold up at the same time. And I wouldn't have this.' She kissed the eagle statuette like a footballer with a trophy. 'Meaning,' she sneered, nodding at the bubble, 'I could hardly have done that!'

Rose felt her words like punches.

'Of course,' continued Medea coldly, 'it would have been quicker and easier, not to mention safer –' she glanced up at the Lake Guardian – 'without your ridiculous change of heart. And if you'd kept your end of the deal, we could have been finished by now. But,' she added, raising the golden eagle high over her head, 'needs must!'

Tilting her face up, she began to turn anti-clockwise, chanting rapidly, her words spilling dark and uneven into the night. Rose noticed the sorceress's face, pinched and furrowed with effort, and felt a spark of hope behind her ribs, knowing that Medea was finding it harder without her help. Perhaps – she tried to think over the wild hammering of her heart in her ears – perhaps, even *with* the golden eagle she wouldn't be able to raise the gold all on her own? Feeling her eyes grow wide, she stared at the dark water around her, hardly daring to breathe as she willed the sorceress to fail.

And then she heard Medea's shrill squeal of delight.

Looking up, she gasped as the sorceress flung out her arm like a flamboyant orchestra conductor to unleash a sweep of caramel light, the colour of rotting apples. Squirming with glowing tendrils, it shot over the lagoon before exploding like hailstones into the water.

Rose felt her stomach flip over as the water instantly began to boil around her. Now, staring down into its depths, she caught a glimpse of something golden, rising like a shoal of glittering fish. She clutched the sides of the canoe, staring in grim fascination, groaning as a clatter of goblets erupted from surface. Behind them, plates, knives and boxes, fashioned from gold, leaped like salmon and splashed back on the swell.

Suddenly a super-sized wave slammed the canoe, throwing Rose backwards on to the floor. For a moment, she stared up, stunned by a rainbow of gold-headed spears that arced over her. Then, struggling to sit upright again, she gaped at the water around her, gleaming with gold figurines and medallions and cups and snake-shaped buckles. A throne with a back carved into a leaping jaguar bobbed madly. Torques and breastplates lolled like flotsam. Pendants the size of ostrich eggs sped over the waves like skimmed pebbles. And everywhere, caimans dived, snapping and grunting after the treasure, snatching it from one another's jaws to return to Medea with it.

'To think of all those years I spent fiddling with wisps of Fleece,' cried Medea, pausing from her chanting to wipe her brow with the back of her arm. 'And now, look at the power I have!'

She scooped up a handful of ancient coins and threw them over the nearest couple of caimans at her feet.

There was a deafening bang, making Rose jump, and she blinked hard as a cloud of bruise-purple smoke enfolded the reptiles. Sneezing against the stench of sulphur that drifted in clouds towards her, she heard a thick, rustling sound, reminding her of umbrellas, giant ones, being opened, and gasped as two huge pairs of wings, long, green and silver-tipped, sprang up through the haze. Flames blasted through the fug as two shimmering dragons stalked out. Each was bridled with a silver harness and snorted fire from their massive nostrils.

But behind them the bubble was shrinking smaller and smaller, and dragging her eyes away from the astonishing creatures, Rose realised that now she could only just make out the pink of Wat's hands, still inside their floppy cuffs, pressed uselessly against the glittering walls as Alex fought on, kicking and punching, jabbing the sides with the shield, stabbing them with the sword. Meanwhile, high on the bluff, the Guardian had stopped swatting at whatever had distracted it and was glowering up the rock at Aries and Jason.

Amused by her horrified face, Medea flicked another bolt of energy from her makeshift eagle wand across the water and sent the canoe torpedoing backwards towards the opposite bank.

Rose sprawled forwards and clung on as the canoe sliced through the water, gasping at the wrongness of everything.

The Nemesis statue was lost.

Alex, Wat, the Gorgon and snakes were trapped in a prison that would crush them out of existence in a few more minutes.

And high on the cliff, the Lake Guardian was thundering towards Aries again.

There had to be *something* she could do.

Crawling to the end of the speeding canoe, she stuck her nose over the edge and saw the sorceress growing smaller in the distance, tickling the dragons under their chins. In desperation, she reached back and unbuttoned the pocket of her shorts and pulled out her own flask of Reversal Potion.

She stared at it, dull purple in the moonlight, biting her lip at the memory of Alex's horrified expression when she'd used it against the conquistadors, his face twisted in fury.

When have you truly seen her magic do anything good?

She scrunched her eyes closed, bewildered. Beneath her, the canoe lurched, bumping faster over the churning, gilded water and for a moment she sank her face against its cool wood in absolute despair. Around her, the waves slapped the boat's sides, bumping it with their flotsam of misery-stuffed trinkets, clattering against its flimsy wood, but as a particularly hefty shield walloped the tip of the canoe, Rose jerked up, blinking. Holding the flask in front of her, she stared at the potion as it slopped and swirled, and suddenly realised something important, something she'd been too worried and frightened and confused to see before now: that this wasn't Medea's magic at all.

It was hers.

There was no pharaoh's bangle here, no Fleece, no gold of El Dorado. Only magic powered by a birthday locket, made from a nugget beloved of the Yanomani people and given as a good wish to her mother.

Gold steeped in love right from the start.

Truly cherished gold.

Not bloated with hatred and suffering.

Which must surely mean that it could not possibly be poisonous?

Energised now, she ripped what remained of the locket from her neck and stuffed it into the flask, gladdened by the answering swirl of blue smoke, spangled with stars that shot up into the night.

Then corking the flask tightly, she took a deep breath.

And dived into the water.

XXX
Croc And Roll

High up on the rock, Aries flew backwards through the air and landed, sprawled like a starfish, the godly gifts he'd carried exploding into the darkness around him. A couple of metres away, the Guardian leered, triumphantly enjoying the ram's breathlessness, and, clearly confident that it had almost won, snatched up a nearby swatch of Penelope's tapestry – Ithaca at sunset – and chewed. Behind it, the smashed tinderbox spluttered and wheezed, spitting out its last sparks like a spent Catherine Wheel.

Slowly, painfully, Aries drew himself up onto his hooves, as behind him Jason feverishly tore at the remaining creeper, tied fast around his left ankle. His back felt bruised, his leg tendons trembled. His muzzle was swollen and his left haunch throbbed where the Guardian's foot had sliced off the harness only seconds before. Worse still, he was just beginning to wonder what had happened to Alex and Wat. After all, that flash of light had been several minutes ago now, which surely meant they should be up on the bluff with him. So why weren't they? And why was the canoe zipping the wrong way over the water, sending up a glittering trail of foam behind it?

Trying to tamp down the bad feeling that plaited his stomachs, Aries watched as the Guardian spat out the tattered remains of the sewing and braced himself for its next attack.

Which is when he noticed the lyre.

Tilted on the rock, it spangled in the moonlight and despite the way the Guardian had tried to chew it, and the drool that now dribbled down its strings, it remained perfectly intact. Unbreakable, able to withstand the roughest voyage, just like Euterpe had said.

Suddenly the gloom filled with the sound of skittering shale and Aries looked up to see the Guardian lurching forward. Seizing hold of the lyre, the ram charged forward and slammed it over the toothy tip of the Guardian's snout. He thrust hard, hard, harder still, forcing it high on to the creature's bumpy nose to jam its frame tight over its jaws.

The Guardian grunted in appalled surprise. Crossing its eyes, it stared down at the strange trap and a moment later began tossing its head, left, right, up, down, snarl, mutter – *twing*, *twang*, *twong* – trying to shake the lyre free. But it was stuck fast. The monster slumped down and tried to bat the lyre off with legs that were far too short and stumpy and, panicked, tried to prise its jaws open. Its neck muscles throbbed. Its cobbled shoulders strained. Muscles bulged fiercely beneath its chin whilst its body rumbled like an earth tremor, quivering and shaking as it strained hopelessly against the instrument's unbreakable frame.

Aries stepped back, cringing as the lyre of Orpheus, famed for its honey-toned melodies, wailed like Scylla with the stomach ache, accompanying the monster's frustrated yowls as it struggled desperately to wrench its mouth free.

But it couldn't.

Whoopee-doo!

Way to go, Aries!

Croc-bopper supreme!

Even Jason was struck silent with grudging admiration as now, thoroughly confused and blazing mad, the Guardian flipped itself up into the air and began its death roll.[60] You see, deep down in his foggy, primitive brain, the Guardian knew that such a move had always led to good things. Except that death rolls in water are one thing and death rolls on a high terrace of rock quite another. Especially when there's a ram standing close by, desperate to find his friends on the shore below, and in possession of the most ferocious kick, which he uses to send a wildly spinning stone caiman tumbling down the slope.

All of which goes to show that gifts from the gods really do what they say on the tin. Well, sort of. After all, the lyre had withstood an epic journey, managed to calm a raging beast and even if it hadn't quite brought

---

60 *In case you're wondering, this is the frenzied spinning that caimans use to pull their prey down under the water, whipping them round faster than a washing machine, until their dinner has less fight left than a pair of soggy underpants.*

the team together in harmony, at least for once Jason had nothing to say. And indeed, how delightful that would all have been, if everyone, and particularly my charming self, could have sat down to a delightful cup of tea and a Custard Cream at that point.

Except that as the Guardian flew off the ledge

W

H

E

E

E

E

!

Alex, Wat, the Gorgon and snakes were finding it almost impossible to breathe inside the shrinking bubble. In fact, Alex was so dizzily close to fainting that he could hardly be sure that he hadn't just imagined seeing Rose drag herself out of the lagoon, blinking and dripping, a few metres away.[61] Beside him, Wat lay half-dazed, slumped in a heap, mumbling under his breath whilst the snakes drooped like wilted asparagus.

But luckily, Medea was busy.

And I say 'luckily' because she was so occupied in chanting and scrunching her eyes closed as she whipped up a storm of magical energy to create her getaway

---

61 *Swimming in the opposite direction from the churning gold, you'll be relieved to hear that she'd been able to keep a safe distance from the caimans. Not to mention setting a new speed record for the under-fourteens' crawl.*

vehicle that she didn't see Rose tiptoe past. Nor, with her head filled by the sort of bone-rattling bangs and hisses that conjuring up a magnificent Greek chariot out of thin air always produces, did she notice the strange trembling that Alex now felt quivering the sides of the bubble. Or hear the rising *chucka-chucka-chucka* noise, raucous as a dumper truck tipping its load of shale, as the Lake Guardian thundered down the rocky ridges towards her.

In fact, it was only when what the lyre finally flew off the Guardian's snout and twanged past her, that Medea spotted the creature at all . . .

. . . spinning like a gigantic totem pole of rock towards her . . .

. . . its tail a blur of pebble-grey

. . . just before it walloped her sideways into the water and crashed on to her spanking new chariot, smashing it to smithereens.

Stumbling to its feet, the Lake Guardian lumbered groggily forward, groaning as the two dragons took gustily to the sky and flapped away. Then, catching a glint of the gold, *his* gold, still clutched in Medea's hand, it scrambled after her.

Now Alex saw Rose sprinting across the shore. She leaped over the Guardian's swishing tail and for a split second Alex met her panic-stricken eyes before she hurled something wet at the bubble. It splashed against the gelatinous sides, dragging them outwards, stretching them, straining and squealing, until the bubble burst with a deafening bang. Reeling, Alex and the others were hurled to the ground, free.

'Yes!' shrieked Rose.

Gasping, Alex glanced up at the rock bluff and, seeing Aries there, stamping his hoofs, safe and victorious, felt a fresh surge of determination. Searching about him, he blinked furiously, scanning the ground for the Nemesis statue. Above his head, the bubble skin spun back out into its original sheet of light and exploded in a shimmer of grey. Momentarily, it lit up the statue's base, and Alex lurched after it. Sensing him, the Lake Guardian swung its head back and snapped ferociously. Desperate, with his sword and shield flung beyond his reach, Alex held the statue out in front of him, swinging it from side to side as the monster lizard plunged forward and clamped its jaws around the statue's head and snatched it from his grasp. Then, seemingly amused by Alex, standing there wholly defenceless, it bit down hard.

There was a sharp crack.

The air bristled as a sudden chill swept over the shore and three heart-freezing screeches rang into the night. Alex gasped, all thoughts of the spoiled weapon lost as the terrible screaming filled his ears, and he scrabbled backwards and grabbed the shield, gaping, as a trio of shadows swept into the air. Bathed in the flood of blood-red light that now poured from the broken statue, the Erinyes hunched together, floating in a circle over the Lake Guardian's head. A low thrumming filled the air and, as Alex watched, three pairs of bat wings emerged from the Erinyes' smoky forms. Black gowns wreathed beneath their feet. Scorpions dripped from their whips and scuttled over the Guardian's back.

Slowly, horribly, the three dog-headed women tilted their snouts to the sky. Now Alex could see their eyes, blazing and red, and their muzzles, matted with rough fur, silhouetted against the dazzling light as they keened together before suddenly snapping their heads down in unison and diving like cormorants for the Guardian. Two slid their hands beneath its front legs, the third seized its tail and together they dragged it into the air, squirming and snapping like a live battering ram. The Guardian twisted and wrestled. It writhed, it wriggled, it roared. But there was no escape as the Erinyes tightened their hold and sped away, rocketing across the lagoon to vanish in a fiery glow.

For a second, Alex stared into the darkness, his ears roaring with his own horrified breathing and the shocked gabbling of Rose and the others behind him.

Then, his eyes glimpsed a movement in the water.

The sorceress was crawling out of the shallows and on to the shore. Weed slithered from her hair. Filthy water streamed over her face, making white streaks in the smears of mud.

Backing away towards the others, Alex watched as she rose slowly to her feet and stood, head down, shoulders hunched, eyes blazing. When she spoke, her voice was low and guttural and spine-freezingly cold.

'How do you plan to send me to Tartarus now?'

she asked, clawing the curtain of sodden hair from her face.

Knowing that Jason must have told her about their plan, Alex felt a flash of fury, but it was immediately swept away by fear when he noticed the gold eagle, smaller now from all its magic, still clasped tightly in her hand.

She smiled gleefully. 'Now that you've managed to lose the statue? And got rid of that tiresome old tooth-bag, too?'

Alex raised the shield, holding it up in front of them all like a writhing, hissing wall.

Medea tipped her head, mocking the squirming snakes with her eyes.

'Alex Knossos, potter, zoo hand and have-a-go hero. Still running around with that ridiculous lump of mutton? Busy poking your nose into my business a second time?' She scowled. 'And you, Rose. Can't you see what a mistake you're making when you have the makings of a truly great sorceress? But then, you're not what you seemed, are you? Or you,' she scowled at Wat, rolling her eyes at his tattered, puffball pants. 'Just look at the three of you. On the outside you're a fop, a fledgling sorceress and a pint-sized hero. But, on the inside you're all the same. Monkeys.' She tapped her nose with her finger, scowling. 'Meddling and sticking these in, trying to mess things up! How very deceiving, don't you think?' Smiling darkly, she stroked the curved beak of the eagle gold. 'All that pretending to be something you're not. After all, monkeys on the inside really ought to look like monkeys on the outside!'

She looked up, her eyes flashing with cold fury, mouthing a curse as tendrils of slime-green light began curling from the gold in her hand.

'No!' yelled Alex.

Instantly knowing what the sorceress was doing, he thrust the shield high in front of the others. 'Get down!'

Pushing Rose and Wat backwards, he lifted the shield high over their heads as the sorceress unleashed a bolt of stinging magic at them. Yet, in that split second he saw the snakes, dark as an after-image, scrunch-faced, bracing themselves against the rancid green glow hurtling towards them and, realising their danger, his mistake, he flipped the shield over.

Instantly there was a heavy metallic clunk, like a sword crashing against the shield, sending Alex and Rose toppling over backwards to land on Wat. The snakes reared up, wailing and snapping around the Gorgon's face as the spell slammed into the mirrored back of the shield, denting it – and, bouncing back, reflected straight into the sorceress's chest.

'Nooooooo!'

Medea's scream ripped through the night, high and shrill. Then her voice began to waver, sliding down the octaves, lower and lower, until there was nothing left but a low, excited grunt.

Blinking against a thick swirl of black light, Rose, Alex and Wat peered out from the rim of the shield to see her staggering backwards, the golden eagle falling from her furry hand. Shaking, her arms and legs splayed out like a star, her fingers fluttering madly, her head tossing from side to side. But now, her legs began to shrink and bow out. Lurching from side to side, she stared down, appalled, as her arms grew longer, until her knuckles touched the mud on either side of her. Tufts of russet-coloured hair sprouted from her face as she shrivelled further down, hunched beneath wide shoulders, her cries growing deeper and louder and thicker, as she began to hoot and yammer.

Gaping, Alex helped Rose to her feet and they stood together, staring in astonishment.

In the place where Medea had been standing, a howler monkey stretched up on to its back feet and, seeing them, began to thump its chest. Its eyes grew huge, as it swung its head, its huge mouth barking and howling and sending spittle flying into the night. Moonlight danced off its flame-red fur – and the single streak of purple that ran down the left side of its body. Stepping back, Rose and Alex edged away as the creature threw itself into the mud and hammered wetly with small, tight fists.

With a start, Rose noticed the golden eagle lying close by its feet and, darting forwards, snatched it up and hurled it far into the lagoon. Then she tossed in the shields and scattered coins and jewellery too. Out in the water, the caimans stopped fighting over the floating gold and swam quietly away in the darkness.

Roaring in fury, the howler leaped on to its back feet, took one last belligerent look at them and spun away. It lumbered into the rainforest and, hurling itself at the first tree, raced up into the leaves before looping away through the branches, into the night.

'Who needs statues or Tartarus?' yelled Alex, throwing his arms around Rose and Wat. Together they jumped up and down, cheering and laughing and gadzooking at the top of their voices.

Seconds later, there was a heavy thrumming of hooves as Aries galloped over the shore towards them, in a blizzard of sprayed mud, and their loud yelps of delight sent the vultures flapping off the trees.

Rose and Alex threw their arms around him and hugged him, too. Even Wat managed a gentlemanly pat on the head or two.

In fact, they were so busy congratulating each other and cheering that no one actually realised that Jason had arrived down from the bluff until he spoke.

'Well done, team!' he announced.

At which nobody took any notice at all.

'Athena will be so pleased with me,' he continued. He ran his hands through his hair, gazing out over the water, now lying still beneath the moonlight. 'Such a huge quest, filled with danger and ending with me choosing to square up to the cruel sorceress of Greece all alone,' he said, beginning to rehearse his story for the Underworld. 'Oh, how the goddesses will swoon when I tell them I trusted to love, only to have Medea viciously try to destroy me. Yet I managed to break free, despatch the monster and, battered and bruised, raced down the bluff to snatch the shield from your trembling hands.'

Behind him, Alex, Rose, Aries and Wat exchanged looks of absolute disbelief as Jason leaped backwards, holding an imaginary shield in his hands.

'Of course, since you'd wasted the Nemesis on the monster,' he went on, staring out at the water, 'I was forced to think on my feet. But that old Perseus shield-flip, eh, Alex? They'll love that. Oh, wait till I tell Apollonius. What a flourish he'll end my tale on!'

Laughing, he glanced back over his shoulder.

And found he was standing completely alone.

Epilogue
Homeward Bound

A few days later, Rose stretched luxuriously in her pink squishy chair, smiling as the air stewardess walked towards her, carrying a tray of lime-green mango coolers. Picking up a glass, she took a long sip, feeling the citrus tingle on her tongue, and watched her father, seated beside her, gazing out of the window, transfixed by the river, twisting through the rainforest below.

Surprised?

Rose was.

Suddenly her father glanced back at her over his shoulder and pointed to something through the aircraft window.

'Jabiru stork!' he cried, his cheeks flushed. 'Rose! Come and have a look!'

Setting down her glass, Rose jumped up and pressed her forehead against the window. Beneath them, a flock of great white birds flapped and wheeled, their black heads gleaming in the sunlight.

'They were believed to be almost extinct!' he said. 'This is amazing!'

Rose turned back to her father, beaming. His eyes were bright, glittering with excitement.

'Yes,' she said, feeling her heart soar like the birds outside. 'It is!'

She sat back down and listened as he gabbled on about flight paths and nesting sites, delighted to hear the warmth in his voice, brimming with all the old enthusiasm she'd missed for so long, and felt a wave of pure joy engulf her.

Even now, she could hardly believe all the remarkable things that had happened since they'd defeated the sorceress. Starting with the realisation that she'd been right about her own magic. You see, when she'd splashed her spell over the bubble, reversing Medea's murderous magic to save Alex and Wat, she'd proved that her magic and Medea's were two very different forces.

The sorceress's magic was big and world-changing. It was driven by the sort of gold that should stay locked in tombs, or left at the bottom of lagoons, because it conjured up murder, mayhem and misery, and ruined people's lives. Rose's magic was smaller and more personal. Most importantly, it was kinder, just like the gold given with the love that fuelled it.

Taking a deep breath, she closed her eyes, feeling the sunshine stream through the window, warming her face. Drifting into her thoughts, she felt an even bigger glow inside, certain now that her worry earlier that week – that dabbling in magic would make her as cold-hearted and selfish as Medea – was completely unfounded. She could stay the same old Rose as she'd ever been, but with her own magic too, magic that would do good things.

Better still, Alex and Aries had believed it too.

Which was why for the last few days they'd helped her brew enough potion to take her father safely back to London.

She stifled a giggle, thinking back to Aries, who'd become quite the celebrity in the village, all decked out with garlands of orchids and his face striped with ochre, stirring the potion in the big scrying pot, a long spoon in his mouth, twirling his tail round and round in concentration. Meanwhile, Wat had busied himself finding the ingredients and Alex had trimmed phoenix feathers, sneezing in a blizzard of copper-brown tendrils.

Jason, as I don't suppose you'll be at all surprised to hear, had been about as much use as a concrete kite. Choosing to spend the time waiting for Eduardo to come to collect them lolling beneath the trees drinking milk from coconut shells, he'd boasted to any passing villager who'd listen. And, oh, how the tribeswomen had swooned when he told them about killing the three-headed cat, simpering at how he'd survived the swarm of army ants and sighing at how boldly he'd led a boy and a ram through the jungle.

Meanwhile, Rose had found it horribly difficult to concentrate on spell-casting, her blood boiling at over-hearing his tall tales whilst she'd worked inside Medea's hut. How dare he, she'd riled, carry on lying and cheating and making himself the big, clever, hero when he'd really done nothing but run away and abandon the others? As you might imagine, she'd had just about enough of people warping the truth lately and yet here he was, bragging and swaggering, leaving her, frankly, flabbergasted that he'd ever become the long-remembered Greek hero up on Earth, fearless and undaunted, in books and movies. At least until the others explained that his fame rested solely on some ridiculous old poem written years after the actual voyage of the *Argo*, because the ship's log had been lost overboard at sea.

Lost?

Tossed, more like, she decided, and, thinking back to what she'd read about him in the journal-scroll, imagined him flinging it into the waves himself, in a rage at reading the true account of his 'courage'. Only for a slim, white hand to dip into the green and retrieve it as a fond keepsake for years afterwards.

'Penny for your thoughts,' said Hazel, jolting her from her light doze.

Rose opened her eyes to see the pop star walking back into the cabin from the sleeping quarters at the back. She still looked exhausted and pale, and when she smiled, Rose noticed that it didn't quite reach her eyes.

'I want to thank you,' said Rose.

Hazel sat down beside her, a little awkwardly, biting her lower lip, and Rose realised that even now Hazel still felt ashamed about leaving her alone in the jungle to find her father. Yet Hazel had tried to be a good friend, she really had, Rose knew that, but Medea was just too smart and spiteful an enemy. She thought back to the spider scuttling over the cabin floor towards Hazel, and shuddered, certain now that the sorceress had sent it, transformed into a lily, simply to split the two of them up. After all, Rose thought, Medea had always known exactly which buttons to press to make people do precisely as she wanted, and Hazel had been easy prey to her.

'I mean it,' said Rose earnestly. 'For everything you've done. For getting me here, for busting Alex and Aries out of the police station and helping them find me, and for flying Dad and me home. And, especially,' she smiled, remembering the sound of the cheering crowds filling the Manaus Opera House, 'for last night.'

Hazel shrugged. 'It's the least I could do.'

'Hardly,' said Rose, handing her a drink from the tray and knowing how far Hazel had gone out of her way to help, offering to throw the freebie concert at the opera house, calling in lots of favours from her musicians scattered all round the globe and flying them back to work day and night through the weekend to make it a success. Meaning that, for the first time since the disastrous first night of *Madama Butterfly* – whereupon Rosita de Bonita had fled to Venice to rest her arias – the building had been opened up again. Hazel had performed to a delighted crowd, distracting just about everyone, simply so that a gang of ghosts could sneak in, unnoticed, to hurry to the statue of Orpheus on the first floor.

Hazel took the seat opposite Rose's father and leaned

forward to listen to him tell her about the lecture he was planning to give on his return: how soon after they'd found evidence of the old tribe there'd been a terrible accident on the lagoon and, unable to cope mentally, he'd been cared for by the Kaxuyana and Medea – a fashion designer, of all people! – until Rose, his wonderful daughter, had managed, with Hazel's generous help, to find him.

Smiling, Rose thought back to the whoops and cheers of the crowd the night before, thrumming through the elegant corridor, as she'd stood with the others. She recalled the matching expressions on Alex's and Aries' faces, triumphant to have succeeded in the quest, but frustrated too, and angry, as Jason shot through the doorway ahead of them and raced down the glistening rocky corridor, back to the Underworld.

'It'll be all right,' Rose had promised them. 'Going home this time will be different.'

Alex had shrugged, unconvinced, smiled and hugged her again, and after several more rough rammy licks from Aries, and a splendidly flamboyant bow from Wat,[62] they'd turned and stepped into the corridor back to the Underworld.

Sighing contentedly, she reached into the pocket of her shorts and brought out the small chunk of gold that

---

62 Yes, Wat too. After all, the young explorer hadn't met a pretty young queen for nearly four hundred years, and particularly not one with a network of portals stepping out all over the world. As you might imagine, this was a far more tempting prospect than returning too quickly to an eternity of croquet with one's parents.

was all that was left of Aries' horn after using it on the gallons of Reversal Potion they'd made. It glinted, buttery in the sunshine. Gold, from a fabulous creature of myth and given with love, gold that had powered the potion, and filled the hut with trails of blue and green smoke, stars and giggles.

And yet, so many things lately had glittered on the surface only to turn out to be something much darker on the inside: Medea's hollow promises, what truly lay at the heart of the El Dorado gold, and Jason's 'legendary' courage. She turned the nugget over in her fingers. But some things had remained twenty-four-carat pure, hall-marked and genuine. Like Alex's and Aries' friendship. They'd come back and protected her, saving her, not from Medea, but from her own dazzled foolishness, bringing her back to her senses before she could have put the wretched El Dorado gold into Medea's hands. She shivered, knowing how close she'd come to making the sorceress unstoppable, arming her with enough power to stir up wars and bring down famines, to turn people against one another, to poison all the good things around her until they were rotted and deadly.

Sitting back, she wondered about the future, certain that her magic had a place in it. But only a small one. After all, it was no match for friends and family. Her magic had rescued her father from the jungle, making him temporarily well enough to travel home to London. But it was the doctors and nurses who would truly heal him, together with his family and friends, the people who loved him. She shivered, understanding that Medea had never known that sort of love in her life. Neglected as a little girl, abandoned by a father who'd spent his days in awe of the Golden Fleece, only to be heartlessly betrayed by Jason, the only man she'd ever cared for, she'd come to rely on magic instead. Ever more powerful, ever more poisonous, ever more twisted, it had given her what she needed and turned her into the person she'd become.

Still, Rose smiled, buttoning the gold safely back into her pocket, Aries' gold, together with the ingredients from Medea's hut, now jammed into the rucksack at her feet, would certainly be useful. After all, she reminded herself, fledgling sorceresses needed something to open portals in London museums when the guards weren't looking, in order to visit their best friends in the Underworld, didn't they?

She tilted her chair back and rested her head on its big fluffy cushion.

In a few hours' time they would land at Dallas and change to the flight back to London. She could hardly wait to see her mother's astonished face when her husband walked into the arrivals lounge, and knew that all of their lives were about to change for the better.

Just like Alex's and Aries'.

As she drifted off to sleep, she saw them again in her mind's eye, walking away, framed by the rocky, torch-lit corridor back to the Underworld: a ram with a broken horn, a muddy boy with snakes looming over his shoulder hissing their goodbyes to her, and Wat, trailing ribbons of stuffing from his ruined puffballs, as the echoes of Jason's footsteps rang back to them. They looked like anything but heroes. Not like Jason, bounding ahead, impatient to delight Athena with his tale as he gave her the rather special present that Rose had sent her, all wrapped and tied with ribbons, to thank her for sending them back and protecting her from Medea.

But then, she smiled, imagining Athena opening her gift, it was always what was on the inside that counted.

'Two treats in one day!' cried Athena, as Jason handed her the gift. 'Not only does our greatest hero return, but he brings me an Earth souvenir, too!' she smiled.

In the flickering torchlight of the throne room of Castle Hades, the goddesses Hera, Euterpe and Artemis clapped wildly, whilst Aphrodite leaped forward and planted a kiss on the Argonaut's cheek. Meanwhile, standing right at the back, way behind the jostling crowd of courtiers and maids who'd gathered at the news of Jason's return, Aries looked up at Alex and Wat, a furious snort rumbling low in his throat. As it grew, people glanced back over their shoulders, tutting before scowling at Alex. Clearly, he thought, expecting him to clamp the ram's mouth shut, the way he usually did.

Except that he wasn't likely to do that again.

Ever.

Instead, he stared back at them, as the trembling bellow grew louder. Soon, it became ferocious enough for people to step aside as they nervously gave Aries a wide berth, accidentally opening up a pathway over the glittering mosaic floor to the two huge thrones at the front.

Now Alex could see Athena clearly, her face beaming as she unpicked the red ribbon of Rose's gift, and he rubbed Aries' head, wondering again why Rose had been quite so keen to send the goddess something.

Beside her, Persephone looked up and, spotting Wat, leaned forward to Jason.

'A guest?' she murmured. 'Have you brought us back some new company, too? You are so, so clever!' Giggling, she slipped off her throne and skipped through the sea of nods and curtseys to Wat, who gave the most splendid bow of all.

'Madam,' he said, straightening up again. 'Wat Raleigh, explorer, poet and soldier at your service!'

'Ooo, goody!' said Persephone, quickly sliding her arm through his. 'How completely exciting. Do tell us all about the quest! Was it horribly frightening? Were you scared?' She glanced down at his tattered satin pants, her eyes like saucers. 'And what happened to those?'

'Fain, it was terrifying,' said Wat, escorting her back to her throne. 'A daring enterprise from start to finish, but, madam, verily it is these two,' he turned back to smile at Alex and Aries, quieter now, who were following behind, 'this brave boy and this magnificent ram, whom you should be prettily chin-wagging with. For the exploit was entirely theirs.' He smiled, stroking his neat beard. 'With a little starring role for myself, of course.'

'Really?' Distracted, Athena glanced up from her half-unwrapped parcel.

'Yes!' snorted Aries, and slammed down a hoof.

'No,' smiled Jason, stepping quickly in front of Wat and offering a dazzling smile, as the other goddesses encircled him, giggling. 'Can't you see the man's a clown? Why else would he be wearing such ridiculous clothes?'

Alex watched them, bristling. He'd expected the twisting feeling in his stomach, the thumping of his heart and the way his skin prickled with annoyance. But actually standing here, watching him preen, offering that perfect, practised smile and switching on those familiar dreamy expressions on the goddesses' faces, it felt a million times worse. Now, watching the Argonaut whispering to Aphrodite, his mind shot back to Aries, lying bleeding and almost extinguished on the Amazon mud and feeling a wave of anguish so strong that it almost took his breath away, he walked up to the front.

'Goddess,' he said. 'Wat is telling the truth. It was he, Rose and I who defeated the sorceress, whilst Aries fought a terrible monster to rescue Jason.'

Athena glanced up, amused. 'Rescue Jason?'

'*Our* Jason?' teased Persephone, pulling a bewildered face at the crowd behind her, making them laugh. 'Whatever next?'

The room rang with coarse laughter.

'I think the sun has addled their minds,' said Jason, as Aphrodite shook her head prettily, holding a hand to her mouth in giggly shock.

'No,' said the Gorgon, raising her voice above the merriment. Flame-eyed, she fixed her stare on Athena. 'It's true, mistress. Alex and the others had to complete the quest, because Jason had run away. It was this boy who turned the shield and destroyed her with her own magic.'

Now the laughter was deafening. It bounced off the walls and swelled though the room, surging and rising like a storm.

Furious, Grass Snake lurched off the shield, boggle-eyed.

'And s-s-saved usss, too!' he cried, his voice lost in the gales of merriment.

Standing there, forced to listen to it, Alex felt as though his head would explode. He turned to the courtiers, and knew that this feeling, tight behind his ribs, was what Aries must have felt, treated like a joke, ever since he stepped into the Underworld. Beside him, the ram drew closer, looking up and urging him on, his eyes bright and excited.

'All right then,' shouted Alex. 'How do you think Aries got these wounds?' He stared into their ruddy, laughing faces. 'From fighting a monster three-headed cat, when a terrified Jason had abandoned us, that's how!'

'Terrified?' Euterpe, red-faced with amusement, turned to Hera, laughing heartily beside her.

'The cat was bigger than the Nemean Lion!' hissed Krait, whipping out in a blur of black and white, sending the muse of music backwards in fright.

'And Alex killed it,' said Grass Snake.

'With arrowsss,' said Adder.

'And the thunderbolt!' said Viper.

'And pure courage,' finished Aries, with a furious snort.

'Enough!' snapped Jason, flapping at the serpents with his hand. 'Goddess, have them removed from the palace. Can't you see how they're trying to grasp some small slice of glory for themselves?' he said, turning to face her. 'Surely you can —'

But his words died in this throat.

Athena wasn't listening.

She was too busy reading over the tattered, sea-stained scroll she held in her hands.

Jason stood frozen, gaping at it, his eyes wide with recognition and shock. Then his eyes slid towards the heap of paper and red ribbons at her feet, the wrapping that Rose had bought in Manaus, clearly unable to believe just what it had contained.

Around them, the crowd watched Athena's grey eyes darken and the smile slip from her face. Now they stopped laughing, their guffaws and wheezing fading, turning into a rush of curious, muffled whispers and then silence, leaving everyone as still as statues. For long moments the only sound in the throne room was a loud slobbering and squeaking as Cerberus chewed his favourite ducky toy, bone and ball all at the same time, until Athena finally looked up. Being the goddess of wisdom, of course, she had immediately recognised the truth of the words on the page and when she turned to look at Jason, her eyes were as cold and grey as ashes from a dead fire.

'Goddess,' said Jason, his smile hollow and held rigidly on his face. 'What foolishness is this?' He reached for the scroll and Athena snatched it away. 'Why waste our time on such . . . such tricks,' he stuttered, 'when I should be telling you how I defeated the sorceress?'

Abruptly, Athena turned away from him, and regarded Alex and Aries with fresh curiosity.

'Actually,' she said, meeting Aries' bright eyes. 'I'd rather hear it from the ram.'

Oooh, I do love a jolly ending, don't you? And this one makes me want to boogie round the front room, just thinking about everyone returning happily home. Well, everyone apart from Medea, of course, and that really has me shaking a tail feather.

Hoochy-scoochy! Waggle my rear!

You see, whilst Athena and the crowd at the palace settled down to listen to Aries telling them what had actually happened on the quest, and Rose held her father's hand as the plane soared above the Amazon, Medea the bug-bitten howler monkey was sulking high in the leaves of a Brazil nut tree. A particularly spiky and beetle-busy Brazil nut tree, I might add, and one thundering with the hoots and grunts of other howlers, honking round her like a herd of windy walruses.

Seemingly nothing more than just another monkey now, she had soon been raucously accepted by the troupe. And I mean *raucously*. Because, for those non-zoologists among you, let me tell you that these monkeys make more racket than a stage full of screeching rock stars trying to be heard over a team of vacuum-cleaner testers hoovering around a passing brass band. And they're even more deafening when they're yammering right into your ear hole. As Medea might have told you herself, save that in that din she'd never have heard you asking, and besides, she couldn't have answered anyway, could she, what with her being a monkey, remember?

To the left of her, a young howler cheerfully sprayed the leaves below with wee – something, I'm afraid, that passes for fun in monkey circles – but comes as a terrible shock to someone who until recently was a snooty-booty high-society sorceress. To her right, a big, russet male appeared to be blowing her kisses, and every time she leaned back against the tree trunk, she was startled by the unwelcome prod of fingers in her fur, as the grandmother of the group, a grumpy-looking monkey with piggy eyes, plucked lice from her fur and chewed them wetly.

Grunting in disgust, Medea closed her eyes and tried to shut out the clamour and the heat and the prospect of yet another fistful of green bananas for dinner.

Things, she decided, could not be any worse.

Which was when the bellowing chorus around her drained away and in the light twittering of finches left behind, Medea heard a new sound. She snapped open her eyes, noticing the other howlers, paused and mute, their faces upturned, their bowl-mouths slack with wonder, as the unmistakable throb of an engine grew louder. Turning her snub nose to the sky, she saw a bright pink plane gliding across a perfect stretch of blue.

Instantly her brain scorched with rage. Fury flashed through her limbs, white-hot, propelling her on to her back feet. She stretched up, she bunched her hands into fists, she waved them wildly over her head, hooting madly after the distant aircraft. Then, snapping her tail out to swing it like a whip – the tail that she should actually have been using to hang on to the branch – she overbalanced and shot backwards off the bough.

Wham!

Bam!

Slam!

– she hurtled down through the trees

Smack!

Thwack!

Crack!

hitting every branch on the way

'!'

'!'

'!'

– hurling monkey curses into the air (curses that I shall not repeat here because I am far too refined for that) to land in a tangled heap in a prickle fig bush.

Moments later, she groaned dizzily, peering up to see the greenery overhead quivering with the other howlers, swinging, dangling and whooping with glee. Then, summoning up the last scrap of her dignity, which isn't easy with a bottom full of thorns, she lumbered away into the shadows.

Don't Know Your Hades From Your Harpies?

Then Take A Sneaky-Peek At The Greeky-Speak Bclow!

Achilles (pronounced *A-kill-ees*)
Achilles was the most famous warrior in Greek myths and fought and died in the War of Troy. Because she loved her little boy so much, Mummy Achilles tried to make him immortal by dipping her baby into the River Styx. Unfortunately, rather than let him doggy-paddle in his water wings, she held him by his heel, so that this part of his body didn't get wet and wasn't protected by the river's magic. Consequently, Achilles was killed when Prince Paris fired an arrow into his foot. Nowadays, we still used the term 'Achilles' heel' to mean somebody's weak spot.

Agora
The *agora* was the Ancient Greek marketplace where various traders brought their wares to sell. Most towns enjoyed a flower market (the flora-agora), a sword market (the war-agora) and a pet market, bursting with dogs, cats and gerbils (the paw-claw-and-gnaw-agora).

Alexander the Great

Alexander the Great was one of the cleverest military leaders of all time and conquered a third of the globe from the saddle of his faithful horse, Bucephalus. The stallion had once been regarded as furious and untamable, but the teenage Alexander quickly spotted that the gigantic neddy was simply scared of his own blooming enormous shadow. Turning him away from the sun, he won the horse's trust and from that day on they were inseparable. Alexander rode Bucephalus into nearly all of his battles and when the horse died, he founded a city in his steed's honour, called Bucephala. Making it lucky, I suppose, that Alexander hadn't named him Hoofy-Pops. I mean, who'd want to live in Hoofy-Pops-Ville?

Apollonius of Rhodes and 'The Argonautica'

Voyage of the *Argo*? Is there an app for that? Yes, there certainly is: Ap-ollonius of Rhodes. He was the Ancient Greek who famously wrote about it around 3 BC in a long poem called 'The Argonautica'. Not much of a poem, though, if you ask me. Waffles on for ages without a single rhyme. Personally, I think a snappy limerick would have been much better, say:

Some heroes of long-ago Greece
All muscles and knobbly knees
Sailed far just to snitch
With Medea the witch
Aries' glorious Fleece

Atalanta

Atalanta was the only female Argonaut. She usually spent her days running wild in the hills and shooting things with her bow and arrows. Of course, having so much fun, she didn't want to have a husband and settle down, and so, to rid herself of any suitors, she challenged them to a footrace. Being so fast, she always won and then executed the loser, saving all that bother with big white frocks and bouquets. However, her luck finally ran out when she raced sneaky Hippomenes, who threw three golden apples ahead of her as they sprinted. Unable to resist their lure, Atalanta slowed down to pick them up, pausing just long enough for Hippomenes to whip past and win. Result: wedding cake all round.

Boreas

The Greek god of winter, snow and frost, Boreas was also the god of the north wind. He had three brothers: Zephyros, god of the west wind, Notos, god of the south wind and Euros, god of blowing draughts up Scotsmen's kilts.

Centaurs

Centaurs have the heads, arms and torsos of men and the bodies of horses. Being a somewhat temperamental bunch, they were often to be found causing havoc around Ancient Greece. Some enjoyed jumping the stalls in the market (shopping centaurs) whilst others insisted on competing in the Olympics (sports centaurs). However, the most troublesome of all were the ones who hoofed on stage in the middle of a Greek play in order to do an inappropriate tap dance. These were known as centaurs of attention.

Charybdis and Scylla (pronounced *Karib-dis* and *Cilla*)
The original Bubble and Shriek of the ocean, you wouldn't want to come across these two terrors on your water-skiing lesson. This is because Charybdis was a ferocious whirlpool that sucked down any passing ship while Scylla was a six-headed sea-monster with tentacles and a ring of howling dogs' heads around her waist. Best friends, these two haunted the sea close to one another, forcing any passing seafarers into a grim choice of being drowned or devoured. Hold on a minute whilst I cancel my Greek cruise . . .

Chiton
Although pronounced 'kite-on' this has nothing to do with tying a diamond-shaped flying toy on your back and running round in circles to see if you can take off. It is the name given to the draped tunics that both men and women wore in Ancient Greece.

Cyclopes
The Cyclopes were a race of giants, each with a single eye in the middle of their forehead. Known for their brute strength, they often helped Hephaestus, the black-smith god, at the forge in making thunderbolts for Zeus.

They also made Artemis's bow and arrows, Poseidon's trident, Achilles's sword and a range of novelty stands to set down hot pots of moussaka from the oven.

Daedalus

Daedalus was a smarty-pants Ancient Greek inventor, who made wings from wax and feathers, so that he and his son, Icarus, could escape from prison. Sadly, being a bit of a show-off, Icarus ignored his dad's warnings not to fly too near the sun and was so busy looping the loop and throwing funky shapes to scare the seagulls that he didn't realised how high he'd risen until the sun's rays melted the wax of his wings. By then it was too late, and he tumbled into the sea, in a flurry of feathers, and drowned.

Drako

Drako was the nickname of the Dragon (or Drakon) of Kolkis, the huge, man-eating serpent who guarded the Golden Fleece that hung in the Sacred Grove. Never sleeping, he often passed the time by playing draughts with Aries, using the dented helmets of thieves for counters. There were lots of these lying around, being all that was left of men who'd crept in to steal the Fleece, only to end up sliding down Drako's long, long throat instead. Games of I-Spy, however, were less fun since the giant snake always spied something beginning with 'T', which when you live in a forest, doesn't make for a very exciting competition.

Eros

The toddler son of Aphrodite was a right little devil with his bow and arrows, and spent his days firing darts of desire into people's hearts to make them fall in *lurve* with each other. However, having shot an arrow into Medea's heart, the little cupid then stopped for lunch. Unfortunately, Aphrodite had mashed up some greens for him. This later triggered a terrible attack of the hiccups, meaning that the arrows he fired at Jason's heart flew into the pond – *hic!* – the trees – *hic!* – and the feathery derrière of a chicken who happened to be passing at the time – *hic!-SQUAWK!* Consequently, Jason never felt the same way about Medea as she did about him, and some people might say that all the horrible things that followed weren't really Jason's fault at all, but down to Eros and the curse of the Brussels sprouts.

Euripides

Euripides was the name of the Ancient Greek who wrote a famous play about Medea in which he made her out to be even more of a moo than she was. (And that is certainly saying something.) His name is pronounced 'Yoo-rip-er-dees', and indeed, had Medea found his pile of writing before the actors, she'd quickly have instructed her familiar, 'You rip-er-dees up!' before anyone else could read them.

Greek chorus

A Greek chorus was a small group of actors who spoke,

sang and acted as one during a play to help the audience understand what was going on. They did this by wearing large masks, depicting happy or sad faces, and going 'Hooray!' or 'Woe! Woe!' according to the play's story. They were also handy at waking up audience members who'd nodded off and were distracting everyone else with their snoring, by lining up close by and yelling 'Fire!'

Grey Sisters

The Grey Sisters were three old ladies who lived in a cave on a windswept hill in Ancient Greece. They had grey hair, grey skins and even greyer moods on account of having only one eye and one tooth to share among them. This situation led to dreadful squabbling, and particularly at Christmas, when there was often something good to watch on the telly and Santa had left them a bumper box of toffees to eat.

Hades (pronounced *Hay-deez*)

Hades is another name for the Greek Underworld and also the name of its king. Consequently the monarch's letters were addressed to: 'HRH Hades, Hades Castle, Hades', which made the postman's job much easier. Or at least it would have done if Cerberus hadn't been quite so fond of chasing him around the royal rhododendrons.

Harpies

Vile creatures with the heads of women, the bodies of giant birds and a wicked way with their handbags, who were famous for swooping from the sky to snatch the snacks of unsuspecting passers-by.

Hecate (pronounce *Heck-a-tee*)

Spooky Hecate is the goddess of sorcery and magic, and is often shown in old pictures carrying two lit torches. Scholars say this is because she used them to light the way when she helped Demeter search for her daughter, Persephone, after Hades stole her away. In actual fact, she needed them each night to find her pets, a pair of badly behaved ghost dogs, called Hocus and Pocus, who loved nothing better than having a roll in the middle of a meadow at midnight. Well, have you ever tried finding ghost dogs in the dark? Quite.

Helen of Troy

The goddesses Hera, Athena and Aphrodite were one day squabbling over who was the prettiest. To stop their bickering, Zeus told Paris, a prince from Troy, to be the beauty-contest judge. Each goddess wanted to win and offered Paris a bribe: Hera promised him power; Athena, victory in war; and Aphrodite, the love of Helen, the most beautiful woman on Earth. Paris instantly crowned Aphrodite 'Miss Olympus' and claimed his prize.

Oh, see,
Paris and Helen,
Sitting in a tree!
K-I-S-S-I-N-G!

Lovely. Except that their romance led to the War of Troy because Helen was actually married to King Menelaus of Sparta, and he wasn't nearly so keen on her new boyfriend.

Hippocrates (pronounced Hipp-ock-rat-eez)

Hippocrates was a real person and is considered the first Western doctor in history. Modern doctors still take his 'Hippocratic Oath', a set of rules rather like the Scout's promise, which includes vowing to keep what the patient tells them a secret and not laughing out loud when they show them the spots on their bottom.

Minotaur

The Minotaur was a monster with the head and shoulders of a bull and the body of a man. He was locked up in a maze beneath the royal palace of Knossos on the island of Crete. This was partly because he kept devouring young men and women, and partly because he caused the most dreadful havoc in the china shops around the island.

Nemean Lion

This monster lion lived in Nemea and ate everybody who crossed its path. No one could stop it because its coat was as tough as armour and ordinary weapons were useless against it. Nevertheless, Herakles – not being the brightest shield on the battlefield – set out to slay it with his arrows. These bounced off the lion – *bing, bang, boing* – thwacking

Herakles on the head – *ping, pang, poing* – until he finally decided to bop the lion with his club and strangle it instead. Then, fancying the pelt as a cloak, he tried to skin the lion with his sword. Duh? The sword was about as much use as a banana. The sun went up, the sun went down and still he tried and indeed, he might still have been there today had it not been for Athena, who suggested he use one of the lion's own claws to do the job instead.

Nymphs

Nymphs are female nature spirits who flounce around forests in floaty frocks going 'Ooo!' (the nymphs, not the frocks). They mostly spend their days singing and paddling their little feet in streams. However, they occasionally throw woodland parties, drink far too much buttercup wine and end up shouting the most unladylike words.

Obol

An obol was a silver coin used in ancient Athens. However, unlike most currency, it could be spent *after* death, too. This was because Charon, the skeleton ferryman, demanded a fare of one obol to take the recently departed over the River Styx and into the Underworld. Being stuck in a spidery cavern with rising damp seeping up your shinbones and an endless procession of customers who were never pleased to see you made Charon rather gloomy. But, luckily for him, those obols kept jingling into his piggy bank so that he was finally able to buy a retirement apartment, with a view of Hades castle, and bingo in the lounge on Sundays.

Odysseus

Odysseus was a right old clever-clogs who came up with the idea of the Wooden Horse of Troy. He also led the soldiers, secretly hiding in the horse's tummy, out into the city at midnight and threw open the city gates to the Greek army, who stormed in to win the war. However, he wasn't nearly so smart at sailing, as it took him a whole ten years to return to his island home of Ithaca, and his wife, **Penelope**, who'd waited there for him.

Olympus (and the Olympians)

Mount Olympus was the home of the most important Greek gods, who were known as the Olympians. However, with so many aunts, uncles, brothers and sisters living under one roof, arguments were frequent. These were made worse when the gods' pets joined in. On such occasions Zeus's eagle would pummel Aphrodite's doves, Hermes's tortoise would tuck into his shell and bowl himself at Hera's peacock and Apollo's swans would snap Poseidon's fish up in their beaks and fling them out of the window. Only Athena's owl, being the most sensible and wisest of the creatures, could be relied upon to behave well and he could always be found under the bed reading a good scroll.

Orpheus

Orpheus was a master-musician whose lyre-playing was

so beautiful that it charmed the birds from the skies, the wolves from the woods and made the trees boogie on down. As one of the Argonauts, his sensational strumming smothered the songs of the ship-sinking sirens, meaning that the crew sailed safely home.

Panathenea

This festival, held in ancient Athens, celebrated Athena's birthday and was famous for its procession of heroes, musicians and poets, all wishing the goddess many happy returns. Her presents included a gigantic dress for her gigantic statue and lots of animal sacrifices. Some people think that one of the marble friezes on her temple, the Parthenon, shows the event. However, despite extensive examinations of the remaining chunks of stone, archaeologists haven't found a single picture of a birthday cake or a balloon. Well, some birthday, I must say.

Pegasus

Pegasus was a beautiful white flying horse that put the 'up' in 'Giddy up!' and the 'rise' in 'rising trot'. Always a bit of a show-off, he enjoyed hoofy-dancing high in the sky, where he performed kicks and twirls in the clouds. However, his spectacular dressage could occasionally lead to an accidental flurry of doo-doo *mess*-age, which ultimately led to the invention of the fabulous Athenian-reinforced umbrella.

Penelope

Penelope, the wife of the hero, Odysseus, waited many years for her husband to return from the War of Troy. During that time, lots of other suitors, who believed he'd died, wished to marry her, but she declined, saying that she would only choose a new husband when she had finished her tapestry. This she unpicked every night so that the picture – a delightful harbour in Ithaca, filled with fishing boats, gulls and snappy-clatters of crabs line-dancing on the shore – would never be completed, leaving her free to stitch and twitch until her husband finally returned.

Poseidon

Poseidon, god of the sea, lived far beneath the waves in a glittering palace of coral. When he was happy, the sea was calm. But when he was angry, he made it rage. Whipping the water into a fury, he'd rise up from the froth to jab things with his trident. Such tantrums caused earthquakes, shipwrecks and tidal waves, not to mention playing absolute havoc with the jellyfish, which were left spinning for days.

Pythagoras

Pythagoras was an Ancient Greek mathematician, most famous for thinking about triangles, and one day your maths teacher might well mention him. The old Greek's work on geometry involved lots of pacing about on the beach, assisted by Adder, who still blushes to recall the day that the old man finally cracked the puzzle, flung his robes up over his wrinkly knees and performed an early version of the cancan in the sea. However, since this is not recorded in the history books, your maths teacher will probably say it never happened.

Scylla

Charybdis's best buddy – see above.

Sisyphus (pronounced *Sissy-fuss*)

Sisyphus was a fiendish Greek king who loved lying and deceiving others and topped off his treachery by murdering his guests. For these crimes, he was sent to Tartarus, the Underworld's terrifying prison. Here, he was sentenced to push a backbreaking boulder to the top of a steep hill. However, as soon as he'd achieved this agonising feat, the boulder rumbled back down the slope again to the bottom, condemning him to repeat his task over and over for eternity. This made him the original King of Rock and Roll.

Sphinx

The Greek Sphinx was a mythical creature with the head of a woman and the body of a lion. She was said to guard the city of Thebes and wouldn't let anyone pass unless they could answer her annoying riddles. If they failed, she ate them. Her most famous brainteaser was:

'Which creature has four feet, then two feet, then three?' Any ideas?[63]

Stymphalian Birds

The Stymphalian Birds were the pets of Ares, the god of war. However, unlike other pet birds, such as parrots, they ate people, pooped poison and had beaks made of bronze. Worse, anyone foolish enough to ask them 'Who's a pretty boy then?' never found out the answer because it's impossible to hear when your head is stuck halfway down a bird's throat.

Theseus

Theseus was the man who killed the Minotaur, a monster who was half-man and half-bull. In order to defeat it, he needed all of his Greek fighting skills, together with a good dollop of bullfighting know-how. Luckily for him, he was as graceful as a matador and swift as a picador. However, once he'd done the deed, he then needed to find-a-door since he was still stuck inside the creature's maze-like prison. This he did by following the trail of wool he'd unravelled behind him on his way in.

---

63 The answer is MAN. This is because a baby crawls on its hands and knees (four 'legs'), an adult walks on two legs and an elderly person uses a stick (making three 'legs' in all). I know. Not much of a punch line, is it?

The Legend of The Golden Fleece

According to Apollonius of Rhodes[64]

Long, long ago, the brave and handsome Jason learned that he was the true king of Iolkos, a city-state in Ancient Greece. However, his wicked uncle Pelias had crowned himself king many years before and when Jason demanded his rightful place back, Pelias agreed to step down on one condition: that Jason sail across the sea to bring him back the Golden Fleece.

The Fleece was a ram's coat made of pure gold and the most valuable thing on Earth. It belonged to King Aetes of Kolkis, who sought to keep it safe by hanging it at the top of a tall tree in a magical glade, where it was guarded by a gigantic, man-eating snake. The serpent never slept. Instead, with its coils wrapped tightly about

---

64 *Being a poet rather than a sailor, Apollonius didn't witness any of the events he described but just wrote down exactly what Jason told him to. This probably explains why the earliest copies of his best-selling Scroll were found with strange, ram-shaped bites taken out of them, and his name scribbled over, to read, 'Claptrap-ollonius' instead.*

the tree's trunk, it watched, night and day, for intruders, its snout resting on the scatter of bones and armour that was all that was left of the men who'd tried in the past. And so Pelias felt certain that since the quest was so dangerous Jason would never return to bother him again.

But, determined to win back his crown, Jason sailed valiantly with fifty of Greece's noblest heroes, as captain of the *Argo*, and after an eventful and terribly dangerous voyage presented himself at King Aetes' palace.

Of course, Aetes had no intention of giving up his precious Fleece, but since it would not be kingly to flatly refuse, he agreed that if Jason could yoke the fire-breathing bulls and plough a field with special seeds, then the Fleece would be his. Aetes laughed secretly to himself, certain that Jason would perish in the attempt.

However, the king had reckoned without his daughter, the beautiful Medea, who was a sorceress. Falling deeply in love with Jason, she set out to protect him with her magic.

The next day, Jason stepped into the field with the fire-breathing bulls, furious beasts that blasted jets of flames at anyone who stepped near them. Aetes smiled to himself, confident that Jason would be scorched to a crisp in trying to put on their iron harness. However, Medea had given Jason a magical salve to protect his skin from the searing heat, and whilst everyone else ran away from the fire and the smoke and the fierce clattering of bronze hooves, he bravely yoked the bulls without harm. Then he stepped behind the plough and began guiding the terrible beasts across the field without injury or fear.

The king was horribly frustrated, but smiled and handed Jason a bag of seeds to sow across the new furrows. But the seed was no ordinary seed. Each seed was a dragon's tooth and as they fell on to the freshly turned soil, an army of bone soldiers leaped up and raced towards Jason, swinging their swords. But Jason cleverly thought to pick up a stone and throw it amongst them. The soldier it hit immediately thought his neighbour had attacked him and fought him instead, and in the following chaos every soldier smashed one another to pieces.

The king was secretly furious at Jason's cleverness and courage, but to keep up appearances he promised him and the Argonauts a feast to celebrate Jason's success in winning the Fleece. But that night Medea warned Jason that her father really intended to kill him and his men, and led him to the sacred oak, where she sent the snake to sleep so that Jason could clamber fearlessly up its slithering, terrible coils to collect his prize.

Triumphant, and a true hero of Greece, Jason carried the Fleece back down through the branches of the tree and returned to the *Argo*, and with his men and his new bride, Medea, sailed home to be crowned King of Iolkos.

AUTHOR'S NOTE

Those of you who like a good snootle through a history book will discover that whilst Wat was indeed shot by Spanish soldiers as he quested for El Dorado, he was not shot in the Amazon in Brazil, but in Venezuela, which is another country in South America. Tweaking the truth like this is called 'artistic licence' and is where writers, who spend all their time making things up, decide to make up a little bit more.

AND FINALLY, A NOTE ON THE AMAZON RAINFOREST

You might be surprised to discover that the Amazon gets its name from the fabby old Greek myths and the Amazons, who were a tribe of ferocious women-warriors. These feisty females spent their days bashing up anyone that annoyed them, such as Herakles, who had run off with their queen's girdle as one of his Twelve Labours. However, it wasn't until hundreds of years later, long after the fall of old Greece, that the tribe's name became linked to the river. This happened in the late sixteenth century, when some Spanish explorers searching for – you've guessed it – El Dorado, ended up sick, hungry and horribly lost in the jungle. Worse, just to top off their disastrous trip, a tribe of wild women who, the Spaniards said, looked exactly like the Amazons they'd read about at school, ran squealing from the trees and clobbered them. The Spaniards' tale spread far into South

America and beyond, and the river quickly became known as *Rio Amazonas,* the River of the Amazons. Nowadays, it is simply called The Amazon.

The biggest river in the world, and the second longest after the Nile,[65] it is about four thousand miles long. It rises in the Andes Mountains of Peru and flows through Venezuela, Ecuador, Columbia, Guyana, Bolivia and Brazil. It carries more water than any other river on Earth and flows up to six miles wide, stretching to thirty miles across in the rainy season. Its mouth (where it flows into the Atlantic Ocean) is around one hundred and fifty miles across. This is why the Amazon is sometimes called 'the River Sea'.

Around it, the rainforest is one of the most spectacular places on Earth, and brims with thousands and thousands of plants. It home to sloths, vampire bats, jaguars, caimans, monkeys, armadillos, poison frogs, boa constrictors and anaconda. More than 1,500 species of birds, including Mr Potoo, live there, together with over two million species of insects and more than two thousand species of fish. Over half of all the creatures on Earth live in rainforests.

According to Greenpeace, one hectare of Amazon jungle can contain three hundred species of tree, compared to a measly old ten in a hectare in England. And just one tree can house more species of ant than

65 Scientists are still arguing about which river really is the longest, and flinging their tape measures at each other in a most unpleasant manner.

can be found in the entire United Kingdom. However, we are not going to talk about that, because I've had quite enough of ants in this book, thank you very much.

The Amazon rainforest is called 'the lungs of the planet' because it gives us one-fifth of the world's oxygen by processing carbon dioxide with its billions of leaves. These plants have also given us more than a quarter of all the medicines we take in the West. In fact, seventy per cent of the plants that we use to treat cancer grow there, yet scientists have so far only investigated a teensy little bit of the jungle.

So, who knows what other wonderful cures might be found?

Well, unfortunately, probably not us, if the rainforest continues to be chopped down at the rate of three football pitches a minute. That's right. Sky Forest Rescue and the World Wildlife Fund have calculated that that's the area being hacked away every minute of every day for furniture, paper, doors, windows and fences, and even fancy coffins. Some land is used to farm or graze animals, but with the poor soil of the Amazon, the ground soon becomes nothing more than a dusty wasteland. Meaning that in roughly the time it's taken you to read this far through my note on the Amazon rainforest, another patch of jungle about ten football fields big has vanished for good, taking with it all the thousands of animals, birds and insects that thrive there, some of whom will be lost for ever, together with the ancient homelands of tribes who have lived there for hundreds of years in harmony with the jungle.

Losing the rainforest would be utterly disastrous for the world. That's why governments and conservation organisations are trying hard to save them, for us and for all our future generations, before it's too late. But it's a tough battle. You can find out more about the work they are doing, and what you too could do to help the rainforest, at:

www.rainforestrescue.sky.com
www.greenpeace.org.uk/forests/amazon
www.savetherainforest.com

Acknowledgements

I would like to thank Tilda Johnson, Debbie Hatfield and the team at Piccadilly Press. Thank you, too, to Helen Boyle from Templar, and to my agent, Jo Williamson, who together first unleashed Aries, snorting, into bookshops and classrooms across the world. A great big round of applause is due to my partner, Jim Chandler, who, with Stephanie Clifford and David Allen, read through the final draft; to Professor Armand D'Angour of Jesus College, Oxford, who put my Latin straight; and to my dear friend Helen Gee, for her historical insights. Thank you to my aunt, Yvonne Bird, for her encouragement, and, of course thank you to my sister, Jennifer, for all the support and chocolate brownies through the post. Last, but certainly not least, an Aries-sized thank you to Melissa Hyder, my super-talented editor on both *Fleeced!* and *Rampage!* for her wisdom, constancy and rammy-cheerleading throughout – not to mention a comprehensive knowledge of The Muppets and cake.